Praise for Michael Patrick Welch and *The Donkey Show*:

"Michael Welch is an awesome, feral talent. His take on the world is tender, fierce, crazy, funny, hateful, deranged and loving. He's the most exciting young writer I've come across."
-- **Jonathan Ames,** *creator of the HBO show* Bored to Death *and author of* The Extra Man, Wake Up, Sir! *and* What's Not to Love?

"New Orleans has turned out another pathos-filled comic genius...Put this one on your shelf and look for the budding Balzac to keep widening and deepening his study of our urbo-cosm."
-- **Andrei Codrescu,** *popular NPR voice, and author of over 40 books of poetry and prose*

I read [TDS] in a single evening -- in fact, it kept me up until past 3 AM last night, and the narrator's voice was so engaging that I found myself dreaming in it when I finally did go to sleep. [TDS] captivated me even as it made me feel incredibly old, tired, and boring. Patrick's stint teaching at a New Orleans public high school... every word of it rings absolutely true. Welch has a near-perfect ear for the black voices of New Orleans. An excellent book... Highly recommended.
-- **Poppy Z. Brite,** *author of famous vampire novels, and New Orleans restaurant industry novels, including* Liquor *and* Prime

"Uncomfortable moments of race relations, the quest for decent drugs, and the search for sex... these are the stories behind the shit-eating grins we flash the tourists. This shit rocks!"
-- **Abram Himmelstein,** *author of* Tales of a Punk Rock Nothing. *New Orleans teacher behind The Neighborhood Story Project*

"Your boyfriend is very, very talented."
-- ***The Kinks' Ray Davies*** *to the author's girlfriend at JazzFest 2003*

Published by Dirty Coast Press

Published in the United States of America
Or, rather, New Orleans

Book design, layout, illustrations,
and cover lettering by Jeff Pastorek
One of the only conscientious, timely collaborators the Author has ever worked with. Visit Jeff Pastorek's website at
www.jeffpastorek.com

Cover image by Morgana King

Rear cover painting by the Author

Visit the Dirty Coast website at www.humidbeings.com

Cataloging-in-Publication Data

Welch, Michael Patrick
p. cm.
LCCN 5047562147
ISBN

1. Costa Rica—wildlife—Florida—Sanibel—Fiction.
2. Man-woman relationships—Fiction 3. Sex and drugs—Fiction
3. 4. Costa Rica (Central America)—Fiction I. Title.

PS5150 OU812   504

QBDreWBrees
10 9 8 7 6 5 4 3 2 1

y'all's problem

by MICHAEL PATRICK WELCH

with illustrations by JEFF PASTOREK

To anyone I ever loved in Florida.

And to my wife, the artist Morgana King who, over the course of the six straight years it took to write this book, rarely seemed to question why anyone would shape their entire life around their imagination.

And for Sanibel. We are truly, deeply sorry.

Thanks to Katey Wallenter, Rusty Singletary, Helen Kreiger, Jonathan Ames, Jon Chiri, Jon West, Phil Fracassi, Rosalie Siegel, Mike Waksman, ABC Pizza, George Popadopolis, and the real Milton Chapman. And to the people of the real Costa Rican village I stayed in on two long occasions while writing this, who were almost all extremely nice and had the most perfect priorities I've ever seen.

BOOK 1: "attack"

(TAMPA, FLA)

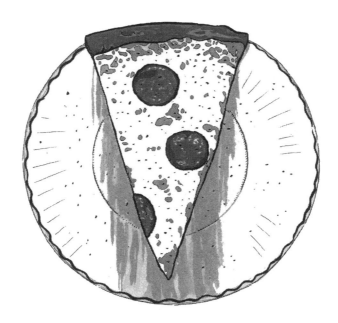

1.1 THE EYES HAVE IT

Her left eye turns in a little bit toward her nose, but in profile she is perfect. You can't even tell. Her handicap only becomes apparent when her relatives wipe her mouth at dinner in front of everyone in Pizza Dive. I'm sure she's always relied on them, and trusts them and maybe no one else, ever. But if she knows trust, then she probably knows embarrassment, so they shouldn't wipe her mouth in public. She's a bit younger than me, 23, maybe. Too young to be old. She dines with the elderly, who trap her in boxy, old lady dresses, imposing their identities onto her when she's too feeble to cultivate her own. Dressed identically, the whole family of four gray women and one old man brings her into Pizza Dive each week after Saturday night mass. Smelling of the church next door — not-unpleasantly stale — they request their "regular table" in my section. She's too young to have a regular table.

The patriarch and the old women bury their faces in their menus as her hands lay folded, her shoulder against the wall, her crooked eyes on her grandmother who sits always directly across. Waiting for their decision, I study the girl's perfect profile: full lips turning out and away from each other and I wonder what it would be like to kiss her — until her grandmother ties a bib around her to protect her polyester hand-me-downs. As the old ladies conspire and finally whisper their decisions to the patriarch, I wonder if their imposition of old age upon her isn't worse than the bad situation God put her in.

Minutes later I bring watery Italian food to their booth. Setting the girl's spaghetti in front of her, I used to warn, "Don't touch the plate, the ceramic is really hot." But then her grandmother always made a big squawking show of stealing the plate away, saving the girl from herself. So now I set the sizzling cheese down without warning. I then inquire whether she needs a refill, but before the girl can form the answer herself, her grandmother chirps, "Yes, more water for her." I stand there, hoping she'll answer for herself, nod or smile. Then I pour the silent girl more water, because this is my job.

No former server – whether they loved or hated their own service industry experience — would thereafter ever have the heart to enter a restaurant five minutes before closing time, as the handicapped girl's old family did last Saturday. I mopped the red tile floor of my section and because big George had already left, our new waitress, Alana, took the family order. The girl's odd eye didn't stare across at her grandmother tonight though, or up at Alana; from across the room she seemed to eye me. I mopped and she smiled and gawked, front teeth pinning down a kissable bottom lip like a newborn's pinky. I jumped back to work, head down but felt her same stare and smile until I set my mop aside and escaped into the kitchen to listen to our manager Tony tell the kitchen staff his sexual exploits in a way both genuinely fun and disgusting. Soon, her family would leave.

Through the Service window I watched their long, slow take-off, before returning to my section. Pumping the grunting mop, I barely felt a hand touch my waist like slow dancing. Alana pushed a paper placemat at me. On the back was a drawing.

"The girl left this picture of you," Alana smiled. I was rattled.

She's worked at Pizza Dive for five and a half weeks. I've distanced myself from Alana, afraid she'll hear my loins boiling if we're close enough to talk. When we have spoken, for work purposes, she maintains strong eye contact but while blinking in slow motion, projecting the compelling softness of dryer-warm blankets. Or sheets.

She's just too much: olive skin smooth as a landing strip, loose black curls down past the back pockets of the same soft maroon corduroy work-pants she wears to work every night. And 17 years old. I was 10 when she was born in some Costa Rican rainforest. Alana was nine as I slept through college Spanish.

She came to the U.S. just months ago and acquired this job through a friend, a line cook. Our manager Tony also manages a network of undocumented workers, setting them up with minimum wage work then helping their friends and relatives come over as well. Tony is very loyal to his kitchen people. Especially to the gorgeous, swarthy Greek and Brazilian girls, Austrian girls, Puerto *and* Costa Rican women all in need of employment. More than a few have college degrees so it surprises me that after Tony hires and helps them they are often grateful enough to sleep with him. In most cases just once.

Keeping Alana at arm's-length, I snatched the girl's drawing from her small pretty claw. "The *uh,* the girl drew this?"

"The pretty one with a bad eye," Alana answered, blinking slowly. Impressed that she'd noticed the girl's beauty, I inspected the placemat's crooked orange crayon drawing of a bald man in a collared shirt bearing the word *pizza.* "It's you?" Alana asked with a languid smile. "No?"

"Am I bald?"

"What it means 'bald'?" she asked.

I leaned on my mop, eyes on the drawing so as not to be overcome by Alana's sleepy blinking. "It means *no hair.*" I pointed to the crudely drawn, orange character, then to my own head: "And I *have* hair."

"She don't give you hair for the picture," Alana explained, "but she draw the picture orange for your *red* hair."

Seventeen years of Florida sun have muted my hair so that now, when I refer to myself as a redhead, most people respond, "Redhead?" I told Alana this.

"No! Red hair is the *whole* person, everything!" she announced. "If your red color dies, you are still red forever." I glowed comfortably, and finally couldn't help meeting her sleepy eyes with no reticence as she claimed, "All my three sisters and my brother Raphael have red hair."

"Really?" I leaned and gazed. "Costa Rican redheads?"

"How you know I am from Costa Rica?" she asked, brow furrowed, and jerked the mop handle from under my chin.

I steadied myself, we shared a laugh and I lied, "Tony told me that you are Costa Rican." Actually, I had eavesdropped when she first came into the restaurant to make work arrangements. Tony interviewed her at the front cash register as a blandly handsome young Latin guy in a ball cap waited, studying the oversized suckerfish in Pizza Dive's 100-gallon aquarium. Working my section, I'd heard Alana say she was to marry this guy after she turns 18 in February. Another good reason to stay away from her. Still, I couldn't help being fascinated: "There a lot of redheads in Costa Rica?"

"Not many that I have see," she replied. "People are stare at my brother there. And men want my sisters because my sisters are..." Her limp hand circled the air, fishing for...

"Exotic?" I offered.

"What is 'exotic'?"

"Rare. Not many around. Endangered species."

"Yes, my sisters are exotic. So even old men want to have them." She stuck her tongue out and shook her head. "These old men are..."

"Gross?"

"Gross," she nodded. "They go for my little sisters, when my sisters are only 12 year olds! It's gross."

"All three of them are 12?"

"And all with red hair! I also have one gringo friend in Costa Rica who have red hair," she continued. "Everybody stare at *heem* too. He is crazy redhead! He is writer also, like you. You would like him. He has a famous book though."

"What's it called?"

"I don't know. I never read it yet."

I laughed. "What's your friend's name?"

"I don't remember." We laughed together as she added, "He even cry for me and I don't remember he name!"

"You're terrible."

"You love it."

Unable to rebuke this, I asked why she thought I would like him.

"Because he is a writer, and because he is very sensitive. Maybe too much sensitive, like you."

"Wait." I suddenly realized: "How'd you know I'm a writer?" I hadn't ever mentioned my writing.

"Tony tell me." She smiled, and her black coils of hair danced off into the kitchen.

* * *

After typing up the church calendar, I spent the rest of my afternoon at *The Trib* searching the internet for a new place to live. New York is off limits; Natalie's there. Maybe San Francisco or... Where else? Anywhere. Must escape FLA.

With a few hours left before my dinner shift at Pizza Dive, I walked across the street from the newsroom to my former college campus to wander amid the beige stucco architecture and stare at all the far away sweet young bodies with underdeveloped brains in them. Beauty swarms the Student Center, the Art and Theatre buildings, the English department, the Dance department *especially*. Some beautiful but not sexy, some painfully sexy though not necessarily pretty, others just perfect, but all torturous. Natalie would've stoned me with laughter had she seen me there sniffing around our old school, wishing, hoping, even aching. Though I am sure that if not for my time with Natalie, all that beauty out there wouldn't now seem so out of reach.

Done dawdling around campus searching for my imaginary class, plus hungry but not wanting to eat pizza at work *again* tonight, I sought the school cafeteria. And upon walking in, I spotted the pretty handicapped girl, her hair trapped in a net, her boxy dress protected by a long, white work-smock. *She's strong enough to hold down a job,* was my first thought, *but her keepers need to wipe her mouth?* She didn't notice me watching from the cash register as I paid for my Taco Bell. Student lunch rush had passed and she stood alone in the empty cafeteria, a giant beige lunch tray pressed flat across her chest. She teetered side-to-side like waiting to cross the street.

She went nowhere, however, as I chewed my chilito and studied her and wondered what it would mean to her to be touched. After just two years alone, I myself feel embarrassingly desperate at times. So overflowing with what felt like empathy I felt like standing, walking over and kissing her before she could even recognize me.

My pulse revved excited as if I were gazing upon something I had discovered.

I rose to cross the cafeteria.

Only her eyes moved, struggling to discern the figure approaching her. I heard Alana's voice say, "The pretty one...".

But when she focused her eyes on mine and smiled bright buckteeth in a happiness-glazed face, I just suddenly couldn't. Kissing her might wake a loneliness asleep so deep in her it was probably almost drowned by now. *Don't reach that far in and stir it,* I understood and swerved past, out the exit and back across the street to the newsroom.

Not until I later rolled away from *The Trib* in the private air-conditioning of my truck did I realize I had left her to clean up my mess, as I so often have hers.

1.2 We Spit in the Food

Without qualification I say: I prefer Pizza Dive to my day job at *The Trib*. I prefer running around sweating, shoveling pasta down rednecks' gullets over typing obituaries in that ergonomic chair, or rushing under harsh FLA sun to the courthouse to fetch files for the 'real' reporters. I make pretty tiny money at Pizza Dive, but feel compensated listening to manager Tony's corny machismo and the constant laughter it elicits from the immigrant kitchen, or smoking pot in the Mop Room with big waiter George. Especially now with the addition of Alana, I've never enjoyed a job more.

Beginning work last night, Alana more than casually inquired about my writing. "I *love* lee-tre-choor," she said, breaking the word up into small, pretty bits. She told me again about her famous red-haired author friend in Costa Rica as she followed me back to Tony's office. There, I warmed up his computer and let her read a very short piece I recently had published on a literary website (she'd *never* used the internet! How charming). I wasn't particularly proud of the piece; it's a little too *true* and so didn't take much imagination. But it's the only writing I've had published outside of pedestrian copy at *The Trib* (if it still counts as "published" on the web):

Remember Mandy

Mandy was my first chance. I was 12 to her 13 when my younger best friend Peter and I rode our bikes past Mandy and her large, white girlfriend playing pool in their condo's glass clubhouse. Actually, only I rode past; Peter stopped when Mandy waved us in.

The following week, watching Peter tongue-kiss prematurely busty Mandy, I felt at a comfortable enough distance to befriend her. She and I ended up blooming into far better friends than she and Peter – closer even than she and her girlfriend who'd traveled with Mandy from Pennsylvania for the summer. Mandy soon began leaving her friend behind and telling Peter her parents wouldn't let her outside, so that she and I could sneak off and swim by ourselves.

My orange eyebrows were bleached green and our skin always smelled of chlorine. Mandy's nipples stared through her pink one-piece suit and she had real *woman's* legs. Still I never felt insecure around her, not even with my shirt off.

For two summers after, Mandy returned alone, to visit *me* rather than Peter. Each summer was more joyously intense, though we never touched; as kids, we still possessed the ability to just as passionately enjoy the *INEVITABILITY*. Or rather, the illusion of inevitability; we never did touch. Still Mandy is remembered as my first chance.

The last time Mandy and I saw each other, my parents were dragging me off on a miserable Key West vacation one week *before* Mandy was to return to Pennsylvania. I didn't want to go! Not *before* Mandy left! So I was happy when my seasick mother barfed over the ship's bow on our first snorkeling trip. Millions of small fish like multicolored sparks rushed to eat her vomit and the other snorkelers were all very grateful — though this began our vacation's downward spiral. I proceeded to fight with my sweet little sister. It began to pour hard, tropical rain. My dad's a skittish driver even in FLA's smilingest weather. He lost his cool at the rain and his bickering kids and sick wife and, swerving on wet Key West roads he threatened, "We'll go home right *goddamned now*! How would you like *that*?"

A LOT! I laid into my sister harder and prayed for more rain until my Dad finally did turn the loaded car around, back toward *her*. He yelled the whole 12-hour drive, still I felt warm and satisfied, and before our minivan could fully pull into our garage, my bike was already racing across our condo development, skidding into her parents' empty parking space...

Empty? No Pennsylvania plates in the lot. I knocked on Mandy's door, expecting her chewing head to pop out and proclaim, 'I'm eating. Be out in a minute!' and I would wait in the parking lot until her family finished dinner. But this time I sat on my 10-speed, spinning my gears freewheel, waiting. I laid on the fresh smelly tar under my bike's thin shade, waiting. I walked around their condo, lolled in the grass between Mandy's bedroom window and the manmade lake, ran my hands along her rough tan stucco, waiting, waiting...

Her parents' condo was soon after repossessed and I never saw Mandy again, except in photos she mailed to me of her winning beauty contests, or cheerleading — activities that seemed in gross opposition to her sweet, smart character as I knew it. Our long-distance calls always ended with shy, quiet "I love you," but we never made plans. Eventually, Mandy admitted to having done scary things like trying drugs and losing her virginity — while I'd begun harvesting acne that would keep me away from those basic social rituals until college. So, intimidated, alienated, it was perhaps far too easy to let Mandy go forever.

Reading the piece again, I thought I'd done an O.K. job describing every pound-per-square-inch of pressure that, at the time, had crushed my heart. But, "That story is like *waaaaaaa*," Alana mocked as I guided her through shutting down Tony's computer. "I like the fishes eating her puke," she tittered, "but most of the words are like a baby going in his diaper."

"Wow. Thanks."

"Pa-treek," she sighed. "Don't be mad. But you say 'I feel insecure with my shirt off' and it is joss...Is like *waaaaaaaaaa*...what is the word in English? It's joss..."

"Whiney," I filled in her blank. "Right. I guess that's why I've only been published on the web..."

"Oh Pa-treek." She touched my hand. "Don't be so sensateef."

Throughout our shift carrying hissing cheesy plates past each other, in broken bits and pieces this amazing teenage girl explained to me how writing should be a celebration, not the blues. "Henry Miller is the one man who write about being happy. I like him best. You probably more like a Bukowski," she grunted, her lazy tongue protruding. During another flyby, I argued that one's writing should consist of whatever one cares about most. She laughed and kept on running.

In the end though, I got the point. I should thank her for that.

Bathed in the distinct smell of a long night's restaurant work, folding the last of the night's pizza boxes, we sat beaming, discussing our mutual love of animals ("Especially animals in the water!" Alana bounced). We debated her claim that there no animals are truly male: "*All* animals are *she.*" Between her fits of laughter and kicks under the table, Alana would leap up from the booth and run away to go milk our ancient hot chocolate machine that sits like a hulking naval-ship bogged down in straws, napkins and cup lids on the wait station's oceanic beige countertop. Dozens of times each night that machine vomits its brown lava into her kiddie-cup. Alana's the only one who ever drinks the hot chocolate. Enough of it, one would think, to kill a 98-pound girl.

She popped her already hot cocoa into the microwave for 30 extra seconds before returning to our booth. Over her steaming cup I asked, "How do you drink that crap?" I test-squeezed and the heat nipped my fingers through the Styrofoam. "It's way too sweet."

"Oh, you shut *up!*" Her features sharpened. "I love this stuff *as hell.*" She gulped the volcanic goo, eyes watering.

Our giggly confrontation paused only long enough for us to watch my last customer of the night, a large sunburned cracker, swing out the double doors of the restaurant — before I admitted to Alana that I had spit in his salad. At this, Alana lunged across our paper placemats and seized my arms, almost knocking over her dangerous drink. "You too!" she shouted. "I do that *all* the time!" Her nails dug in and my blood fizzed like fountain-fresh Sprite. My heart tickled, expecting more. But knowing there would be no more, I escaped her grasp. She sat back and declared, "If a customer talk to me like *sheet*, I *speet* in their drink. Or I *leek* these part of their cup…what is *these* part called?"

"The lip?"

"Yes! I *leek* the *leap!*"

Her evil admission surprised me; she floats angelic around Pizza Dive, smiling softly, impossibly long hair flown back and sleepy eyes blinking so slowly I would've never suspected such venom. I assumed she'd have developed a humor-based coping mechanism for all the times customers abuse her. Not that spitting in someone's Coke isn't funny. I'm sure she laughs…

"This one man come in tonight with stupid loud kids," she confided. "He was *real* asshole and I *speet* in his water. But my speet was *theek*. When I stir it with the straw, it turns into a little tornado with pieces of food in it *from my mouth*." Alana lost her words in another long laugh. "But it was too easy for gringo to see," she continued. "So I dump out the water and make a new one."

"Gringo?"

She laughed proud and loud, unafraid of Tony, who would definitely consider her spitting in his customer's food an affront to the tradition of neighborhood excellence that is his family's 25-year-old business. Pizza Dive may qualify as one of the oldest buildings in FLA, as anything over 10 years old is generally torn down and replaced with new, stucco and pastel monstrosities, at least in Tampa. Our restaurant owes its years of economic health to its cheap prices. A family of four can feasibly dine for $25 ($22, sans tip). Many of our regular customers walk to the restaurant from the surrounding neighborhood because they don't have cars (unheard of in FLA!) because they are poor. Disabled vets, single moms, and families like the handicapped girl's who are financially crippled by medical bills consider Pizza Dive their big night out. But affordability also attracts stone-dumb, straight-up mean Florida rednecks.

Usually I chuckle off customer abuse at Pizza Dive and just neglect any jerks. I only took this part-time job to save money to move away; it's not my real life. Thus, even at its busiest, Pizza Dive is, for me, a low-stress environment. Unlike most restaurants, Pizza Dive throws no huge menu at waiters to memorize; all of our food items are pre-printed on notepads, and we simply *circle* the custom-ers' orders. Instead of battling a computer ordering system, we pass paper tickets directly through the service window to the cook. When our customers are through, they take their own check up to the front counter where Tony cashes them out, meaning we waiters do no math and touch no money save our paltry tips. Pizza Dive doesn't expect us to adhere to any tableside service 'technique,' or sweat-out mountains of side-work before we're allowed to go home. So I'm rarely stressed enough to let customer abuse fray my nerves.

But if I *did* "kook-out" (as Floridian fratboys say), Pizza Dive isn't like corporate places where standing up for yourself gets you fired regardless of right or wrong. Tony *understands*. The other night when big George told a customer to fuck off, Tony merely pulled George aside and whispered, "Hey, don't do that, *malaka*."

Tony is Greek-American. He fractures sentences with an accent, as if English is his second language, when really the only Greek he knows are the cusswords — *malaka* means 'jack off.' Pizza Dive's cooks are obsessed with this word, *malaka*. Its comic impact never lessens. I abuse it too; when customers ask what type of salad dressings we serve (we serve only one, a secret white house dressing Tony makes himself at the restaurant *only* after the staff have all gone home) I tell them, "We have a lovely homemade *malaka* dressing. It's a *creamy Greek*." The customers respond through sometimes-tooth-less smiles, "Ooh! That sounds *wonderful!*" and I can't wait to run tell the kitchen guys, who cackle when I hit the punchline, whether or not they understood its preceding joke.

This is the most fun I've ever had at work. So I never thought of spitting in food — until the end of tonight, when that large hick sat in my section wearing a T-shirt with a picture of the Confederate flag flying from the dome of the White House. Beneath the White House taunted the slogan, "*I Have a Dream.*" So I spit in the rac-ist's salad, then massaged it into the wet iceberg lettuce and *malaka* dressing on my way through the dish pit. I felt as if he'd given me permission.

Leaning against the cooler watching him eat it (because what's the point if you don't watch?), I cringed and shuddered, my silent eyes beaming laughter until Tony stepped to me. "Malaka, why you staring at that guy?" he asked, brow furrowed.

"I dunno." I straightened. "Just zoning out."

As he squinted at the redneck, I studied Tony. He is an amazing character I never tire of studying. His feathered brown helmet of mousse — lightly frosted blonde and covering just the tops of his ears — seems strapped to his head by his small goatee. Tony is 5-feet-4 (same height as musical genius Prince, who also enjoys much *munaki*, despite — *munaki* is *vagina*), and when he stands close enough, I'm afforded a view down the neck of his Pizza Dive polo shirt to the diamond-cut herringbone necklace nestled in his chest hair. "You spit in that guy's food?" Tony accused more than asked me.

I spun to face him, stunned, impressed. Still I admitted nothing.

"Don't spit in people's food, malaka," he grimaced, strutting back to the kitchen, mumbling orders for me to finish cleaning my section.

I mopped around the bigot's boots then slid my smelly bucket in beside Alana's and sat back in the booth with her and her cocoa. We watched the guy finish his spitty meal then limp out of Pizza Dive without tipping, leaving us alone in the dining room, laughing in tribute to our evil.

But during an inevitable lull, I observed Alana's mood decay. She finished her third hot chocolate and didn't dart off for another. "Hey, what's the matter?" I finally asked.

"He is not calming," she whimpered, scanning the empty restaurant over her thin shoulder.

"Calming?"

'To peek me up!" she snapped. "He is not calming to peek me up!"

"Your boyfriend?" I wondered why it hurt to speak that word.

"Yes. He is very late." She then shrugged: "Fock heem."

I joked, "You shouldn't cuss."

"What is *'cuss'*?" she sighed.

My laughter drew Tony back into our section. Little pursed beard and plucked eyebrows aimed down at me. "Ey, *malaka!* You're sitting around trying to get the *munaki* and you haven't even emptied your mop bucket. C'mon! Finish this shit, man!"

"I'll be right back," I assured Alana. "Stay here." I rose from our booth to drag our big, yellow mop buckets of dirty bleach-water (mine *and* hers, though Tony didn't dare yell at Alana) through the dining room, then the kitchen, the greasy prep room, Tony's greasy office, through dry storage and out into the perfect December night. If I miss anything about FLA when I leave, it will be the winters; following every abusive summer, like some inverted spring fever, FLA's winter crawls cool down your shirt, simultaneously exciting and satisfying. But even winter couldn't keep me from hurrying back inside to Alana. I splashed bleach on my regulation-blue jeans, rushing to dump the mop water, rinse the buckets and lay them upside-down to drip-dry in the mop room.

Back inside I found Alana slouched in our booth, sobbing on a placemat. With more concern than may have seemed fitting given I don't really know her, I squatted on the tile beside her, rested my chin and elbows on her table and said, "Hey, don't cry, Alana."

She wiped her eyes and wailed, "He *abandon* me!" Anger sat her up out of her slouch. "And it is *Mami* and *my* car he has. He was supposed to peek me up a half-hour ago!" Then, half laughing at herself, she deflated back down.

I wanted to place my hand on her small shoulder, but simply continued trying to make her laugh long-distance: "Hey, at least you didn't have to empty your mop bucket."

"Yes, I did," she shot back.

"No, I just did it for you," I pointed out, finally hazarding to touch her. "You don't need to lie to *me*, Alana," I smirked.

Again, she straightened. Her tears retreated back into her eyes. Slapping my hand off of her shoulder, she stood and swore, "I don't *never* lie!"

She stormed off, leaving me there squatting.

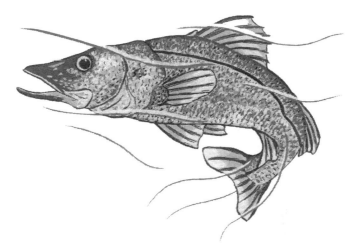

1.3 THE ANIMALS ARE TOUCHED

Having met this afternoon's deadline, I wasted the company's next few hours trying to compose a more celebratory (and more fictional) piece for her:

Alana and I arrived for lunch shift at our terrible job simultaneously, only to find the restaurant burned down.

"What we do now?" Alana giggled.

"I have a *press pass!*" I divulged. "We can get in lots of places for free. *The Trib* would fire me for abusing it but... Ooh, the Florida Aquarium has an amazing seahorse exhibit right now!"

She grabbed my arm: "I love seahorses!"

"Oh man this one seahorse they have, the most beautiful, amazing, ornate..." I described as her eyes widened, grip tightened — "...superfluous, decorative alien!" Her mouth hung in wonder akin to horror like I'd just opened my dry palm and SHOWED her the seahorse lying there gasping for water. "I'll take you there now," I said, and she dug her nails in.

Outside The Aquarium stood smaller aquariums: big glass bubbles containing not water and fish, but big women selling tickets. The Aquarium was about to close, so my *press pass* easily slid us past the large ladies.

Inside, we were immediately met with signs begging:

PLEASE, DO NOT STICK YOUR HANDS IN THE TANKS.

We both silently realized that we had been given our challenge.

Dusty sun shone down from skylights high above. The Aquarium was as usual deserted. Still we began timidly. At the first chest-high tank, designed to emulate muddy mangroves, I spotted none of the aquarium's volunteer security guards, and so reached in toward a mammoth redfish. When I barely touched its scales, the bull red swam a scream of ripples to the tank's farthest side.

I then stepped back to stand lookout for Alana, who reached over the glass toward a snook on its obligatory lap of the tank. She stroked its black-striped side with her knuckle and squealed. But rather than swim away, the fish stopped, backed up, and lingered before her, unblinking.

"It wants more," I said of the pining fish.

"*She* is not '*it*,'" Alana sternly corrected, running long fingers across the snook's broad head. "She is SHE!"

"How can you tell?"

"All animals are `she'," claimed Alana, who then glanced over my shoulder and "Oh!" She jerked her arm from the water.

I turned to see one of FLA's many white-haired old white men, 20-feet away in a golf hat. He smiled at Alana then turned back to the fake mangroves. Alana shook her arm like a drying dog as snook, mullet, sheepshead, turtles and nurse sharks all crowded the side of the tank at her back. She walked on not noticing the fish all follow her down the glass, past the old man and hit the wall as we left for the next room. Running to catch up I glanced back and saw the man, one sleeve rolled, shaky hand reaching in...

Next, we approached two small blue-billed ducks, afloat on eye-level water. They snapped at our reaching fingers, so we waited until they ducked underwater to reach in and hold them submerged for longer than they'd intended. They surfaced squawking, rushing the edge of the tank. Our laughter further agitated the ducks, but they calmed as we calmed, until soon they swam back under — at which point we held them down. Each time they bobbed up gasping, flapping, screaming, spinning circles, tossing violent wingsful of water — angry, but wanting more. Which we gave. Until a little-old-lady guard found us being attacked by small ducks.

"The aquarium's been empty all day," she apologized. "They get a little attention crazy when they're alone for too long."

Her withered hand shooed them as a recorded voice boomed through the high, empty room: "THE FLORIDA AQUARIUM WILL CLOSE IN FIFTEEN MINUTES!"

Alana and I broke for the seahorse exhibit, but paused at a realistic cross-section view of a sandy Gulf of Mexico shoreline that even smelled exact. Through a wall of live sea oats shined a giant picture window onto Tampa Bay. The sloshing tank harbored mullet, amberjack, nurse sharks, and a school of small stingrays gliding synchronous like air-show planes, their wingtips intermittently cutting up into our world. When Alana bravely poked one of the passing rays, the entire school swung back around, back to her, to be poked again. She poked harder with each pass, and each time they returned faster, flapping harder. Soon every ray in the tank hovered before Alana, their flat heads bumping the glass, splashing water onto her work-shirt. "Senoras! Calm down!" Alana ordered, doling out affection. "You get me wet!" Her nervous eyes met mine as alien heads bobbed, wings overlapped. For the first time ever Alana seemed scared.

"THE FLORIDA AQUARIUM WILL CLOSE IN FIVE MINUTES!" threatened the intercom.

"All right ladies!" Alana scolded the animals. "You are too een-TENZ! I must go!"

But before she joined my side, one stingray leapt from the water, landed briefly on the tank's edge and seemed to watch Alana, before dropping onto the formerly dry floor.

"NO! Poor *baby*!" Alana screamed. The ray spun on her back, wings and long blurry tail slapping cement. "Patreek! *Put her back*!"

I took a step to run for the security guard but — upon contemplating our situation's explanation — I realized what all this would look like, and so stopped and suggested, "Let's just go."

I grabbed Alana's arm. "Any minute someone will come around to check and make sure no one's locked in, and they'll see it — HER, I mean. They'll take care of her." Tugging Alana's Pizza Dive polo, I gestured to the EXIT sign.

"No!" Alana jerked free, rearranged her panic into anger and aimed it at me. "Put her *back!*"

"Hell no!" I pointed down at her stinger. "You want to drive me to the hospital with that stuck in my neck?"

"PICK! HER! UP!" `

I'd never heard Alana yell like that. I grabbed my work-shirt's collar and in one invisible motion, ripped it off, threw it over the flopping ray and lobbed the entire package back over the glass, into the fake ocean.

We watched the white Pizza Dive logo float to the sandy bottom like a dead jellyfish. We then sprinted a wet trail past the seahorse exhibit we hadn't seen, in front of the duck tank, and out past the fat lady ticket-taker.

We cried laughter on the car ride home, though I felt self-conscious with my shirt off.

Back in real life, Alana grabbed my arm with both claws. "Oh Pa-treek!" she cried. "These story is not whiney! *These* is *strong!* I love it *much* more!" As if squinting at me for the first time, Alana admitted, "You are like you really *know* me!"

1.4 BROTHERHOOD

Alana's "Mami" and 14-year-old brother Raphael flew up from Costa Rica recently to stay a couple months until Alana's wedding. In the interim, Alana made Tony give her brother a temporary job in the dish room the two slow nights a week when the Guatemalan guys with the Masters degrees are off. Tony pays Raphael less than minimum wage, but it'll translate into a fortune in Costa Rican colones, I'm told.

I hadn't believed in such a creature, but Raphael is indeed a Latin redhead. He's slightly darker than his sandy sister but somehow seems to glow pale, possessing the same ambivalent beauty as the blind sea creatures scientists find when they sink cameras lower into the ocean than humans could stand. Raphael's freckles stand out like stars against his skin, buzzing around his cheeks and arms gnatlike. I often marvel at him, staring as if he'll suddenly swim away down deeper, disappear, and I'll never see anything like him again. At work, only Raphael distracts my eyes from his sister.

Tonight, as Alana and I mopped our sections and her skinny brown ghost brother ground soap bubbles into round, silver pizza trays alone in the dish room, I asked her, "So, when do I meet your redhead sisters?"

"They don't come to the United States. Not everyone in my family can come." Because it was too expensive, I assumed. She dunked and wrung her mop, looked past me into the dish room and admitted, "Raphael come because I love him more than my sisters."

She just *says* these things.

Afraid I might spook Raphael, I whispered, "He looks delicate."

She then asked me to explain *delicate*. And all I could think of were the soft, brown gullies where her neck meets her shoulders. Whenever Alana bends to buss tables, I peer over our customers' heads, down into the wide V of her Pizza Dive polo and I fantasize about pouring sweet-tea into these divots and drinking from her. Her neck and shoulder bones look dangerously breakable, like balsa wood under her perfect skin. So after checking the dish room again to confirm Raphael's distraction, in an odd burst of confidence, I tugged Alana's shirt collar down, exposing one sweet tea hollow. "*This* is delicate," I said.

Her nose scrunched like a question mark but she didn't object, didn't ask *What in hell are you doing?* She simply laughed, "I don't understand."

"Yeah, it's not really the best example..." I stammered, flushed, released her and managed a laugh and, "I may have just been using that as an excuse." Admiring her straight little bright smiling teeth, I wished I had as much courage with women my own age.

Melancholy peaked when Alana placed a hand on my ribs, closed her sleepy eyes and said, "Pa-treek," then opened them, "I like you."

I've heard that from women before, always followed by "but..." and then something discouraging. But Alana just likes me. That's all. And she wanted me to know. Everyone at Pizza Dive likes me so much more than others seem to. Especially my co-workers in the newsroom. I've never felt as accepted, as *liked* as I do at Pizza Dive. So I must keep in mind that Alana's liberal flow of affection is simply a cultural phenomenon, and not a sign that she wants me to stop her wedding.

"Bot what is 'delicate'?" she repeated.

My eyes found wine glasses high atop some cupboards. Tony keeps wine glasses though we're prohibited from serving alcohol because of some archaic FLA law regarding the church next door. Whenever churchgoers ask for beer with their pizza I tell them, "Sorry. God's fault."

On my tiptoes I plucked one of the thin, dusty glasses off the cupboards by its stem, explaining, "*Glass* is *delicate.*" I punctuated this by flicking the rim. We both flinched when the glass exploded and sprinkled into our stringy mop-heads.

"Are you O.K.!" I asked. She looked angry.

"Raphael is not like *that!*" she shouted, "Raphael is *strong!*" She stomped away, leaving her mop handle standing magically upright. When her hair trailed around the corner into the kitchen, the mop finally tipped *smack!* against the red tile, and Raphael in the dish room finally looked up, beaming at me with his usual strange admiration.

Like his sister, Raphael acknowledges me as a redhead. He's quiet, but talks and talks when it's just us. One recent slow night we hung in the small, hot-wet, four-walled dish room discussing The Secret Redheaded Brotherhood that will eventually overthrow the world, and the all-redhead punk band we'll start—*Stepchild*? *The Hateful Red*?—to provide the revolution's soundtrack. "Everyone loves my little sisters because of they have red hair," he told me as we leaned against the hot, metal dish cave. "All lots of men like them. But most of girls make *fun* of me!" Alana would have smacked him for being whiney, but I almost hugged him because it is true; red-headed girls are treated as rare gems, the boys as freckled freaks.

A second "Raphael is strong!" brought him out of the dish room to watch his sister drag Tony from the kitchen by his hairy hand. Behind the cash register lay the pile of money Tony had been counting. Any male who approaches Tony while he's counting money is told, "Buzz off malaka." But he'd left it all exposed to the world for Alana, who now stopped before me and challenged Tony, "You wrestle Raphael again!"

"Again?" I looked down into Tony's eyes. "You wrestled a 14-year-old kid?"

"No malaka, she wants me to *arm* wrestle him." Tony does have well-toned arms. He keeps himself in very good shape. But he declined the challenge: "You're gonna get me arrested for child abuse, Alana."

"*HA!* No-ho-*ho,*" Alana laughed. "Raphael *always* win! He beat Tony *every* time!"

The kitchen flooded out into the dining room in a wave of laughter as Tony and Raphael sat and locked hands in a non-smoking booth. Alana counted, "Uno, dos, *viate!*" And before we could even yell encouragement, Raphael was the humble victor, his buzzing freckles lit from behind by blushing cheeks. Alana screamed as if he'd won an Olympic medal. Tony shook his feathered head, walking off to finish counting. She hugged and dug fingers into my neck so deep I emitted an involuntary, "Yow!" and pushed her off. Quickly realizing what I'd done, I went back for a milder victory hug but now she pushed me away, and darted off again into the kitchen.

I know, I knew. I should have stayed away.

His lurid red dining room finally empty, Tony ordered Raphael to clean his bathrooms. Not thinking this fair, I made a big show of asking Alana to finish mopping so that I could go help her brother.

In the men's room, Raphael sniffed the air: "Damn, who been smoking the *mestuda* in here?" he asked. *Mestuda* is Greek for marijuana.

"Me and George smoked in here earlier," I admitted, not wanting to seem ashamed of doing something truly harmless. Besides, though Raphael's a teenager, he seems older than me.

I wire-brushed toilet-bowl grime while Raphael chiseled at the grout between the bathroom's million tiny, white, neglected but perfectly straight teeth. Aided by the fluorescence, my eyes secretly explored the peculiar dynamic of his freckles and skin and the cow-licked back of his hair so much redder than mine — until finally he caught me gazing and, rather than question me, disclosed, "My sister says you are a writer."

"Well, I write. But I haven't really been published," I answered, dipping my brush into the toilet.

"What is 'published'?"

"Um. It's like when someone puts your writing in a magazine or makes a book out of your writing," I explained. "It's the same as when the record company put out Queen's songs. Queen has been published." Though Latin men are supposedly the most macho on the planet, the kitchen guys all love the band Queen. *All* of them worship Freddie Mercury and will not accept that he is dead and that his band is no more any sooner than they'll admit he was, "queer as a football-bat" (one of Tony's sayings). They speak of Queen in present tense, i.e. "If Queen have to work at a restaurant," Raphael said, attacking the grout, "then they won't have time for make their music. So maybe if you don't work, Patrick, you can be published!"

"Yes," I agreed, dipping the brush again into the toilet. "But until then, here I am. So I don't know if you'd call me a *writer*."

"Alana have a friend who did published a famous book."

"I know, I know."

Maybe Raphael noticed my slight jealousy: "You are good writer, man," he nodded, stirring the freckles calmly orbiting his nose. "I can tell. You are smart. So...you will help me with something?"

"Yeah, definitely, Raphael." My heart quivered. "What's the matter?"

"I have a tutor in the daytimes so I can go to school while I am in America. He give me homework, but Mami and Alana are too busy planning the wedding to help me."

I know, I know...

"I don't remember what you call in English," Raphael continued, "but I have to write some-sing to make ah...make someone believe some-sing. A *personal*... No... A *pers...pers...*"

"A persuasive essay?"

"Yes! You will help me?"

"Of course I'll help you, Raphael."

When the entire bathroom shined white, I sat on the porcelain sink above Raphael and explained the mechanics of a persuasive essay as he jotted notes. He's so sweet that I felt wrong teaching him to *persuade*. Looking down into his innocent eyes, I imagined him in a couple years, *persuading* women to look past his odd beauty and... From there I imagined his *persuasion* evolving into *manipulation*. And it will have all started with me, in a bathroom reeking of bleach and pot. I am no teacher, no example. Raphael, the sweet beautiful kid, deserves so much better.

1.5 THE TRICK I DO WHERE I BLIND MYSELF

Saturday morning I drove two-and-a-half hours south to Ft. Heathen to spend Xmas with my parents. There were frowns, there was an under-appreciated meal that took hours to prepare, there were dinnertime stories of illness and failure and warning, drawn-out and repeated for lack of anything else, and there were three loads of my laundry.

First dragging the laundry into my parents' too-clean condo, I didn't kiss Mom. I haven't since I was about 12. That may also have been the year she started intermittently claiming she hates me, though I've never taken that too seriously. She still finds occasion to repeat the sentiment about once a year, but I always assume she just has a bad temper and a sloppy mouth, and every six months when I come home, I make myself at least hug her. This visit though, I couldn't, since hugging her would put my eyes too close to the nasty, freshly-stitched scar on her neck where skin cancer had been surgically thwarted days earlier. The scar runs from behind her ear, six pink inches down her neck. I could have tried closing my eyes and hugging her, but once my chin was over her shoulder, my face would have been *right there* and I wouldn't have been able to not peek, knowing *Someday that'll be my scar...*

So, my laundry saved me. Though it also meant not hugging my Dad, who I get along with O.K. and have no problem hugging when I haven't seen him in months. Still, with exaggerated strain I carried my laundry past him up the pale teal-green, carpeted stairs, and his mouth turned down in a frown that looked almost insincere given the innate sunny-ness of his lips; this year the FLA sun gave his lips cancer, and the doctors burned their top layer off so that Dad could start over, cancer free. At 60 years old he now owns the new, puffy, pink lips of a 17-year-old runway model. I myself sprouted a skin cancer this year too, a resilient, scaly pink blemish on my temple. My doctor froze it off with nitrogen on two separate occasions and on my way out of his office the last time he was still warning me to call him, "If it comes back again."

My sister was the first to gleefully note our family coincidence over sulky Christmas dinner: "You've all had cancer!"

My parents didn't laugh when I followed my sister's bleak revelation by joking, "Well, my cancer's *you guys'* fault for moving me to Florida."

Because no one else in my family was blessed with red hair, my parents never empathized with the particular needs of my pale species and as a result my skin remained singed throughout most of my childhood. I once fell asleep at the pool and burned so badly my eyes swelled shut and I had to stay home from school for three days. In college, I finally learned to apply a layer of 50-SPF sunscreen every day — though I also learned that one's skin cancer fate is determined *before* they turn 18, so I'm already doomed. Which is why seeing Mom's surgery scar up close would have been like looking into my own damned future; if they're *brunettes*, and *they* can't escape it...

After dinner, my sister went drinking with high school friends and, left no other option, I conceded to watch TV with my Dad. During a commercial, we lay as lumps on parallel couches and he brought me up-to-date on my half-brother, David, my Dad's son from a previous marriage. David's a skinny, commercial truck driver from Iowa. Every few years David stops by the condo while driving some shipment down into FLA, but I haven't seen him since high school. "You know, David's gotten really bad," my Dad said, his eyes glazed with television.

"Yeah, you told me," I replied, not wanting more but…

"Well, now his mother is having the trucking company send her his checks, so he doesn't go spend it on dope," my Dad huffed. "I always thought he was just smoking marijuana. But that's where it starts I guess…"

"Oh god. That's not *true*, Dad," I defended, my volume unintentionally admitting my own habits. "Don't blame weed. Weed's probably less harmful than cheese or peanut butter, definitely not as bad as alcohol."

"He's 40 years old!" Dad repeated. And I wondered if I'll still smoke pot every day in 13 years; if I'll grow out of it, or graduate up, like my half-brother.

"Yeah, his mother's in charge of his money," Dad continued. "David's not even allowed to pump his own gas. When he needs to fill up his 18-wheeler, he has to call his mother to come pump his gas for him. Can you imagine? Forty years old and your mother's pumping your gas?" Meanwhile, upstairs, mine is folding my underwear, as I impatiently anticipate escape.

I can rarely stay in their condo very long, not with all the cancer and white wicker and mauves and teals. Now I was trying to leave the same day I arrived, which, as usual, surprised my Dad. "What? So soon?" he protested. "At least stay until morning." But I barely heard him as I listened for the dryer's rumble to cease and set me free to drive back to bleak Tampa, sleep in my own bed, wake alone, type the obituaries of those who died on Xmas, then return to Pizza Dive, and Alana.

These past weeks, things have really changed between Alana and me. Now, when we fold pizza boxes in the wait station and I make a joke, she falls into me, laughing. Big George and the other male employees all stand around bug-eyed unbelieving when this perfect girl squeals, presses her cheek to my diaphragm, cups her cold, soft hands around my neck and digs in. But while they suffer mere jealous pangs, my heart truly suffers, because she's getting married.

It stung so badly this past week I finally couldn't help asking loaded questions like, "Does this guy you're marrying, does *he* make you laugh? Is he smart? Do you guys have good conversations like *we* do?" I wouldn't have attempted such brave and questionable behavior had Raphael been there. But on his night off, Alana held my eyes until finally I suggested, "You should run off with me when I leave Tampa."

"To see your parents?" she laughed.

"No. I'm moving soon. I mean you should come with me when I move. Be my roommate!"

"Oh yes?" Her eyebrow arched. "When?"

"Soon," I promised, throbbing.

"To where?"

"I don't even care where at this point."

"Oh! Move to Costa Rica!" she sang. "I miss it *so* mosh. It is *so* beautiful there Pat-reek!"

"And you'll come with me?" I taunted, testing with mock-persuasion as behind my eyes I pictured her in 20 years, crazier, meaner, yelling at me loud to be *heard over the louder cries of our children and when she screams at me in Spanish I feel so far from her I wish I'd never...* But I realized that my wild, negative imaginings were just reverberations from growing up with my particular mother, or else the more recent shock of Natalie. Just six months after we met, Natalie and I began screaming at each other, and it took four years before we stopped and finally let go. I've never seen two people who claimed to love each other fight so often, so hard, so *loud*. That had to be an anomaly though, and I shouldn't project all that onto much more soulful, realer, happier Alana. And so, I eventually began to believe myself more deeply each time I advocated, "Dump that guy and come with me."

As I prescribed evil, Alana did not notice me snatch a plastic coffee creamer from the counter. I also stole a fork then asked, "Would your fiancé do *this* for you?" I turned so she saw only my profile, and cupped my hand around my left eye like looking into an imaginary telescope, the creamer hidden inside. I breathed deep and dramatic then swung the fork into my eye: white creamer burst forth and Alana fell against me once again, laughing in the trail of white liquid dribbling down my work shirt. And though I suffered another kind of hurt, for the first time in almost two years I didn't miss Natalie one bit.

For some reason though, my eye also ached. I slid from Alana's grip and walked through the restaurant's blinking, buzzing video arcade to the newly clean bathroom. At the mirror I drew my eyelid down by the lashes: a dab of blood dripped from a tiny fork-hole just above my eyeball's outline. I ran my pounding heart back out to the wait station. "My god Alana!" I broadcast. "Look what happened when I did that trick for you! I *stabbed* myself!"

Alana gasped at the blood, covered her mouth and gripped my wrist. "One centimeter lower," I continued, "and I would have stabbed my eye!" Her nails dug in when I added, "I almost *blinded myself* to make you laugh! Would your boyfriend do that for you?" Her cheeks rose behind her hand. "You shouldn't get married, Alana," I reiterated, in total belief.

In answer, she unveiled her smile and placed her hand over mine on the fake-wood counter by the giant, steam-belching hot chocolate machine. "Patrick, I like you," she repeated, then closed those slow eyes and ran her fingers across my stomach on her way back to her section.

In her place, big waiter George slid up, grabbed a sheet of white cardboard and began folding. Inserting slats into slots George recommended, "Tag her, bro. You need to. Like, now." He nodded his crewcut. When I didn't respond, George set aside the now 3-D pizza box, picked up another flat sheet and proceeded to work its pre-programmed origami. "You know she's only marrying that guy to stay in the country," he said.

"He's not from Costa Rica?" I asked, watching George's muscular arms maul the box into shape.

"Nope," he grinned. "He's Cuban. From Miami. She's just marrying him because she wants to be a citizen. She's only known that dude a couple months." George set another box aside. "She likes you. It's *so* obvious, bro. You should tag her."

"'Tagging' her would be illegal," I reminded him. "She's 17, George."

"But she's smarter than most people our age. And *that's* what matters," he countered. "Since when do you respect The Law anyway? They're the idiots who make pot illegal. And if it wasn't for pot we might not be friends!" Which is true; nights and nights smoking in the mop room before, during and after work have indeed bonded us. "We're only not allowed to tag a minor," George continued, "because we *supposedly* dwarf them mentally. But that's not the case here."

Though I followed his logic, "I don't think she really likes me like that way."

George chuckled, laid another box atop the teetering white stack, patted my back and lumbered off to the service window to collect his meatballs.

* * *

I carried Alana with me all Sunday morning at *The Trib*. The reporters had December 26th off, leaving me alone to write the Xmas obits and distribute faxes to empty desks, while my imagination kissed Alana. Intermittently, she and I paused to laugh and talk about art and languages and "*lee-chre-choor*" like we do at the restaurant. Smiling her imaginary smile wet with our saliva, Alana cooed the same words she had last week in real life, "It's been so long time since I've had smart talking." And again I kissed her, while emailing completed obits to the bureau on the other side of the bay.

I left the newsroom knowing she'd be at Pizza Dive when I arrived at 5, and that we would flirt until 10, or later. Walking in, I would receive a hello kiss on the cheek, Costa Rican style, with feeling, but without misrepresentation — though she doesn't really do it to anyone else in the restaurant. Readying for Pizza Dive — tying on my stained apron, adjusting my plastic straws, picking out reading material for after the rush and after the boxes are all folded — I also grabbed Richard Brautigan's *The Abortion* for Alana, because she wants to learn more English. But I rolled up to Pizza Dive and ran for the back service entrance, accidentally leaving the book in my truck. Which seemed smarter anyway; later in the night I would casually mention, 'There might be a book in my truck you could borrow. Something you'd like, maybe. Let me go check...'

But in the kitchen the bad news smacked me in the smile: "You better be on your toes tonight, malaka," Tony literally cried, chopping onions on the line. "It's gonna be just you and George tonight. Alana ain't working."

"She's not?" My face heated. "Why the hell am I even here then?" I tried to chuckle. The kitchen guys smiled at me without understanding. "Where is she?"

"She's not feeling well. She's sick," Tony explained, wiping his eyes with an apeish, knife-wielding hand. "She has an upset stomach. She got herself knocked up."

1.6 TAKE MY VIRGIN

Three years ago on my very first day at *The Trib* I lit up upon seeing her red hair. Or what seemed to be red hair. I'm most attracted to women representing my visual opposite: swarthy, healthy-looking. But I'm also innately attracted to fellow redheads. Brown-spotted pale skin makes me well up hoping *Maybe she's like me inside too...* Though really, the redhead women I've known have all seemed spoiled from too much positive attention. We've shared nothing special in common. Still the hope haunts me whenever I see one.

Anyway, the first week that she trained me, my redhead-seeming co-worker hung over my shoulder, her spotless pale cheek close to mine as she taught me the procedure for writing a proper obit. I thought my new job might be worth showing up for. But in the following weeks, along with realizing she dyes her hair red, I noticed she wears too much makeup and hairspray, and hangs out at dumb sports bars in Ybor City. So I distanced myself, and disliked myself for it; she's so sweet, and honestly appreciates me, still I don't give her a chance.

So, this afternoon I finally forced myself to do the right thing and ask her out. The fake redhead girl beamed and pinched my uneven stomach. "Of course, Patrick!" And I could only think

Why not, if Alana's fucking pregnant?

I've been brooding on her pregnancy, but decided not to ask her about it — a plan conveniently congruent to my *inability* to ask her. Because what if she answered, 'Yes! I am pregnant! I'm so happy!'? And what if she expected me to be happy for her? I just couldn't. So I did not grab her soft, olive elbow and plead '*Don't* have a baby Alana. Damn. Serious.' I simply folded boxes in the wait station, head down, or else escaped into the kitchen to be with men who don't understand my words, but make me feel understood in more important ways.

The kitchen's flow of love and laughter is surely thickened by the language barrier between the English speakers, the Greeks, the Spanish speakers and Brazilians; it's easier to get along when a word limit is imposed. The kitchen's so giddy they sometimes seem to be flirting, cackling like dolphins, kissing cheeks and patting asses even man to man, often while Queen plays on the kitchen radio. It's beautiful, but as tough to categorize as the flow of love between Alana and Raphael.

Alana didn't notice me ignoring her tonight. She focused on her brother who, as on any slow night, leaned against the cooler just outside the dish room, throwing his slight shadow over refrigerated bowls of iceberg lettuce, 10 pounds of truly great potato salad and 15 gallons of malaka dressing. I watched his sister stomp toward him balancing dirty plates in one small hand as her other grabbed for Raphael's dick in passing. He blocked her shot, swatted her away, and she managed to maintain her soiled dishware's balance as she trotted on, smiling her little beak.

Alana's impish smile differs from her sweet one, where her small but full lips curve into a smooth, inverted arch. When she's mischievous — like after spitting in a mean customer's drink — the sides of her top lip hike up, forcing the middle down into a tiny, pink beak of flesh. Alana placed her plates in the giant silver cave and stepped back out of the dish room to tug lightly at her brother's baggy jeans and invade his space with her little beak in his ear. She hissed too-fast Spanish to him, the tip of her nose bouncing off his head as all the while she watched me from the corner of her sly eye, perhaps wondering if I understood her, maybe hoping I didn't. I took two semesters of Spanish in college but then never traveled anywhere to practice, so by now it's all lost.

The way Raphael's face clenched, I knew Alana was just spitting intimidating, older-sister sadism. Rough play. He forced a look of boredom, as if whipping the cooler with his smelly dishrag interested him more than the wild woman in his ear. Alana's blurry Spanish grew louder. Raphael wrapped the rag around his knuckles, unwrapped it, wrapped it again and lightly punched the cooler glass, leaving a greasy mark. When he tried to step away into the dish room Alana grabbed his pockets and jerked him back into her rant. Watching it all made me miss talking to her, conspiring.

Alana gave Raphael's jeans one last hard yank down. He grabbed his big belt to keep from being pantsed. I sucked-in my gut as she ran her nails across it on her way out to the dining room. When she'd gone I stepped to the cooler and asked Raphael, "What's she bitching about?"

"Oh, she just talk crazy sheet." He shook his head and wrung his rag.

"What was she saying though, exactly?" I nudged.

He whipped the cold glass again with his rag. Looking through the grease streaks at the salads he answered, "She say she is going to suck my penis…"

My body stiffened. "What?" I helplessly envisioned that scene. "Nuh, uh. She didn't say that."

"She always talk just crazy sheet."

"So she's not serious?" I made sure.

"I don't know."

"*You don't know!*" barged out of me. I then felt silly for yelling, because '*I don't know*' holds different meanings for those not so adept with English. Alana wields '*I don't know*' as a defensive *and* offensive tool. She says it sweetly to avoid a subject, while leading you to believe she's a victim of misunderstanding. Then other times, when she actually *doesn't* understand your English she barks, "I don't know!" irritated, like you're stupid for asking. Either way, people back down from her *I don't know*. Never have I seen such power in such a lithe, pretty bird.

"No, I mean, she is not serious," Raphael assured me. "I mess up my words. She is joss crazy…" he repeated, before his sister tiptoed in through the dish room's side door. Over his shoulder she glared at me, placed index finger to her lips, reached up between Raphael's legs and in one graceful motion, unzipped his fly.

Startled Raphael scrambled for his crotch then turned and raised a threatening backhand. Alana's eyes lit furious. She seized Raphael's jaw in her little hand. His freckles blurred, chasing the face she jerked back-and-forth. Of her fastest Spanish, I understood only "*nunca!*" and assumed Alana was warning him *never* to retaliate.

Finally she released him. White fingerprints lingered on his blushing cheeks. Staring down at the red tile, Raphael zipped his fly. Alana's beak again blossomed as her language slowed, quieted. She petted her brother's strange red hair, smoothed it like a housecat, tugged a bit, hard, and then, talking calmly, smoothed him back down. Her fingers danced down his neck and spine, patted his behind, and Alana skipped away across the dining room.

"What'd she say now?" I asked, eager, anxious, frustrated having to rely on others to understand her. "She was pissed you acted like you were going to hit her?"

"Yeah," Raphael answered, ashamed. He wrapped his dishrag around his knuckles and softly punched the cooler. "She say if I pretend to hit her again, she gonna take my virgin."

"Your virgin?" A hodogentric garden statue of Mary holding Jesus came to mind, protected by half a bathtub. Then I understood: "Your *virginity*, you mean?"

"Yeah. She say if I raise my hand she gonna take my virginity. She's a fokeen crazy," Raphael mumbled then sulked back to his post.

Before I could make sense of it (or concede that I couldn't) I glanced toward the service window and met Alana's eyes. With a sweet, beakless smile and curled index finger she beckoned, "Patreek!" I walked over, forcing my own smile. "What is your work schedule?" she asked.

"Well, I work five afternoons a week at *The Trib*, but I only work here Thursday through Sunday night. Why?"

She flipped her yellow server's pad over and I watched her write on the blank back: 'Th – Sun'.

"Why?" I repeated.

"Don't have the wrong idea," she qualified, watching the dining room over her shoulder. "But I only want to work when you are working." Then her food slid out the service window and she ran it to her table.

Alone and confounded I assumed, *Tony must be harassing her.* I enjoy Tony, but he's the biggest pussyhound I've ever known.

He's truly funny, Greek-style forward, and pretty successful with women, but he can never conquer enough of them to quench his hard-on. It gets him in trouble. He recently fought a sexual harassment lawsuit aimed at him by a 16-year-old waitress; one night, as she knelt scrubbing the kitchen cooler, Tony, for the laughter of the kitchen, stepped up behind her, unzipped, and laid his penis on her shoulder. Neither the girl nor Tony admitted to the judge that they'd already been sleeping together and she'd simply seen an opportunity to tap into Tony's family's pizza empire. Proving that she'd previously *enjoyed* his penis wouldn't have helped Tony in court; he eventually won by claiming that the limp cylinder with which he knighted her shoulder was not, in fact, his genitalia, but manicotti pasta.

And even that didn't tame Tony. He still wolf-whistles at every woman who passes in through his red doors. So when Alana told me she would only work 'Th – Sun' I figured Tony was sexually harassing her. *But why only when I'm not around?* When Alana hummed past me again I grabbed her elbow: "Is someone in the kitchen messing with you? Is Tony being weird?"

"No!" she huffed like a magical, beaked colt, and jerked from my grip.

"You wouldn't lie to me?"

Her smile straightened like she would leave prints on *my* face. "I *never* lie!" she scolded — then stood there. Looking far back into my eyes. Waiting.

"O.K. All right. Jeez, sorry."

She turned and marched.

"But why do you only want to work when I'm working?" I shouted at her flapping hair. In her absence I theorized, *Maybe her fiancé hassles her about working here with all these worshipful men.* A valid concern for him, as restaurant jobs are indeed like rabbit cages. Every restaurant I ever worked in, the staff finished their end-of-the-night side-work then met up at bars to turn their tips into alcohol and pair off to go home and make mistakes with each other. Natalie finally cheated on *me* with an 18-year-old busboy at her restaurant job. And since Latin men are reportedly super jealous and possessive (though there's little evidence of that at Pizza Dive), I leaned against the service window, imagining Alana's defense to her boyfriend, 'No, at work I only talk to my friend Pa-treek. No one else.'

But when I couldn't imagine why he'd allow her to talk to *me*,

I remembered how, when I first asked Natalie out, she'd laughed, "I thought you were gay!" We'd met at a party and I was being happy and animated, and my laugh is higher-pitched and cuts through a room, but I'm not gay. Once in an elevator at *The Trib*, alone with some nice-smelling businessman, I did wonder with a remarkable intensity if I didn't want to kiss him. But that's what cologne is supposed to do. Plus, it had been a year since Natalie left, and after so long without being touched, I was starving, and when you're starving you hallucinate. I may be in this same trap now, with Alana.

But I accept that my laugh sounds feminine. And I've been laughing a lot more lately, with Alana. We all need someone to help pass the time at work or else we'll go crazy, but Alana specifically needs someone who won't try and 'tag' her. So she clings to me because I'm not a sexual threat. She doesn't love me; she feels *safe*.

Which hurts to know, but at least something makes sense.

1.7 FIGHT NIGHT

Despite our impending date, I avoided the false redhead girl yesterday at *The Trib*. Crossing paths in the newsroom she'd smile and I'd feel seasick. Then later I arrived at Pizza Dive to a wedding invitation tucked behind the time clock, inviting us all to, "Come celebrate the holy giving-away of Alana Ephraim to Carlos Whatshisfuckingface." I counted eighteen tiny lavender flowers around the invitation's border. Two children sat in the center: a girl and a boy holding hands, their backs to me. Tearing it up would've changed nothing.

"Only a month till the wedding, bro," big George's voice and timecard breeched my shoulder. Punching in, he prodded, "Better hurry and work the magic with Alana."

Neither she nor Raphael worked tonight, and since George was off the night she'd verbally molested her brother, I filled in some plot holes for him as we passed through the smiling, laughing kitchen, past Tony at the front counter to the wait station, where we stopped to fold boxes — our lives are measured in pizza boxes. Measuring out our lives, I told George everything.

In the end, George scoffed a spec like a white flea that landed beside my shirt's Pizza Dive logo: "You think she thinks you're gay? Bro, you think too much."

"But she's used to macho Latin dudes."

"Man, it's cool that you're humble," said George. "But if you can't even *accept* that a girl digs you, then… Bro, don't be so sensitive."

"I'm not humble," I replied. "I just really don't think she likes me that way. She just doesn't think it's weird to be *nice*, the way white girls do. She's getting *married* George!"

"I know! So you better tag that soon."

This response seemed very Floridian, and again I wanted out. I thought to bring up her pregnancy, but feared George would say something I didn't want to hear. So I silently conspired with myself: *Leaving Tampa will solve this Alana problem too…* I debated quitting Pizza Dive right there. George continued, "Tag Alana, tag Alana, tag…"

Finally I shouted, "George! Fucking *drop* it. Serious."

George rolled his eyes, tossed an unfinished box aside and lumbered off, leaving me with guilt. George is just about my only friend these days. And our friendship was built partly on sharing harmlessly sleazy evaluations of female customers. We laugh and laugh, impersonating Tony debating which teen girls he should or shouldn't "tag." George doesn't know I might be in love with Alana, so why would he speak any more respectfully of her? That's not real logic but… I just shouldn't have snapped at him. So, later as we mopped together, I apologized and invited George to a punk-rock concert that my old friend Jake was promoting in Ybor City.

Ybor was once the Cuban ghetto — the only culture in the entire state, just about. When I first fled to college, Ybor's art community flourished because no one else in FLA wanted to live in *old* buildings. But by senior year the city had forced the Cubans and artists out, deemed Ybor the "Historic District," ripped its guts out and replaced them with a shopping mall, 20-plex movie theatre, a too-shiny bar district, and a perfect example of FLA's identity crisis. Ybor's buildings now have dead, glassy eyes. And weekend nights find Ybor's red brick sidewalks burdened with thousands of drunk nine-to-fivers finally free of their neckties, but still voluntarily tucking their shirts.

The plague hasn't yet reached Ybor's far end though, where my friend Jake still books shows in a little club called Our Bar. Jake and I played in a band together in college, but our friendship has since been reduced to his letting me into concerts for free. Our Bar wasn't crowded when George and I arrived in our smelly Pizza Dive uniforms. George proceeded inside while I lingered in the doorway with Jake, a position that afforded us simultaneous views of both the band on stage and the thick human flock crowding the main strip blocks away. Jake and I lamented Tampa's sad cultural state until a white kid with a Mohawk fell into Jake. The punk grabbed the door-frame to support himself, squinted swimming eyes and asked, "How much it cost?"

"Don't worry about it," said Jake's big red beard — he's bald beneath his Tamp Bay Bucs cap, but Jake's definitely a redhead; another reason we've remained friends. "You can go in. Just let me X your hand."

"You see a punk dude come in ear?" the kid coughed on me.

"Nope. Just you."

The kid fell back out the door and Jake tucked his money and marker into his Hawaiian shirt's pocket. "I'm done man," he griped, walking away from me. "I don't know why I bother. If it's not 80s night, no one in Tampa gives a shit." Jake stepped inside to sit at the bar with his back to me like the kids on Alana's wedding invitation.

I went in too and stood beside the stage with George, keeping one eye out the window on that dramatic scene with the Mo-hawk kid, who now slouched drunk on a girl's shoulder. Because tears streaked her makeup, I assumed she was his girlfriend. Her young hips were packed into tight, plaid pants, like some perverted private-school uniform. Her lips were those of a FLA *cracker*: thin redneck lips, the evolutionary result of many generations drinking beer exclusively from cans. She struggled to support her sloppy beau before finally she eased him down against a skinny tree planted in a brick sidewalk. I envied his safety — until she backed away, and a large skinhead swooped in and attempted to sober the kid with a black boot to his shoulder. The skin yelled down at the Mohawk like a corner-man rallying his broken, slack-jawed boxer. I couldn't hear the skin's words for the loud band, but saw him slap the kid's soft face a few times, until his moussed Mohawk drooped over. No one watching the band noticed as this scene outside grew rougher. The girlfriend finally stopped crying, as if satisfied that her boyfriend was now being taken care of. She chewed on a glow stick and watched the big skin cock his leather arm back and punch her boyfriend in the teeth. The kid followed his hair's trajectory down to the red brick.

"Holy shit!" I slapped meaty George's shoulder and pointed out the window. "That guy just knocked his friend out!"

Though shorter than me, George is twice my breadth, and so walked straight out and hovered near the punks, glaring at and eventually conversing with the big skin. Beside them the splayed-out Mohawk kid bled from his teeth. Between songs I heard the kid's studs and chains rattle against the pavement. He was having a real seizure. I dashed into the bar and ordered Jake to call an ambulance. Back outside I found George nose-to-nose with the skinhead like on a boxing poster. Unable to get a hand around George's arm, I jerked his work-shirt and urged, "C'mon, let's go. No more. Jake just called an ambulance. Fuck this. Let's go."

Luckily, George is pacifist enough to turn away from a fight without much coercion. We stepped over the shaking, bleeding Mohawk kid and his dry-eyed girlfriend.

As we approached the main strip's chaos from its snaking side, the world grew louder but George remained silent. Soon we were swallowed by Ybor's human sea. Steamy skin and breath killed the cool air FLAidians live through summer for. Through what felt like six feet of bathwater, I followed in George's big shadow. He cleared our path of yuppies and led our way — until I collided with his bulky back outside Club FUN. During my sophomore year of college, Club FUN was The Stone Lounge, where Jake booked great concerts. When the owners couldn't afford Ybor's rising rents, they sold the lease to whomever gave it that horrid new name and aimed for the high-end, dress-code crowd who've recently — along with the younger suburban crackers — discovered rave culture. Club FUN now plays weak Orlando break-beat, and techno that shouldn't exist outside of aerobics classes.

"Hey bro, I need to use the bathroom!" George shouted at Club FUN's giant bouncer. "Can I go in for a second!"

"Sure! It's free tonight!" the mean-looking, bald bouncer yelled back – one guards every Ybor doorway these days. "We're trying something new tonight!" The bouncer aimed his big thumb at a poster: *LIVE BOXING TONIGHT! TOUGH MAN CONTEST! ALL COMERS! $100 PRIZE!* "Come in and check it out!"

"No!" I protested. "*No*, no, no, no, no. I don't want to see that *at all.* I've had way more than enough punching for one night, George."

"I need to use the bathroom before we drive home. And there's no line here," he shrugged and disappeared inside. On the street, the khaki-clad living dead staggered, bumping me, their dress-shirts wet with sweat, spilled drinks and vomit — until I too sought free refuge inside Club FUN.

Some of the best shows of my life happened at the old Stone Lounge, but Club FUN was unrecognizable. A dusty spotlight hammered down onto a full-sized boxing ring, the world around the ring receding into blackness. We'd arrived between rounds. Two big meatheads still in *their* work clothes (tan pants and tucked-in polos *sans* logos or aprons) slumped in their corners, glaring across the ring at each other, adjusting headgear and sipping giant plastic cups of beer. Hateful modern rock music filled the cavernous space like invisible cement. When the volume lowered and the bell rang, the drunken men plodded to the center to artlessly wail on each other. I hate fighting of any kind but I accept that, though brutal, real boxing is real art — whereas Club FUN's *tough-men* flailed sloppy windmills, their shirts untucking as they vented frustrations on the stranger before them who now represented their bosses, parents, the women who deny them. Considering how many on Ybor's Main Strip are looking for the smallest excuse to punch each other anyway, I'm sure Fight Night will become as huge a Tampa phenomenon as massage parlors and full-nude lapdances.

I need to move before The Trib *deems this a cultural phenom worthy of a feature,* I happened to be thinking when I spotted the fake redhead girl, my date for tomorrow night. On the opposite side of the ring, she bounced and screamed at the fighters, wasted, falling over herself. I turned and dashed back outside to wait for George.

I was wound on the drive home. And we had no more pot. We were silent. I might have explained to my only friend how I've always appreciated that FLA is at least slow, safe and understandable, but really it turns out I don't even understand the ground I walk on — or more to the point, *drive* on. Instead I silently dropped George at his parents' house, returned to my apartment, hit the bong then crawled into bed to have a hopeful but calming dream, about being eased down onto the pavement, safe.

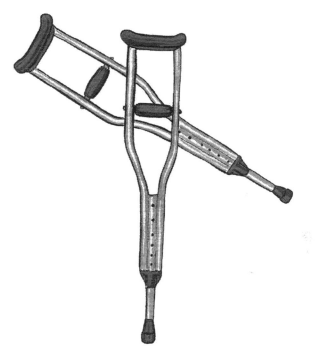

1.8 WE WORK TOGETHER

This week's traumas provided impetus for me to finally begin the exit process. Today, I actually handed my editor my two weeks notice — or at least slipped it in his mailbox. Either way, I now have no choice: goodbye fair newsroom, and good riddance FLA. Though where to go? Must decide quickly or risk trapping myself in parental condo purgatory. To make sure I won't balk, I called the realty office and warned them I'm moving out in February. The secretary later called back and said they'd found a renter for January. I conceded. Fated? Exciting!

But it also means I must quit Pizza Dive soon, and before that, find closure with Alana. I will drag it around forever if we don't have our moment before I leave. I'll brave that limb soon; as of tonight I'm positive she wants me in some way. And I never would have known had I not gone on that date with the fake red — Christie.

Her name is Christie.

Today Christie called in sick at *The Trib*. Assuming this meant she would also cancel our date, my queasy stomach calmed enough that by lunch I decided to treat myself to my favorite salad buffet restaurant. There I ended up seated near two of the newsroom's young female reporters. Despite my two years fetching their faxes and court files and sneaking studies of their sleek gray skirt-suits (I always imagined them as beautiful sharks swimming by my desk), neither woman recognized me. And thus I was free to listen. Over the squawk of the lunch crowd, they detailed mild infidelities against their husbands.

One reporter has Alana-like sandy skin. Her mouth like a flower full of teeth crunched lettuce. Her blonde colleague across the table attacked her own plate and playfully admonished: "I can't *believe* you let that guy *do that* last night. In front of all those people! His hairy hands all over your ass? Do you even remember his name?"

"Tony? Maybe? I didn't know *what* was going on. I drank them mojitos, girl," the sandy one snorted, "I couldn't even *feel* his hands down there! He seemed cute though. A little short but…" I'd never seen either of them laugh. In the newsroom they always acted as if social warmth impedes the climb; they treated me like an office supply. So, despite their cruel conversation, I liked watching their personalities spill out: "You started it anyway," she continued, "dancing on the bar! Everyone could see your underwear!"

"I didn't *kiss* anyone though."

"Not this time."

Their hands over their mouths suppressed laughter and chewed vegetables, until finally the blonde channeled my biggest question, "What would your husband do if he knew you let some guy touch your ass?"

I noticed a diamond like a fat tick feeding off the sandy one's finger when she laid her fork aside and squinted out the window at the white FLA sky. Her squinted lids folded like thin lace handkerchiefs. "It doesn't matter," she claimed. "I know I love my husband, and *he* knows I love him, so it doesn't matter. He'd be mad. But he shouldn't be. It doesn't matter."

What should have sickened me somehow had the opposite effect. *Why be so sensitive?* I asked myself, and for a moment everything weighed less; this week's anxieties and fistfights and wedding invitations faded, and for the first time I envisioned going on this date with Christie and just having fun and not worrying about how much I do or don't like her. Working on my third plate of rich salad I rationalized *It's just a date. I don't have to love her. It won't kill her if I don't kiss her goodnight...*

A feminine "Oh shit," woke me from this epiphany. The reporters had recognized me. The chewing mulatto evaluated me for long seconds then, "You're not married are you?"

"Not even a girlfriend," I admitted, then for some reason lied, "Not even looking."

"Men don't ever stop looking," she said, "they only stop trying."

I nodded because it sounded true.

"So, you're probably gay then," she continued.

"Not at all." I then blurted the last thing I wanted them to know: "I have a date tonight actually. With a girl."

"Christie the red-haired editorial assistant," stated the blonde. She'd already broken the story.

"*Head* editorial assistant," her friend added. "And she *dyes* her hair." Then back to me: "I'm just messing with you. You don't seem gay. Don't be so sensitive."

We were reading each other's minds! She'd sensed inner confusion and, though she was using it to try and spook me, I felt suddenly close to her. Then her smile straightened: "So, how much of our conversation did you hear?"

"Enough to scare me away from women forever," I smirked.

"Really?" She turned to her blonde friend. "Forever?" They smiled. "I had no idea I was so *powerful.*" We all laughed, together.

The blonde rose: "I'm gonna use the ladies room." The other reporter stared back out the window. Not wanting to leave her, I continued eating, despite my stomach's pleas. Because I equate vegetables with *health*, whenever I visit the salad buffet I consume and consume until I'm miserable. I cram my intestines so full of *health* I can barely fold my body in half and slide it into my truck and drive it back to the newsroom. Cleaning this last plate I followed her squint's trajectory into the sky, to *The Trib*'s huge logo blaring across downtown Tampa. I imagined her contemplating her job, quitting it and running off to do something insane and beautiful. Her imagined whirlwind divorce of her burdens so inspired me that, upon the blonde's return, I announced to both women, "I'm quitting today."

They nodded affirmation like weak handshakes and unsheathed their cell phones, making sure they weren't late. Slipping hers back into her purse, the sandy reporter looked down at me and asked, "So, that's tonight you're going out with the redhead?"

"She's not a redhead, actually," I reminded her. "But yeah, I guess I am."

"Well, good luck then," she sighed. "And congratulations."

I watched them depart out the window in separate SUVs, then hoisted my food-logged body up from the booth and drove it back toward that logo in the sky.

Back at work they resumed office rules: no fraternizing with the help. I ran errands for them as it seems I always have. She pushed papers at me — "Fax this" — with no more regard for my spiritual aspirations than she would those of a stapler. But they had already helped me up onto a wave of optimism I surfed for the rest of the day. I did not dwell on them, or Alana. Only my impending date.

And as I exited the newsroom, this momentum led me to slip a letter in my editor's mailbox, explaining my decision to finally escape FLA.

* * *

Back at home I called the fake — Christie. I called Christie and asked what time she would pick me up. Part of enjoying this date meant that if she liked me, if she wanted my attention, then I would not pick her up, or drive her around, or pay for her meal. And let *her* deal with nausea like at a job interview, the way I often have on dates.

But on the phone, she said she couldn't go. She'd stayed home today with a twisted knee, unable to even drive her stick-shift. But before dialing her number, I'd loosened-up with some pot and two beers and now really wanted to go out and laugh and keep drinking and see what happened. "Aw, c'mon," I prodded. "I've been looking forward to this all day!" She seemed suspicious of my sudden enthusiasm, but I disarmed her by offering to wait on her at Pizza Dive. "I'm an excellent waiter," I promised. "They can't sell alcohol but we can bring our own good beer!"

"I don't like beer," she giggled.

"We'll buy wine at Publix then and head over to Pizza Dive and have anything we want as much as we want for *free*! I'll drive!"

She loved the idea, and recited directions to her apartment.

Readying for my first date in forever, I drank more and sang loudly in the shower, not caring who saw me through the chest-high window above my bathtub. Mine is the only two-story house on the block and I bathe in full view of the entire one-story neighborhood, sometimes forgetting that from some angles my head and shoulders are visible to every neighbor as I sing with my mouth open or masturbate. Still, the shower's windowsill provides an excellent place to set a beer, and cold beer in a hot shower is a magical combination that sometimes makes me sing with my mouth open, not caring who sees. After toweling off, smoking a little more then brushing my teeth, I was really ready for *fun*!

En route to Christie's beige condo, I picked up a six-pack. Upstairs she greeted me dressed and perfumed. She wrapped around my neck for support and I helped her hop down three flights and out to my truck. No woman besides Alana has touched me in forever, and Christie's soft warmth felt good.

Swerving to Pizza Dive I asked, "So, what happened, exactly?"

Her eyes rolled. She has pretty eyes. *Melding Christie and that handicapped girl would produce one perfect looking woman*, I chastised myself for thinking. She continued, "I went to some stupid boxing thing in Ybor and I was all drunk and jumping around and twisted my knee."

We both laughed, for different reasons.

Then for a while the weed kept me silent, leaving empty air for Christie to fill with the story of how, "My knees have always been screwed up. When I was born I came out backwards and for some reason the doctor had to break my legs to get me out. I still have the tiny little casts they cut off my baby legs. I walked pigeon toed until I was like 14. The messed-up thing is, I think they gave my mom the choice of a cesarean; the doctor's could've just lifted me out, but I think she actually *chose* to have them break my legs." I didn't tell her that my mom would have chosen the same. I let Christie ramble, "The umbilical cord was like wrapped around my neck and my eyes were all black and swollen shut and supposedly I was dead for like, the first five minutes of my life."

"Damn."

"Yeah, it's true. Then as if life hasn't been hard enough," she casually confessed, "today I started my period."

And though I hadn't contemplated sleeping with Christie outside of that first workweek, when she mentioned her period, the thought came instinctually: *No sex tonight...* My instincts still function! Christie then disappeared behind my menstrual contemplation: I'd forgotten about periods since I ceased sharing my life with Natalie's. I used to think about them in some capacity every day, saw their wrappers in my trashcan, knew their smell, waited for them, blamed them for things. I now barely remember fetching 4am ice water for Natalie, wiping away her cramp-induced tears (happy that, this time, the tears weren't my fault) and always waiting for those few days every month when her cycle blessed us with the freedom to do it the way it's meant to be done. Now I don't even read magazines or watch TV where ads would remind me that periods still happen.

Finally, these thoughts faded into whatever story Christie finished as we pulled up outside Pizza Dive.

Tony spotted Christie from behind the register and bound around the front counter. "Hey malaka, who is *this*?" He helped her through his red double doors, asking her questions, complimenting her, giving her all the attention she probably deserved.

"Hey boss," I interrupted, "you mind if I go make a pizza for us? Maybe some salads?"

"Yeah, yeah, do whatever you want, malaka." He waved me away, concentrating on my date.

The kitchen guys peeked up over the service window like soldiers in the trenches, checking Christie out and patting my back as I stood on the food line, layering on too many toppings. "A stoner special," Tony calls the overworked pies George and I make for ourselves.

I slid the heavy thing into the oven then carried Christie away from Tony into the back section. I set her down in a booth and stood at the head of the table. "Everything is taken care of this evening madam," I announced, ceremoniously uncapping two beers with her *Club FUN* bottle-opener keychain. "Your food will be out shortly."

We laughed and drank and laughed — until I noticed Alana over Christie's shoulder. Had Alana not supposedly synchronized her schedule to mine, I'd never have brought a date to Pizza Dive. I tried to avoid comparing the two of them when Alana stopped at our booth and forced a smile. My thumping heart filled my cheeks with blood as I introduced the ladies. Alana bent down to peck Christie's cheek and crippled Christie rose to meet Alana's beak. They performed an awkward version of the Latin greeting kiss. Christie blushed, sitting down. Alana rolled her eyes.

"What do you want to eat?" Alana then asked, staring at the pen pressed to her yellow server's notebook.

"I guess Tony didn't give you the days off you wanted?" I asked.

"What do you want to eat?" Alana repeated.

Surprised, I laughed.

"What do you want to eat?" she said again.

What the hell? Christie's eyes implored me.

"Uh, I made my own pizza," I finally answered. "It's in the oven. I'll get it myself. Don't worry though, we'll still tip you for having to clean…"

Alana abandoned my sentence for other customers, and Christie asked aloud, "What the hell?"

"I don't know." Then I couldn't help gushing, "She's usually really cool, an *amazing* person, crazy but smart. One of my favorite people, actually. We have a lot of fun working together."

Christie looked past me. "She's very pretty."

I turned to watch Alana gallop back at us. "Hey Alana!" I shouted as she fled past. Supplying straws and smiles to her customers, she accidentally met my eyes, then jerked them away, and marched out. "Hey Alana! Wait!" I slid out of the booth and wobbled to my feet. "I'm gonna go check on our pizza," I told Christie.

My heavy head like a blood-filled balloon led me through the blurry dining room, past Tony at the register and into the kitchen, in pursuit of Alana. Through the guffawing kitchen, the prep room and Tony's office, I chased Alana, close enough to have grabbed her hair. "Alana! The other day we're best friends and now… Alana! Stop! Serious!"

She rushed on and on through back rooms until we hit a dead end in dry storage. There, alone together with boxes of dried pasta and giant sauce cans, she turned on me like she might bite my face. Instead, shivering, she proclaimed, "I *HATE* NOT WORKING WITH YOU!"

Like a bucket of cold water, confusion, elation, sadness and hope all dumped over my head... Then she stormed back through me, left me alone again.

My joints unstuck slowly and I creaked back through the maze of rooms. The kitchen guys stared at me; they'd heard her yell but probably hadn't understood what she'd meant any more than I did. I stuffed my shaking hands into a pair of over-sized, silver mitts and through the service window I watched Alana slow her gate outside the dining room, wipe her eyes and re-apply her service industry smile. I reached into the oven: the density of toppings caused the pie to bake slowly, so I slid it back into the heat and shut the heavy door. The kitchen snickered at me on my way out.

Back at our booth Christie opined, "You know, I think that girl is *jealous*."

I'd held that idea at bay. But when an actual woman claimed that Alana seemed to care, my heart and smile blazed. Opening another beer, I kept the smile, but changed the subject: "Oh hey! Guess what! I quit *The Trib* today!"

"What?" Christie frowned.

"I'm moving!"

Before I could admit I have no idea where I'm moving to, Alana returned, struggling under the weight of my pizza. Her arms shook, lowering the pie down before Christie, its round shadow looming over us like some mothership. Alana sighed relief and stepped back. Below her raw eyes, the little beak appeared: "These is for you," she said, patting Christie's shoulder, fanning us with her slow-blinking eyelashes. When she'd gone again, I let Christie serve herself a slice and surely eat the spit of the girl I love.

Christie and I didn't talk much while eating, and she didn't eat much. When we were full, I rose with difficulty and traversed the dining room to retrieve a to-go box. In a corner of the wait station, Alana folded a box that seemed equal to her size. I leapt forward and snatched it from her hands. She glared up, then turned to flee. When I grabbed her arm her eyes opened wide and she felt frail in my hand and *Oh shit, what am I doing? I'm drunk and being rough...* But her fear quickly dissipated into sadness. Her wilted face turned away:

"What do you want?"

Her despondency gave me confidence. My skin felt tight. I guided her face to mine and assured her, "I would much rather be here, working with you."

When once she would have given me only a smile and sharp fingernails, Alana now wrapped herself around my chest and squeezed all my cool confidence out my open mouth. I heard my pizza-box hit the tile and almost pushed her off, shouting, *'Alana you're having a baby! Either don't get married or leave me alone!'* But before I could lose my mind I remembered that each moment passes and I should savor each one. I squeezed Alana gluttonously. She pressed into me like a child scared of thunder — so small and young-seeming that I fingered the rings of her spine, counting to make sure there were at least seventeen.

Then finally remembering Christie, I tried to ease from Alana's embrace. "When do you work next?"

"No!" She anchored her nails in the back of my neck.

The more I tried to pry her off, the harder she dug in. I couldn't help laughing: "Hey, I gotta go. Serious. I'm sorry. I wish I wasn't with her. I wish I was here with you."

She released and backed off, tearing but smiling. I thought it better not to tell her now that I'm moving, and instead just repeated, "When do you work again?"

"New Year Eve," she answered.

"Cool. So do I. We'll do something together that night."

"I can't," she frowned. "I have other things."

Like, a fiancé... "We can celebrate at work then," I accepted. "Just you and me. We'll sneak out to the mop room and smo..." *She's too young for drugs...* "We'll think of something." Then again, "I gotta go."

Alana raised her skinny elbows like a bird sun-drying wet wings, allowing my hands under and around her back again. I pulled her in and we hugged perfectly. Before we could become a diamond from the pressure, I broke away, bent down for my to-go box and walked back to the fake redhead girl.

I remember nothing else about our date except that I spent it fantasizing how *I'll help Alana raise her baby! We won't have much money at first but there's always free pizza... I'll teach the kid preten-*

tious sloppy English and Alana will bestow beauty and passion. Amid Alana's family I will wish I were dark too, but will probably fit in better than I've yet to anywhere else...

So rapt with this fantasy was I that, dropping Christie off, I didn't even think to kiss her goodnight, or help her up her stairs.

1.9 OUR (ACCIDENTAL) MOMENT

fter all this time without it, I forgot how happiness makes my mouth sloppy, my hands slippery. Happiness increases gravity's pull, my rare joy triggering rockslides that block my path to future happiness, if not full-on bury all hope.

George was away on a New Year's vacation visiting friends in Miami, and the rest of Pizza Dive were scheduled to leave early to go watch the ball drop with their loved ones, so I agreed to stay and close the restaurant with Tony. I didn't care that I would share the first moments of the New Year with a bucket of gray bleach-water, as long as Alana and I could enjoy some private celebration at some point during work. Something needed to happen.

The restaurant filled with customers from 5 to past 10 p.m., keeping us so busy that Raphael was forced to bus tables. Alana and I didn't get a chance to talk until around 10:30 when she laid hands on my stomach and asked me to monitor her last table while she used the bathroom. "Take good care of my customers," she requested and punched me hard in the gut.

"Of course," I gasped. But when she disappeared I rushed to

the dessert cooler, slapped two thick slices of cheesecake on small plates then darted to the ladies room to wait outside. Alana emerged buttoning her corduroy work-pants, smiling at the cheesecake and me. "Let's go out back," I suggested.

She did not question my intentions: "First I check my customers," she said, as if her customers were really hers. "I meet you at my car in minutes."

The car Alana has lately shared with her visiting mother is tiny, red, and round like a pill. It's a newer model, but already sprinkled with nicks and dents. It sags low to the ground, looking sad and exhausted. Mosquitoes tickled my wrists beneath the dessert plates as I peeked in the car's windows looking for evidence of Alana's life outside Pizza Dive. Squinting through my reflection smeared across the glass, I discerned what I assumed to be a Costa Rican flag dangling from the rearview mirror, and wedding invitations scattered between the front seats. I also made out dozens of small blue boxes littering the floorboards, with cocktail straws protruding from their tops: fruit juice containers, probably. *Maybe Alana's Mom's addicted to sweet drinks like her daughter...*

Finally Alana rounded the stucco corner, her black hair shining silver beneath the lot's fluorescents. Loud clouds of bugs plinked against the lot lights and dive-bombed the steaming cups in Alana's hands. "Take it," she sleepily commanded and pushed one at me. I didn't want disgusting cocoa but it was such a sweet gesture, I balanced the cheesecakes on her car's roof and accepted a cup. As she fished her pocket for keys, her lips lowered to her drink, but flinched back from the thick heat steam. She blew across its foggy brown surface.

"Too hot?" I gently taunted.

"Never it's too hot," she bragged. "I eat everything hot as hell."

"I know."

She unlocked the passenger door and winced as the chocolate burned its way down her throat. "We will sit in the back," she smiled, eyes watering.

I opened the door and tilted the front seat forward. As she climbed in back I was struck silent by the strip of tan skin exposed between her belt and work-shirt. Focused so intently on that strip and the possibilities within our *moment*, squeezing it so hard to wring out everything it could be worth, that I never found breathing room to ask about all the little blue boxes on the floor. I realized only, "We need music. Keys, please." Alana passed me her key ring. To get at the radio, I slapped the passenger's seat back into its natural position. Following its gun-like *click*, a huge silence cried out to me. The neighborhood's New Year's parties fell silent. Bugs ceased plinking. Something bad had happened.

"What?" I asked the suspiciously still air.

When Alana didn't answer I peeked around the front seat and wished I were dead; from her soft face, steam rose, cocoa dripped. She looked as if she might cry, but whispered only, "I am burned."

Our moment dissolved. I feared for us both. The hot cup in my own hand now felt like a weapon. *I don't deserve a woman,* I knew, running into the restaurant to retrieve napkins for Alana — as if napkins would sooth the burns.

When I careened in through the red doors, a redhead college girl playing the crane-game smiled at me and I reflexively paused — before guilt shocked me back into motion. Over the pound of my pulse in my ears I heard Tony yell at me from the register, some blurry question beginning and ending with "malaka." I didn't stop.

Napkins in one fist, cocoa sloshing and burning my other hand, I ran back out to Alana. From her dark backseat she did not respond to apologies. Her trembling hand took the napkins and everything inside me collapsed. Tremors from the collapse spilled burning hot chocolate on my leg. Carefully, I set the cup down on the blacktop.

"Drive me home to change clothes," Alana murmured. I scrambled around to the driver's side and heard the ceramic plates slide off the roof and shatter in the lot when I squealed her little car out onto the street. In the rearview I saw Alana's sad, red-splotched face. I did not look up again. Alana muttered directions to her house which, somehow, I already knew. Like this had happened before.

Her tires crunching her gravel driveway turned the heads of many slouched, mustachioed Latin men in baseball hats, all holding canned beers around a New Year's bonfire. Alana sprinted out and through the quiet revelers all staring not at her powerful beauty, but rather, her wet clothes and eyes. She disappeared with a big, metal *clang!* in through the front door of her one-story house. The house's walls and roof looked made of graham crackers, like it might blow over or simply dissolve in FLA's next storm. I studied it, hoping it would tell me about her. It seemed to say her family was poor but... I wanted to be happy to finally see it but... I did not see her fiancé amid the men in the yard and wondered if any of them was her father. I wondered where her mother was, and wished I could tell her I love her daughter and that I hadn't meant to burn her.

Each Latin man slowly turned to me. I looked away, down at my feet, and noticed one of those little blue boxes under the clutch. I plucked it up by the straw and read its side: *CORNSTARCH*. I didn't understand. But at the time I didn't care either, and so tossed the box in back with the rest.

Soon, Alana returned wearing a fresh Pizza Dive polo and amazing lycra pants. Eyes now followed her for the right reasons. I jumped out and ran around to open the passenger door. "I'm so sorry," I offered again as she ducked in.

Alana paused, straightened: "Where is your hot chocolate I made for you?"

"I'm sorry," I repeated, turning from her splotches. "I set it on the curb outside the restaurant. I got scared. I'm sorry."

"Quit saying you are sorry," she scolded, pushed the dreaded seat forward again and slipped in back.

Chauffeuring her to work, I silently practiced the lies I would tell Tony about where we went for so long; if I admitted what really happened, Tony would run back to the kitchen and pantomime my entire stupid accident for the staff, making sure everyone got their laughs.

Raphael was too busy catching up on New Year's dishes to notice our absence. But Tony stopped me at the door (letting Alana run off to her tables). "What the fuck is *wrong* with you, *malaka*!" he raged. "I had to wait on your goddamned customers myself! *Moto Christosu!*" Meaning, 'Fuck Christ'.

Tony's rare disciplinary rant ended when I had no choice but to admit the whole truth to him.

"Oh my god!" he laughed. "That's no way to lure the *munaki*, *malaka*!"

"I'm not trying to *lure*..." But he didn't hear me, laughing his way back to the kitchen.

Alana and I worked the rest of the night in silence. I couldn't look at the red side of her face. But after punching out she approached me, untying her apron, Raphael in tow. "Monday Mami use the car," she said. "And I need a ride." Raphael patted my back, smiling, oblivious. "I need to go turn in papers at Tampa *ee-me-gration,*" she explained. "You ride me to *ee-me-gration* in your truck." This was not a question. It was penance. "At my house you come get me," she ordered. "Seven o'clock Monday morning." I did not need directions.

Alana kissed my cheek a fleeting happy New Year then floated out the doors. Raphael followed: "Pa-treek!" he shouted, "Happy New Year, brother!"

From the window I watched her tiny car roll away through broken plates and smashed dessert.

Soon after, I entered the new year, a fool.

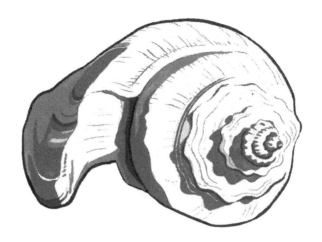

1.10 STOPPED AT THE FRONT OF THE LINE

6:30 a.m. Monday I ran out into the perfect winter in such a nervous rush to pick her up that I forgot to apply sunscreen. Outside the driver's window, sunshine danced in my orange wrist-hairs and cooked my arm – I at least burn like a true redhead.

Alana sat out on her particleboard porch in a garden of New Year's party debris, wearing her Pizza Dive polo. When I pulled into her driveway she stood and kicked empty cups and dead, black fire logs on her way across her yard. She opened my truck's door whistling, smiling. Raphael waved to us from the front window as we pulled away.

She touched my arm to guide me ("Left here" "Turn now" "Right here"), but granted few other signals. Her pink cheek faced the window.

Immigration and Naturalization Services wasn't open yet when she hopped out and stomped ahead of me across the fresh FLA tar. Her hair flew past a line of Latins, Asians, Arabs and Arians wrapped around the glass building. She stopped at the front of the line and shook her papers at a rotund black security guard sitting outside the metal detector: "I need to turn these in *today*."

"Not without an appointment." The guard pointed at the long line. "These people all have appointments."

"This is my last day!" Alana announced. "I have to turn these in today or they will kick me out from the country!"

I walked away to sit in the grass and watch them argue. The still-growing line didn't seem to understand what Alana was trying to do; they waited patiently, their early-morning stares aimed at the cross-cultural phenomenon of a beautiful 17-year-old girl. I sat beneath the winter sun, picking fossilized seashells from the matted runners and thinking how I've never met a girl who strong-armed so gracefully. Still the guard hiked up his belt and his bulk and shook his head *no*.

"You *have* to let me in," she commanded. "I can't be kicked from the country! I'm in the middle of making my Master's degree!"

After minutes of lies and debate, he conceded to find someone to help her. "Just go sit by your boyfriend!" He gestured toward me and waddled in through the metal detector. Alana smiled wide the beak as she skipped over.

Against my knees she knelt in the grass, leaned in close and pulled her collar away from her throat. Down her work shirt, pretty hills of soft sand slept in lacy white cups — serene and perfect down in there, save for the red splotches. She shouted in my face, "You burned my tits *as hell!*" The long line all faced Alana's loud, high laughter. I couldn't help laughing with her, just as loud and high. The white January sky brightened when she was happy and I was forgiven.

She unrolled her body across the itchy grass vines. Watching her stretched out, arms above her head, I realized I've only ever seen her in work clothes. Despite my skin's hatred for sun I lay down beside her and whispered, "Do you *ever* take that damned shirt off?"

She sprang up: "I have to *work* after here!" She backhanded my stomach. I hiccupped on laughter, in heaven. The line then witnessed the ambivalent moment when Alana gently pushed my shoulders back onto the grass, followed me down, kissed my neck and rested her burnt cheek on my heart. Discounting Christie, I haven't had a woman against me since Natalie. Though I'd fantasized plenty about lying with Alana, when her thin leg draped over my knees and I heard her pluck grass just outside my car, it all felt *heavy,* not unlike too much salad buffet. Her small weight crushed me. My mouth hung silent as the sky cooked my face.

When she tucked her hair behind her ears I noticed a fleck of dried chocolate on her lobe. I reached down and lightly pinched, secretly wiping away the brown. My hand lingered against her face and I wished she would push it away. I faked detachment: "So, what did your family say when you told them what I…what happened?"

"I don't know," she hummed against my heart.

"Oh, c'mon. Don't pull that. They had to notice something."

"I tell them nothing."

"You had to have told them *some*thing," I corrected. "I mean, all those guys saw you run inside the house. And your *face*…"

"I *told* them Tony did it," she revised, "that it was an accident."

"It was an accident."

"Oh really? I thought it was a gift on purpose. I thought you are telling me again to run away and marry you." Again she laid her face down. My sales pitch had never mentioned marriage…

"Your family's gonna hate Tony," I laughed, then remembered, "Wait, you said you never lie?"

"I *don't*!" she reiterated. "I only lie so Mami will not hate *you*."

"Aw. Thanks. Then you *are* currently getting your Master's degree?" I poked my pinky into her small ear. "A 17-year-old genius!"

She squealed, squeezed me with her whole body then rolled off onto her back. Now able to breathe, I sat up on my elbows and studied her the way I do every chance I get: a Latin Ophelia on her blanket of hair, eyes closed, work-shirt hiked so that her bare brown belly smacked the FLA sun and I remembered the baby inside her.

But it didn't matter. Maybe because I'm moving, maybe because she kissed my neck. Unafraid for the moment I admitted: "I brought a book to work for you that night you called in sick. A book called *The Abortion*. Isn't that weird?" She remained unmoved. *Maybe she doesn't know the word 'abortion'…* "When Tony told me that you were…that you weren't coming in…" I paused. "It's just weird that I happened to bring that particular book for you on that particular night."

Small laughter shook her. At the appearance of her beak, some dumb little hope exerted itself in me, that Alana was about to crack open and cackle *'I was lying! About everything! No boyfriend, no wedding, no baby! Ha! Ha! HA!'* Hope never seems like a bad con-cept until it leads me somewhere stupid like that. Suddenly embarrassed, I changed the subject: "I forgot to wear sunscreen today," my voice unraveled. "No one else in my family has red hair and when my parents moved us down to Florida they never put sunscreen on me and I'd hang out at the pool all day getting burned it was horrible and then when I went away to college I read that…"

I'd told her all this before. Her slow-blinking eyes above me interrupted. Her head eclipsed the sun, cooled the air. Her fingers tickled up my chest, over my Adam's apple to land across my mouth and shut me up. Her other hand covered my eyes. Lost in her sweet-smelling darkness, I heard her whisper, "Don't worry Pa-treek. I protect you."

1.11 Another Accident: My Blind Fault

T he guard eventually waved Alana in through the metal detector. Ten minutes later she bounced out, hair dancing celebratory circles around her as we skipped back past the inert line of hopeful immigrants to the parking lot.

I'd told *The Trib* I had a dermatologist's appointment, so Alana and I could drive around spread-out Tampa forever, talking and laughing, her hand lying palm-up across my knuckles between us like a dead mouse. But for the privilege of leaving Pizza Dive early New Years Eve, she'd accepted a double shift today. So when George called and asked me to cover his night shift, I gladly accepted the opportunity.

When Alana finally leapt out of my truck to go in and work for 12 hours, I mooned, "Good luck. I'll be here to join you at 5." She leapt back into the cab and pecked my neck again before running in through the red doors of her job. Our job.

I drove home alone, the sweet afternoon weather working like anesthetics, allowing me to just be dumb and feel wonderful. None of my problems had been solved, but not wanting to take serenity for granted, I pondered only my imminent escape from Tampa. *Moving will be exciting...* At my apartment, I surfed the web for nude redhead girls and ideas about where to move. I've never been anywhere; amazing, considering my Mom owns a travel agency. She herself hasn't even been to San Francisco — which looks amazing on my small computer monitor. But S.F. would be too heavy a financial burden. Same with New York, where Natalie moved to get away from me. I abandoned the web, hit the bong then the mattress, until Alana.

The kitchen laughed upon my arrival. The guys leapt out of my way as I stepped through to the time clock, like I might accidentally hurt them as I did Alana. I laughed along, lighthearted, worried only that our comic commotion might alert Raphael to my having burned his sister. But the schedule taped to the clock said Raphael was off. Hopefully by his next shift the laughter will've died. Until then I whistled back into the kitchen, where Tony joked, "Malaka, you won't have to worry about killing anyone with hot chocolate anymore." He slapped my back. "Cause tonight we're getting rid of that piece-of-*scata* machine."

Alana rounded the corner: "No!" she cried, "No!" the way she hadn't when I'd burned her.

"Alana listen," Tony grew serious, "we'll get a new one someday. But that one makes disgusting brown diarrhea and no one buys it. It takes up all the counterspace and you're the only one who drinks that *scata!*'" No one laughed when Alana stomped out of the kitchen, lips quivering. But Tony stood firm; the old, steam-belching hot chocolate maker would soon be gone. And because things rarely change at Pizza Dive, a big deal was made in the kitchen's many languages.

Alana though barely spoke all night. We shared several sad smiles and she ran fingers across my stomach in passing, but the evening rush kept us mostly separate. I didn't worry though, left her alone, sympathized from afar. Until later, as she and I mopped the empty restaurant, Tony rounded the counter to impose upon me the honor of pallbearer: "Carry the machine out back to the dumpster, malaka," he commanded, straightening the collar of his identical Pizza Dive polo. "I'm dressed too nice for manual labor."

Alana and I paused mopping. I entertained quitting, right there.

"Tony, it looks way too heavy to just, uh…"

"It's not that heavy, malaka," he groaned. "Don't be a baby."

I didn't care about the machine, yet still thought to push my mop aside, turn to Alana and declare, 'I cannot do it, Tony.' But I am loyal to Tony too. Instead of walking out in a contrived show of allegiance, I simply made sure he knew, "You're breaking her heart."

Tony threw up his hairy hands. "*Malaka,* man! Just take the damn thing outside!"

He left us. I leaned on my mop. "I'm sorry about this Alana."

She frowned down at the red tile. I would have told any other friend to just get over it, but for invisible reasons, I indulge Alana's dramas. I reached out and tilted her face upward: "I'll bring you hot chocolate every day from the gas station if you promise not to be sad. I'll stop and buy cocoa for you every night before work. Just don't be sad. O.K.?"

"Really?" she barely smiled.

"Yes. I promise. And I *never* lie." We laughed together. "But the deal's off after you get married," I amended. "After that, your stupid husband can get it for you."

"O.K.," she smiled, allowing me to perform my duty.

First, I checked the empty dish room, wishing Raphael were in there so I could pawn my task off on the strong one. Instead I faced the fake-wood counter and Alana's beloved machine. The old monster had handles on its sides but, doubting my strength, I grabbed it from the bottom and pressed my chin down on the top grate from which its steamy breath once blew. I inhaled deep and lifted. The machine's weight immediately dragged me forward, across the wait station and out into the dining room, where I tripped directly over my yellow mop bucket.

Tidal waves of bleach rippled through the restaurant as the metal grate slammed my chin, jarred my teeth and knocked me back. My head bounced against the red tile. Staring at the ceiling, dumb but not yet in pain, I laughed along with the approaching kitchen guys, who all stopped laughing when their ring of black moustaches and ball caps hovered directly over me. I did not understand why their faces cramped with worry, or who or where we were. Lolling in bleach, I saw the hot chocolate maker beside me like a mangled airplane carcass. *Was I in a plane crash?* A shrill note screamed inside my skull and brought my hands to my ears, where I felt a warm wetness. *Marinara?* I wondered, inspecting my blurry red fingers. Then all delusions faded into the reality of my bloody hands. I panicked thinking my brain was leaking out — until Alana came into focus above me, laughing. *She's so pretty when she laughs...* She pointed at my chin: "*Delicate! You* are a delicate!"

She helped me up and pressed against me, held my face and laughed, "Oh, baby. Poor baby." And everything was fine.

Now *she* handed *me* a thick of napkins. Her other hand rubbed my chest. I checked the staff's faces, making sure they all saw how she touched me. They didn't seem jealous. They winced and mumbled Spanish and Greek.

Tony peeked out of the kitchen: "*Moto Christosu!*" He ran to me. "Malaka, you need to go to the emergency room and get some stitches in there!"

"I wone die farm a cutchin," I slurred. "Ahm fine. Everthin's fine."

Tony studied my chin like a jeweler discerning a gem: "I'm worried, malaka," he frowned. "Your chin looks like an eye socket with no eye in it — looks like a munaki. Go to the doctor now. I'll pay for it. Don't worry, I'll pay."

Alana snatched up another giant fistful of napkins along with Tony's money. "I will drive heem to the hospital," she announced, leading me off by the hand.

Mami had earlier brought Alana's car to work for her. Riding to the hospital, I drenched 15 napkins — whereas it takes only 10 to soak up the orange grease lake atop a Pizza Dive pie. Alana and I laughed over this stat, and everything else, because we laugh always, even driving to the hospital. My smile threatened to rip my chin open further so the ER doctors would need to sew my face back on. I felt insane. But insanity allowed me to ask, "So, what are you going to name the baby?" Alana stopped laughing. Nighttime outlined her breakable frame, and imagining it stuffed with child, I wiped my watery eyes and suggested, "'Patrick' is not a very Latin name, but it would sound really *exotic* in your country. Especially for a little black-haired kid, which is all you're gonna have — your stupid husband's definitely not gonna give you a redhead, that's for fucking sure..."

Her beak appeared: "I'm not pregnant," Alana set me free. "I lie."

I lie: like the sweet tone of a vibraphone ringing clear over her little car's engine and my wailing brain, cutting through everything to reverberate sweetly inside my chest. For one shining second I felt in control of this life. Like I could stop my own bleeding, from the inside! "You don't even *know*, Alana!" I wheezed laughter through the bed of red napkins. "You just *don't know*! I've been so fucking *sad* about this and... Man, I want to *kill* you and kiss you and..."

Eyes on the road she confessed, "I just say I'm pregnant cause I don't want to work that night." She flipped the dome light on, pushed my hand away, plucked a smoky wisp of napkin from the blood. "Poor baby," she laughed, inspecting my gash. "Tony was right. It does look like you have *poosy* on your chin."

I reapplied the napkins before my heart could pump a geyser out my face. "So, you're *not* pregnant," I fact-checked. "And you *do* lie?"

Oncoming headlights lit her wet eyeballs. "Actually, I have a bad time with honesty," she admitted, seeming sincerely troubled by her honesty problem.

"Tony might get suspicious," I said, "when your stomach doesn't grow."

"Next time I don't want to work," her beak replied, "I just tell Tony the baby die inside of me."

"Oh Jesus Alana. That's horrible."

"You love it," she replied, skidding into the hospital lot.

I did not admit that I do love it, only added, "It's called a miscarriage."

"Huh?"

"When the baby dies inside you, it's called a miscarriage. When you tell Tony, remember to say, 'I had a miscarriage.'"

"Oh." She opened her door. "Thank you."

Stepping out, I once again noticed the many small, blue boxes on her floor. "What are all these little cornstarch boxes from?"

"I don't know." She slammed her door. I didn't press her.

The waiting room moaned, full of bloody, broken accident

victims and empty-eyed pill poppers grinding impatient knees into their chests. But we were happy, Alana and I. Lying across white plastic chairs, we cooed and sighed. She pressed her face against mine, cool, soft and comforting, and pulled away with my blood stamped onto her cheek, camouflaging her fading burns.

On a TV above an empty snack machine, Chris Elliot appeared on David Letterman and we screamed laughter. The waiting room's broken sufferers (who, if not for the fresh blood, could've been a roomful of Pizza Dive regulars) all hated us as we *leaned into* our glee, turned the waiting room into our black comedy—until our laughter ignited my lump, and I had to lay my head down against Alana's corduroy fly. She stared down, touching my bloody face. "It is beautiful," she claimed.

I was a baby in the lap of a 17-year-old girl. Looking up I wondered, *How could I ever take care of* her? She pet my hair and, wishing it were red as her brother's, I remembered to ask, "So, what's up with all that crazy sex stuff you say to Raphael? He told me you threatened to take his virginity? That's creepy, Alana."

Surprised, she answered, "I only make fun with heem. That's all. I just make fun with Raphael."

"Don't you think that saying that stuff will screw up his head?"

"Boys in Costa Rica are not like boys here," she scowled. "Boys are not shy in my country. Not the way how you are shy."

"How *I* am shy?" My pounding lump still warping my mind, I sat up on my elbows and kissed the corner of her mouth. She offered no defense, so I kissed the beakless center. She did nothing to stop me, but didn't participate either. For the first time in our short history, I think she didn't know what to do. I kissed her again, longer, and she neither leaned into me, nor away. I laid back down in her lap and admired more of my blood on her young face and before I could feel guilty — or worse, old – they called my name.

The nurse instructed Alana to remain in the Waiting Room. But she demanded to watch my operation. After some debate, Alana got her way and sat rapt beside me even as the nurse recorded my blood pressure and allergy history. In the doctor's empty office, we counted each other's heartbeats with a stethoscope. I was on the verge of stealing another kiss when the doctor walked in on us: a short Asian man with thick, curly hair. He scanned both of our bloody faces: "Which of you first?"

"Unless you're also a psychiatrist," I said, "then I'm the only one you can help right now."

Alana planted her small fist in my diaphragm.

The doctor's eyes widened. "I see," he said, then gestured with his pen to Alana's face: "I thought you needed to be sewn-up too. You two must have been…hugging." He shot a large needle full of anesthesia into my chin and the whole bottom of my face fell away. Alana gasped, squealed, pointed and made fun, but never blinked as he sewed my flesh. Despite the doctor's light-hearted hair, he scolded us, "Stop laughing! Hold still! And if *you* don't stop *making* him laugh Miss, you can sit outside!"

At exactly 2am, Alana gave the nurse Tony's money (I was too dazed and distracted to remember I still have health insurance via *The Trib*). Alana loaded me into her car. "Where do you live?" she asked, and drove us there directly.

* * *

Beneath my bedroom window she killed her engine. My numb, stitched face impeded my smile when she said she was very tired, and asked to come up and lie down. Remembering my 10 p.m. curfew at her age, I asked "What will your parents think when you're home so late?"

"I don't know." She gripped the wheel and stared ahead as if still driving.

"Would they approve of you going up into some older guy's apartment at 2:30?"

"I don't know."

"Won't *Mami* be worried?"

"I don't know."

"Alana. Quit saying that." I laughed to sound jokey, though I do want to be the one person at whom she never wields *I don't know*. "Your dad will kill me if he finds out I took his little girl up to my…"

"Papi is dead," she interrupted, smiling. A fun smile, not a *covering up grief* smile. So I waited for further signs of humor before I let myself feel bad. The signs never came.

"How did he die?"

"He had cancer on his skin."

"No way! I just had one on my temple!" I pointed to my little pink scar. "I've never heard of anyone *dying* from it though. Jesus. I'm sorry." I was full of questions, but continued waiting for her to point and laugh at my gullibility. She smiled but never laughed, or criticized me for apologizing. She opened the driver's door.

I followed her close up my stairs, her dangling curls tickling my nose. My heart pumped crazy blood and nothing could keep my lips from forming an inverted rainbow that shined madly inches from her back pocket — another accident ready to happen.

Up on her toes behind me, Alana watched me unlock my door. Inside I kicked my shoes across my small, dark living room, and followed them to my bed. I laid down and watched Alana trail me into the blue-black shadows, her hair floating behind like Dracula's cape. She stood over me like a doctor over a patient, staring and smiling. Her long fingers hooked her hair behind her small ears: "What do you want to do?" she asked.

I shivered, not just in reaction to her question, but because FLA has thinned my blood so that my teeth chatter when it drops below 70 degrees, as it recently has. I feel ridiculous though, turning the heater on when it's 64 outside. So to warm myself in recent nights I've conjured half-dreams of Alana lying against me, talking softly, her clean warm breath in my face. It works. But when my fantasy scenario finally became real I stood from my bed: "I need to pee real quick."

In the dark bathroom I discerned the shadow of my favorite zipper-down sweater heaped like a sleeping person against the toilet. My skin still smelled of marinara and iron, but I was too tired to find clean clothes. I left the light off, locked myself in, collected my sweater and zipped it on over the blood and food. On the white sink beside my toothbrush teetered my lighter and glass pipe. I longed to smoke and collect myself but didn't want Alana knowing. I stepped into the tub; in the window's dark reflection I saw my five black stitches like the lashes of a sleeping eye. I unlatched the window to breathe blue smoke out the mosquito screen and survey the night-soaked, one-story neighborhood. With each hit, more questions I'd refused to ask myself back in the sunny grass at INS attacked me: *What am I doing with her? Or to her? What am I doing to me? Is her fiancé gonna kill me? What the fuck am I doing?* No answers followed, just pain in the lump I pictured on the back of my head like a rhino's horn filling with questions. Pot has never made me paranoid; I was stoned to heaven when I first interviewed at *The Trib*. So it had to be blood loss, anesthesia and sexual tension that had me kneeling for a moment on the cold tile floor, mouth open over the bowl.

Luckily, my first esophageal contraction woke my self-preservation instinct: *She'll hear. She'll smell my pukey breath…* I rose, blew the last dirty hits outside, shut the window, rinsed my face and smeared toothpaste across my teeth (my half-brother David told me truckers call this a "whore's bath").

Back in my room Alana lay in my bed watching the ceiling fan and rubbing her stomach under her shirt. Her face turned to me: "I *am* pregnant. I lied again to you." Her smile glowed in the dark. I held my breath and lay down with her for the second time today, now without the sun.

"You know, the fact that I haven't ever accidentally impregnated anyone makes me scared I might be sterile," I admitted. I'd never told anyone that. Alana said nothing. *Maybe she doesn't know what 'sterile' means?* "Not one pregnancy scare, ever," I continued. "And that Natalie girl and I quit using protection about a month into…"

"Don't," Alana whispered, sleepy, or something close to sad. She faced away.

"Don't what?" I lowered my voice, hoping she'd roll back to hear me better.

She spoke into my pillow, "Don't talk about your love with other women."

I dammed my pulsing chin with my palm. "Why not?"

"I don't know."

"You're getting *married*, Alana."

She rolled back to me, lips pursed. "I hate you!" she squealed and lifted her knees to her chest. Her feet on my hip, she grunted and pushed like birth and I braced the wall to stay on the bed. We cried laughing as I leveraged back onto the mattress, stood on my knees and grabbed her foot. Stumbling to full height, I pulled her feather weight up by the ankle like a fisherman having his photo taken. When only her shoulders touched the mattress her leg growled *krrr-r-r-r!* I panicked and let go and she bounced down onto the mattress. "Shit! I'm sorry, Alana. I'm such a clod."

"No. It feels good!" she said. "You stretch my leg. It feels good after all day of work. Make my other one go *krrr-r-r-r!*"

Again I stooped and lifted her by the foot until her knee cracked, then her hip, then her spine. When her body silenced, I eased her down like ballet. Breathless beside her I blurted, "I feel so good with you here. Not that I usually feel *bad*," I lied. "But right now I feel better than I have in forever. It was worth the blood to get you here."

"Ah, no," she waved away my sentimentality then caught me off guard: "You are just smoke weeds."

"No, I'm not. I mean, I didn't. How can you tell?"

She held my fingers to her small rosebud nose. "I smell it on your hands and your mouth. You don't have to lie, Pa-treek; I smoke *mota* before sometimes. It's not this bad thing."

"*Mota* means pot?"

"Means *weeds* too, like in the garden. But I don't think there is nothing wrong with smoking weeds," she said, still holding my hand. "Mota make people nice! It is good for your...inside you your..."

"Soul?"

"Yes. Mota is good for your soul."

My dream girl... "Well it's not because of *mota* that I'm glad you're here," I said, "Either way, I don't think you should get married."

"Why not?" she asked.

All her possible responses: *Patrick, no...Patrick, stop saying those things...Patrick, I'm in love with someone else.* But she answered "Why not?" And I heard, *Talk me into it.* I rolled over. My arms quaked, holding my body over hers. Despite her encouraging question, I seemed to make her nervous now — a beautiful rarity. She flicked the zipper dangling at my neck: "Take your sweater off."

"What's wrong with my sweater?"

"It's a girl sweater."

"No it's not. It's my favorite sweater." I unzipped and shed the sweater then slid back in beside her, shivering as our food-stink rose up around us.

"I like you in that shirt," she said, her eyes on my white *Pizza Dive* logo in the dark.

"My work shirt? I think the sweater looks better."

I lay back on my bed and let the peaceful quiet plus one dinner shift followed by three hours in the Emergency Room conspire to put me under. A restless dream of flying led to a feeling of falling that snapped me awake to find Alana no longer in bed. I rolled over, searched the mattress. Gone? *Gone!*

Then I found her, standing beside the bed again. I expected an announcement of her departure. When she lifted her work-shirt up over her head and pulled all that hair out the hole I thought I might cry. Or worse, tell her "Don't." But I managed to hold everything in, even as her dirty workpants and bra landed atop my gay sweater. When she was just skin and hair and small, white underwear, she climbed on top of me like a cat readying for sleep. She slid a hand under my bloody shirt, lifted the rough cotton off my stomach and ducked her head inside. We laughed at the sound of ripping seams as she shimmied up my bare chest like a rat up a palm. Inside my shirt, her warm breasts made every bad thing not matter. Her head finally emerged from my collar, her face against mine. Her moist beak landed between my eyes, skied down the slope of my nose to my lips, and my eyes did water when she kissed my mouth.

I kissed her back while rolling her underwear down her size-zero hips. Her hands, trapped between our stomachs, struggled with my belt. I kicked my bloodstained jeans down my legs and we saw only each other's eyes as I entered her: she winced like drinking too-hot chocolate. She whimpered moving her hips and the sound magnified her youth. I worried for her, and then, again, for me. But though I could feel that she hadn't done it a lot, I wasn't *taking her virgin* either, and all worry dissipated inside her. Wound in my shirt, our slippery maddening feeling seemed to go on *somewhere else*, separate from the magician in a straight jacket tussling farther down my bed, until Alana finally slid out of my shirt and the rest was visible. The rest was freedom.

Upon conclusion, there was blood; at least one stitch had popped out, lost in hair and blankets. I laid on top of her, enveloped her, smeared red between her sweet, long breasts. She dipped two fingers in the blood to paint quarterback lines beneath my eyes. I asked if she'd ever read *The Bell Jar*.

"I don't know," she answered, biting my lips.

I'd never felt so even, perfect, and scared. Guilt can persist all it wants on behalf of infidelity or pedophilia or whatever, but this was the most romantic moment of my life. I needed it.

When our moment calmed, we laid back discussing work, Tony, Raphael and "*lee-tre-ture.*" Alana gushed on about Latin authors I hadn't heard of aside from Marquez. When I finally broke the mood to ask her what she will do now that she'd betrayed him, Alana leaked melancholy laughter and led us into our own magic realism, wherein we run off to Costa Rica to lay low for a while, explore her wild, gorgeous country, and get married.

"Far as I'm concerned," I let her know, "we can leave tomorrow."

"No, I have to stay here longer to pay back Mami," she sobbed. "Oh! Mami spend so much money on the wedding! And to fly here! I am such a asshole..."

I shut up for fear of tainting our moment even more than it was inherently tainted – and thus never managed to tell her I'm moving away soon, regardless of all this.

Only the whir of my heart and the ceiling fan existed in our silence, until Alana sleep-mumbled, "You know I never been with no gringo before."

"How am I different?" I whispered to not wake her, though I suspected she may have been playing a little girl game.

"You are my baby," she said.

Only waitresses have ever called me 'baby'. And it's not something I've missed. My Freshman-year dorm-mate used to placate his ferocious long-distance girlfriend on the telephone with, "Baby, I know. Baby, calm down. Baby, I know, baby." He would roll his eyes and smile at me as she grew louder on the other line, despite his "Baby, I know, baby. Please stop, baby." But really, 'baby' wasn't comfort; he was accusing her of *infancy*. 'Baby' was the last word, and he wanted it. For two semesters I slept on a metal bunk above, "Baby, calm down, baby. I know, please, baby, *baby*." And since then I've never cared for *baby*.

But it sounded sweet from Alana's beak. Soothing. It massaged me into comfort followed by a sleep from which I did not wake for her last kiss goodbye, or the creak of my front door, or the sad purr of her little car driving her off to finish her own sleep, in a bed that was not mine.

1.12 WHEN WILL YOU QUIT?

The smell of her and us hides in ever corner of my apartment, despite my staying home all day blowing pot smoke in its face. Wrapped warm in bloody blankets, I again begged the internet for clues about where to move. My eyes glazed over the monitor as my nose and mind full of her turned into words that forced themselves out my mouth; I found myself announcing to her that I was moving away, that I would miss her, and that I loved her. Every few paragraphs, I would catch myself, stop talking, and feel dumb — but then a minute later guffaw over some imaginary retort Alana hadn't, in reality, made. I finally decided to channel this schizophrenia into a letter, which I would drive to Pizza Dive when her shift ended. While there, I would also break the bad news to Tony. I swooned composing, emoting (then editing a couple times):

Dear Alana,

Amidst all of last night's insanity, I never got around to telling you that you make me so happy my head hurts, my stomach cramps, I drop hot-chocolate machines. Fading in and out of sleep beside you last night, I also forgot to thank you for driving me to the hospital, and I forgot to tell you that I love you. So much.

I also never found the right moment to tell you I'm moving away soon. I'm not sure where I'll go, but I'm leaving FLA. That and your impending marriage make it easy to admit that I love you. I can say it now, knowing it will only make you smile, not complicate your life the way it might if we kept sharing the same job and city. So everything's turned out for the best, right?

I'm not sure either.

Really, I'm scared that I ever felt this in the first place. I had stopped hoping for love, until laughing with you (goddamn SO much laughter!) poked a pinhole in my heart big enough to see through to the other side where I now glimpse POSSIBILITY. And I'm afraid cold air will forever whistle through the hole, keeping me awake nights, haunting me wherever I end up moving to...

O.K. that does sound WHINEY. I just needed you to know that you've changed my life and I will always remember your dark humor, your passion and anger, your amazing arrogance, your intense love for your brother and for hot chocolate. It's gonna be so SAD to leave Pizza Dive! I like everyone there so much! Even Tony. But only YOU will make me miss mopping the floor.

If the death I've wished upon your husband ever visits him, you can always be mine, any time, forever.

Love,
Patrick

By the end I was a snotty, wet mess. The feeling of not wanting to leave her was unbearable, the knowing I was *almost* not alone. Exhausted by sadness, I narrowly avoided passing out. I folded all these words Alana mightn't understand into my copy of *The Bell Jar*, and drove two miles to the nearest convenience store, for cocoa.

* * *

In through Pizza Dive's red doors I found George and Raphael making good use of all the new counter space: their elbows dug into the Formica, hands locked, "1 – 2 – Go!" Big George could flick Raphael's head and crack it like an egg. Raphael barely exists. So their equal stress and strain while arm-wrestling looked like a puppet show. They ran even for a good 30 seconds before George slammed Raphael's hand down and sang, "*Weeeeeeee are the champ-yuns, my frie-hend!*"

"George!" Alana raged into the frame. "If you hurt my broth-er!" She punched George in an arm the thickness of her head.

"Ouch!" George cried. "What?"

"You leave Raphael alone! You are big and older!" She jerked Raphael to her by his collar.

"Whatever Alana!" George rubbed his arm. "He almost beat me!"

Alana held her anger as she silently formulated and con-jugated and finally declared, "'*Almost*' still mean '*no*'! Leave heem *alone!*"

As she flew toward the kitchen I caught her attention and held up her cocoa. Her eyes shone a striking brightness that remind-ed me of the way pregnant women are described — I realize now that it was love. I'd just never had it aimed at me like that. She raised an index finger: "One *me-nut*! Go to my car!"

I followed orders. Soon, Alana exploded from the restaurant and wrapped around me like a car around a tree, knocking her co-coa to the ground. She kissed my mouth and stitched chin. But not having expected us to carry-on past last night, I wasn't sure how to feel. I backed off and handed her the empty cup and book. She un-folded the letter and read, smiling the softest smile...at first... Then her eyes shrank, her lips twisted. She punched me in the chest with a loud paper *smack!* I gulped air against her car with the letter landing on my shoes. I could only watch her storm back in through the red doors, *The Bell Jar* under her arm.

Tony sauntered out the back entrance to dump a bucket of suds down the storm grate. Raphael followed, carrying two garbage bags and sneering at Tony's mini-mullet. Tony kicked his bucket aside, lit a cigarette then noticed me clutching my diaphragm: "Mal-aka, what the hell you doing out here?" He thumbed his restaurant: "Don't come around here on your days off distracting my employees, malaka. I'm happy for you two, but leave her alone when she's work-ing."

A loud *clang!* echoed through the cool night when Raphael

lobbed the trash into the dumpster. Then, "Pa-treek!" he yelled and ran across the parking lot on drinking-straw legs. He smiled into my eyes like he might kiss me.

"Hey man!" I wheezed, and slid my arm around his waist. Between him and his sister I'm beginning to feel loved and lucky.

"So," Tony interrupted, "when were you planning on tellin me you're quitting?"

"I uh, came down here to tell you," I stuttered, surprised Alana would disclose anything to him. "I'm moving away!" I cheered. "You should be happy for me! Of course I'm gonna work the next two weeks, or however long you need me. I wouldn't leave you hanging."

"They're gonna kill you in Costa Rica, malaka." Tony smiled and smoked. "Central America's dangerous, bro."

"That's not true!" Raphael shouted too close to my ear. "Costa Rica is beautiful! You will love it Pa-treek!"

When I finally understood what they meant, what all this meant – that Alana had told them she loves me! — I felt like the winning contestant on a tedious game show that had dragged on my whole life. I palmed my chin to bend and snatch-up my letter and giggle away like a freed man.

In a red booth across the red dining room Alana bawled, head down on *The Bell Jar*. Though her crying over me made my own eyes well up with happiness I shouted, "No, no! Alana don't!" The kitchen guys peeked over the service window and I loved them for not laughing — before a wildly flapping bird sailed in from my periphery, into my eye. Or a book. Eye watering, I reclaimed The Bell Jar from the tile and chased Alana's blur deep into the restaurant again, as it seems I always have. Back in dry storage she sadly boiled, then sprung, grabbing fistfuls of me. My pulse lowered, and lowered. "I didn't think you were serious, Alana," I barely said. "I thought it was just bedroom talk. If you want me to come to Costa Rica of *course*. That would be fucking perfect."

"Don't curse words." She couldn't stop crying but a wet smile trembled on her face.

"Is that what you're upset about?" I double-checked. "You want to be with me?"

Her tears and grip eased. "Mami was so mad when I tell her," she choked.

My uneven breaths pecked like finches in my lungs. "I'm

sorry." I wiped my eyes. "Did you tell your…did you tell him?"

"No. I'm just leave America." Before I could form an opinion, she cried again: "But I have to stay and save money first, for paying back Mami."

My first instinct was to loan her the little I'd saved working two jobs. But I suppose I'll need it for my own travel expenses…

1.13 THESE GIFTS MUST BE RETURNED

The next night, Tony sentenced me at the time clock: "I don't need you tonight, malaka, or anymore." Kitchen guys laughed and poked index fingers through the O.K. gesture, assuring me that our tale had already been translated into several languages. "Since you worked for malaka-number-two here while was on his little New Year's vacation," Tony thumbed George, who was busy personalizing a meatball sandwich on the line, "he'll pick up your last shifts."

As little money as I made at Pizza Dive, two more weeks wouldn't have benefited me much. But I wasn't ready to leave yet: "No, no, it's cool, I can work." My voice cracked and made the kitchen snicker. "I want to work, it's not a probl—"

"No, don't worry about it," Tony said. "You're free malaka, fly away."

I had assumed he'd be upset to see me go. I felt dumped. "I still have to work at *The Trib* so I might as well keep on…"

"No malaka, I don't need you here making goo-goo eyes with Alana," claimed mister *manicotti-on-the-shoulder*. "I'm trying to run a business, not a dating service. Plus we got a new malaka coming in tomorrow, some chick I hired today. She's Cuban." He growled, "I wanna train her myself. But I'm too busy. Lucky George here gets to train her."

George's name lifted his eyes from his meatballs. He saw me: "Bro! I *knew* you could hook it up! Right *on*! Costa Rica!"

Before George's reminder of my new impending life could re-elate me, Tony interjected, "Not that I wouldn't follow Alana's munaki to the ends of the Earth myself, but you're brave going to Central America. You might want to use this time off to take some self-defense courses, some Judo or something."

I turned to George. He shrugged mountainous shoulders: "I dunno, bro. You know more about the place than I do. I've heard there's a lot of pickpockets there…" He bit big from his sandwich, mumbled "and monkeys," then lumbered off into the back rooms.

Exiting the kitchen, I shook hands with Raphael as Tony added, right in front of the kid, "Hey malaka, good job by the way, taggin Alana! That's some sweet munaki!"

Her brother's freckled face became a storm cloud of boiling blood. I always found Tony a harmless, funny cartoon, but when I tugged Raphael's elbow and his skin shocked me, Tony wasn't funny anymore. I thought the huge man inside Raphael — the arm-wrestling palimpsest of strength and age beneath his freckles — might burst forth and strangle the libido out of Tony. And waiting for that, nothing was funny. Love, so often, is not funny at all.

Tony walked away lighting a cigarette. I tried calming Raphael. "Hey brother, he's just being silly," I claimed. "Don't sweat Tony. Tell your sister he said that and she'll kill and skin him herself."

Raphael's red anger seemed to level off. I departed to the dining room, pausing when he shouted, "Patrick! Why you have bones on your back?" He stepped forth and plucked a small, wet chicken bone from my collar. Confused, I inspected the bone: around one knob a paperclip had been wrapped and bent into a hook, like a homemade Christmas ornament. The kitchen guys cackled.

"What?" I asked.

Their laughter led Tony back into the kitchen. "When you're in Costa Rica," he smiled through his smoke, "you're gonna need to keep on your toes, malaka, watch your back. So the guys here…"

"That's not *true!*" Raphael slapped his thighs. "Costa Rica is *nice!*" The family resemblance showed itself when he stomped out.

Though Alana would never turn away with so much anger left in her.

"Anyway," Tony dismissed the boy and aimed his cigarette at the cooks, "malakias here are gonna train you to watch your back."

"By hanging bones on my shirt?"

The cooks leaned on the wall, sucking the yellow meat off of the tiny, Greek chicken wings Pizza Dive serves in small Styrofoam cups. They shifted their eyebrows suggestively and I couldn't help laughing, which triggered more of their laughter: a sound I love, even when it's aimed at me.

Still Tony kept digging. "If these malakias here can sneak up on you, then so can some Costa Rican fucker with a knife," he sneered. "Every time these guys hook something on your back without you catching them, you're dead."

Dead. I'd never really thought of being dead. One time I slipped in anger and told Natalie I would kill myself and while I was locked in the bathroom the cops came. Tony's strange new, bad attitude toward me wasn't quite as traumatizing as riding in the back of a squad car to a public mental health institution at midnight to be prodded by grad students. But it did change my mind about him. I've always defended Tony from his critics, but as he attempted to plant fear in me, he did finally seem like just a jealous little scumbag — who'd now *fired* me.

"The kitchen guys pulled the same test with me before I vacationed to Mexico last year," Tony continued. "Got to where I could catch em every time." He tossed his lit cigarette into a box of wilted lettuce and took a moment to evaluate his staff: "Malakias," he decided. "Mexicans still picked my fucking pockets."

"Whatever." I mustered cockiness. "Alana'll be there with me and she'll…help me figure out what's what." I'd almost said, 'She'll protect me.'

Knowing though, that I should only accept this breed of information from Costa Ricans, I abandoned the kitchen to find Raphael. On my way out the cooks sent up a wave of laughter that made me reach for my shoulderblades. But this time it hung from my belt: the greasy, white lid from one of their chicken cups, run-through with a garbage-tie hook.

I was dead, again.

Hadn't felt a thing.

Pizza boxes teetered on the wait station counter when Raphael pounded the Formica, demanding a re-match: "C'mon George! Fokeen *c'mon!*" Mad as Tony'd made Raphael, I'd have bet on the kid. But when I approached, the challenge was dropped and their enthusiasm attacked me. "You're gonna love Costa Rica!" Raphael promised. "It's beautiful! Tony lie!"

"Bro, that is *so* cool!" shouted George. "When are you leaving?"

"You will be here for my sister's birthday?" Raphael asked.

Their high-velocity interrogation continued, but my thoughts stuck on her birthday. I'd forgotten she would be legal soon. I haven't celebrated a girlfriend's birthday in years. "When's her birthday?" I asked.

"*Marzo seis*," he replied. "But me and Mami are going back home sooner because Mami so mad."

"I'm sorry."

"I'm not!" Freckles chased Raphael's nose as he shook his head. "I am happy! I *want* to go back to Tiburon. And you are a *mosh* better boyfriend!"

Raphael's benevolence scared away Tony's hex. I hugged him and realized for the first time that he is taller than me. Rocking in each other's arms I pictured us in tuxedos at some breezy beach wedding. "Honestly Raphael, I have no idea when I'm leaving, or what I'm doing," I admitted. "Your sister and I haven't really talked about it. Give me her phone number, will you? I'll go call her now."

Raphael plucked a pen from George's apron and scrawled on a napkin. I kept careful watch through the kitchen so as not to be symbolically killed on my way to Tony's office — still when I plopped down in his swivel chair and dialed, another wire-rigged chicken bone dropped to the linoleum. Death. The phone rang slowly.

"Hola?" answered a deep female voice.

"Yes, hello, can I speak with Alana, please?"

Alana's mother, I assumed, spoke fast Spanish in a questioning tone, her tongue sounding fat in her mouth.

"I'm sorry, no hablo Espanol," I copped. She replied with heavy breathing like she'd just run a race. Then I remembered, "*Puedo - hablar - con Alana – por favor. Esta – Pa - trick.*"

She yelled some fast vocab words before the phone died.

I tried, "Hello? Hello?" even, "Hola?" then dialed again. Alana answered. "Oh! Hey!" I cried too loud, too happy, her mere voice seeming to deliver me from pickpockets and muggers.

"Pa-treek!" she scolded.

"What?"

"Don't call here! If he *answer, oh!*" I pictured the irritated face she surely wore, but felt no guilt because I believed she should be honest with everyone involved. As she lectured, my eyes wandered Tony's unopened mail, un-cashed employee paychecks, multiple hairbrushes. I picked up and flipped through a *Playboy* as Alana explained, "If you call and he answer it will be so bad. *Do not call.*"

"Don't you think he's going to know the wedding's off when your mother and brother *leave?*" I asked a striking redhead bunny lying arch-backed on a fur couch white as her skin.

"I tell him they're coming back."

"Oh Jesus."

"Patrick! You do not *know!*" she snapped. "Don't *cree–tea–size!* Just do not call! I see you at work."

I closed the Playboy. "Listen, I don't even know what's going *on*. We *need* to talk. Don't yell at me. I'm *understandably* worried! I've never been outside of the country. Don't be a jerk."

After a pause she quietly gave-in: "I'm sorry."

Her apology seemed a magnanimous gesture. And before I knew it, I'd returned her apology, despite not feeling sorry. False apologies: another love ritual I'd forgotten about. My instincts do live.

"Is Costa Rica dangerous?" I asked. "Tony's trying to scare me."

"No, no, no," she laughed like blowing bubbles. "It's beautiful, baby!"

Its beauty won't save my life, but the word *baby* distracted me from the issue, made me remember, "Hey! It's your birthday soon!"

"But we can't be together for it…"

"Alana! Why?" I was prepared to compromise, but not to sneak around like Natalie and her teenage busboy. "Why don't you just *tell* him?" I asked, picking the *Playboy* back up and again searching out the redhead.

"I can't Pa-treek. He will be so mad."

She sounded like she might cry and I couldn't help but back

off. I chose diplomacy: "So, then, what should I do?"

Her voice smiled, "Just go to Costa Rica, Pa-treek. I will be there after my birthday. You are so unhappy in Tampa. Go and be alone for some weeks. Alone is good. Then I will come meet you." Beautiful people think *alone* is a rare thing of value because they don't have to run from it. "It's your chance!" Alana exclaimed. "Go and write all the time! Be happy and write some-sing beautiful until I come to be with you! Write some-sing for *me*!"

I closed the magazine and thanked her for making so much sense. The receiver then exploded again in a loud string of raging, fat-tongued Spanish. Alana covered the mouthpiece and shouted back at Mami. After a short, violent volley, Alana returned to me sobbing, "I am sorry Pa-treek. I have to go. I love you."

She'd never said that before.

"I love you too," I responded for the first time out loud (when she could hear it).

"Come to the restaurant tomorrow night," Alana said over that fat voice railing in her background. "I tell you how to go to Tiburon and to my home."

"Tony doesn't want me at the restaurant anymore," I told her. "He fucking *fired* me because of this. Because of us."

"We will talk," she cut me off. "But don't call."

"All right. I'm sor—" I began to lie again. But she'd hung up.

I wasn't ambushed with bones and lids, coming back through the empty kitchen. I made it to the dining room alive, despite feeling a bit dead. Raphael toiled in his dish pit. George looked up from folding a box: "So, how'd it go, bro?"

"All right."

"Good," he smirked. "There are some customers in my section — I told them you were leaving and they want you to wait on them one last time. I hooked them up with silverware but haven't taken their drink order."

Confused, I borrowed George's pad and pen and loped around the corner into his section. At his biggest table, three old women and one gray man all stared into menus on behalf of the handicapped girl with the beautiful lips. I spun on my heels and attempted silent escape but heard them all laugh behind me (*at me?*) with an haughtiness I wouldn't have expected from them.

"Funny, George." I tossed his pad back at him.

"Not as funny as..." He reached around my back and un-hooked from my belt a long bread bag full of air, like a windsock.

I left the restaurant, fine to never return.

* * *

Today I cleaned off my desk at *The Trib*. No more obituaries, birth announcements, religion calendar or campus news. No more fetching faxes. No more uncomfortable flirtation from Christie — actually, she pretty much gave up once word mysteriously spread through the newsroom that I'm "following some young girl to Costa Rica." I do have to hand it to *The Trib's* reporters.

The task of sorting newsroom mail, however, will be missed; creeping away by myself to slide envelopes into slots alone at my own pace. The duty also gave me clearance to open any packages, in order to filter out all free CDs, event tickets and magazine subscrip-tions sent to reporters by hopeful PR hacks. Journalistic ethics dic-tate that these gifts must be returned or donated to charity, for fear that a reporter might falsely inform the public that a crappy band crappy band is *good*, simply because said band gave said reporter their crappy record *for free*. But sorting mail for the last time today, I encountered a rattling manila envelope and opened it to find a pro-motional red pocketknife key-chain inscribed with some corporate logo, which I stashed in my bookbag, thinking *I might need this to defend myself in Costa Rica...*

This can't possibly be the right attitude before embark-ing upon a liberating experience. But I don't know what I'm doing, or what to believe. I know, "It's beautiful, baby." This week fed me strange, conflicting reports from disparate sources. Some internet travel sites say Costa Ricans will steal your teeth, but that they're non-violent and if you catch them with their hand in your mouth they'll scatter like silverfish. Then studying court files today in search of one last newsworthy case to bring back to the reporters, I told the courthouse clerk why this was my last day, and she warned, "Latin men'll *kill* you if they catch you lookin at their women." Thankfully, Alana has brought my staring habit into remission, or at least fo-cused it on far fewer points. Still I pocketed the knife in case I relapse while alone in that brown skin sea.

Of course when I told my parents half of the truth — "I'm

going to go concentrate on my writing; a self-imposed, self-funded residency." — they warned me that I would die. But despite owning a travel agency, Mom is not worldly. Our family travel has been limited to many trips to the beach, and to Disney World. Seventeen years ago I did see a chunk of America from the U-Haul window, driving from Indiana to FLA, but other than that... On my one visit to New York with Natalie (Mom warned I would die there too), I gripped my keys between my knuckles on the subway, ready to unlock the throat of anyone who encroached. But on that subway, and today stealing that pocketknife, I wondered if I could ever really stab someone. I've never been able to even punch anyone. I've always walked away. I should have had more fights back when the worst that could happen was a split lip; physical altercations now, at my age, involve not only denser muscles but years of built up dissatisfaction and anger all projected into the toe of one boot to my face. I could only hope that whatever stranger I was fighting had been less mistreated than I have; without physical strength on my side, I would have only the harsh memory of Natalie's busboy.

Just before Alana, I was still angry enough about the whole thing to fight. After Natalie admitted they'd slept together, she continued waiting tables, he continued coming behind her to clean them off, and I set my heart on wanting to fight him — or thinking I should. In bed I would talk out loud, formulating the most powerful way to challenge him whenever I eventually saw him in Ybor or wherever. Really, Natalie deserved my fist more than he did (when I explained the situation to Tony, he almost made sense: "That guy has no loyalty to you malaka, he was just getting his."), but I decided I should beat the busboy up because he knew she was my girlfriend. She'd told him we were struggling, and he took advantage of our weakness. So he deserved...something. But I never did see him out when my iron was hottest, or even since Natalie moved to New York. But I can still, as I type now, feel my hatred simmer. Holding on for so long seems petty, but I've *never* picked a fight, so I feel like if hatred still wants me after all this time, I should just let hatred have me. And whenever I think of him, I hope to see him soon, and rise above non-violence.

Nice to know he no longer matters. Unless I happen to see him tomorrow morning, before I escape Tampa forever.

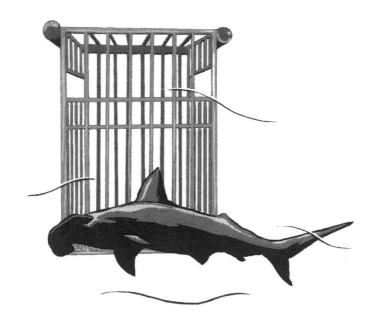

1.14 THE SWEETNESS OF NEAR MISSES

S old my furniture, boxed my clothes, books, records, guitars and drum machines, and canceled all utilities. I haven't communicated much with Alana outside of her brief phonecalls from Pizza Dive and the package she left today. Still I remain stress free — with a beautiful plan! A vision, actually, visited upon me in the bed I no longer own:

Alana and I are getting married, far from view of land. Our 50-foot wooden ship rocks under a storm-gray sky. We wear matching Pizza Dive shirts. From my side of the family, only my sister's white face stands out amid Alana's dozen brown relatives. Three small sandy bridesmaids stand in V formation on the ship's bow: Alana's sisters, though in this dream, none of them have red hair (not even in dreams can I adequately imagine redhead Latin triplets). In the tradition of bride's maids, wicker baskets hang from the girls' toothpick forearms. But rather than rose petals, the baskets hold chunks of fish, which the giggling sisters scatter overboard, leaving a brown sheen on the choppy water.

Alana's mother yells at the girls in English to be careful and not bloody their blinding-white little dresses. Though her voice sounds as it did on the phone, Alana's mother is not fat; she looks exactly like my love only taller, and with beautiful, wise wrinkles. She is not mad at us for derailing the previously planned wedding. Despite clouds grumbling overhead, everyone is happy. After much thunder and many hugs, Alana's mother calls for the wedding music, and speakers mounted in the crow's nest sing a long, mellow shriek. I somehow know that this *music* is actually the cry of injured whales. In our waking lives this soundtrack would unnerve, but it elevates the attendees of our dream-wedding to greater levels of happiness. The bridesmaids toss chum chunks and Alana's beautiful mother weeps joy into the oily water.

When the time comes for vows, Raphael — our preacher in the ceremony — leads us to a towering silver cage hung overboard. We three step into the cage and the guests howl, waving goodbye as we lower, sans scuba gear, into the sea.

Underwater, Alana now wears a traditional white gown that, like her long hair, floats upwards, as if attempting escape. Her wedding bouquet of six dead amberjack aims up at her face. I wear a white tuxedo shirt with black bow-tie, and feel like a different kind of waiter. Raphael reads the underwater vows through gray clouds of fish blood and the whale cries grow louder as in the distance, vague blue sharks began to appear. I assume this has been the point all along.

The cage is soon circled by two-foot hammerheads, hulking Lemons, Makos big as Alana, boat-sized Great Whites, dozens, hundreds, thousands of endless silent, hypnotic sharks, peering at us on their way past. Terrifying but so fucking *interesting* — the *perfect* wedding!

Alana and I smile our way through the threat and the vows and eventually mime, "I do." The cage is lifted back onto the boat into a party that now includes my own smiling parents and my half-brother David. Traditional organ music has replaced the shrieks, and a bright, clean sun glimmers off the flat, blue ocean and our big silver cage.

* * *

When I tell people that I'm leaving, and why, and that I'm unprepared and clueless, some say it's admirable, romantic, brave. I've tried to feel that way too. This week I divested myself of almost all possessions, and didn't let it frustrate me that I've missed her whenever she's stopped over. I remain ill-informed, but it *is* romantic, how Alana and I hang in the imbalance. It is easy to relish the painful sweetness of near misses.

Tonight, I returned home to a map tied with an orange ribbon on my welcome mat. I brought it inside, sat down on the tan carpet and unfolded Costa Rica across my unfurnished living room. All over her country, Alana had scribbled notations regarding my trip. I'd never seen her handwriting before (except when she'd jotted my work schedule: "Th – Sun.") and I giggled in anticipation of all the little things I still have to learn about her. She'd circled the capital, San Jose, and written beside it, "Only big airport in Costa. You fly in here." A long orange highlighter arc outlined my trajectory to tiny Puerto Tiburon, which juts out into the Pacific in the southeast of the country like the Florida of Costa Rica, complete with its own little Gulf of Mexico: *El Gulfo Tiburon.* Here she'd written, "This is my home where I meet you in some weeks."

The next day I called Mom and bought a plane ticket to San Jose, then hauled my bed over to Jake's house. I returned home late to a phone message from Alana in giddy, mischievous Spanish speckled with sweet laughs that broke the language barrier: *she loves me, misses me, we'll be together soon.*

My truck sat out front, stuffed full of my belongings, ready to be driven to my parents' condo at 6:30 a.m. I slept on my floor where my bed used to be, the pocketknife beside my head where my nightstand once stood. And in the same way I slept through my alarm and woke at 9:30, I didn't hear Alana knock. In the morning, on my bare front step lay a long cardboard strip divided into several weeks worth of days, each day a different color. There was also a note:

Dear Patrick,

I came by to make fun with you before you go away but you were stupid and not here. Your truck is full but you are not here? I will steal from your truck! But when I do steal from you

I will sell things to pay Mami so I will come meet you in Tiburon faster than some weeks. So you don't mind if I steal? No you don't. Good.

This long paper I made for you is all the days I will not be with you. I made it from a pizza box ha ha! You will rip off a piece every day in Tiburon and when there are no more pieces I will be with you!

Tiburon is very small. When I come home you will know everyone. There are good people for you to be friends with and many gringos there now. A gringo man with red hair curls is the writer I was tell you about. Talk to him. He is quiet and don't talk much and is crazy, but he is sweet and nice like you and good writer! But not as beautiful like you. He is from Florida! I don't remember his name. Don't tell him I don't remember because he is very sensitive.

My family house is by the BIG pier NOT the small one. You will know it. Mami sleep in the big house and mine house is the last small one of three small ones. Mami and Raphael will be there and PLEASE talk with Mami and make her happy. Ask her for to stay in my bed. Make her happy so that she likes you and we can be happy.

I love you and I will miss you at work and on my birthday. Write something beautiful for me! Practice Spanish! And take sunscreen for you do not die like my Papi.

I love you again,
Alana

1.15 Swear On My Mother's Life

Tomorrow I fly to Costa Rica but I don't even know what time my plane leaves. Mom booked the trip and my parents will drive me to the airport, so I haven't bothered to check my itinerary. I hate relying on my mother when I don't even think she likes me. My parents derided me for tripping off to C.R., but then compulsively did too much to help me get there. So much help. I hate it.

Still, I followed Mom to work this morning. We faced each other at parallel desks across her tiny travel agency, me flipping through brochures and making lists as she handled the last of my travel business. Somewhere in it I admitted, "You know, when I'm here with you guys I feel like nothing bad can happen to me."

"Because we take care of you," she recontextualized my complaint and blew forth smoke. All day, surrounded by full-color fliers, she gazes out her picture window onto a lot full of palm trees and over-abundant handicapped spots and she smokes Winstons, then sprays freshener over the smell, then smokes, then sprays over it, then smokes, then sprays, smokes, sprays, all day, alone.

"I know it sounds weird," I continued, "but I like to uh, feel my mortality a little. It's disturbing not to."

She typed over my voice and claimed, "You won't find a place to stay in Costa Rica for under $100-a-night, Patrick."

Not that I believed her, but still this news worried me. So I sat in that smell with her until noon, not telling her I was leaving to drive my truck around to used car lots. I didn't tell Mom because the truck was their graduation present to me. But it is mine, and if I ever moved back to the U.S., it would only be to a city with good public transportation; Florida's is mere novelty. Leaving the agency I stopped at Mom's desk. She peered into her computer monitor, her crystal ball into my future. I noticed the stitches on her neck have healed up shiny and white (her only comment regarding my stitched chin: "Don't fall on your face again now that you've pissed away your health insurance."). So I bent and kissed the brown roots of her white-gold hair.

When I pulled away, she looked up and said, softly, "You know, Patrick, I'm really afraid you're gonna fuck this up."

I wanted to yell about how *difficult* this all is, even *without* her discouraging bullshit. And I wanted to tell her not to cuss; Moms aren't supposed to say the F-word.

Instead I just left.

The first car lot gave me $4,600 cash. I filled out paperwork and the salesman drove me back to the condo in my former vehicle. Natalie and I had sex in that truck. And in the bed I sold to Jake for $35. I'm selling her off bit-by-bit…

Lunch awaited inside the condo, along with much parental criticism. They didn't appreciate me selling the truck, but since I did, they thought I should have gotten more money. Eating turkey sandwiches, potato chips and cottage cheese, I soaked up their slags and imagined Alana in Tampa, her mother screaming at her about me. At least my parents weren't screaming; they don't know about Alana. They simply talked, and talked, and talked down to me as I chewed and stared at the conch shell centerpiece on their white wicker dinner table. Mom scoffed, "You know Patrick, you're gonna go through that truck money so goddamned fast in Costa Rica."

Worry surged again. *What if I can't talk Alana's mother down from her anger?* Seems feasible since she speaks no English… Mom kept squawking. Finally I turned to Dad: "Please make her stop. I'm worried enough already."

He took in a silent fork-full of cottage cheese. He rarely goes against his wife. Which I understand; she came to him before I did. I would rail against anyone on Alana's behalf — except maybe Alana's imposing mother. "Do you know, Dad," I continued, "her last words to me this afternoon were 'You're going to 'F' this up, Patrick.'"

"Never!" Mom shouted. "I *never* said anything like that you little liar." Then to Dad, "He's in*sane*! Making things up! I swear on my mother's life! I swear on *your* life! I would *never*!"

I set my last bites of sandwich down, rose from the table, skulked up the teal stairs to go lay down in my room (*mine*, though they painted over my personality the day I left for college). Soon my Dad creaked open my door. "Go in and apologize to your mother," he requested. "She's in her room."

"No. No way." I frowned at the teal ceiling fan. "She *definitely* said that. Why should I apologize?"

"Just do it to appease her," he cajoled. "You really upset her."

"No, her own words upset her. Maybe hearing them will make her stop saying that shit to me."

He shut the door and I lay there conflicted, wondering if I refused to apologize because it would indeed be unhealthy to let her think she was right, or because she'd taught me how to hold my apologies down like small vomit in my throat.

An hour later I came down to them lying on their couches watching television. Mom sat up on her elbows and offered, along with a forgetful smile, "Let me take you to Wal-Mart, get whatever else you need for your trip: bug spray and sunscreen and stuff." Though I hate pretending like nothing happened, I needed sunscreen.

She and I spent a pleasant, impersonal hour shopping. On the way home I stared out her Lexus' window trying to remember the shark dream that had inspired me to confidence, because I was again feeling ignorant and unprepared. But instead my head filled with the loud, sharp *crack* of my spirit when Mom began, "I'm just sick about you selling that damn truck for so little money."

Baby please, don't baby, please, I thought, wanting to wretch into the Wal-Mart bag at my feet.

"You're gonna spend all that money then come back here and want to live at our house," she said. "I just know it."

No baby, c'mon baby, I promise... I didn't tell her how ridiculous her accusation was since I can't stomach Ft. Heathen for more than a day. Nor did I remind her it's a *condo*, not a "house." I said only, "That's not gonna happen, Mom."

"Well, it better not." She lit a cigarette. "You just don't want to work. You just want to run away. And when you come running back..."

"Where do you get that from?" I laughed. "I've worked two jobs for the last year."

"Well, I know how you are. You don't want to..."

"No," I interrupted, "you don't know how I am." *Baby please, baby...*

"Oh yes I do. You'll spend all that truck money, come back and expect *us* to..."

"Mom, you realize you're telling me I'm gonna fuck up, just like you swore on Dad's life you didn't."

"All I'm saying is, when you run out of money, we're old now and don't need you coming into our lives and..."

"That's not gonna happen."

"Good. But when it does I just don't want you..."

"It's not going to. Jesus. Enough," I commanded.

"We have our own lives, and when you need a place to stay, don't..."

"Enough." Baby, please, baby c'mon...

"When you blow all that money and..."

"Shut up."

She gasped, "Don't you dare."

"Then just stop. *Now.*"

"I'll tell you what buddy, we won't ever help your little ass again if you..."

"Shut up!"

"You little mother*fucker.*"

"SHUT *UP!*" I lost it. "STOP! JUST FUCKING *STOP!*"

"Patrick, I'll tell you what," she growled. "You are the biggest disappointment of my whole goddamned life..."

"SHUT - *THE FUCK* - UP!"

"You know what?" She calmed to a sizzle at a stoplight. "I hate you, you little son of a bitch."

"I'm *your* son Mom." And before she could wish that I weren't, I opened her Lexus' grand white door and stepped out into the sun.

No more fighting. I fought enough with Natalie. Never again. If I have to quit talking to my parents until they both die, I will not argue with anyone, ever again.

She didn't try to stop me. Her Lexus pulled past me down the four-lane road. I figured I'd catch a slow, inconsistent FLA bus somewhere, the mall maybe, and hang out for a couple of hours. By the time I returned home she'd be pretending it hadn't happened, I would accept her lack of apology and in the morning fly away from it all — or maybe in the afternoon. I'm not sure. *Some*time tomorrow...

The January air was mild, and fast traffic blew me breezes, still I soaked my shirt, walking in the fake-seeming grass runners along the roadside. Nearing the bus stop I spotted a big white dog lying dead out on the dividing line. As I passed her, the dog lifted her cheek from the concrete and eyed me over her shoulder, merely wounded, unable to get up. Traffic blurred so thick and fast, if she could've moved, even two-inches, she would have been hit again, fatally. We watched each other, her eyes less worried than mine, her panting tongue flapping like the Red Barron's scarf whenever a car buzzed too close to her face.

I hopped around waving my arms, trying to stop traffic and run out and drag the dog to safety. But SUVs flew by and by. Finally I spotted a small break in the cars ahead. I decided to just step out into the road; the insensitive cars would *have* to stop for a human. But when she sensed me coming for her, the dog's face furrowed, and when my shoe hit the tar, she stood up, backed away and...

Before I could whip around to avoid the sight, I saw the white dog fly high up into the air over the rush of vehicles, followed by a long string of red blood against the blue sky. Behind me tires screamed and metal shrieked.

When the world silenced, I plopped down in the grass to wait for cops or medics to ask for my story, and to stare at the twisted cars like giant hot-chocolate machines dropped by a clumsy god. The car that killed the dog was now half its original size; the second car was a crumpled metal accordion — the EMTs wrapped a neckbrace around its lady driver and carried the stretcher past the dog. Sobbing, chuckling, wishing I were in Costa Rica, I watched the last car's unharmed driver inspect her smashed grill. She was 20 years old, gorgeous with long brown hair and a dark sweat stain creeping down the front of her small workout unitard. I calmed at the sight of her walking my way.

She squatted beside me, her outfit the same gray as the street. "You all right?"

"Yeah. Nothing happened to *me*." I lay back in the grass, hands over my eyes. "It's just so fucking sad."

"What happened?" she asked. In my darkness I heard the grass shift where she sat down beside my head. I told her the story, omitting the argument with Mom.

When I finished, I heard her lay down. Her voice beside my ear asked only, "How do you know the dog was a she?"

"I guess I don't."

She laughed. She was very kind; despite her trashed car, she cared about the dog, and me. We lay there for several minutes, close enough I could smell her minty breath. Finally she sat up straight and asked, "Do you need a hug?"

For some reason I lied, "No. I don't."

1.16 A Soft Voice Like Forgiveness

It's dead here now in Ft. Heathen, on the pier in the condominium complex where I grew up. Two miles away my parents lie on their couches watching TV as I sit beside the Gulf of Mexico, under the stars, drinking beer and smoking pot and typing on my laptop, which I'm not bringing to Costa Rica; I can't risk it getting swiped. As promised, I will document my time in C.R. before Alana arrives, maybe make it into a little book for her, but I guess I'll scribble it all out by hand. Another nice change…

I've also never drank a beer on this pier before. I haven't been out here since before Natalie convinced me to take my first drink, try drugs, and have sex. I underappreciated this pier, back when I was a virgin. I only thought to ride my Dad's beach cruiser down here tonight because Alana's last letter mentioned her pier, and because I couldn't watch my parents lay on those couches like coffins.

Earlier, around sunset, when the bus dropped me back at their condo, Mom was indeed back to pretending our air was clear. But when I tried telling them my dead dog story, they shushed me, not wanting to miss a word of this week's *COPS*, shot on location in Ft. Heathen.

Since my last time out on this pier, a huge new pointy patch of oysters has emerged beside the boating channel. There's less water now, even given low tide. And I don't hear mullet jumping in the night like they used to. Many people used to fish out here. My parents always came home with buckets of crabs, trout and sheepshead, a snook sometimes. But the yellow webs of crabtrap rope are all gone now. FLA changed so fast. I should have enjoyed it more when it was still alive. I plan to sit and fish on Alana's pier as much as possible.

The two-mile bike ride down here through the condo complex was full of memories. And swimming pools. If I never come back to FLA, I will miss the unnatural-blue miles of pools. On the bike just now I passed the pool outside Mandy's old condo — it's been half my life since we swam there all day. The Condominium Association's since built a seven-foot wood fence around it. The main straightaway leading to the pier — once an empty field run by burrowing owls — is now dense with cheap condos. I remember driving the first thousand-dollar car my parents ever bought me down to that baron straightaway to see how fast I could get it going. Around 100 mph I turned off the headlights — for no real reason, just that *I-sort-of-want-to-die-but-I'm-confident-I-won't* feeling that middle-class white kids get — and after 20 black seconds, I flicked the headlights back on to find myself screaming up on a 10-foot alligator. Had I not swerved, she would have rolled my new, used car.

Now streetlamps light the straightaway and the entire visible bank of the Gulf. I see them from here. Counting the new lights, I try to remember the good things about FLA. But aside from cool winter air and swimming, FLA reminds me mostly of Natalie; Natalie prettier than the palm trees behind her, Natalie shimmering brighter than the Gulf, Natalie bobbing her head and singing campfire songs sincerely on the drive to Orlando. Disney World might actually be as magical as alleged; even our family has had fun there. And Natalie and I got along great at Disney. So we went there a lot.

My strongest memory of Disney World is from just before Natalie and I broke up. Our relationship was dying and we huddled around it, intending resuscitation. But at the time we couldn't afford the Disney ticket, so instead drove all the way from Tampa just to ride the free park monorail from one themed resort hotel to the next.

We ran through sprinklers at the Western-style ranch, then dried off with towels from the faux New Orleans plantation. We lounged in wet swimsuits in a baseball glove-shaped couch in the Sports Hotel's lobby, watching cable on a giant Disney TV. And when night descended, we stormed the Rock-n-Roll Hotel with its guitar-shaped pool.

Though she tried to feel differently, Natalie had lost all physical attraction to me. In teary speeches during nights when she wouldn't have slept better against any other man, she convinced me that she was helpless to re-ignite desire. Women, more than men, see past visual unimpressiveness when they love you, but when they stop, reality takes hold. Far past our expiration date, though I wanted her, Natalie wouldn't touch me. Emasculating, knowing that within minutes of our breakup, she would find someone new to sleep with — she had already, actually, not including the option of my "friends" who all lined up, waiting for a possible turn with her. Natalie and I had screwed *each other* up, made *each other* unfit for emotional consumption, but when you're that beautiful no one cares how shell-shocked you are. And no hot tub bubbles, or guitar-shaped pool glowing like a white-blue diamond could dilute the fact that I would waste years trying to fill the void she was about to leave.

Still, as the Disney sun set and we changed into our bathing suits in separate restrooms at the empty rock-n-roll pool, I was happy and hopeful that something good would come of this trip. In the men's room, I removed my jeans then pressed my ear to the mauve wall between us, listening for anything suggesting the beauty going on in there. But the windy palms obscured all sound, so I grabbed my swim trunks, peeped out my door and in a rush of hope and stupidity, broke naked through two feet of night to the lady's room. There Natalie and I stood together in the tiny, damp, concrete changing room, naked together for the first time in bitter months.

"What are you doing?" she asked, breathless.

"I dunno, what are you doing?"

"I'm changing."

Because I feel redundant and dumb telling women they're beautiful, I said only, "I wanted to change with you..."

To break our sad tension she hugged me, pressed her warmth against me, then looked down, tying her bikini on over her smooth, beautiful breasts. I touched her hip to recapture her gaze, but she laughed as if it tickled, as if she'd rather not. So I jumped into my green nylon shorts and we stepped out onto the painted poolside.

Two teenage boys who'd commandeered the hot tub giggled at our exiting the lady's room together. The pool glowed like that healing pool in the movie *Cocoon* that gave old people the power to never age or die. Staring into the guitar-shaped light, I thought to joke how *we* might jump in and save our dying thing — before Natalie tested the water with her perfect toe and, "It's too cold..."

So we wordlessly slipped into the hot tub with the two muscular jock boys. Natalie and I spat water at each other, the boys' presence impeding our conversation. Down through the hot, white water, my flaccid skin made me wish I were better, physically irresistible like her. I suffered her beauty. At one point she embraced me again — or I pulled her to me — and as her face nuzzled my wet neck, over her shoulder I caught the boys scanning her back, shoulders, thighs, and I ached knowing that either of them had a better chance of bedding her.

"Let's get out," I suggested.

We dried off. Natalie wrapped a towel around her like a strapless dress, and I crawled inside my shirt. Dark palms divided the pool from a manmade body of water that whispered like real waves — beautiful and amazing FLA's most questionable incarnation. Thin slivers of blue pool light peaked through the palms like ghosts onto the deserted Disney beach. We smoked a joint traversing a beach-cricket course as the wind whipped Natalie's towel against her thighs ahead of me.

Seemingly far enough away from humanity, she reached under her towel and magically removed her bikini without exposing herself. She wrung it into the Disney-sand and I sighed loud and dumb. Balled-up top in hand, she leaned back against a tall palm and smiled convincingly: "Oh, Patrick," she said in a soft voice like forgiveness, then opened her towel like a flower.

I felt cold and damp and inadequate walking to her, thanking her for trying. She let me put my mouth on hers. Our last kiss. And I had my damn shirt on.

We then tightened our complimentary towels around us and set about exploring the rock-n-roll hotel, beginning with the first floor, reserved for Disney-themed activities, board meetings and BINGO. Most FLA businesses run their a/c wide-open during the summer, giving us summer flus. But nowhere is worse than Disney World. My girl shivered like a freshly bathed kitten in those frigid halls, and so allowed my arm around her. We giggled down the pastel corridors. Well-dressed humans shot us mean looks for dripping on their thin, loud carpeting. Finally we slid to a wet-footed stop at double doors opening before us. An older man limped out and down the hall. Inside mulled dozens of old women dressed like elegant wedding cakes. Gray men in suits all stood in line for free booze beside a band playing Jimmy Buffet (as all FLA cover bands eventually do). In the room's center stood a 10-foot island of extravagant desserts. The slow doors closed on the glory.

"Did you see that *cake*!" Natalie exclaimed more than asked. Water dripped from her shivering hair as she bounced on the naked balls of her feet. "Let's go in! Let's go! *Let's go*!"

We debated the implausibility of our wet hair and towels, then decided to just run in, grab desserts, and run out. We reopened the double doors. An ice-carved palm sprung from a table layered in whipped and iced creams and elegant, dripping, chocolate chaos meant for the rich and dry. But no one seemed to mind us. We approached Dessert Island and picked out two ice cream cakes blown up like puffer fish on chilled-glass plates, then went so far as to collect free Jack-and-cokes. Amidst the elderly we danced and drank and dug confidently into our desserts with huge silver forks. We booed the Buffet band and laughed hard because we knew it would be over soon. All of it. We ate and drank it all while we still had it. Smart, since Natalie and I don't have it at all now. None of it. I wonder what she's doing in NY tonight, while I'm out here writing about her and crying off the pier, rehydrating The Gulf... Maybe it's just the beer and pot. Either way, it's good I'm leaving tomorrow for new memories. I need new ones.

There! A mullet splashed! The last fish of my FLA life.

O.K., I guess. Here we go.

BOOK 2: "sustain"

(COSTA RICA, CENTRAL AMERICA)

2.1 ON MEMORY AND MAMI

Dear Alana,

    I remember my family's U-Haul caught fire driving from Indiana to our new home in FLA, 17 years ago, the LAST time my geography really changed. I remember my ears popped, high in the Smoky Mountains where my Dad emergency stopped. But though I'd never before witnessed mountains, the Smokys themselves are now just a vague brown chocolate smudge across my memory — me, who's been accused of "holding onto memories, white-knuckled."

    But forget all that in favor of the second mountain skyline of my life! Opening before me like mile-high knees! A vast green rising and falling landscape! Although YOU Alana, affect me heavier than any NATURAL wonder, I WILL remember THIS taxi ride forever, confident that I have every right. It is painful though, how much I wish you were here.

Nor can I really share my excitement with this taxi-van driver who now shuttles me to some San Jose youth hostel. I did practice Spanish on the plane though, seated beside a well-off artist whose business card read: HOCHI SMITH, ARTIST. He was butterscotch-colored, half Black, half Chinese, fluent in English and Spanish. He wore a sleek, gray sharkskin suit, a healthy wristwatch, and shaved black hair like a film of charcoal dust. Hochi was being flown to the University of San Jose to lecture on photography, so he liked my answer when he asked why I'm visiting C.R.: "To concentrate on writing, and life, and hopefully make those two things ONE." Waiting for take-off, Hochi decided to speak to me only in Spanish. We shared many awkward volleys, until the warming jets drowned out soft-spoken Hochi, and we lapsed back into English, then silence.

I then fell into a TERRIBLE vivid nightmare about your brother and Mami! No reason to share the details, other than to admit that I don't know HOW I'll win her over without SPANISH on my side... I could explain to her that I NEED my clothes washed, or NEED to cash a check, but...

I'll figure it out. For you. I promise. In the meantime ONWARD! In the meantime...

I love you,
Pat

* * *

Jesus I hope that was a dream.

I dreamt I was on the same plane, Hochi beside me, every detail exact. Except the cabin lights stuttered off. Just dusty sun lit the passengers, who all hushed as the engines wound mysteriously down. When their collective mumble resumed, Hochi prophesized, "In Costa Rica, you will meet a nice, sweet girl — likely much younger than you — whose family will take you in and provide everything you need so you can concentrate *just* on writing."

Before I could divulge Alana, the plane re-lit. Then stalled again. The pilot's drawl filled the sunny cabin: "Well folks, seems we're havin a little lectrical trouble which'll delay the flight a bit. I do apologize."

This time though, the passengers remained silent, and I followed their unified gaze down the aisle — to Raphael! I stood! Sat! Stood! Happiness stifled my voice — much like in a dream. The craft's small windows spotlit freckles caught in Raphael's gravity. Hochi proved himself the artist by commenting, "Celestial little fucker." Raphael looked different though, in dress pants and white long sleeves: sturdier, more real, an allusion to traditional beauty. He looked dressed to attend a wedding, and I smiled remembering that he would not be.

But Raphael's eyes over his shoulder watched, along with the passengers and flight crew, a 300-pound Latin woman in a blue muumuu, squeeze sideways onto the plane. I sat back down, anticipating Raphael's surprise and studying the woman's smooth, sandy Latin face, large and round as a pumpkin. Straight black hair swept down onto her thick brown arms, and elbows that bent like marshmallows as her hand lifted to her mouth a thin cocktail straw protruding from one of the small, blue boxes I recognized from Alana's floorboards: *Cornstarch.*

Mami *drinks* cornstarch?

Each of her monstrous steps down the aisle took days. Between days, Raphael spotted me and beamed: "Pa-treek!"

"Raphael!" I leapt up. "*Mi hermano!*"

Mami wrinkled her small pretty nose over her son's slight shoulder like a hippopotamus behind a dandelion. Upon sight of me, she reached around Raphael's face and smacked her big silver rings hard *clack!* against his teeth. Raphael squinted and grabbed his mouth. The tiniest shriek escaped his knuckles. The passengers' eyes grew. I slumped back down and leaned into Hochi's sharkskin to make room for them; neither scowling Mami nor whimpering Raphael acknowledged me in passing.

"I take it you know these two?" Hochi asked.

Stunned, I answered only, "I worked with that kid in Tampa."

Hochi turned to watch them sit in back. I wanted to dissect her too, to look for Alana in her and find no trace. Still all of me faced forward, stiff.

"His mama's a real ass kicker!" Hochi laughed. "Find a big girl like that when you get to Costa Rica! She'll whip you into shape!"

Then the cabin lights flickered back on.

"Well ladies and gentlemen," the pilot drawled, "seems the problem has fixed itself! Soon as everyone's buckled up, we'll continue on to our destination, San Jose, Costa Rica!"

"The problem has *what*?" Hochi asked the air, then whispered a rosary.

For the duration of the flight, despite FLA in my past, Hochi at my side, and a new life ahead, I felt deprived knowing Raphael was *right* behind me and I couldn't even…

No. It was a bad dream.

People don't *drink* cornstarch.

2.2 HOSTEL
TERRITORY: SAN JOSE

D ARLING ALANA,

I'm here! Safe at the hostel. Which has an internet café right across the street. I should have set you up an email account before I left. Or I shouldn't have promised not to mail love-letters to Pizza Dive — though I do understand how quickly Tony would pin them up beneath the time-clock. I will continue shouting then, into the San Jose wind (which is surprisingly cold). Maybe I'll bind these letters — full of pretentious English words you'll enjoy looking up; never would I patronize you — in the bark of some native tree and give it to you to read upon your return.

Whoa. That means, as you're reading this, we're together! STOP READING! Save the past for the future and come to me NOW!

In the real NOW though I sit silent on a bottom bunk, surveying the other bottom bunk, where I've spread out everything I brought with me: tape recorder, blank tapes, notebooks, a disposable camera, razors, padlock, secret money belt, five T-shirts, three pairs of shorts, one pair of jeans, one towel, no underwear, tiny gold fish hooks, Avon's Skin-so-Soft (to ward off sandfleas: 'No-see-ums,' FLA calls them), windbreaker, Strindberg's *A Madman's Manifesto*, Vollman's *Whores for Gloria*, Jonathan Ames *The Extra Man*, *The Sorrows of Young Werther*, *Death in Venice*, *Lolita*, a book called *On Love*, plus some glossy Central America travel materials from Mom's agency.

My Dad's fishing pole also leans against the bunk. He couldn't comprehend my sudden desire to fish. Last night, oiling the reel's every tiny gear and replacing its line for me, he recalled my traumatic LAST fishing trip. I never fished much (I will make up for that here!) but when I did it was not in the ocean up the street, but in a shallow, artificial estuary beside the community pool, where fish as long as my childhood forearm would become trapped. These big fish were always starving whenever I tossed live lizards out into the water and I loved studying the bass' eyes before they ripped through the water with the ferocity of great white sharks. Plus it's just easier to catch what was already caught.

But this last time, at the age of 12, on my first cast out, my orange plastic lure snuck up and grabbed my head from behind, the treble sinking in above my ear. I panicked and ran, dragging my rod-n-reel across the grass. Mom heard me scream and ran out to retrieve the rod-n-reel off the ground, and follow behind her son like a kite being flown.

So, thanks for this second chance, Alana. Seriously. Thank you.

LOVE!
Patrick

* * *

Leading downtown, away from my hostel, skinny *Avenida Central* is hemmed in by tall, cracked white-beige walls choked by vines and algae, and freckled with what look like bulletholes. At the feet of these walls run narrow sidewalks, like building ledges above *La Avenida's* mess of mean little red taxis. Down these precarious sidewalks, my temporary roommate Eduardo walked twelve steps ahead of me — then suddenly froze, assuming the focus of a pointer dog when *Avenida Central* became a lively glass-front shopping district, closed off to all cars except cops busting unlicensed street vendors peddling pot pipes, jewelry and small plastic toys. Thousands of beautiful Latins circulated through. I imagined San Jose as Southbeach Miami circa 1970, with less color (beige, mostly), more dirt and less money, to the benefit of its soul.

"Veemen, veemen," escaped Eduardo's dumb parted lips like *vehement, vehement.*

Even after we had thoroughly met, upon each re-entry into our room he repeated, "I am Eduardo!" because English was his third language. I don't remember which was his first. Eduardo was gray-faced, athletic, traveling alone, and believed he, "cannot leave vithout I make love viz a beautiful Costa Rican geerl. Do you understand, Patrick? I *most*," Eduardo mumbled, "I *most*..." So wound up, he never noticed my crusty stitches.

He was correct about San Jose's women though: so beautiful, and of so many shades, from pearl black to sandy like Alana, they could have all hailed from separate countries. On *La Avenida*, Eduardo's frantic eyes panned. "Hey!" he'd bark into the crowd, followed by a plowboy's whistle. And packs of women actually turned to meet his desperate eyes — my first instance of culture shock. Most of them quickly returned to their original destinies, except the one woman Eduardo had wanted, standing still in the distance, meeting his gaze, hand on hip, waiting. Eduardo would squint like a jeweler then, "Nah," he'd say aloud to himself, "she is not so perfect geerl." And his quest resumed. For some reason I followed until eventually Eduardo did dart off to collect. And though he promised to return, I'd already accepted my abandonment.

For once though, I felt better alone, and spent until sunset exploring Costa Rica's gray, greasy, funny, sad, supposedly most dangerous streets. I let two very drunk and dirty construction worker types buy me beers with my overcooked rice and chicken (at one point the two working guys even hugged me, which was a bit unnerving but), then I had two more beers for the extremely low price of one, in a glass bar on a hill lit by bonfire. Throughout the day I talked to and trusted many natives, and am thrilled to report not one chicken bone on my belt!

2.3 PUERTO TIBURON

Oh DEAR Alana!

We're passing through the whites of God's eyes!
Now we're out.

I'd planned on sleeping away this flight to Tiburon but DAMN I'm glad I didn't! UNNERVINGLY beautiful! The tiny plane doesn't pass through clouds so much as we are overwhelmed, SWALLOWED. Every window's blocked-in screaming white. Heaven hurts the eyes still I stare out and wait for the pilot to lean over his right shoulder and announce to all dozen passengers that, "the problem has fixed itself..."

And we're out.

SO DAMN glad I didn't take the long, cheap bus to Tiburon. I changed my plans after the hostel's front-desk lady told me the bus station is a wonderful place for a gringo tourist to experience an authentic San Jose mugging. The plane ticket cost 23,000 colones (I've never OWNED 23,000 of ANYTHING save freckles!), but from the moment a boy younger than Raphael flapped orange-painted rags to lead us into takeoff, this flight has been worth 23,000 of anything.

TURBULENCE! Eesh. It's tough to write with the plane's vibrations plus my heart slamming against the cage bars in there. The white people all around me sleep as I'd planned to. A middle-aged hippie guy with matted black-and-white hair snores against my nearest window, mouth open, partly blocking the view of endless blue waves trimmed in foamy red tide outlining green mountains with roads carved into their chocolate tops. It all takes my breath as only you ever have.

Haven't spotted any volcanoes though. My guidebook says your country is famous for volcanoes, rainforests, beaches, coffee and prostitution. The hostel provided great breakfast coffee for free this morning, and tangled rainforest beaches sing up to me now, but I've seen no trace of the other stuff... No rush though. If after we land I can hold onto even a fraction of this new optimism, I won't care if I never see volcanoes OR hookers. As the pilot announces Tiburon coming into view below, I need only you, here.

Yours,
Patrick

* * *

We plunged toward the trees with no airstrip in sight. Thankfully the pilot had no trouble sliding us in beside a field of miniature white grave markers: hand-carved headstones and statues leaning every direction like drunks chatting at a funeral. I dragged my bags and pole off the plane to the knee-high wall around the graves, to look for Alana's dad.

Out in the middle, their family name, *Ephraim*, lay beneath the stone feet of a naked angel. I imagined his obit: *Survivors include one son, Raphael, Puerto Tiburon, Costa Rica; four daughters, Alana Ephraim...* and wondered how cemeteries survive here so close to the ocean. Tiburon's air is even wetter that FLA's. Her dad's bones must swim in Costa Rican groundwater.

Turning from the angel, I found that salt-and-pepper hippie on my wing. On the plane he'd introduced himself as Jacques, from

Quebec, and described the catering business he and his wife operate outside of Tiburon. When I told him I know nothing about Tiburon, he offered to, "show you where the gringos hang out, once we land."

"I'm not necessarily partial to gringos," I spoke up. "But you can show me where the redheads hang out..."

"Oh, there are a surprising number of those here as well," he'd smirked.

Now back on Earth we studied graves together until a little Toyota pickup exploded onto the tarmac: a fenderless, white version of my former truck, painted with a full-body tattoo of peace signs, yin-yangs, ankhs, infinity 8s. A middle-aged gringa with a malicious tan and long split ends leapt from the truck and into Jacques' mouth. They kissed, their shoulders like chopsticks struggling to grip marbles. Their shirtless gringo driver sat patiently in the truck, his Alana-length dreadlocks coiled like a snake atop the gearshift. Finally Jacques pointed at me and announced into his wife's mouth, "He knows nothing."

She gave a sympathetic but questioning grin: "Aw. Y'wanna ride intuh town, sweet-awt?" Her accent was drunken New Jersey.

"Into town?" I repeated.

"The village's a coupla three miles from here, sweetie," she clarified, and I shuddered: *I would've been stranded in a real-life jungle!* But I then dared believe that my luck is *good*, that I am blessed. That I'm usually, in the end, swept up-and-out, saved.

High atop a cooler in their truck's bed I sat surrounded by crab traps, bait buckets and tent bags, my feet up on a spare tire: a fool's throne. The truck tumbled through my first ever jungle down almost-roads between fields of barely fenced-in grass nibbled by strange, gray humpback cows. Small, open-air tin shacks appeared every half-mile, then slightly sturdier shacks, which soon led onto an official dust road lined with low buildings made from awkwardly disparate materials. Chickens did scatter. This was not San Jose. This was much more what I expected.

On this hot Main Road, locals squinted from the glassless windows of their tiny grocery store, hardware store, liquor store, bar, bar, butcher shop, bar, internet café (out *here* even?). Costa Ricans peered from their tiny shoe store (*zapataria*), bakery (*panaria*) and concession stand (*soda*). The entire village seemed to be roughly the size of Ybor City, surrounded by trees into infinity.

We stopped finally, here at this gringo restaurant. Desk fans roped precariously to the ceiling now flap posters advertising *Mangrove Kayak Tours! Sunset Dolphin Tours! Sportfishing! Rainforest Mountain-biking! Shelling Expeditions!* Shelling? The restaurant was as empty then as now, save a bulky, sulking, Costa Rican waitress, and a cook hanging his moustache out the service window — reminding me that no matter where I go, I am never in the minority as a member of the service industry! There exist millions more waiters than redheads.

"Grab a bite here with us before we head out to aw place," Jacques wife commanded. "I want to talk to you." Jacques convened with their driver, who then moseyed off down the road to the internet café, which Jacques says their driver owns. Leading me up the restaurant's many high steps, his wife — "Uhlivya," she mispronounced her name — admitted she'd drunk a carafe of wine while waiting for her husband's plane. This I blamed for her staring at me across our white plastic covered picnic table, her smile knowing, also expectant.

We all ordered beer from the dour waitress. Jacques ordered tacos then quietly informed me, "Tacos aren't traditional Tico food, but gringos come here expecting tacos, so this place gives em what they expect." He fell to a whisper, "You can actually eat better for cheaper elsewhere in the village. But the gringo who owns this place helps us get supplies for our catering business that local places can't, so…"

I did not ask about the word Ticos – I'll assume that's what Costa Ricans are called, though I'm surprised I've never heard it – still I proceeded to betray my self-preservation instincts: "So, where exactly is the pier from here?"

"You haven't looked at a map?" Jacques gestured like banishment: "Go left down The Main Road past the internet café and the school, then cross or circumvent the soccer field, cut through the trees and that's *El Gulfo Tiburon*. To the left is a fun little bar that gets pretty crazy at night, *Nos Barra* — a good mix of locals and gringos. But if you instead go *right*, over that little bridge, you'll see the little fishing pier…"

"And just past *that* pier," Uhlivya finally spewed, "down the beach is *Ilka's* pier!"

I knew she meant my love's mother. The cornstarch drinker.

She was on to me.

"Ilka and I have been, I guess you could say *friends*, for a long time," she winked. "I had already knew Alana's new American boyfriend was showin up. I guessed you were him. Boy, that red hair," she laughed. "No wonder..."

I held back, *No wonder what?* It didn't surprise me that news would travel fast in a village with just two roads, but I was determined not to expedite secondhand news. Jacques looked worried over his wife's wine words flowing, "Ilka had that pier built with her hubby's life insurance money. In his *honor* y'know." Her eyes rolled. "So she don't want blood all over it — fish blood, I mean. Everybody just sticks to the first little pier." I silently, helplessly practiced answers to the questions I was sure Uhlivya would ask about the cancelled wedding, the age difference, my stitches. "I just *love* her kids though!" she laughed. "Alana is *so* gorgeous! Sweet-awt you're just *so* lucky! Everyone in the village loves her. And the triplets, my *gawd*! A litter of cute little tabby kittens! And little *Ra-fy-al*? Uh *angel*!" She paused. "Ah. I just feel *so* bad for the little guy sometimes..."

I allowed myself only, "I can't wait to see him."

"If you're ever lucky enough," Uhlivya cackled. "The Ephraims live sorta separate from the village. Ilka keeps little *Ra-fy-al* on a *leash*! Comes right home from school. That is if she ain't keepin him *out* for some reason or anotha. *I* didn't tell ya this, but Ilka's kinda *distant* to her redhead kids. Her husband ran off with a lil redhead tourist chicky..."

"Honey, c'mon." Jacques and I both smiled weakly.

"No, he was a *great* guy! Wasn't he Jacques? We loved him. That shit he pulled was a long time ago. Alana was a baby..." She turned to Jacques, "Gawd, we been here f'*evah*. Ilka was *thin* when we got here!" Jacques smiled weaker still. "He did the right thing and came right back," she continued, eyes slightly swimming. "Got a good job teaching at that nice school and wanted more kids. But cause he had jet black hair, when Raphael came out with that *red hair*, and then a few years later the girls... It was spooky. And let's just say it caused a rift."

"You don't need to finish that beer," Jacques frowned, motioning the waitress over. "We need to get you out of here."

"Yes," I laughed casually, glad though that she'd warned me that in Tiburon, telling someone means telling everyone. Until Alana arrives I abide by those signs on FLA beaches: *take only memories, leave only footprints.* Tiburon is my *No Wake Zone.*

My garlic-baked fish had been dry, but my bill with rice, fries and three beers, came to only $7. So after they said their awkward goodbyes and the dreadlocked internet café owner drove them off in the direction of the Gulf, I continued drinking and writing. I could certainly afford to. Jacques also scribbled down directions to $3-a-night lodging! Even this gringo restaurant rents $10 rooms — $90 less than Mom predicted. I'll have no trouble finding accomodaFUCK I LEFT MY DAD'S POLE IN THEIR TRUCK!

2.4 LYING LODGER

D ear Alana,

Maybe Costa Rica doesn't surprise you anymore. Maybe Tiburon is your Tampa. But my blood's bubbled like CHAMPAGNE since landing here! Tiburon's so bucolic! So REAL! So YOU! I pen this letter against a six-inch-thick mattress — previously three-inch-thin, before I folded it over and tied it with bed sheets so the rusty springs won't stab me. $3-a-night to sleep in what were surely once stables, though a horse couldn't fit in this room now.

Sorry I'm staying in a CABINA. I just need one night to decompress before heading down to the Gulf to fix our lives, tomorrow, I promise...

Until then, I could spy on my neighbors through the gaps in these teal slat-board walls. We breathe each other's air, and benefit from each other's light: authentic bare, white bulbs illuminate black bullseyes burnt into the cement floor by previous tenants' hotplates. A slab of wood hacked from this wall leans against my bed, in case I want to 'close' the 'window'. But I leave it open, knowing at least that if I'm eaten by a panther, my obituary will include Cause of Death — info *The Trib* omits, unless the death is "interesting." They'd exclude C.O.D. if I died of heatstroke in this sweatbox, with its impotent waist-high fan slouched and decrepit, missing its face and squealing louder than whatever that is outside my 'window.'

PERFECT room!

Except for the communal bathroom, where my feet sank into what I HOPED was algae. When I turned the slimy shower spigot, the pipes shrieked to wake the entire village. I quick-spun them back OFF, and in the silence of Tiburon's ever-present jungle percussion like distant marching bands, a heavy snot ball SMACKED the bare skin that protects my heart from the world. A giant tree frog! Scientists can supposedly gauge an environment's suitability for humans by its abundance or lack of frogs. When I first moved to FLA, we couldn't open the door at night without frogs big as human hands jumping blindly from the porch light, peeing on us mid-air. But frogs seem to have evacuated Florida. One more reason for you to COME BACK HOME! QUICK!

QUICKER!!!
Patrick

* * *

From the shadow of low tin structures, bored-faced Tica grandmothers supervised baby granddaughters playing in the Main Road's dust as I assume they have every day of Alana's life. Ticos in baseball caps leaned and laughed against pick-up trucks with complex metal roll-cages like coral reefs growing from their beds: taxi-trucks waiting for capacity loads of backpack-burdened gringos to transport into the jungle. As I dragged minimal belongings up the steaming, staring Main Road, the cabbies all hollered smiley Spanish. I waved clammy palms. "*No neccesito! Estoy* local," I said. And they all laughed harder.

For the moment, I denied the questionable gravity of the shaded Gringo Restaurant, trudged on in the direction of the internet café and the school: some of the only Tiburon buildings that look born of blueprints. Gravel and chainlink surround the school like a prison courtyard, but cute brown children in sky-blue shirts and navy slacks chased each other freely in-and-out, sucking juice-bags with mouths full of missing teeth. A classroom stocked with beautiful children watched their young, attractive, curly-haired Teacher, or else gazed longingly out the window through me, to shirtless boys attacking a ball on the vast soccer field. Directly above the boys, two flocks of huge macaws smashed together in a red, blue, yellow, clawing, biting, screeching explosion — then just as suddenly shrieked off in every direction. A single blue feather floated down onto the battling boys, who never once looked up from their ball. I paused to search the schoolyard for Raphael or his little sisters. Spotting no redheads, I dragged on.

Rather than continue down to the second pier where I've yet to make peace with Ilka, I veered onto Tiburon's only other, less busy road. Wild iguanas lay like fat housecats in the thick wet trees, all warning me with the same head-bobbing dance as FLA's small anoles. On the dusty street, two police guards hugged sawed-off shotguns outside the diminutive bank — directly next door to my new, temporary home, *Cabinas del Mar.*

Del Mar's white stucco facade looked almost Floridian, with shiny bamboo railings across the second-floor balcony. Directly below said balcony, a Tica inside a service window smiled at me, bobbing her head of tight curls, like the iguanas' dance, but welcoming. *"Neccesitas un quarto?"* She waved me in. Assuming that clean, white *Del Mar* was another gringo-owned joint charging gringo prices I lied, *"No neccesito."* She bobbed sweet acceptance then filleted and cooked my lunch of fish, beans and rice, toast and avocado while explaining at a sympathetic pace that her name is Rosie, and she owns and runs *Del Mar* with her husband, who also drives a *collectivo* (taxi truck) on the Main Road alongside his six brothers. Rosie slowly described the many beaches and rainforest national parks the *collectivos* drive to, and from her mouth I understood every Spanish word! Even her inquiry regarding my stitches.

I apologized for my inability to describe my accident, but did admit to safe-seeming Rosie that I'm Alana's boyfriend. Her laughter and clapping hands frightened jungle parrots into the sky. "Oh! *Si, si!* Alana! *Mucho gusto!*" She then paused, pointed again at my mangled chin: "Alana?"

"*No,*" I laughed, *"pero, si,"*

For food that did taste better than the Gringo Restaurant's, Rosie claimed I owed her only 1000 *colones*. $3.25? Her prices trump even Pizza Dive's! I gladly paid, and wondered if her room rates might also surprise: just *two thousand colones* for a clean, thick mattress with fresh sheets, which Rosie promises that her daughter Mimo will change per my request. Sparkling white tile spreads into a clean bathroom that boasts a hot water shower, and is mine alone! There's even a TV, something I chose to never have in FLA but... Though not as large as my Tampa apartment, this cabina's nicer and certainly cheaper!

Damn I would love to gush to Alana about all this! If I hadn't promised her I wouldn't be so comfortable...

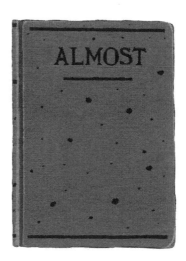

2.5 It Takes a Village

Alana would have us splashing in El Gulfo Tiburon right now, not hovering over her village at this Gringo Restaurant again. The patio's now frantic with clean new backpacks and fishing hats, maps fanning air hot with Germanic languages. Alana surely hates it all. I should patronize only Tico watering holes. But it is interesting how gringos here sit and just start telling me things. They seem lonely, though so do Floridians, and the only Floridians who were ever friendly out of nowhere were Scientologists, Jehovah's Witnesses or other cultists. So, I was skeptical when a balding gray German sat here with me and volunteered his story: for one month every year, he explained, he leaves his family in Germany and drags 100-pounds of digital recording equipment into Tiburon's rainforest to document jungle noises. Fascinated and ashamed of my previous apprehension, I now had many questions. But on freshly rested knees, he left. And I decided to henceforth be kinder. Even to white people.

Tiburon's next desperately friendly tourist emerged from the beaded curtains of this restaurant's office, carrying a small pink paperback and a journal the same brand as that pinned under my elbows. His young white face framed in long neat sideburns and thick-rimmed glasses paused smiling above me. "They usually have a great book exchange in there," he said, volunteering info that might turn out to be valuable, since the dragging flow of Tiburon time has already eaten through *A Madman's Manifesto* and half of *Death in Venice.* "But today," he amended, "they only have copies of *this.*" He handed me the pink book, titled *Almost.* I was first to crack its binding, flip its powdery pages and read atop one page after another the name: Milton Chapman.

"Oh, I've heard of this guy," I said, though unsure. The back cover featured a blurb from my alma mater, *The Trib*:

> 'Milton Chapman does for the state of Florida
> what Peter Benchley did for sharks. A
> passionate but patient novel...a beautifully
> disturbing debut.' - *The Trib, Tampa*

I did recognize the name. Chapman's blurbs hailed exclusively from FLA publications, still I remembered *Almost* was popular enough to sell at Wal-Mart, meaning even Mom read it, thus I never did. But I'd heard enough about Chapman to fake it: "He teaches at Florida State."

"Actually, he lives *here* now, in Tiburon," the guy corrected. "I haven't run into him yet. But every new load of used books is immediately traded for copies of *that...*" He pointed at the novel, pink as my hands. "It's so good that I even bought this second copy for my friend Buck. But I guess if I want new reading material though, I have to beat Chapman down here!"

Studying the author's photo, I wondered if I hadn't seen him up on this patio. But no, I'd remember the shoulder-length curls and long catfish mouth across the wide black-and-white face on the book's back cover. "Have him autograph this for you," I lightly mocked, handing it back.

"I plan on it!" the tourist laughed, so easy-going as to be almost abrasive. "He supposedly lives right down by the pier. The big private one."

"My girlfriend's family owns that pier," escaped me.

"Whoa! That's woman's your girlfriend's *mother*?" His shock immediately faded into an embarrassed grin. "No offense."

Without asking him to sit with me, I pointed to his journal:

"Let me guess, you're in Costa Rica escaping your job to concentrate on your writing?"

"How the *heck* did you know that?" he laughed again. In my blunt silence he volunteered his name, Jonathan. Other than that, we are the same: with English degrees, we both worked in journalism's margins, Jonathan as a freelance music writer in New Orleans. We saved money at restaurant jobs (he as a cook) to escape to C.R. to write. "Man, that's amazing!" Jonathan reveled in our similarities. I felt factory-made. As he explained other things about himself that I already knew, I gazed down onto the Main Road and wondered how many more of me I will meet here.

Still, finally, "Need a beer?" I offered.

"No way," he said. "Fuck this place. I only use their Book Exchange — or try to. Especially since coming to Costa Rica, I don't like gringos so much any more."

On cue, a shirtless young Tarzan with long, wet, sun-blonde hair and full, feminine lips leapt the patio's steps three at a time. "Jonathan!" the Tico beamed. They hugged. Jonathan introduced him as Orlando – "Tiburon's welcoming committee, ha ha" — then waved goodbye with his copy of *Almost.*

Alone with me (and a dozen chatty white tourists), Orlando placed a strong hand on my shoulder: "Peter?"

"Patrick."

"Pura vida, Patrick..." he trailed off, eyes on a middle-aged man at the next table, the only other Tico up here. I assumed he was Tico; he looked like an old-style organ-grinding Italian, with dirty painter's cap shading a fat moustache and nose. "Dass my friend Jordano," Orlando explained. Jordano whispered with a small but tough-looking old gringo undercut by a bad orange toupee, whom I recognized from *Cabinas Del Mar.* Theirs were heated, perhaps shady dealings. So Orlando sat with me to wait and watch tourists on the Main Road below squeeze their gear between trucks, and packs of half-naked teen Ticas pushing baby carriages over gravel. "You want I could point out who is a hooker for you," Orlando laughed, but just to buddy up, not because he was joking. I laughed along. "They *all* putas, mae! All of Tiburon girls," he continued, not as funny. "S'why I only have gringa girlfriend. Foke all of them while you are here, many as you can, but don't *never* pay more than fy-thousand for a hooker." Before I could correct Orlando's thinking, "*Her* is one!"

He pointed across the road to a Tica older than Alana, showing more soft brown skin than neon green clothes. "Her is definitely one I know." Her black-burning eyes met Orlando's. They waved to each other. Because she's Orlando's sister.

"*All* are putas," he repeated.

Jordano finally dragged his chair over to us and dove into a manic Spanish conversation with Orlando, but soon swerved to engage me: in rushed English like he might sprint away, he asked how long I've been in Tiburon, how long I'm staying, and why I came. All my answers felt like clues that would lead him to shout, 'Oh! You're Alana's boyfriend!' But he allowed my repetition of the same half-lie: "I came here to write."

When I offhandedly told him I wished I'd brought my laptop, Jordano closed in and whispered, "When a you need laptop by? I get for you, no problem."

"No, no, no" I laughed him off, but he seemed like the guy. "*Pero neccesito mota?*"

"Sure, sure my friend!" he nodded, smiled. "And hey, you don't a have to speak a Spanish with me, mae! We're *friends!*"

"But I want to learn…"

Jordano shrugged. Orlando leaned out and cast his shadow over a passing large white woman. "Hola chica, pura vida…" he mouthed, with that mouth. Orlando is a traditional hunk; manager Tony aspires to Orlando-ness. But breathless beneath her backpack, the woman reddened deeper, pushed sunglasses up her sweaty face and rushed along. "*Chica!*" he shouted at her wide back fading down the Main Road, "You not wanna talk to me?"

My safety concerns dulled by beers, before every eye in the village I handed Jordano the extra 5,000 colones Jacques had suggested I carry at all times to pay off the inevitable crooked cops. Jordano fled, casually, down the stairs, "into the mountains to see my friend," he said. "Meet you here, 15 minutes!"

Two slow hot hours have since melted away. In that time, Orlando returned once to invite me to the beach with him, his pretty gringa girlfriend Jennifer, and her two friends Jennifer and Jennifer. Instead I stayed here waiting, writing, drinking – all the while watching a short, very drunk Tico down there, hose in hand, watering the Main Road so it won't dry up and float off into the atmosphere. His eyelids hang half-closed over what look like a secondary, wet pink pair of vertical lids closing like elevator doors. A big, perfect round dent in his temple is exactly the size and shape a hammer would make. The weight of the hose might pull him over onto his scabby face. He looks to have been buried alive, and clawed his way out.

And still he cares if the road floats away.

My hungry eyes raised from the gringo menu at the sound of Jonathan's voice: "You been here this whole time?" Rather than criticize, Jonathan suggested we eat at a Tico-owned place. By then, freedom was worth losing the 5,000. More than I disliked Jordano, I hated that gringo hole for eating my day — I still haven't even seen the Gulf.

"Pura vida, mae!" Jonathan smoothly replied to the *collectivo* drivers' solicitations. When asked to translate, Jonathan explained, "'Pura vida' is an all purpose salutation like 'aloha.' 'Mae' is just 'dude.' 'Pura vida' also has deep meaning though. Like, Ticos aren't lazy but, they don't sell their whole lives to their jobs like people in the States. They only do what they need to, to live. Pure life. They seem to spend most of their time with their families. They have good priorities."

Finally we approached the Other Road, and Jonathan's "favorite Tico-owned restaurant," Rosie's service window. Rosie and Jonathan kissed and cooed familiar, speaking Spanish like pros. When I admitted to them that I'm better at speaking Spanish than hearing and understanding it, Jonathan claimed he'd never met anyone with my linguistic inversion. Rosie laughed, "The *most* people understand *before* they speak. You are the *wrong way!*"

I spoke Spanish again only to order beans, rice, fish, homemade cornbread and a cold, blended fruit drink — Rosie doesn't sell beer because, "*She'sveryreligious*," Jonathan rushed so she wouldn't understand. Which surprised me since he seems ultra polite. Almost too *nice*. For one, he'd driven his van all the way from New Orleans through much rougher parts of Central America, simply to drop off a friend who'd procured a chef job at "one of the gross gringo sport-fishing lodges outside of Tiburon." Jonathan doesn't rent from Rosie only because, in Costa Rica, it's legal to camp up to 50 feet past any high-tide line, so he sleeps in his van on the beach — whereas, I've been kicked off FLA beaches in the middle of beautiful sunsets…

Throughout Jonathan and Rosie's alienating Spanish

conversations I did things like take note that Rosie's address on postal letters reads: *Puerto Tiburon, Costa Rica, Junto al Banco*. I leaned out to peer down her white tile hallway, now lit for nighttime. In a room at the end, a small TV illuminated a gory crucifix hung above two brown toddlers hugging pillows on a couch. Beside it a tiny glass office housed a dozen room keys on a pegboard, and an old, blue-glowing *computer!* But before I could ask Rosie's permission to use the PC, I heard her get slightly angry with Jonathan, tapping hard his copy of *Almost*: "Meal-tone Chap-man take money for *collectivo!* And for kayak!" she said to me in English. "He take money and he is not Tico! He is *bad* man. Bad."

And though I hadn't planned on partaking in anything touristy, I couldn't help contemplating kayaking with a semi-famous author…

Jonathan then quietly invited me to the gringo-owned internet café. Despite having no one to write to, I tagged along, wanting at least another glimpse of that thin slice of Gulf water reflecting silver moonlight like a giant blade stabbing between the trees. But as we approached the soccer field it seemed El Gulfo Tiburon had disappeared? I squinted into the night: no Gulf?

Then finally, slowly, the silver sliver came into view, bit-by-bit as if from behind some eclipse. Freed moonlight illuminated the trees, the goalpost, and the cause of the eclipse: at a glacial pace toward the village, moved the unmistakable size-and-shape of Alana's mother.

Ilka.

No dream.

She moved with a grace I hadn't noticed as she'd wedged herself onto the plane. I heard rocks crushing to dust beneath her, though she seemed to float toward the village, toward me.

"On second thought," I tripped backwards towards Rosie's. "I've given gringos enough money for one day."

"Um, O.K.," Jonathan laughed. "Swing by Nos Barra later!"

2.6 A Semi-Famous Author

My Dear sweeeeet Alnaa, I'm so drunk with love.

EVERYONE's SOOO goddamnd much NICER here! Excpet your "red-haired writer" friend you suggested I meet. He nees to wear sunscreen more than anyone I have ever known but his personality is REFRESHINGLY raw. Negative but hilarious. I met him tonight at Nos Barra. HOW could you forget such an interesting, weirdo's name: Milton Chapman. He told ME "John" though, to hide his identitiy I think — he's not just a "writer" but an AAUTHOR you know (who maybe thinks he's more semi-famous than he is.

Other than his disgusting burns and blisters though he's zackly how I like my redheads: like some strange, rare creature, less like me than Raphaelk — who I haven't seen yet but I promise to seek out tomorrow… Sorry I'm at Del Mar again tonight drunk as hell typing on the computer I'm renting trhe rights to for n extra dollar a day. Above the frog-generated sub-bass and the jungle's tickticktick like arrhythmic hi-hats, I hear Rosie's kids giggling on the other side of this office wall. Rosie just barked at them to stop — sounds like the whole family sleeps in one room. Now they're all giggling together… How can I REALLY apologize for being here at Del Mar?

But Milton: Milton is the blessed antithesis of every other gringo I've met here. Definitely not chatty. At first, he barely gave me half-a-word per minute — until II got him high for the first time in his LIFE! and he went on a hilarious storytelling BINGE. He related the story of how you two met, how Orlando's younger cousin Rolando was taunting Milton on the Main Road, walking alongside him, chewing the inside of his mouth in imitation of Milton aand asking "Are you COOL, mae? You COOL, DUDE?" The he said you stepped up, flipped Rolando's hat backwards and kissed the little brat on the mouth. "Kid bout pissed his shorts!" Milton guffawed. "Yr girl's the shit, dude." The whole night he never spoke you name, reffering to you always in his most distinguished Florida drawl as, "Yr girl." I liked that.

After a while though Milton grew too loud, aggressive, overwhelming. "Playful antagonism" Milton dismissed it as but he was cursing merceleslly and Ticos were frowning. It was my fault for getting him high. He started really freaking out, something about his mother and gambling. He said Mama WAS deep into milder forms of gambling: BINGO, lottery cards, slots. He was kneeling on his barstool all worked up telling me how the shape of the bar reminded him of this four-sided MOUSE ROULETTE table Mama USED TO play at the FLA Fair (I am guessing she died recently?). In the middle insread of Tweety the bartendress there would be a big spinning wheel with numbered holes and gamblers would bet on a number before a carny removed a small wooden box from his overalls, slid it open and dumped a live mouse into the wirlwind of numbered holes. Milton perfectly described the little pink poor thing flailing and in fewer words than I just wasted, he conveyed the feeling that HE HIMSELF was the mouse whose pick of hole determined whether Mama won or lost. I NEED to read his book!

Fro now though, I will climb back upstairs to sleep before sweet Mimo finds me passed out on this keyboard, their office thick with my toxic breath.

Though I barely CARE where I sleep, without you.

Lovepatrick

* * *

I woke to a single-engine plane barreling down at me from the white popcorn sky but my cement blood wouldn't circulate to move me out of harm's way. I laid watching the propellers through slits, enjoying the breeze while waiting to be chewed up... But not even my ceiling fan's extraordinary wingspan could keep the morning sun from blaring through these electric pink curtains and baking me out of bed, into the bathroom to vomit. A simple joint would quell my pain, but it would also mean walking out under a sun I trust even less now after meeting Milton.

Last night, *El Gulfo Tiburon* was a vast black-and-silver ghost: an epic black velvet curtain surrounding just one glowing car headlight rigged atop a pole, out on the tiny pier. Night smothered all signs of Ilka's big pier in the distance. From outside, Nos Barra provided but little light, camouflaged by small trees. I stood outside the bar, peaking in through its cage bars, watching middle-aged Ticos in baseball hats drink beer beside handsome local teens playing darts versus shirtless gringo jocks. Middle-aged sport-fisherman propped expensive sunglasses on gray-or-bald heads to better leer at underage Ticas across Nos Barra's wooden, mouse-roulette mote. I didn't see Jonathan in there, but recognized the pretty Teacher from the village school, looking a bit haggard in black stretch-pants and a tube-top the same hot pink as my cabina's curtains. On a school night. Far be it from me to tell her to go home to sleep off the deep darkness around her eyes.

I was about to leave when I recognized, inside, hair curly as the Teacher's except *safety orange! Alana's writer friend!* Whose long catfish mouth tied all the ends together for me: Milton Chapman, Semi-Famous Author.

Three skinny bar cats scattered from me in the doorway. I followed one to the stool beside Chapman, picked her up, took her seat and transplanted her to my lap where she squirmed and clawed, trying to wriggle over to him. I held her firm. The Teacher occupied Chapman's other side, her yellow eyes watching his pink eyes observe some Tica schoolgirls. *Almost's* black-and-white author's photo didn't do his hair justice; it's as flouncy as Alana's, but not long enough to protect his badly burnt neck and ears. I swelled with empathy, studying a profile of lips like chewed purple gum, cheek pink like a Victorian maiden's, and one freckled arm, singed hairless. He sensed my gaze — not the Teacher's, or the cats begging up from below as if Chapman had, or was, food — and he faced me. His large, pink face hosts freckles in tight congregations around far apart sad gray eyes; an oddly handsome specimen, if not for a deep maroon cut running up his bottom lip, into his mouth. I winced at the gash shining wet under Nos Barra's tracklights.

"Fucking *what,* dude?" he demanded of me.

"What happened?"

His big, damaged face turned away.

"Your lip I mean. What happened?"

"Sun." As I waited for more, my tabby broke free and maneuvered onto Milton. She rammed her snoring muzzle into him until he slapped her down.

"Sun, huh?" I persisted. "Watch out. My Dad got cancer on his lips. And I had a pretty tenacious one on my temple. We should *always* wear sunscreen. Especially here. Especially *us.*"

"Us?" His pink forehead creased white.

"Yeah. *Us.* We have to be extra careful."

"White folks?"

"Redheads!"

He eyed my hair skeptically.

"Well, not as red as yours," I admitted. "It used to be. But I guess as a child I wished too hard. Now the only proof I have that I'm a redhead are..." the furry orange knobs of my wrists, which I displayed.

"That ain't yr head, bro." Milton's longest sentence so far — his was either the voice of slow-and-simple wisdom, or the stupidest suburbs of FLA.

But to me he seemed more sad than rude. So I kept on: "You're from Florida, right?"

He discharged an equine sigh. His pink eyelids closed like

tired clams.

And then I said the secret password: Alana.

"Oh no *shit*." He turned his whole body to me. "At's yr girl? At's *you*? Damn dude. Well shit."

I felt the smaller of us though we're the same medium size discounting his fluffy hair. Feeling the need to even us out, I added, "Alana couldn't remember your name. What is it?"

"Really?" His cracked lips flatlined, greenish eyebrows lilted. "Well, Ticos don't give a shit about my name," he said, words coming slowly as if he were reading them while typing. "At's one reason I'm here; Ticos don't care who I am."

"Well, I'm Patrick."

His burnt hand extended, "I'm…John, man."

I thought to call him out on this lie. Instead we shook on it.

He called the bartender Tweety — a big sensual, sly smiling girl, eyes pulled back tight by a tiny ponytail – her thin tank-top showed a cartoon Tweety Bird on her full bra. Still, she looked too young for bars. "*Dos guaros,* Tweety, *por fah-vor*," Milton ordered.

When Tweety had poured us two clear shots of "guaro" Costa Rican Cactus tequila, I toasted over the jungle's loud bug orchestra, "To Tiburon!"

"Where there ain't shit to do but burn," Milton added.

"Hey. No." I set my full shot down. "That's not funny. You *need* to wear sunscreen…John."

He barely laughed and took a tiny sip. *What kind of author sips?* Despite his gruffness he's clearly not really the Norman Mailer type in this one regard; he winced like the alcohol stung his cut. I didn't believe the sun had done that, split his mouth like a grilled hotdog. As the night wore on, a punch in the face seemed more likely. He minced another sip and his eyes filled with pink watercolor tears.

I downed mine purposefully. Old Ticos across the bar saluted me and covered their mouths, capping imaginary vomits. I patted my fast-beating heart, and felt in my pocket the small joint I'd rolled from the mulchy brown *mota* Jordano eventually delivered to my cabina: 5,000 colones ($15) for a small, hard tinfoil nugget that grew and grew as I broke it up into almost a half ounce of dirt weed. "Um, John. Come smoke?" I stood.

"Smoke?" asked Milton, master of the one-word sentence. "Grass?"

"Yeah," I laughed. His stale colloquialism dated him at about eight years older than me.

"Nah."

"It's good for your soul," I quoted Alana.

"Nah. Too much booze makes me yappy and I assume grass'd do the same," he claimed, though he'd obviously drunk much and wasn't yet loose. I yearned to get him loose.

"You've never smoked?" I asked.

"Hardly never drink neither."

"Why tonight then?"

Silence but for the singing jungle. "C'mon outside." I leaned over the bar for matches.

"Get away god*damnit!*" Milton shouted — his bleary eyes aimed down at the cats still fetishizing his flip-flops. *What kind of author doesn't like cats?* I wondered.

The Teacher watched the felines and me trail Milton out of the cage.

The town drunk with the dented skull, whom I'd seen watering the road, fished with a friend in miniature out on the small pier. "He looks like he was hit in the head with a hammer," I grunted, holding in smoke. Within the intense jungle noise, over what sounded like a monkey war, you could hear your cells dying and replicating out there, and clearly discern the town drunk's bait hit the water 100 yards in the distance.

"Good guess," Milton mumbled. "He was." I pushed the roach at him. "Nah." I reeled it in...then immediately pushed it back. After one more "nah," Milton amateurishly pinched it. His inhale displayed strong lungs that obviously don't smoke and could probably really *yell*. He sucked too hard and coughed a loud storm across the water. The startled men on the tiny pier pulled in their hand-lines.

I took it back and puffed. "What did he do to get hit with a hammer?"

Milton sniffled, shaking it off. The fishermen stared our way, as if they too waited for more of Milton's words. But nothing. When I sadistically volleyed the grass back, Milton wiped his eyes on his white T-shirt, tucked his curls behind his ear and sucked, gently now. His moonlit eyes were now placid. His bloody swollen lip began to droop. Finally the far away fishermen sat, and lowered their lines back down.

I tried again: "So who hit the dude with a hammer?"

"S'wife."

"Why is that?"

Milton took one more hit and the door finally flew open: "Cause he's a fuckin drunk is why." He laughed and chewed the inside of his mouth, his foot tapping as he explained, "Dumbass dude gets wasted out on that pier every fuckin night which, I love the ocean m'self, but when the dude's fuckin *family* wants to see him ever, they gotta go out there while he's gettin shitfaced! So anyway, one night they're *all* crowded out there, spending some high-quality *family time* together, half of em drunk as shit, and that stupid bastard goes an knocks their fuckin *baby* in the water, if you can believe that!"

I could not believe it — the *difference* in Milton! Much more what I expected from an author, and a friend of Alana. "In the time it took him to set his beer can down and kick his shoes off while his wife's beating her fists on his back," Milton continued, "long comes this *huge* fuckin shark and *WHAM!* shark snatches little *bambino* up in one fuckin *gulp!*" He laughed nastily, snuck a tiny last puff then, "Here y'go man. I'm straight."

"Whoa."

"I know dude!" Milton growl-laughed again. "At's such a *killer* story I almost wish it'd happened to *me!*" That remark made me decide to bring my tape recorder next time I come to Nos Barra. Milton cackled on, "Now he's gotta keep fishin till he catches the fuckin thing! Till then his wife's in San Jose — she said goodbye to him with the hammer. Ha, ha! Ol' *Hammer*head! There's been talk a kickin ol Hammerhead outta Tiburon cause the ugly sonuvabitch scares the tourists with how fuckin drunk he gets *now!* You go out on the pier nowadays, dude's *passed out*, pole tween his legs, weird fuckin eyelids all crisscrossed."

"That's horrible," I smiled. Until it sunk in: "So, there are a lot of sharks here?"

He squinted at me then scoffed in my blank face, "Man! I can't speak Spanish for shit and even I know *tiburon* means *shark*. Damn, bro." I love sharks, as I do all pure-intentioned animals, but not in a way that would allow me to swim freely in *Shark Gulf*.

As I worried over this, a different Milton sighed, "Wow, Alana. Yr a lucky summbitch. Where you stayin till she gets back?"

"I'm supposed to stay at her place," I admitted, "but I haven't been over there yet. It's up by that big pier?"

"Yeah they have a bigass compound behind my place. Big piece a land, kinda sunk down."

"I am supposed to go stay in…she has like a separate house or something?"

"Yeah where she sleeps. You want, I can lead you right to her door."

Before I could know how to feel about that offer, the Teacher stepped out of the cage, smiling a missing tooth at both of us. Her curly hair isn't as long, but it's otherwise eerie how much she looks like a late-30s Alana. "Oh shit, Patrick, dude," Milton said, staring at her but leaning so far into me I feared his lip might stain my shirt. "You kin help me out?" he whispered. "Kin I borrow 5,000 colones, bro?" Milton looked seasick by now, his flushed cheeks and forehead overripe. I shouldn't have pushed pot on him after he'd drank so much. I forced him into a state where he probably stupidly went and bought his own pot or some other crazy thing with the 5,000 I loaned him… "Damn dude, I owe you!" He loped an arm over my shoulders, and also the Teacher's. They obviously know each other though I didn't see them speak once in the bar. "Sorry fy was bein fucked up before," Milton laughed. "I was just tryna scare ya. If *at's* yr girl, I'm sure you don't mind a little *playful antagonism*. Man, enjoy Tiburon," he said, releasing me but not the Teacher. He seemed a completely different newly happy albeit blurry person now. "You'll be fine. Costa Rica's easy. Whole damn country's set up so the most ignorant white motherfucker can land cushy and never have a problem. N'as fer sharks," he drooled, "ain't been a shark in that smelly-ass Gulf since that slaughterhouse down the shoreline stopped throwin cow heads and shit into the water — cept this one shark recently, and it's prolly long gone by now. Hey!" He slapped me hard in the chest. "Tell you what! Meet me on the Gulf tomorrow afternoon and I'll take you on one a my famous *sunset kayak tours,* show you some *amazin* shit! I usually charge 50 bucks but since *at's* yr girl I'll take you for *free!*"

"Ill take you up on that!" I said too loudly, and felt the heat of Milton's skin through his shirt when I slapped his back. He howled into the jungle. I cried out in response, "Oh Jesus Milton I'm so sorry! You *have* to wear sunscreen from now on *please!*"

He breathed like he'd been kneed in the testicles, as the

Teacher lugged his burnt body down the seawall, into the night – in such pain he hadn't heard me use his real name.

2.7 AN EXTREME GULF

A lana love,

I'm on The Gulf, baby! Finally. Supposed to meet Milton down here later. Till then though, I sit alone on the broken stone steps leading down into the water from this tiny pier Rosie calls EL MUELLITO. In FLA they'd call it 'dry, splitting boards across a pile of rocks.' So much more…HUMBLE than your family's pier, which I see gleaming white down the beach. I'm working up to it… But for now my ankles and ass remain submerged in the reasonably blue water of "Shark Gulf" — you should have translated that for me earlier! I still woulda come!

Sad you're not here to see my leg-hairs wave underwater like orange anemone, inspected from every angle by hundreds of silver-dollar fish gleaming and popping all around me. More fish than water now, probably attracting that shark but WOAH! A HUGE BLACK-AND-WHITE-SPOTTED STINGRAY just swooped in and gracefully scared off every other living thing on her way past my legs! Behind me shrieking macaws just exploded from the jungle, chased away by that same slobbery little plane I flew in on.

Now all's silent again. The ray's circled back, closer now, but I still haven't pulled my legs out. Because despite sharks, I feel strong and unafraid lately, Alana. And I can't thank you enough, for wrenching me free of FLA, and launching me into THIS!

>   love,
>   Patrick

* * *

I'd been wondering where Hammerhead and his partner were, and now here came their skinny boat, coughing between sandbars toward the pier. I climbed up out of the water. Down the pier and back on land, I watched them drag their boat up the stone steps and onto the wood. Scanning the watery horizon populated with dirty, scrappy little boats, I wondered why he didn't just tie to the seawall, or anchor off the beach with the rest, and I fantasized that their mysterious dry-docking had something to do with the shark they're after. The haggard men flipped the vessel over and sat atop its white belly, staring frustrated, sipping beer, affording me a perfect view of that unnerving dent in his skull. Hammerhead looked mauled, physically and spiritually, radiating an aura of defeat that forced my eyes away, down, to the water, where I noticed…

…a glint, down there between the big gray rocks, a white spark underwater like a far away mirror alerting airplanes to poor souls stranded below. First I thought money, maybe. *Or a ring? A wedding ring I could some day give to Alana!* Still eyeing the men, I scaled the rocks and scooped up what were actually *two baby octopi!* Each the size and gleam of a quarter. I held them up, my flat palm the stage upon which they slimed over each other like liquid glass. So amazing. Worried that the sun stung their clear skin, boiled their translucent blood, I searched for a container.

Tiburon suffers more than enough litter, but the novelty of Spanish logos on soft drinks and snack packaging made the trash around the pier look more like *decoration*. I smiled as wide as the yellow cartoon dinosaur printed on the ice-cream cup I filled with saltwater, and then octopi.

Rounding the seawall past shacks bearing hand-scrawled signs — *Hay Pescado! Bien Fria!* — I spotted a pelican in the channel off the pier. She bobbed alone on the water, looking serene and beautiful to me, despite my having grown up where pelicans were as abundant and respected as rats in NYC. I studied the pelican's greedy gray waddle until suddenly but silently a broad, gray shape like a small truck's bumper surfaced, threw brief shade over the bird, and calmly snuck her under, with no warning music, and ripples subtle enough to impress high-dive judges. More like the big shark had popped up for a breath of dry air and accidentally inhaled the pelican like second-hand smoke — so quietly, the men on the pier never turned. Holy fuck.

Back along the soccer field, I forgot sharks and kept such a hard eye out for Ilka that a tentacle pricked my finger before I noticed one octopus had crawled out onto the cup's lip. I poked her back down. Not until I found myself hiding the cup from Rosie, rushing past her up to my room, did I start to feel guilty. But I also felt nice and cool, under my room's giant madly whirling ceiling fan. I balanced their cup on the edge of the sink, removed my shirt, laid down and...

Fell asleep. Too much naptime here. The dragging high of Jordano's brown dirt weed synchs me with Tiburon's creeping pace, helps me *feel the texture* of time barely passing in this place, though it's also given me more excuses to nap, plus the difficult cough that finally jerked me awake from that last one. Must find more to do. *Cough, cough.* Must find Jacques and get my fishing pole back. *Cough, cough.* Can't believe I won't have it tonight when I kayak with Milton.

Fifteen long minutes hacking under a steaming shower would clear my resin congestion, I thought, stepping in. But the *agua caliente* Rosie initially bragged on is a mere plastic filter attached to the showerhead, from which small purple lightning shot when I flipped the *caliente* switch to ON. I hopped out and at that moment noticed that the octopus cup was empty. I dropped down and scoured *el bano*. Under the moldy sink, between the festering pipes, in close on my own dried vomit flecks and pubic hairs. I hoped they didn't creep down the drain, which Jonathan told me leads directly onto the hot Main Road.

The medicine cabinet too was empty. But then shutting its mirror I found one, frozen in an escape pose, a dried snot streak up the mirror. Translucent blood on my hands. I continued hunting for her partner, chasing my tail around a small room that seemed to shrink with my every painful cough, and hotter and stinkier even as the sun faded outside my pink curtains. Finally I needed out.

Then stepping from my cabina mid-hack, I was met with honey. Honey in a long silver spoon held by long brown fingers leading up a thin brown arm attached to a beautiful young girl: Rosie's teenage daughter, standing so close I noticed she was taller than me. A headband accessorizing her blue school uniform pulled her black hair back tight and shiny as a killer whale. She touched the spoon to my lips, looked down into my eyes and commanded something I thought was "Open up!" So I opened. Mimo lay the cold spoon on my tongue and fed the honey into me. I closed my eyes and pictured hummingbirds drinking sugarwater as I swallowed.

When I came to, Mimo smiled, turned and unlocked my neighbor's door. And in the two seconds before slamming it shut, we saw a panicked, white hand snatch an orange toupee from the nightstand. The Teacher pinned bed sheets across her chest and I thought what every man thinks upon seeing any couple other than his own: *She could do so much better...*

Not embarrassed just exasperated, Mimo pushed fugitive black hairs back into their headband, as I've seen her mother do while cooking. She then pointed to my door and sighed something about cleaning my room. "*No neccessito,*" I lied, simply not wanting her near my dirt or vomit, not wanting her sweeping my pot seeds off the tile, or scraping away a dried octopus' corpse. I tried telling her I would clean up my own mess. Finally she gave up and went away before I could thank her for soothing my cough.

Had this been a letter to Alana, it would have read only: Get home quick baby, before I kill everything.

* * *

Today the Gulf did disappear. Not figuratively, behind Ilka; the whole thing left for sickly low tide. The pier's naked rotting front legs rose from mudflats that even *smelled* the same as FLA's: a thick vaginal mist, undeniably alive, if not inviting. The gray flats drained all color from the formerly powder-blue sky and the now-stale chocolate mountains beyond the once silver water. In the few hours since my first visit, paradise had transformed — the result, I fear, of my sins against nature.

Hammerhead continued wading ankle-deep off the pier though, tossing his hand-line into the channel. He was in the right spot. I walked in the opposite direction along the crescent shoreline past closed Nos Barra and a whale-sized, rickety blue boat stranded in the mud. Smaller boats of all shapes and low-budget personalities littered the dried-up Gulf, all unceremoniously dry-docked until the tide returns. *They'd never let that happen in FLA*, I knew, entering a thick of mangroves. Stepping lightly down a muddy hallway, across a carpet of short purple knees shaded by a thick ceiling of tangled trees, I recognized their wet clicking sound before coming upon the vast swarm of fiddler crabs. In perfect British Army unison, hundreds of pink backs fled into holes. Other mysterious holes on the lunar mudscape puked up viscous gray stew, or hosted fleshy periscopes. Between the holes were stamped the prints of some huge quadruped. *A panther?* I worried, lighting up. *Makes sense since FLA has panthers too...* Inhale. *Or do they still?* Exhale. I followed the prints across softer mud to a half-buried car engine, corroded orange, plagued with oysters and barnacles. *Beautiful...* Inhale. *Readymade...* Exhale.

Above the engine, a sort of window cut from the trees framed the mountains, and Ilka's glorious far-away pier, pitiful Hammerhead fishing, and a dog running free across the stinky flats — the exact white dog I killed in Ft. Heathen. Except this wild Costa Rican dog ran free and *wide* open, too fast for footprints or ownership. Coming around the big muddy bend she launched herself at a team of gray gulls. Having cleared the flats, she proceeded to gallop straight at my honey-coated cough...

I didn't look down into her eyes or her growling wet gums against my calf. She sounded like she hated my guts (for reasons I felt I understood). After some tense minutes, she lost interest and trotted off to pee on the rusty engine. My stomach relaxed when she lifted her leg — er, *his* leg...

He finally perched out back of Nos Barra so I continued deeper into the low-tide mangroves, through more grassy puddles, around a corner where a crow-sized Jesus Christ lizard sprinted across a boating channel. Florida doesn't have those! Nor loud macaws like those above, arguing with silent iguanas. But halfway through my joint, the exposed mangrove roots began looking like where a croc would stash a body, letting it rot for supper. Aggressive mud sucked off my gym shoes. Oysters stabbed my ankles. *I'm too far from the village,* I realized, just as I noticed, up ahead amid the continuous gray: red hair!

"John!" I remembered the correct lie.

Sitting flanked by green mop buckets, seeing no escape, Milton scowled at his muddy, pink knees. I approached, shoes in hand. His split lip had been washed bloodless, likely the result of a good saltwater swim, but the rest of him had suffered even more sun. Amid the branches of his weeping-willow hair, two purple blisters gleamed congruent atop his ears like orioles' shoulder markings. "I don't member invitin you to my spot."

"Your spot?"

Silence. He unsheathed a pair of garden spades, stabbed them into the wet ground between his legs and began to dig.

Inhale. "What's in the buckets?" I grunted, stepping closer to peek. *Exhale.*

"Hey no!" he demanded. Before Milton could jerk the buckets away causing a clatter like dishware on a moving truck, I glimpsed a dozen fist-sized mollusks engaged in a writhing, snotty orgy. The other bucket jailed just one mollusk big as a Christmas ham.

"Holy shit!" I gasped, "What are those?"

"*Shhhhh*ut the fuck up!" He hissed, guilty eyes panning. "Thoser King's Crowns, dumbass. Big one's a Lightnin Whelk." The huge, sweaty black snail hung limp from her shell.

"You dug these up?"

"Na. You only gotta dig for Angel Wings." Veins sizzled across his scorched forehead as he tossed scoop-after-scoop of mud at his shoes. "It's a bitch. But I git good money for Angel Wings."

"And what, people make stew with them or?"

"Hail naw," he spoke into his deepening hole. "Thoser big-ass *Pink* Conchs folks eat. I sell the shells."

"By the sea shore?"

No reply.

"To tourists in the village?"

"You ever see me in the fuckin village, bro?" Buried to his shoulders, working intently, Milton didn't notice a small bat tumble from the dusky sky toward his nest of hair, but abort at the last second. "I sell em to shell shops back in Flor'da," he chuckled, digging and digging. "Same shit here as there." *Dig, dig, dig.* "But a perfect pair a Angel Wings ain't no easy fuckin..." He suddenly sat up straight, tossed his spades and excitedly sifted through mud until he found a clam, like pure white parakeet wings carved from rock candy. Frilly wings feebly wrapped around a...foot-long jellyfish sausage? A translucent dildo? Milton held the creature up.

"What's that in it's uh...mouth?" I asked.

"Its fuckin *body*, man." The vulnerable white meat pulsed, afraid; Mother Nature had given her the wrong glass slipper. *So many helpless creatures...* "They hide way-the-hell down in the mud cause they're so delicate," Milton mused, and I thought of Raphael, and wished I were with him instead. "Ah *fuck!*" Milton crowed. "I cracked these. Fuckin worthless now." He lobbed the Angel Wings onto the mud *crack* like an egg on linoleum.

Before I could cry, beyond Milton I noticed another seashell. I passed him the joint.

"No, no, no," he scolded. "I start yappin like a dumbass."

I didn't tell him the dumbass had been a lot cooler, just plied, "Hold it for a second. So it doesn't get wet."

Milton obliged and before I knew why, I'd stepped over onto hard sand to collect the shell. Beneath a clean coat of scum shined a lacquered deep orange, I noticed, as the little orange monster inside whipped out and stung me. I squealed. The shell thudded wet sand.

"Fightin Conch," Milton snorted, holding in smoke.

"Am I poisoned now?"

He coughed, wiped his eyes, smoked again.

"What the hell did it sting me with? John?" I sucked on the papercut, frustrated having to *draw* lifesaving information from him.

"Operculum," he answered, standing and picking the Fighting Conch up, fingers far enough from the orange tongue's lashing little hard brown operculum. "Its foot," he said, kissing the roach with white-scabbed lips again before finally blasting off: "They use the operculum to walk and to close themselves up inside there safe and — least they *think* they're safe! *Ha ha!* Most shells have operculums, but Fightin Conch got sharp ones to t'crack open other shells an killem and eatem. Any serious shell collector keeps the operculum. I got a whole wall um back at Mama's place. Mostly from bigger shells though, Horse Conchs an shit." *Exhale.*

Atop the Fighting Conch's long thin antennae, white eyeballs stared into mine. He tossed her into the bucket with his other shells all calmer now, drowning in dry air. We stood in silence, red eyes scanning the sandy foreground across which, I only now noticed, dozens upon dozens of Fighting Conchs flopped and struggled, fighting an invisible enemy. Milton slid two black trashbags from the waist of his swim shorts, flapped them open and uttered the correct phrase in the wrong context: "Help me."

"If you need me to."

"I don't know bout *need* but..." Deep red parentheses bookended his sad, singed smile. He pushed a trashbag at my nervous chuckle.

Trading joint for trashbag, I questioned nothing except, "Are there always this many out here?"

"Aw hail naw. This some kinda special occasion. Some rare moon shit," he answered, the few puffs he'd taken making an audible difference. "Mama circled it on the tide chart tacked up back at her place..."

"Your mother lives here too?" I dared, knowing she's dead, just hoping he'd tell the story.

Milton silently gathered conchs. He'd collected over a dozen (I continued staring at my first violent little beast, who stared back) before a gray-haired gringo couple rounded the corner. From beneath straw hats the tourists watched us as they too collected conchs, lobbing each into the channel.

"What the fuck?" Milton asked himself. Then loudly, "Hey what the *fuck* y'all!"

The couple hurriedly bent and plucked and bent and plucked like FLA tomato pickers, their shaded faces scowling as they liberated conch after conch. Milton dropped his trashbag: "Hey now! Stop!" He flip-flopped toward them. "Damn y'all! *Stop!*" Meeting them in the middle of the sand flats he demanded, "What the fuck!"

"Don't use that language with me!" creaked the little gray woman. She deadeyed Milton, but either his sun damage or his obvious existential sadness forced her eyes away. "We're saving these poor creatures," she said, "before you *kill* them all for profit!"

"*You're* killing them!" Milton claimed on his tiptoes, casting his shadow over her, reminding me of the racist adage stating that a redhead's shadow touching you means bad luck — *not* for the redhead. "Why you think they're all up here on land like this?" Milton challenged. "Why?"

The man unclipped the sunglass attachment from his bifocals and listened to his wife. "Well if there are *this* many then they're probably mating," she said. "I'm not sure, but I am sure that if—"

"They're not *mating*!" Milton roared. "Look around. You see any *pairs*?" We all surveyed the sand: each lone conch bounced a yard from the next. "Actually, ma'am," Milton condescended in a much smarter sounding voice than his own. "The water's currently lacking in oxygen as an effect of Red Tide. They crawled up on land for oxygen. When you toss em in the water, they drown."

The woman checked her husband's face. He diddled his digital camera. "Well, it's a more natural death than you're giving them!" she attempted.

"Wait a minute!" Milton squinted. "Y'all think we're *shellin*! Oh, no no *no ha ha!* We ain't *shellin.*"

"No?" The woman gulped. "Oh, I..." The husband gripped her shoulders, bracing her for the answer to her next timid question: "What are you doing then?"

"We work for the Puerto Tiburon Environmental Protection Agency," Milton answered. Her hand slapped her open mouth. Milton continued, "We're collecting these to take em to the uh, *other* coast." The woman moaned, mortified at her presumptuousness. "No, no ma'am." Milton touched her arm. "There's no way you coulda known. You ain't know."

"Wait," the husband blustered, "why are you taking them to the Caribbean coast?"

"Cause there ain't...*enough* over there," Milton stumbled, then, "Y'all wanna help?" He handed the couple their own garbage bags and set them to work picking clean the entire flat — the funniest thing I've ever witnessed and the worst most evil...

By sundown the murky flats lay finally inert. I overheard the couple mention their rental truck to Milton, and their willingness to help transport the shells to the "other" coast, where there "aren't enough."

"No, no, no. Y'all've helped plenty," Milton laughed outright, a big stoned guffaw that aroused no suspicion. "I got my own truck. And by the way," he added, "I also give *environmental kayak tours* on the side, if y'all are ever interested." They exchanged information.

"O.K. Well. Thank you," the woman sobbed. "And again, we're so, *so* sorry about the... I'm so embarrassed. I just hope you can... I hope *God* can forgive us."

"He will," Milton smiled, painfully.

When they'd faded around the corner out of earshot Milton howled, "Dude! Now *there's* a story you can write! That was fuckin *awesome!*" Around us, full garbage bags popped and jerked as if possessed. Milton plunked down to open bags and count his loot like a post-Halloween youngster. "You wanna come help me clean these?" he offered, ignoring the tiny monsters' violent swipes, as well as the big white dog that from nowhere charged him.

"John!" I said when there was still time.

But because his name is not John, he didn't look up in time.

Some big dogs have a *prey drive*, meaning they view all similar-sized animals as prey. Sitting in the mud, Milton was only slightly bigger than the dog, whose mouth opened wide enough to accommodate a human face, or neck or, in the end, Milton's foot. *"Noooooo!"* he screamed. I turned away. *"AHHHHFuck!"*

The dog bolted out of the groves and I turned back and dove upon Milton's injuries — or lack thereof. He elbowed me off and stood. "Fuck!" He spiked his spades into the mud. "Bastard stole my fuckin *flip*-flop!"

He limped between the beach and his truck, loading all his buckets and lively bags, then left without goodbye.

Maybe we'll kayak tomorrow.

2.8 FLOUNDERING

My angel sans wings,

Today I revisited the Gringo Restaurant, but only to acquire your friend Milton's novel, *Almost*. They usually stock it there but the owner told me they were out: "He's sold more copies in this crappy little village than in all the United States," the guy claimed. His exact words. I am surprised you didn't grow up to hate white people...

When you return, let's start a cooler Tiburon bookstore! You could talk Milton into giving a reading there. Or we could open an internet café for locals; Tiburon's current one is sterile, expensive, and its dreadlocked gringo owner has my fishing pole, he confirmed, though he didn't bring it to work. I only went in there to GOOGLE Milton.

His book's only amazon.com reviewer gave his book five stars, describing it as, "a loving portrayal of a Florida mother leading her impressionable son into ecological evil." Shelling, it's about. I found very positive reviews of it from FLA papers and an excerpt too, a long piece that felt short; autobiography, I assumed, about young Milton spending an entire day chasing and finally catching a giant flounder with his bare hands on a sandbar off Sanibel Island. Flounders are those flat, bottom-dwelling fish with their faces all crammed together on top of their bodies like a Picasso painting. With remarkable economy Milton described every BREATH he took chasing the flounder through the grasses, every corner he backed it into, its every narrow escape as the sun slipped down by inches. Very *Old Man and the Sea*, in that straightforward style favored by so many surly white writers. I can't wait to read the whole novel!

I also found an interview from a Texas webzine where Milton admitted his mother wasn't speaking to him anymore because, though billed as FICTION, *Almost* was a little too true. Milton and his mother hunted seashells on Sanibel Island, Florida, for years when it was the "Live Shelling Capital of the World," and in the interview Milton expressed much guilt over having helped cause the island's current TOTAL BAN on the taking of live shells — though, I saw him shelling just tonight, and while he did look SAD, guilt seemed oceans away…

Wait. Now I'm gossiping. I'll shut up and respect your friendships, however strange they may seem. Besides, what's that weirdo jerk done to deserve any part in OUR story?

I will tear this letter up now, and throw it away.

      * * *

I walked up behind Nos Barra as that old German tourist, the altruistic recorder of jungle sounds, was blocking Milton entry. The German fumbled for the author's pink hand: "It ease a great honor to meet you Mr. Chapman!" He beamed like spotting a certain illusive rainforest beast. Shameless awe, for some reason. Milton sighed down at his new flip-flops.

I stepped around them, up into the bar. Milton's feline fanclub scattered from the doorway — every day here is the same. Except tonight bartendress Tweety winked at me, old Ticos gave me thumbs up and shirtless Orlando (orbited by his teenage cousin Rolando, his beautiful girlfriend Jennifer and her two friends Jennifer and Jennifer) blew me a fat kiss. Never in my life!

Eventually his shoes slapped up behind me and in my pocket I clicked on the tape recorder I'd this time remembered to bring. "So,

John *Chapman*, is it?" I quizzed.

"Sure," Milton sighed, occupying a stool one away from mine. Every Tico's smile dissolved upon his entrance. Orlando and Rolando frowned beside their trio of horrified white girls all wearing sundresses over bathing suits. Jordano feigned indifference. I barely wondered why they all disliked him, just accepted that I was damaging my reputation by offering to buy the Semi-Famous Author a guaro shot, or whatever he might need to quit being a grumpy dick and open up.

"Nah."

"Why would you come here and not drink?"

I followed Milton's pink-eyed stare to a pack of giggly Ticas bouncing on a plastic patio table near the dartboard; certainly pretty, but young to the point of physical underdevelopment. The skinniest of them smiled silver braces at Milton, despite his face's shiny burns, which get worse every time I see him.

I ordered us two Imperials and half-finished mine before continuing our secret interview, "So, how long have you been in Tiburon?"

"Few months," he answered, eyes on the distant pubescent. Queen's "Big Bottom Girls" charged from the old, spider-webbed PA chained up in the corners, blurring my recording. Ticos around the bar nodded to the music, their hearts filling with Mercurial passion like Pizza Dive's kitchen staff — I miss those guys. Even Orlando now frowned at us as Queen ended and "Eye of the Tiger" erupted.

"So how'd you end up here?" I tried to continue. "In Tiburon?"

"Depressin fuckin story."

"Depressing? This place seems perfect for a writer. *So* many characters!" I motioned across to Jordano, who winked back, but aloof. "So much peace and quiet. You should get *tons* of writing done!"

"I don't know who told you I write."

"Um, this girl named Alana," I huffed, irritated that he would try to build more lies. "Alana told me."

"Oh, right." He flushed. Her name does that to many of us. "When's she get back? I *really* fuckin like that girl. She is real."

"Why did you quit writing?"

"I used't, I guess."

"And you stopped?"

Again his eyes closed and I saw the freckles on his lids obscured beneath tiny blisters. He had to have fallen asleep in the sun. Or else he's frying himself on purpose

We stood out back on the lonely seawall, above that big chipped boat stranded on mud shiny and wet as raw liver. The Gulf hasn't come back yet, still. Nor was the ghost of that white dog anywhere around. The screeching, whooshing two-million-piece jungle philharmonic filled in for Milton's absent voice – so when he barely hit the joint then passed it back, I urged, "Keep it."

Unselfconscious of my recorder's tiny red light glowing through my shorts in the night I asked, "So tell me more about your little shelling operation."

"Man. What are you fuckin *interviewin* me?" *Inhale.* "I don't do interviews. And don't you worry bout what *I'm* doin, bro." *Exhale.*

I didn't mentioned to "John," his web interview I'd read today. I let him hog the joint a minute then tried again: "So how much do you get for say, those Angel Wings you worked so hard to get?"

"Four dollars for a perfect pair." He passed it back.

Inhale. "Four dollars?" *Exhale.*

He sat down, legs dangling over. "Shit I only git about 25 cents for King's Crowns," he admitted. "50 for Fightin Conchs. Three or four bucks for that big-ass Lightnin Whelk — ain't much in American money, but it here it'll keep you in…whatever you need I guess."

I felt Alana's frown looming behind us big as the mountain skyline. "All those poor animals though," I said. "Does Alana know you do this? She'd be mad as hell. She loves animals so much, she might never talk to you again…"

His glass eyes looked up at me with worry. "How the hell else I'm suppose to *live* here, man?"

I didn't mention book royalties: "Don't you give eco-tours?"

"Look, dude," he said like I'd tricked him into something, "don't you tell *nobody* bout me shellin here. You hear? I don't even remember inviting you. Don't tell *nobody*. Understand?" He stood back up.

"Why? Is this illegal?" I remembered the loud signs in the Gringo Restaurant advertising *Shelling Excursions!*

"No!" He stood. "I just don't need to be competin with

anybody for *me and Mama's* fuckin *spot.* You understand?"

"Easy."

"Naw man. Not easy. I'm fuckin serious." He lurched toward me. "You understand?"

Face-to-face with his crispy face, I thought to mention sunscreen again, but instead conceded, "*Si. Claro.*"

"What's that shit mean?" he growled. "Speak English: *Do - you -* under*stand* me? Keep your mouth *shut.*"

"Yes, Jesus, chill out."

Despite the possibility of a free kayak tour soon and whatever other interesting worlds Milton could expose me to, I now doubted Alana's judgment. For some reason I did not leave though. A thick silence sat between us after that, until a boat's farting motor broke the night.

Milton and I watched Hammerhead's weighed-down vessel swerve through the channel between sandbars. The men's faces flashed a new manic energy. "There's yr boy," Milton said to me, as their boat disappeared beneath the dock. The Ticos' disembodied voices blasted orders at each other and finally in unison shouted, "Uno! Dos!" And up onto the dock thudded a 10-foot hammerhead shark. A Semi-Famous Author could not have adequately described my feelings. My first instinct was Francis McComber's. Still I chased Milton's loud sandals down the seawall and out onto the pier.

To me, the shark may as well have been a fucking dinosaur, a sasquatch or any other creature I never thought I'd see like this. An orange-handled screwdriver protruded between the beast's far-apart dead gray eyes, still her jaws snapped weakly. Small white mushrooms of flesh bloomed along her sides: bloodless gunshot wounds, at least ten riddled across the most amazing thing I've ever seen. I wished I had my camera instead of my tape recorder.

The men shed victory sweat, tucking their guns into their boat. Unsheathing their machetes. finally noticed us, and froze. Our eyes conversed. Up close, Hammerhead and Milton looked similarly scabby like they'd been dragged across cement. Hammerhead's second set of wet pink eyelids closed vertically beneath his heavy, primary lids. "Do no tell," he spoke slowly into my hidden recorder, grinning alcoholic teeth.

Time unstuck and their machetes lashed into the giant shark. Blood and white specs flew like someone's nightmare — my nightmare, if sleep is ever again possible. They exposed more and more guts to the open air, and over the copper scent of blood and saltwater I smelled beer in the men's laughter. At last they smiled upon the shark's bloated purple stomach. I was not ready for a dead child pulled from the wreckage — an outcome these men hoped to god for, whilst smiling. Their insane glee died when the bulge in the shark's stomach, yanked out and displayed, was just a pelican. The jungle insects' drumroll announced the sound of spirits breaking, and Milton's barely veiled scoff. Hammerhead's partner patted his back, lobbing the slimy bird carcass into the channel.

That wide, once-in-a-lifetime head attached by flapping flanks of meat to a majestic, gray tail, all jerked and flinched between him and me on the pier. I'd have assumed the shark was overage, the meat too tough, but the Ticos filleted the monster and cut out her jaws before each placed a foot on the body and rolled it off the dock. The shark's remaining nerves ordered her to swim; she shimmied a dozen feet into the shallow shadows until only her long sharp tail was barely visible. There she stopped and sank.

The men wrapped the bullet-riddled meat in a copy of *The Tico Times,* followed the packages down into the boat, solemnly started their engine and farted back off into the night. When Tiburon was as silent as it ever gets, Milton began, "I hate pelicans," then proceeded with the succulently detailed account of his childhood volunteering at a wildlife refuge on Sanibel Island, where 12-year-old Milton had been in charge of chopping enough frozen sardines to fill two buckets, which he would drag out to a batting cage housing a long, blue swimming pool for dozens of one-eyed, one-legged, one-winged pelicans: permanent guests of the refuge. "I'd bring the buckets out and they'd all come limpin at me fast like goddamn zombies bout to eat my fuckin brains, man!"

Such a great story, I momentarily forgot the bloody surreality that had just occurred.

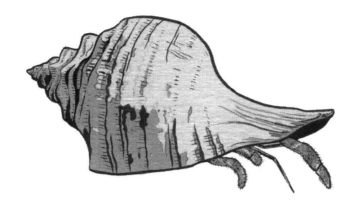

2.9 THE WRECKAGE

Rude sun bakes me out of bed most mornings — the early rise equaling a false sense of accomplishment — yet I've managed 10-and-a-half-hours sleep each night. After three in a row of these sleep-gorged nights, I'm forced to then consume at least one huge portion of blaring insomnia. That's now, coughing instead of humming. After another fruitless 3 a.m. reconnaissance for the missing octopus, I tried stabbing pen-to-paper in honor of Alana, but couldn't wade through my head full of sharks and shells — it's easier to think of them as *shells*, though they're as animal as those poor octopi, or the cats at Nos Barra, or the white dog I killed. As animal as Alana and me, or Milton.

The sun's almost rising. I'll bet that bastard's already down there hunting shells, and anticipating the sun's abuse.

* * *

No. I'm alone out here now on the beach — the closest I've come to Alana's family. I can't see their home, but their extremely nice and totally unpopulated pier shines down the beach to my right. Too early to bother them... The sun's barely awake but I'm already protected by SPF 50 and a T-shirt, which I wear, like a fat kid, even when swimming – not that I'll ever wade in this gulf again. Despite low tide, knee-deep saltwater somehow still laps this sandy stretch between the two piers, and lolling in it just now I gargled some saltwater hoping to help my cough but its bitterness made me wretch. I coughed myself into a sitting position. My hands dug into the sand and accidentally excavated the broken brown crown of a Lightning Whelk, and also, *teeth*. Teeth mounted in a large white jawbone that looked human but. Probably a remnant from the gulf-front slaughterhouse Milton mentioned. Regardless, *El Gulfo Tiburon* basted my white shirt yellowish, and I will never again allow its stagnant, urine-warm water to invade my orifices, sharks or no.

There's also a new stench in the air, deeper and thicker than normal mudflats' stink. The death odor that might precede Lucifer himself. The sun rises behind the mountains, pushing the thin layer of silver water toward — *Milton!*

"Milt-!" I partially shouted at the human head bobbing out in the channel *right* where that pelican had become food. I dropped the jawbone and jogged out onto the flats. "John! Hey! Don't swim there!" A beached boat covered by a blue tarp blocked my sightline. "John! That's right where it happened!" I cried, until I could see him again, still alive, not yet eaten. The mud slowed me like a frustration dream. My struggle scared translucent minnows to the ends of the puddles holding them captive. The death stench swelled and the mud sucked so aggressively I leaned on a boat to remove my shoes, directly beside one of Milton's green buckets, empty but for one leopard-spotted shell.

The smell was unbearable near enough where I could discern Milton's sun-ravaged face. "My *god* what's that smell?!" I asked no one before I lost him again behind another boat — in the shade of which lay like a long, destroyed kayak, the remains of last night's hammerhead. Such a privilege to study up close! Watching fiddler crabs clean their claws in the bloodless bulletholes' saltwater puddles, I momentarily wanted one of these of my own, taxidermied, to look at anytime, to look at with the kids Alana and I will have. *One I caught myself though*, I thought, followed by, *What the fuck is happening to me?* Whatever it was, I couldn't help attributing it to Milton.

I forced myself to continue toward the channel, where he

floated, cheating death. Closer up he looked purple. "You shouldn't swim in this Gulf," I repeated, "and that's right where I saw that shark eat the..."

Milton ducked underwater, inflicting silence. I waited. Waited. Breathed in the stink and waited. He emerged spitting brown water, his sopping orange locks pasted down the purple bridge of his nose. "The thing's dead, dude. Relax yr asshole. Breathe deep. That's the smell a *safety,* bro."

"A shark's not a 'thing.'" I shivered, picturing an attack upon him so clearly it registered as *impatience.*

"That'd be an *awesome* way to go though, wouldn't it?"

"Shark attack?" I tried to laugh. "Well, the newspaper I worked at in Tampa wrote about shark attacks but not ones in other countries." I knew they would write him up regardless, being who he is.

"Tampa?" the bobbing head puzzled. "You from Flor'da? Soam I!"

"You're fucking kidding me. Yeah, Tampa's where Alana is now?"

"Wow! Na she ain't know *where* she was gonna end up once she got there. She musta put down roots in Flor'da at my suggestion! Goddamn! Wow. Wow." Again I pictured him attacked, but now didn't shiver. "Anyway ol Pat, don't you fuckin worry bout me," he flowed so open I suspect he'd bought his own pot. "When I *do* die here, you'll get the scoop, journalist guy."

"If you die of skin cancer they'll just dismiss it as 'Natural Causes'. *The Trib* only expounds on *interesting* deaths."

He ground his jaw as if dying to admit that *his* cancer would also mean the death of a Semi-Famous Author. "Y'ain't never heard a nobody dyin a skin cancer though, have ya?" he baited.

"Uh, my girlfriend's *dad.*"

"Side from him."

"Maybe it's rare," I admitted. "But as you know from shelling, *rarity*'s not always worth much."

He ducked under one last time, swam to the pier's stone steps and climbed up and out, his full violet body like an open wound. "Hey man, grab the green bucket behind ya, will ya?" He cast out *zrrrrrrrr!* His bait landed right where he'd just swam. Retrieving his single shell bucket I studied the dead shark another minute then continued onto the pier, the big bucket knocking my shins. "What kind is this one?" I asked, setting the bucket before Milton.

"Cone Shell," he answered, laying his pole down on the dock. He plucked the shell up and admired its equidistant black freckles. "Gotta be careful with Cones, they got little poison spears. It's like a fuckin spider if it—" My lesson was interrupted when Milton's fishing pole leapt high into the air and out over the water like the flying fish that tag alongside cruise ships, his voice chasing after: "*FUCK! NO!*" But it was long gone.

His trembling head leaned over The Gulf: "MY DEAD FUCKING *MAMA* GAVE ME THAT POLE GOD*DAMNIT!*" He punted his Cone Shell into his bucket, "*FUCK!*" then shouldered me out of the way.

"I'm sorry," I said as his fried ear passed my mouth.

"Jesus fuckin Christ, man," he snarled. "Quit fuckin apologizing."

After Milton stomped off, I squatted out on the mud trying not to choke, staring, studying the carcass up close. Amazing. Though all the while I couldn't help feel the stare of Alana's family's far away pier. Ilka's pier. I couldn't bear to steal a glance back at it. When I did, just as the Gulf began getting truly dark and buggy, I saw a tiny, sobbing silhouette at the end of the big pier. I thought it might be Raphael.

I did not shout, just started walking. *Now would be the perfect time*, I thought, *to confront my fate head on, as promised to Alana.* Maybe, now, I could bring Raphael with me to help with his mother, to translate between us, to vouch for my worth. I approached the pier: a pure white, rail-straight half-mile protrusion into the dusky dying light. From a closer angle (the closest I'd yet been) it looked to stretch all the way across to the Gulf's mountainous far shore. I noticed nice fresh white rod holders and long unused white cutting boards stationed at intervals along the dock, ready for action, with no action forthcoming. Its complex crosshatched underbelly, dry at low tide, came into focus, all of it just as white: the type of sturdy structure you could hide beneath in the rain.

Raphael was indeed silently but visibly sobbing. When I hissed his name, he bolted up: "Patreek!"

"Shhhhhhh Raphael! Yes it's me."

In the near dark I heard a pack of elephants run down the wooden boards to meet me. He came to the edge and leaned over, glowing like a giant lightning bug. "Where have you been Malaka?" he whispered, letting me know my fears were not unfounded. "You been in Tiburon this whole time?"

I almost blurted that I was sorry, but instead remembered *Jesus fuckin Christ, man, quit fuckin apologizin...* "Are you out here crying, Raphael?" I asked. In the dark I did not see tears on his face, just a big white smile. Still I asked, "What's the matter?"

"Alana's birthday is today!" he shouted again, whether or not this was his answer.

"Shhhhhh! Wait. What?" The dark was really closing in now. The pier's row of pristine street lights above remained off. To my right the pier disappeared into the jungle, presumably ending near Ilka's front door. "Hey help me up," I ordered. "Alana's birthday?!"

"It's easier to go down to the end of the pier and..."

"Listen strongman," I faked lightheartedness, "just pull me up real quick with your superhuman redhead strength."

He reached down and gripped my hands tight. His wrists surprised me, feeling hairier than mine. He lifted me off the ground a couple feet easily but the angle was awkward and I fell back onto the sand. We tried a couple more times, with Raphael doing better each time, almost as if he was getting stronger rather than more tired. By my third harsh fall we were crying laughing – which angered the gods. Thunder boomed from the jungle: "RAPHAEL!"

And suddenly he was gone before my pulse had even risen, leaving me alone with the forbidden pier as if with an awkward stranger.

I did not follow my brother into the jungle. I marched back down the beach to the lonely jungle payphone I had noticed earlier at the base of the shitty public pier. Given the lack of cellphones here, I assumed and was correct that it worked. I did not posses her home phone number and so on a whim dialed in my debit card number and called Pizza Dive, unsure even of the time in Florida.

Tony answered. Strange hearing his voice ever again, much less while standing on mudflats gazing across at the silhouette of a mountain range.

"Hola, necesito a hablar con Alana," I said as if with plugged nostrils. I rambled confusing, incorrect Spanish about her birthday, not stopping until he barked, "O.K! O.K. Chill out, chill. I will go get her." Thankfully there was no hold music; I enjoyed the comfortable background clang of metal lexans.

"Hola," she finally answered.

For some reason I whispered, "Alana, hey, it's me. Happy birthday..."

"Patreeeeeeeeeeeek!" she screamed like an ambulance.

"Shhh. Pretend like it's Raphael. If Tony knows it's me..."

"Patreeeeeeeeeeeek!"

"Shhhhh!" I laughed. "How are you? Happy birthday!"

"Thank you!"

"Do you still love me?"

"YES!"

All weight lifted. "It's beautiful here, Alana, really. And the people are really nice. The Ticos I mean."

"Aw, you say Tico now!"

"I could live here forever. It's so sexy too. Makes me so horny for you. My 18-year-old woman."

She giggled, "I am a horny too!"

"Not too much longer eh?"

"Very soon. Agh, I cannot wait to leave. George quit after you, so now I work with all assholes. Tony is such an asshole."

"Well you'll be rid of him soon. God I can't wait to see you. I love you so much."

Her voice went high and odd: "I love you too, malaka."

Then it returned to normal: "Hello? Patreek?"

"Alana? How did you do that? You still there?"

"I am always here for you, malaka," said the warped voice, followed by Tony's baritone, "What the fuck you doin callin and botherin my employees during the rush, malaka?"

Again Alana's ambulance sounded. The line went dead.

That was not enough...

Still I smiled, skipping almost, recharged with hope on the way back to my rented room.

2.10 JUNGLE LOVE

Holy BEAUTY Alana!

Because, as you surely know, tiny Tiburon can feel like a pointless story cramped with too many minor characters, MAN did I need a goddamned break. And this break, out here, is perfect. When you return, we should live like THIS, in a treehouse perched on the lip of an enormous green bowl in the middle of nothing, yet everything. Half-drunk and stuffed, I, Jonathan, Buck, Buck's wife Madeline and their infant daughter (who only ACTS drunk) lay strewn across the smooth wood floor of Buck's 'dining room.' Our half-closed eyes barely watch a toucan fly back-and-forth across a sun setting seemingly for us. Her beak bigger than her body drags her from one corner of Buck's balcony, across the pink sun to the opposite corner, where she stops... turns... flies back... repeats... repeats... Though she's not INSANE, unless she thinks she'll get a different result...

I hope you're not bored with these jungle phenomena baby (how could you ever get tired of this same rainforest symphony EVERY day and night?), because treehouse life seems to me now a far better option than any the U.S. ever offered me — this lack of electricity, lack of walls...

Over dinner, in a New York accent he swears is "the way REAL New Orlins natives tahk," Buck explained how primitive jungle engineering keeps out even the angriest rain. Buck relished describing his family hiding up under their bed's mosquito net to watch lightning and broken palms fly over the jungle. I really like Buck. He looks like a pothead rugby player, with a brown beard shaggier than his crewcut, yet he exudes CAPABILITY. Mere weeks ago he capriciously decided his family should escape "dirty-ass New Orlins" to raise their child in "an even MORE primitive setting." And almost instantaneously, Buck has become a well-paid chef at the same fancy fishing lodge that loans him this brand new treehouse free of charge. Inspiring! The house's ripe, fresh-cut wood smell serves as pungent proof that things CAN turn out right.

This odor of positivity permeated our whole evening. I'd met Buck's friend Jonathan before and hadn't really liked him at first, but tonight I came around. Because the treehouse's nearest neighbor is five miles away, Jonathan is GIVING Buck his wimpy minivan before Jonathan flies back to the U.S. Or else Jonathan might stay here to work 8-hrs-a-day FOR NO PAY on an organic farm whose owner CHARGES volunteers for room-and-board — just TOO magnanimous. After tonight, he and Buck are my valuable allies.

They're also AMAZING chefs! A banquet of fresh shrimp, fish, peppers, rice, yucca, bananas and cantaloupe plus many beers incapacitated us. And now that toucan like a pendulum across the sunset hypnotizes us all to sleep — all but Buck's baby girl, wide awake in mom's armpit, gazing at the bird like it's television. Buck's baby, like lucky you, will grow up with the privilege of screaming into the void and having SOMETHING scream back. She will take her first steps across this same fresh wood floor I now press against, pretending it's your smooth, warm back...

Just one more long week to live through before we are

here, together, in paradise, forever.

Drunk and sentimental from the hopeful heart of the jungle,
    Ol Pat

* * *

Earlier today, before dinner, I had caught Jonathan pulling away from Rosie's service window. He'd tried not to stop for me. I stepped in front of his van. "Where you off to?" I smiled, gripping the sliding door's handle. "You're lucky you can just leave at will!"

Jonathan replied with a Miltonian nothing.

"Are you O.K.?"

"Yeah," he told his steering wheel. "I just gotta get going. I promised my friend I'd drive out to—"

"Can I come? Please?" I didn't care where. Didn't care if he wanted me there. I squealed gratefully when Jonathan barely conceded. Tearing his door open, I temped fate, "Can I run upstairs real quick and get my..."

"I'm kinda rushed, man; maybe we should just do this another time."

"No! No, no." I leapt in, no supplies, not even *mota*. We didn't speak the whole drive out, and not just because the terrifyingly dynamic landscape is so involving. I was glad to see Jonathan concentrating so hard, driving along sky-high cliffs that bled soft red dirt from scars above where large boulders had recently dropped off, with more threatening to fall any moment. Plus sublime streams, waterfalls, white-faced monkeys — talking was rendered obsolete.

Only after some beers at dinner did Jonathan and I finally begin laughing in the same key. We teamed up to fill Buck and Madeline in on all Tiburon's characters: desperate Hammerhead, hunky Orlando and his Jennifers, his punk cousin Rolando and shyster friend Jordano who can get you anything you want. Against better judgment, I even spilled some, 'Semi-Famous Author' stories – the safer, legal ones. Jonathan, a big fan of Milton, was incredibly impressed.

But at one point when he descended into the jungle to pee, and Buck's wife had fallen asleep beneath the mosquito net, Buck slapped my back as I cleared their table, "I'm glad you came

out tonight, Pat," he said. "I think I almost didn't get to meetcha..."
Because Jonathan had told him we didn't get along.

"Really?" I chuckled, stung enough to lie. "I wasn't aware."

"Huh. Guess it was just Jonathan didn't get along with *you*
then." Buck's beard smirked. "But whatev. Just now he toll me you
seem a lot coola den he thought. So dare ya go: ya cool. Jonathan is..."
He thought. "He's the best most loyal person I know. He's just... Not
uptight. But he does have the ability to politicize anything. *Anything*,
bruh. And I notice this about a lot of the white boys who love it here.
But he's a killa friend, the best."

Steering us back home to Tiburon though, Jonathan did
suggest I meet him at Nos Barra later (right now!), to drive out to
some full-moon dance in the jungle. And I'm glad to accompany
him.

Anything but more murder, more shelling, more Milton...

2.11 FULL-MOON DANCE

D

ARLING!

Currently EVERYONE and I drink at Nos Barra, revving up for some jungle cotillion. EVERYONE. Every fisherman, waitress, bank guard and teller, every grandma who washes tourists' clothes for 25-cents-a-pound — EVERYONE, roaring louder than the bar's REO Speedwagon tape. It's easier to catalog those I DON'T see over my beer glass (con hielo): Rosie (too religious), Milton (too misanthropic) and Jonathan, who initially offered to drive me out to this dance, but still hasn't shown.

I'll just tag along with Orlando and Rolando, who've been acting as everyone's HOSTS for the evening. Orlando tows his three Jennifers around the bar giving everyone their own personal "pura vida" and cheek-kiss, while I sit among Rolando's own sub-faction of teenage Ticos all wearing nighttime sunglasses and ball caps. Shy with their English, the kids kindly excluded me from their conspiratorial laughter, until they'd drunk some beer and

I whipped out my tape recorder. Loving it, they gave me every English word they knew, as did the brace-faced little Ticas who follow the boys like baitfish. Several old men have patted me on the back, mumbling QUOTES into my recorder en route to EL BANO. Your people are all so damn NICE to me.

Just now a work-dirty middle-aged Tico bought me guaro and let me openly record our conversation. He was an electrician away from his wife and kids on a special month-long job in Tiburon. He's gone now but I taped him saying, "I never been to Florida, but I have frient in Miami who do ANY-TING for me, mae. Gimmee da phone, mae, I'll fokeen call Miami right now! He give me whatever you need…or ah, give you whatever I need or -— foke mae, my English es no good."

Me: It's better than my Spanish.

He: Foke you, mae. [my laughter] Leasen, few EVER go to Miami mae, I give you my frient number…

Me: I was just in Miami a couple weeks ago.

He: Oh no! And you didn't talk to my frient! Jew miss jore big fokeen chance mae! [my laughter] But real mae, real. My frient can-—

Me: It's 'REALLY'.

He: What da foke?

Me: When you say 'real mae' you mean 'REALLY mae.'

He: Foke you mae! [my laughter] Leasen! In Miami, tell my frient my name, and he will get jew whatEVER jew want: de cocang, de joink…

Me: The what?

He: De joink mae! Joinks! Many as you want!

Me: I do like joints…

He: And de cocang! Jew want ANY kind of cocang, just go to Miami in dis address [grabs my wrist, pulls the recorder to his moustache], two—eight, a two, a one, Miami, in Florida, seven, a two…

Me: [laughing] Actually I've never tried cocaine. I'm pretty sure I never will.

He: What? Jew no like a little [SNORT, SNORT. Mutual laughter]? No? EVERYBODY like a some [SNORT, SNORT. Mutual laughter]. You no like cocang you fokeen gringo mudder foker?

Me: YOU like it though, eh?

He: Foke you! I don't do dat shit; I got a family modder foker. Joss a little bit ever once in a while.

Me: I'll bet it's easy to buy here, huh? With Colombia so close.

He: No. It joss start coming in Cost Rica now since da gringos. Jew can't get shit in Tiburon. Or maybe you can. How da foke I know? I'm not from Tiburon, fokeen PINCHA DE LUNA!

Me: Pincha de...? What does that mean?

He: Pincha de luna.

Me: Right. What does that mean?

He: Pincha de luna! Moon Deek!

Me: Moon Dick?

He: Pincha de luna!

Me: I know, but what does it MEAN?

He: MOON Deek!

Me: But QUE SIGNIFICA 'moon dick'?

He: Fokeen MOON DEEK mudder foker! PINCHA DE LUNA! Is like 'shithead.'

Me: No, because I look at a piece of shit and know I don't want THAT to be my HEAD. Whereas 'moon dick' – maybe it means my dick stretches to the moon? Maybe it's a GOOD thing?

He: NO mudder foker! Moon Dick! Pincha de LUNA.

Me: What the hell does it MEAN!

That went round-and-round until now I gotta quit transcribing my life and go live. Tweety's pushing everyone out early so she can attend the dance too. I'm so EXCITED! Though I can't help feeling that maybe I should wait until you and I can share my first ever dance...

'Don't be stupid,' you would say. 'Go.'

So O.K. Here we go.

Hold this for me while I dance...
Patrick

* * *

I woke alone in Milton's tent full of thick morning heat and fish-stink, and pushed aside the flap to the sight and intensifying smell of a hundred skinned Pompano lying single-file up a fallen palm tree. Beyond the curing fish raged the real, violent ocean: tall white waves freckled with surfers navigating jagged brown-red rocks. This is where all the Gulf's water's been hiding. From a lean-to fishing camp in the jungle, a primitive-looking Tico family smiled and waved at me. Milton was nowhere. No truck. He'd left with the Teacher in the night.

Tying my shoes on, I held my breath and contemplated breaking down his tent and taking it; an easier task now in the daylight than it would have been last night, had he and I tried. Thankfully, Orlando's sister and the Teacher had spoken little English but could *expertly* pitch a tent — which now in the morning I finally abandoned, to trudge up the beach, away from the stink. Wandering, worried how I would get back to Tiburon, I nearly stumbled over Orlando's Jennifers, beached and bathed in gritty sun. I attached myself lichen-like to these, "borin, rich hippie cunts," quoth Milton last night. The girls conceded to let me follow them to the roadside to wait for a *collectivo* after a good hour more of the Jennifers silent sunbathing. I waited and waited up in a tree's shaded armpit, watching pelicans dive barely out of reach of deadly ocean rocks. The closest any Jennifer came to normal sarcasm, *playful antagonism,* was after I said, "Sorry for being such a lame tag-along," and Orlando's girlfriend responded, "It's O.K." I laughed alone.

Last night, I followed Orlando's comprehensive village convoy out to the dance. Trudging across Tiburon's low-tide mud last night, I shared only smiles and joints with the Tico kids, enjoying a personal silence. Despite minor anxiety walking through the mangroves and Milton's "spot" (no one stopped to collect shells) I contentedly absorbed the parade's drunken Spanish, the jungle's screams, and the sound of flip-flops slapping the night like an amphibious herd.

Until finally we stood outside yet another cage, a 75-foot chicken-wire rectangle. A giant crabtrap, essentially, empty save two bored bartenders and *Los Hurricanos*, a Tico quintet on stage in white tuxedos. Contrasting brightly with the rural atmosphere, the band plugged vintage amplifiers into a belching gas generator. To the amusement of gringos at white plastic tables, Tweety spun a tiny Tico grandfather across the empty, hay-strewn dancefloor. The majority of Tiburon leaned against trucks in the grass parking lot. We began lining up at a cage door beneath the streetlamp — until

Orlando, at the front of the line, turned and announced *why* the cage was empty: "*Cuesto cinco mil!*"

He stuffed his Velcro wallet back into his surf shorts and a good-humored groan rose from the lot. Our line morphed into a circle of consultation, of which I stood outside, deciphering their quick Spanish: *This costs too much. We'll go to a party on the beach! But who will drive?*

Tico teens slapped Rolando's palm and my back, flip-flopping off into the black jungle. His troops now diminished, Orlando led us to a hole cut in the far end of the cage, from which bartenders sold beers — a line easily three-times longer than the ticket line. We stood outside drinking and watching *Los Hurricanos* running through synchronized salsa dances, shooting hateful glares at all of us too cheap to enter.

To the right of the big cage stood a rickety, sombrero-shaped stadium: "A bullfighting ring," I overheard one Jennifer explain to another. "They don't kill the bulls in Costa Rica though, just taunt them then put em back in their pens." The ring was boarded up but I followed along the plywood, searching for at least a peephole. Instead I spotted a bushy silhouette, spying on us from between trucks. I managed not to yell his real name: "John! *Hey!*"

The silhouette flinched and ducked when Rolando hollered: "Meal-tone! What the foke hue doing, hue weert mudder foker!"

Milton fled into darkness. I chased after — "Hey! Wait!" — imagining many things for which he might be angry at me. Or maybe he just didn't want to explain why Rolando had called him 'Milton'. I pretended I hadn't heard. "John! Where you going?"

He stopped, surrendered.

"You alone?" I asked.

An irritated sigh.

"You walked out here by yourself?"

"Drove m'truck." He slapped the dented hood of his giant, stone-aged red pickup.

"Come hang out!"

"Alana with y'all?"

"She gets back in a week or so. I'm with these guys." I glanced back at my Tico friends. They all stared at Milton, their collective mood visibly soured. Still, "C'mon man. I'll buy you a beer."

"Naw. I'm too fuckin old to be hanging out with little kids."

"I'm not?" I weaseled. "That's why you *need* to come on over."

I smelled sad alcohol when he gawked over my shoulder at The Jennifers, who'd separated from the herd to press against the cage, watching the band. Milton stared at them, the streetlamp lighting a thin white force-shield or halo around him: a layer of peeling skin. Orlando cared not; Milton is Semi-Famous and interesting, but physical beauty trumps all.

"I'ma drive to the party. Less go," Milton finally said and flip-flopped back into the darkness.

"For free?" Rolando asked me as we hesitantly followed. Taxi rates here are pretty much the same as in NYC.

"I would hope it's free. You think he'd charge?"

"He charge all other times. He the only white collectivo driver." Orlando nodded witness.

"He won't charge us," I promised.

"O.K. den," Rolando shrugged. "Hif hiss a free ride..."

Without enough room in the bed for all the kids, Milton shifted the unenthusiastic Jennifers into his cab. The truck roared and rattled down a skinny sand road, headlights illuminating a continuous arch of white branches above, tangled together like human arms. With remarkably little difficulty, Rolando rolled and lit a joint. Over wind I joked he better keep it low if he didn't want Milton to suck it all down.

"Meal-tone never smoke a pote, mae!" Rolando's wind-warped accent seemed to represent a new ethnicity every few sentences — that clipped British 'pote' — as if raised by tourists from disparate lands. "At Nos Barra he cree-tee-cize!" Rolando shouted. "He tell us we are all stupid for smo-keen! What it's called when somebody say somethink is wrong, but dey do it demself?"

"Hypocrite!" I laughed, accepting the joint.

"Meal-tone ees a fokeen *he-po-creet,* mae!"

Confident of our privacy I bellowed, "He told me his name is *John!*"

"Oh dass right!" Rolando laughed hoarsely, a smoker's laugh at 17. "Beak, famous book writer lie to tourists about his fokeen name so they don't bother him even though they don't give a *foke*! I have to make fun of heem for dat!"

It offended me that Milton would view me as a tourist. Still, "I think some people are interested in him for his writing! I am!"

"He ees good writer, really? He seem like a dumb shit!"

"Yes, he's very good!" I attested, though I'd only read that one excerpt. "And in his writing especially you can tell he's essentially a good person! He's just depressed! Pot though seems to make him feel…not *good*, but! At least better! It seems! He talks a lot more! He sort of freaks out actually, it's sort of hilarious." I immediately felt bad and checked the back window.

"Milton all foke-tope about his mudder die!" Rolando informed before the truck's headlights died. The Jennifers squealed as the truck revved faster in the blackness. Finally, the truck slowed, re-lit the jungle, and Milton's head tilted back, laughing too hard.

"He's a weert mudder foker!" Rolando continued. "At Nos Barra, right before Alana leave!" He paused to let her name sink in. "She meet Meal-tone that night, first time! He try to fuck her all night. She just think that's funny. They were talk about Alana dad, who was died a time ago, and Meal-tone mom, who joss die! They were so dronk until they both start to *fokeen cry*, mae!" Rolando laughed hard against the wind as I tried not to picture her crying with Milton. "Alana not cry much dough," Rolando amended. "She try to calm Meal-tone down. But he joss cry more and more, say he want to *kill* hisself because his mudder hate heem! In front of all Nos Barra he was cry like a poosy!"

All this was knocked from my brain when we were all thrown against the roll cage, then a few inches into the air — over the cab I caught glimpses of the jungle road, now roadless jungle. Climbing an almost vertical dirt wall, Milton's truck threatened to tip. Jennifers' squealing resumed. Orlando laughed. Rolando and crew continued the joint. Even I remained calm, maybe desensitized by FLA's finely detailed theme parks where every visceral experience runs on safety-tested tracks.

We pulled into a muddy grass lot of well-kept SUV's surrounding a palm-roofed patio with an in-the-round bar like Nos Barra's but newer, carved from stone, featuring it's own new oven, stove and dishwasher — like the set of a cooking show with no walls, run by a big, tattooed German bartender lady. A small herd of surfers Milton's age, all burned (not nearly as masochistically) and on the flabby side of muscular, chatted up leathery "Earth Mothers" (Milton called them) all wearing worn sundresses over salty bathing suits — same uniform as Jennifers, who anxiously fled Milton's cab to follow Orlando into the crowd. Milton and I lugged a beer cooler from his truck to the picnic table Rolando and his crew filled on the patio's outskirts. Jimmy Buffett assaulted us from hidden speakers. I sat beside Milton, cracked a beer and announced, "Hey Rolando, twist up another and *your boy* here will give you each a beer. He may even do a little dance, once he's high."

"Easy," growled Milton.

"Sure mae," Rolando smiled like accepting a bet. "I wanna see *John* here smoke."

We watched Rolando pick apart brown mulch and toss seeds over his shoulder. I petted one of the party's many medium-sized brown dogs. Working away, Rolando casually asked my age. "Hey!" he replied to my answer, "Dass exactly 10-years younger than *me*, mae!"

"You mean older."

"Yeah, yeah, older I mean." He licked the paper. "I'm a seventeen, you a twenty-seven." He lit and puffed then passed it, along with an anecdote, which I recorded: "Dares diss book I see in church, with a list of tings everybody gotta do before he die. It say every man gotta climb a mountain. But I do dat every time I go visit my *dad* house! So tross me, it's a no big a deal. You don't gotta do dat wan." He looked to his friends for laughter, but they hadn't understood his English. They watched the party guests like Inca griffins, tiki flames polishing their stoner sunglasses. Rolando passed them the lit joint, continuing, "The book say you gotta get marry before you die. My dad say, 'Get marry before you're 30.' Pa-treek, you still got tree more years — not like over-da-heel fokeen *John*! Over da fokeen *mountain!* You better watch out Patrick, Meal-tone gone try to take from you Alana and marry her!" Milton ignored him in favor of calmly but rudely toking Rolando's joint over-and-over. Rolando finally came to his *playfully antagonistic* point: "The last ting da book say is, before you die, you gotta write your *own* book." Rolando lifted his glasses from saggy, old eyes. "But *John* already *write* a book! Right *John*? Beak *famous* book, right *John*?" Pointing at 'Margaritaville' floating invisible above, Rolando prodded, "*John* is beak famous Florida guy like Buffett!"

I felt Milton heating up beside me.

Rolando coughed and laughed, "So since you already write

a book, *John,* you can go head kill yourself now, like you promise! Maybe if you do dat you can be famous for real."

Milton watched Rolando translate this exchange for his friends before — with more than a rational amount of quiet anger — he declared, "You ain't accomplished shit in your life, Rolando. And you won't. *Ever.* You'll stay out here in the middle a fuckin nowhere smokin weed, and you'll never learn what it's like havin strangers wantin shit from you, wantin to talk about yourself *all the time.* You won't *ever* know what that's like, bro. So shut the fuck up."

Rolando's flatlined friends watched their leader laugh: "O.K.! O.K. mae! *Hahahaha!* Don't gif me no shit! You are a *beak* star. *Haha!* I'm a sorry."

Milton turned away and chewed the inside of his mouth, pushing on the blistered outside of his face. As Jimmy Buffet sang, "Fins to the left! Fins to the right! And you're the only bait in town!" my recorder rolled and the pot took effect on him: "Man, Jimmy Buffett, dude. Fuckin children's music for adults. Only real job I ever had was at this restaurant on Sanibel where the Parrottheads used to meet: Buffett's fanclub, right? Dude, you think Deadheads are dumb sheep? Parrottheads may be the opposite demographic from Deadheads but at least Deadheads kin hold their drugs. Buffett'd come to town and the Parrottheads'd all play hooky from their office jobs to come in and drink Margaritas and Coronas until they're pukin, pissin even sometimes shittin *outside* the bathroom. Guess who got to clean *that* up? That shithole had three dinin rooms, each one blastin a *different* fuckin Buffett CD, then out on the patio they'd have a fuckin Buffett cover band! No goddamn *escape*! I never in my life tried to hear one a that dude's songs, *ever,* but to this I day know the words to *all* um. I hear him now, I break out in a fuckin *Buffett-itus* rash." He scratched at his red arms.

SUV's streamed in like spaceships from the jungle, delivering more out-of-shape jocks and Earth Mothers. Milton's shiny pink eyes scanned the crowd intently. "We need chicks," he hissed, chewing his mouth. He pointed to two white girls perched on a distant, bubbling fountain. Tricky tiki shadows obscured their features, but they couldn't have been 15.

"Too young for me," I said.

"Ain't yr girl like 17?" Milton asked.

"She turned 18."

"You ain't gotta fuck anybody man, I'll take um both," Milton said. "Just come over with me and be nice for a minute so they don't feel, uh..."

"Threatened?" I guessed. "Alana wouldn't appreciate that."

"Hey, I wouldn't take the slightest chance of losing that either, bro. But just cause you're on a diet don't mean you can't read the menu."

"Who wants to read the menu when they're starving?"

"You starving ol Pat?" Milton cocked his smirk. "Yr girl ain't give you nough lovin?"

"Not in the *three weeks* we've been *apart,* asshole."

"Easy," Milton shook his head, then said the exact right thing: "Don't be so sensitive."

"You're right."

Having drank just one beer (to Milton's two suicidal guaro shots) I rose to use the bathroom and found myself in line behind the internet cafe's owner. He informed me that Jacques and his wife are getting divorced, but I only cared about my fishing rod. He promised he would leave it at the cafe for me tomorrow. I entered the bathroom newly excited and noticed the soap dish was actually a jumbo Fighting Conch, clouded in milky soap scum, but bigger than Milton's biggest! I didn't wash my hands, excited to get back out and tell Milton! But I returned to the nauseating site of his exposed, overcooked shoulders and taught red gut. Still unsure how to address him, I looked away and settled on, "Dude, why do you have your shirt off?"

"So I can fit in at the party, bro!" he mocked for those within earshot. Some noticed, most didn't hear. "Don't wanna *stand out,* right?!" He shouted then mumbled to himself, "Motherfuckers wanna stare at me all the time I can *definitely* give em something to fuckin stare at." He turned his bare back on the crowd.

"People are staring at you, Milton?" I laughed at his delusion. "I can call you Milton now, right?"

"It was twice as bad in fuckin Flor'da. One of the reasons I left. Ticos don't give a fuck, but white people won't leave me alone." Beyond him, a dozen uneasy eyes were now indeed tuned in to him. Before I could credit him with real literary celebrity he spun on his stool and I realized they were all staring at the huge tattoo across Milton's back. On the dark pink sea of his burned flesh floated a map of Central America, a bit puffy like the brands black frat brothers burn into themselves. *Masochist!* I cringed, leaning in to find Tiburon, but when I couldn't even pinpoint the capital city I quickly understood this was not a map or even a tattoo; I was scouting the geography of a long, purple blister. My gag reflex spoke up. I turned away and met the surfers' troubled eyes.

"Motherfuckers starin..."

"Milton! It's your fucking back!" I cried. "You're gonna die, man! Seriously!"

"Easy bro."

"No! At least die in private! Put your fucking shirt back on. I'm not gonna watch you kill yourself."

"Then don't." His face resumed its default setting somewhere on the sad side of apathy.

I backed off, let it go, considering all Rolando had told me on the ride out. Oblivious to Milton's blister, Orlando tapped me: "Iss a lame party mae, when the best looking cheeks are a Ticas." He pointed out two dark women sitting up on a table across the patio, their legs draped over two doughy gringos' shoulders: the men's balding, pink heads gave the illusion of being choked from behind by the nice brown legs of the Teacher and Orlando's sister. Sis looked as humidly sexy as on the Main Road, but the Teacher seemed well rested now, happier. Milton finally noticed them too and shouted, "Alana!"

"That's not Alana, Milton."

He pulled me away with him.

"Where are we going? You need to put your fucking shirt on Milton." I walked in front to not see it.

"Shut the fuck up. Sit." Unsure why, I obeyed at a two-top near the Ticas. Chewing his cheek, knee bouncing against the underside of the table, Milton straddled his chair backwards, his back to the women. The Teacher didn't notice him, but smiled a missing tooth at me. She looks so much like some version of Alana that my eyes dove away, down to her bare stomach like hot fudge barely melting over the band of her black stretchpants. "If we knew ten words a Spanish between us," Milton thought he was whispering, "we could jack these chicks away from these dudes like nothin!"

"I know way more than ten words."

"Well *talk* then, bro! Shit! Say something! Tico girls err *easy!*" Before I could remind him why that would offend me, he continued, "A white boy even *tries* to say 'Come back to my room,' you can be sayin it wrong or whatever the fuck, but just makin the effort'll get you the pussy here." His singed eyebrows lifted: "How y'say 'Come back to my room'?"

As I slowly translated, the two women noticed his blister and bolted up, eyes wide. The Teacher instinctively reached a hand out, but stopped and touched her lips. The girls' flutter caused their gringos to look at me, Milton's blister, then away, disgusted. Milton spun and faced them all — in the process, twisting and tightening the blister. Fluid threatened to bust all over our table. Milton repeated what I'd told him, "Venga a mi cuarto conmigo," then something about "vamos" and "playa" and "dinero," as if quoting them a price on a ride to the beach.

Almost instantaneously, Rolando's shaking my hand *goodbye,* hyper-sincerely, like a sappy old drunk and I worry he'll tell Alana that Milton and I left the party with two women. I do not know why I even did it. I do know I would never cheat on Alana, and I recalled some sense Milton had made when I first caught him shelling, "I ain't doin nothin wrong. Folks get the wrong idea, at's *y'all's* problem," he'd said. Still, back at the truck Milton dug crumpled colones from every pocket, handed them over to the Teacher, and I climbed into the bed alone, confused by what I was doing, and why.

* * *

Moonlit whitecaps churned in and out of faint view on a deep, navy blue panorama. The world *felt* huge, looming, crushing. Perfect. Milton tossed down a small canvas bag not big enough to hold one tent and declared, "I got tents." Thankfully, both women competed for Milton's attention. The Teacher finally seemed to win by picking an aloe leaf and laying Milton across the fallen palm where next morning I would wake to rotting pompano. She massaged the plant's clear gel straight into his blister — all of us winced in chorus. Orlando's sister pranced over and crouched beside me in the sand. Her black shining eyes bored into my profile. To break the tension I squeaked, "So hey Milton, let's set these tents up."

"Aw man," Milton moaned, "I'm too wasted to mess with that shit right now." Softly, as if talking to the Teacher he added, "It's nice outside. Lay back and look at the fuckin stars."

I huffed, but then looked up and "Holy *shit!*" The Earth pulled my head back onto the sand, forcing my eyes upon the starriest sky I've ever seen. As much white as black. *Could I have missed more than two weeks of* this *by simply not looking up?* I couldn't recall Tampa's stars either — could they have also been so beautiful? So extraordinary was this sky, it took me a second to notice Orlando's sister leaning over me, pouting down. My skull just missed her jaw when I sat up: "Seriously man, before we get too comfortable, lets put these tents up."

"Dude! Just do it yourself or else spread the canvas out flat and lay on top then if yr so afraid a gettin sand in yr pussy."

The women must have understood. They rose in tandem in the gorgeous starry dark to bend and crouch and slide poles into slots. When the single tent was erect, the damp-skinned Teacher reassumed her post astride Milton. Her squishy massage continued. Orlando's sister returned her hot breath to my temple. To block fantasies of this young perspiring jungle woman and me crammed into the tiny tent, I trained my nervous eyes on the stars. They might have burned my retinas by the time she finally gave up. I watched her hips sway away down the beach, and before I could dwell too darkly on the very rare options I'm afforded here, I realized *I passed! This was a test, and I passed!* A hot smile crossed my face — which Milton cooled with, "Hey bro, since there's two of us, and only one a you, we're gonna take the tent, few don't mind…"

"No way. You get the comfort of a woman," I campaigned, noticing the Teacher's hand crab-walk across Milton's inner thigh; she didn't seem to understand me. "And I get the comfort of a tent. You get the better night either way."

"Fine. Whatever."

Wow. We've had longer arguments than that about…seashells. I attributed my easy win to his impatience, a willingness to cut through anything to get his show rolling. Regardless, I'd won! Victorious, I crawled directly into the tent, laid on my back, molded my shoulders and ass into the canvas floor — and immediately realized I would rather be outside.

But now I was trapped, staring at the shark-gray ceiling,

listening to their spitty mouths collide. "Tienes condon?" the Teacher gasped, before the ocean's cyclical *whoosh* finally put me under.

2.12 OUR TRIP

L eft his tent behind and walked along the beach, worried. A mile down the Jennifers sunbathed on the beach outside last night's bar. Orlando was nowhere. I hid under the bar's shade with no money, hoping to catch a ride back with the girls somehow. The big grungy German bartendress didn't remember any of us: "Last night is a crazy blur. Did you enjoy?" she asked, then, "Vait!" she beamed, "You're the *writer*! I *heard* you vur here last night! Your red hair gave you away! I heard you got rowdy last night." She smiled about whatever she'd been told.

"Yes," I answered, and let her buy me an afternoon beer, tempted to add, 'I am indeed Chapman. Could you help a semi-famous author find some good whores?' Because fuck him for stranding me on the beach.

The Jennifers in wet towels joined me but we didn't talk. I sipped and scribbled, and paid maybe too much silent attention to the arrival of a skinny, sun-dressed young gringa with short curly hair, crooked front teeth, the warmest laugh and clearest skin. She had also a shirtless gringo boyfriend with identical curls. This irresistibly small-featured woman took a stool beside me and we both listened to her boyfriend blow hot wind up the Jennifers about "plant spirit medicine," and some jungle bird that isn't a toucan "but *visitors* often mistake it for a toucan." He went on to describe the house he'd just built on his "property."

Quietly his lady laughed to me, "Like daddy didn't pay for it all..."

Later one of the Jennifers exclaimed something to the others about all the prostitutes at the party last night, sending another Jennifer into a rant: "Tica girls are sexually active and pregnant way too young. It's sad. But there's nothing else for them to do here. I wanna start like, art classes in Tiburon, or music lessons, or like, a storytelling program, to let these girls know there's something they could be doing, besides having sex." At that moment Milton's big red truck skidded up to the bar "Lookin fr *you* Pat! Git in!".

Jennifers were desperate enough to accept his invitation too. Calmly furious, I rode with him up in his cab, to hear what he'd say. For some reason, I always want to hear. His truck smelled of weed, still he said nothing. His burns looked ghastly fresh. He looked vibrantly alive, and just as dead. Silent and distrustful, I turned away, studying roadside farms. Milton nudged me with a story: "Last night right before I seen ya, I walked down to the flats cause I forgot m'flip-flops. As I'm leavin, this little ol Tico dude runs up waving his arms, tryna ask *me* to git rid of that dead shark's stinkin up the Gulf. Course I'm like, '*Hail* naw!' Till he shows me this sweet rod-n-reel — after I *just* lost Mama's! So grandpa gits a rope, and I tie it around that big ol head and drag that motherfucker across the mud. I'm just *chokin* on flies, man! And cause I know the dude will want his rod back if that thing washes back up, I *swam* the body out into the channel! And man I'll tell ya, lookin back over my shoulder at that evil-ass head swimming up behind me in the dark — you were right, bro, I realized, shark attack ain't how I wanna go..."

Now I was silent for different reasons. Pity overcame anger. We trucked between miles of humpback cow pastures. Eventually I spoke: "I wonder what kind of shrooms those crazy beasts produce."

"Shrooms?"

"Psychedelic mushrooms. Wait. You're from Florida and don't know about shrooms?" He really had no idea. "They grow in warm cow manure," I explained, "and they are hands down the best drug. Like LSD but gentler, more organic. Supposedly you trip because your body's fighting off poison. But shrooms are *definitely* on any list of 'things you *need* to do before you die.'"

Rrrrt. His truck halted along barbed wire.

"Oh, well... Right *now*? If you're not in the right frame of mind," I warned, "they'll turn on you. They kind of take however you're feeling and magnify it. Plus, though I don't think shrooms are illegal, I do know that Florida cops will bust you for trespassing — unless the farmer just shoots you in the ass with a rifle full of rocksalt. That happened to a friend of mine in Florida. In Florida they'll..."

"S'ain't Florida." Milton shouldered his door open and hopped down into nature.

* * *

~==ALANA, sweet fuse lit at both ends==~

I hope you haven't tripped yet at your tender age, but I hope WE do someday, together. SO goddamned beautiful ALANA! Communing earlier with YOUR water, YOUR mangroves, YOUR intense stars, YOUR boy Milton and I were honest-to-god telepathic CONJURERS adjusting the sunset's color, and the pitch and volume of the surround-sound jungle symphony. Even now, as I chill down, every pore of my skin is an ear with perfect pitch hearing far-away oceans breathing and my loud heart pounding.

Just PICKING the shrooms was revelatory — a grown-up Easter egg hunt! We uncovered FRISBEE-SIZED caps and checked their stems for the telltale purple skirts before choking them down straight from the shit. Milton licking brown crumbs and tiny white bugs off his blistered lips made me wretch at first but we laughed harder and harder as herds of humpbacked cows galloped straight at us, strange faces asking WHY ARE YOU PLAYING WITH OUR SHIT? Scary! Milton would bark loudly and the cows would all pause and read us with droopy (or angry?) eyes — eventually stepping forward until he literally barked, "WOOF!" And again every creature on the field paused, all of us suspicious.

Or maybe it wasn't so dramatic. We certainly cackled madly struggling back through a knee-deep mote of TECHNICOLOR

QUICKSAND SWAMP MARSH: scary wading in, but SUBLIME coming out, our skin mouthed-at by yellow flowers, yellow reflecting from our teeth and eyes and petals tangled in Jennifers' armpit hair and Milton's orange mop and I wished and wished and cursed GOD herself, hoping you'd somehow MATERIALIZE right at that moment.

Then kayaking! Just me and a Semi-Famous Author navigating tight twisting tunnels through mangroves. Milton's voice vibrated spiderwebs caught like rotted parachutes between branches. Finally out on the open ocean we found no dolphins but the TALLEST sunset loomed over us orange and red as my tour guide. We attacked the water, along with many of my long-held oceanic fears: Underwater hands gripped and tugged our ankles as waves rose above us like giant hands, their fingers folding over into fists that SMASHED down upon us LIKE WE DESERVE! The last of today's sun shined through one big wave, illuminating a flock of stingrays! We kicked free and heaved ourselves panting onto the sand to turn and watch the devil rays fade into the foam. Dude! I'd never entered the ocean at night, ever, and have rarely swam in saltwater deeper than my head, but Milton brought scuba masks and beneath the black water we counted zillions of green-white glowing phosphate beads coating our clothes and skin like ghost dandruff. Dude!

On the clean, wide beach (no footprints but ours!) we ate an amazing, drippy sunset-orange melon plus cinnamon cookies and ice water — the best most tactile meal of my life! We rolled around wet, coating ourselves in sand as if in deep-fry batter. The shrooms began working like truth serum on Milton and for almost an hour he unleashed a HUGE autobiographical narrative that felt memorized, but not cheap; his soul flowed in a rare way, not having to struggle around his usual antagonism, sarcasm, pain, sadness, bullshit. We ended up crying together like at a Sweat Lodge but without the wet bear hugs. I COULD've hugged him, but…

I do believe this was all real.

But not realer than WE'll be, in just 26 hours! I wouldn't have believed my heart could beat any harder…

Soon,
Patrick

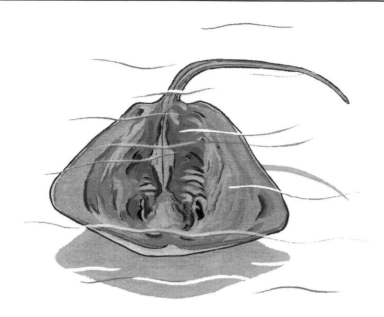

2.13 THE REST OF HIS TRIP

Back at my cabina I realize my tape recorder had drowned. It rewinds with a dying sound and you can barely discern the "moon dick" debate I recorded (which, in reality, the electrician had ended with, "Costa Rica is *my* fokeen cone-tree, fokeen gringo!" I didn't tell Alana that). But Milton's long, amazing, tearful rant about his career and his mother, which I had hoped to transcribe later on, comes in more clearly: "Cause it hurts like shit, bro," I hear Milton's voice sob, followed by garble. "But I cain't fuckin *enjoy* it!" Then his drawl again drowned. Shit. I should transcribe what I can now.

First the set-up: Milton and I made plans to meet again in a bar for a kayak tour, and he dropped me off at *Del Mar*. Color, light and sound surged in my skull, sunscreen-laced sweat seared my eyeballs, and I craved a cold beer with such otherworldly intensity, I detoured into a bar not billed as Ticos Only, but only mid-day drunk locals stared at my frenetic pupils adjusting to the darkness. A skeletal bartendress served me a quick brown beer along with free happy-hour appetizers: two steamed sea-turtle eggs, powdery like new ping-pong balls but pliable, with discernable hot nugget centers. I was appalled, though the eggs *were* amazing to see, to knead and knead and... They looked and felt so...*sensitive... Don't be so sensitive...* I freaked and dropped them and dashed out through Ticos' roaring laughter — straight into Milton, burnt but smiling on the Main Road, leaning on the fence that surrounds the school.

Holding bags of groceries for our trip, he admitted, "I'm waitin to catch another glimpse a the most beautiful things I ever *seen*, man! Or *think* I seen! Could be the shrooms but I *think* I just seen three Tica girls with *red fuckin hair*, bro!"

"Triplets, all *12*-years-old," I informed him, my heart and jaw muscles throbbing. "They're Alana's sisters."

This did not dull his horns. I could have fixated on wanting to see them myself, but thought it best for all involved if Milton simply forgot the girls, completely and forever. "Ooh, Alana. When's she getting back?" he began. Fortunately, Mother Nature's distant breathing across *El Gulfo Tiburon* distracted us away.

The tape's first clearly captured moment has my 'friend' Jonathan snarling, "Screw you guys," and quitting Milton's tour. At the beginning, Milton had warned me that "some tourist rube," who'd paid $50, would be joining us. From the first, Jonathan beamed in Milton's presence but, clumsily entering the groves, I could sense Jonathan beginning to feel alienated by our pre-forged redhead bond. Or our fungus-induced schizophrenia. A $50 tour should have included handshakes, backslaps, lunch, and a comprehensive verbal map of our journey. But Milton's big pink clam head dribbled only silence from the corners of his wraparound mouth. He wouldn't give me kayak instructions; it was Jonathan who finally showed me how to slip smooth and quick through the skinny mangrove tunnels like blood through a vein. Rowing pumped the psilocybin into my muscles and mind. My oars churned up fish both real and imagined. "Whoa *look*!" I shouted. "That giant redfish's tail! Poking out the water! See the spot on the tail!" Frowning, Milton remained absorbed decoding the water's ripples. I grew to fill his lack, squealing out names of animals I recognized from FLA — species Milton knows too, but now wouldn't share. Despite Jonathan's total ignorance of

Tiburon's ecosystem, he told Milton that the Gringo Restaurant had offered him a job as a kayak tour-guide. "You'll just learn as you go," they'd supposedly said, needing only an able white body. So while loudly identifying reptile after bird after shore-bound vermin, I fantasized *I could be a tour guide here! I already recognize that, and that and,* "That! Oh *man! Look!*"

"*OK* we see it! Now *be quiet!*" Milton woke from his watery contemplation. "I don't care whose boyfriend you are, shut the *fuck up*, dude."

My face and neck boiled. Jonathan almost lost his glasses in the water, laughing. His laugh echoed over the green water. Milton finally pointed an oar at him: "Dude! You too! Shut the fuck up. I'm trippin *balls* bro, and your laugh is annoyin as fuck. Laugh again and you kin keep yr fifty-bucks and just *go!*"

That's when Jonathan snarled, "Screw you guys," and headed back.

Unfortunately for him, had he waited, Milton's psyche finally pitched too high and couldn't control his mouth, which thereafter named off every monkey, bird, lizard, snake, insect and fierce-looking flower around us. But in my new silence I leaned toward bad thoughts. I worried that all this dynamic beauty would end in another animal holocaust on another ugly mudflat. *Is he taking me to skin dolphins?*

I was saved when the mangrove ceiling fell away, and we emerged onto an eternal high-tide ocean streaked with startling sunset sky forever into the distance. Large but calm waves rolled white-green, pushing us to the beach. Stars were just beginning to twinkle, bounce, twirl, pulse. We paddled onto the sand, totally fucked-up. On land we smoked a joint to multiply the stars. The far-off mountains closed in then dashed away. The tape has us audibly slurping melon. Then: "This would be better with some cornstarch to wash it down," Milton laughed.

I've tripped enough that I was able to keep this new screeching, sparking train-of-thought simply parked at my mental depot. I told him I didn't know anything about cornstarch. "The shit you stick down yr pants to keep yr nuts from sweatin," he said, smiling devilishly. "Yr girl toll me her mama started eatin cornstarch, plain, just out the box, in order to plump up, to punish her cheatin daddy. And now the bitch cain't stop! She's addicted. An people think

I'm crazy!"

I threw up my only defense: "What about your mother?" And we were on.

Milton proceeded to unfold his life story, which I will transcribe now as best I can *(AUTHOR'S NOTE: text later edited [but not changed] for coherence and readability. Ellipses denote larger inaudible chunks of varying lengths):*

"Yeah, Mama was kyna mean, you could say. Or just competitive. Even with me. We only ever got into it about shellin though, out on Sanibel Causeway... We moved to Sanibel from Lutz and dude, You shoulda heard the *accent* I had! But you couldn'ta had a better childhood, fishin and shellin. The island was just gorgeous. Like Tiburon, cept clean. And more animals. After storms, we'd find walkin catfish in our driveway! Live shellin capital of the world. Whatever tourists couldn't find, they'd buy from shell shops, which were all buyin shells from Mama an me...

"Away to UF and studied under Harry Crews, who had this ugly Mohawk at the time and was drunk most classes. Which is actually why I never been into drinkin — not till I got here, really. Here, I just been so fuckin depressed...

"It was just my senior thesis, not a *book* yet. Only my teachers ever read it, besides Mama. But right after I graduated Mama started bitchin about how there were more tourists and less shells on Sanibel. Not cause her an I raped the Causeway for 10 years, right? No. My unpublished fuckin manuscript about shellin caused a boom in the shellin industry? Hail naw not yet it ain't...

"West of Orlando to teach depressin-ass tech writin at a depressin-ass community college, which fuckin sucked but at least there was a beach. I kin tolerate *any*place with a beach; just turn my back to the land and all the humans crawlin on it, and I'm O.K. I did make one real good friend in that stripmall town though, guy worked at a copy shop, was also in bands and puttin out his own music CDs. He said all musicians put out their own CDs. He was *the reason* I self-published *Almost*. He tape-bound it for me *so* cheap, skimmed supplies, gay-me discounts. Shit came out sweet and tight.

"Since I was from Sanibel and had been dealin with these

shell shops all my life, I started sellin my book in those same places. Mama got *pissed*. But ain't no way I'm gettin my self-published shit in real *bookstores*, right? I just wasn't waitin round for nobody's permission...

"When I was teachin in Tallahassee, Mama was easy enough to ignore. For once in m'life. I didn't appreciate it at the time, but FSU let me build a whole class myself, bout self-publishin. Fuckin awesome. Along with hiring me they also "officially" published *Almost*, so I'm a hypocrite before my class even starts cause *real* self-publishing dudes work their asses off at bein ignored while I'm teaching *their* subject and gettin reviewed in newspapers and I can't go back to Sanibel without journalists callin me and tourists' cameras in my face and Mama screamin her...

"Made it so no one was allowed to take more than two a each type a shell *per day*. She didn't think it was OUR fault. Just MY fault. My book's fault. Either way, Sanibel *po*lice had a helluva time gettin Mama to abide by that one. Without shellin money, Mama couldn't really afford to live on the island. She had to go work at Sanibel's one grocery store — at 56-fuckin-years-old! She had no love for me after that...

"Agent sold the rights in Germany for $5,000 and I called to tell Mama I'd pay her rent and bills – cause see I got to hallucinatin I was gonna get money from each separate country in Europe. Why would just one country pick up on it and not all the others? So I quit my awesome teachin job like a dumbass – my co-workers were pretentious dicks anyway. Dude, on my last day, OH lord (*long laugh*), on my last day I wrote this arrogant curse-out letter, and slid a copy into every mailbox, includin the head a the fuckin department. Oh lord was I a idiot.

"Book was sellin real good, so I moved back and rented an awesome condo on Sanibel with an extra bedroom for Mama. She wouldn't even come over. 'I'm too busy workin at the goddamned GROCERY *store* Milton!' she'd scream and fuckin hang up. I had to mail money to her right up the road...

"Readily became apparent that fame don't exactly equal fuckin fortune when I had to start workin for this little Sanibel paper called *The Mullet Wrapper*. I wrote articles AND delivered papers for extra money and still couldn't afford that condo...

"...guy was some well-known writer-author-journalist

dude, I guess. I'd never heard of him. He recognized my name from *The Mullet Wrapper* and hunts me down all excited, loves my book; nice old white dude with white hair, white suit, says he just wants to get me drunk and talk about writin. An since I'm no good at drinkin, course I end up tellin him my whole goddamn life story, an bout Mama down at the grocery store hatin my guts. An within two months the whole thing's in a fuckin full color MAGAZINE. Big article, all bout famous Flor'da writers. You know Kerouac drank himself dead in St Pete? Anyway, this dude's article went into great fuckin detail bout shellin, an Sanibel an... I sold some more books cause a that. But Mama ain't like it one goddamned...

"Screamin bout I'm ruinin *her* life, when it's me who cain't even ride my bike up-and-down the main road without tourists telling me they came to Sanibel SPECIFICALLY for shellin — SPECIFICALLY cause a me. They finally enacted a FULL ban on live shellin, which was only bout the second time Sanibel's changed anything at all in about 100 years. Mama had to go to work full time at the store, and I had to agree that it WAS all my fault. The bigger I got, the more I was crushin her. And MAN I didn't mean to, didn't wanna — she's my fuckin Mama! I love her! Loved her! Too much to ever fight with her. And MAN did she wanna fight. I know yr girl Alana don't give a fuck bout always fightin with her Mama, but I just couldn't take it. This one time we's fightin and I pushed over her big ol wicker bookcase. Had about half a her personal shell collection on it. Some *rare* shit... It got bad..."

"Couldn't pay my rent, just kooked-out man. Had a breakdown. Went, slept on dirty-ass Nigger Beach a few nights cause no *way* the cops'r lettin you sleep on *Lighthouse* Beach and I just had to be outside. Fur three days or so I swam in the dirty water and slept in dog shit and sunburned myself into a fuckin *episode* man. Kinda like I'm doin here (*chuckles*) cept this time I'ma finish the job cause...

"When I finally dragged myself back to Mama's, she's *gone*. Her condo's empty sep fur the water stains on the ceiling she ain't had money to fix cause she'd been savin the money I give her to buy a house in Tiburon: no windows, roof is mostly gone, got no lectricity, just a gas stove. But four acres right on the Gulf was only eight grand!"

"Bussin fuckin *tables* at that Jimmy Buffett hellhole I toll you about, and every once in a while some tourist'd recognize me and wanna take pictures with me in my dirty-ass apron. They all thought I was on some Andy Kaufman type shit. Super fuckin humiliatin. Eventually I saved enough to follow Mama out here to Costa..."

"Saw me and man did she scream. Then scrammed. Had herself convinced I was gonna write about her new spot here in Tiburon, and that everyone and their shell-collectin Mama'd be elbowin in. I chased er all over Costa Rica for a little bit – a $3 bus will take you almost across the country you know, so she ran around for a little bit till I finally cornered her in San Jose, stayin at this place Hotel China: pretty much a whorehouse. (*Long pause*). Can you even imagine? Yr Mama stayin at a whorehouse? (*pause*) She answered her door and shrieked like (*sob*), like I fuckin stabbed her. Then she tries to run away but just fuckin (*sob*) falls over onto the dirty floor and (*sob, sob*)..."

"Tico taxi driver's somehow (*sob*), *somehow* navigatin all that crazy San Jose (*sob*) rush-hour traffic while Mama's fuckin floppin in my lap shittin all over an I'm thinking 'Man if this heart attack don't kill er, she'll die a embarrassment later.' (*chuckling sob*) But I gotta stop talking now man, cause it hurts like shit, bro. Hurts *bad*, y'know..."

I tried to point out that he has had an amazing, fortunate life and is living some people's dream. "But I cain't fuckin *enjoy* it!" he wailed. I found myself lecturing him about the dangers of skin cancer, despite knowing I should've focused on the dangers of suicide.

"You *are* killing yourself, Milton!" I too bawled.

"Duh!" he leaked pink watercolor tears. Though I don't have the proof on tape, I know he then said, "Pat man, I'm so grateful to you, bro." I sniffed for sarcasm. Smelling none, I thought we might hug when he leaned his orange reef of hair over my lap — but only to slip into my ziplock for my sunscreen. He then sat back, squeezed almost the whole expensive tube into his hand, and slathered it across his not-quite-as-morphing face, beneath stars now firmly mounted in a much calmer black sky. I was coming down. And our whole scene suddenly reeked of druggy insincerity.

I suggested we paddle back to Tiburon, and we did, in silence.

2.14 THIS LATEST ATTACK

Weeks wasted, but now here I stand. Or crouch. Finally. Cowardly. Camouflaged in palms above the two-acre hole that is The Ephraim Compound. The moon is bright enough that I can see, down in their hole, a grand wood-and-tin shack trimmed in yellow curtains, bolstered by modern siding-and-stucco add-ons. Behind the Main House squat three smaller, newer, yellow-trimmed tin sheds like healthy baby ducklings following a ratty mother bird. The farthest shed is where I've been instructed to meet Alana tomorrow morning.

Given all I've learned about her family these past weeks, I now find it difficult to cross this razor wire. Their Compound's topography begs intimidating questions that (especially in my post-psychedelic state) quickly twist into dark puzzles, inner battles. I should definitely wait until the drugs totally wear off to wonder, *Who threw that little pink bicycle onto The Main House's roof?* And, *Which Ephraim plies their living pushing that dented ice cream cart?*

And, *Why nail a three-foot ladder to that four-foot palm tree — a ladder to nowhere?* And if I ever want to make it down there, to her room, I will definitely avoid the heaviest question: *Was this all built with blood money?* as has been intimated. *Cancer money,* at best.

Then *SCREEEEEEEEEEEEEEEEE!* The alarm sounded. I hit the ground, inconsiderate of Tiburon's many large insects. The siren was a pair of macaws grappling on a branch above, screaming into each other's beaks in that particularly mean way Milton attributes to parrots being "one a the only other animals stupid enough to mate for life." I stepped back to avoid being shat on, and to study the birds in the dark, but they were obscured by a fog. What I assumed was a lingering hallucination, seemed to billow in over Ilka's roof, into my eyes and throat. Choking parrots chose flight.

I followed the smoke around the razor wire and through some trees, to a free-standing maze of cement walls: a 'house' with no windows, and no roof above 'floors' of dead, gray grass. A trail of swim-shorts and cellophane wrappers led from a hammock in one room through sandy, rain-damaged paperbacks and plastic shelling buckets that rattled, thumped and kicked. In the center of it all, lit by the moon, three pots of water hissed and foamed atop a hulking gray stove. Milton turned down the burners and added a fourth pot.

"I knew anything *this* awful-smelling would lead to you," I said. He'd obviously gone shelling after we split up.

He looked on me, frowning, then returned to watching his pot quickly boil. He gestured to a weakly writhing Whelk in a bucket at my feet. I lifted her to him. Milton dangled the Whelk over the pot by her long tail then *eased* her down in. Steaming water slopped unnoticed onto his purple toes. The boil ceased, then slowly returned. Parrots screamed to the clanging of pots, until the thick stench peaked in a foaming green-gray orgasm. Despite lack of roof, the gross/vaginal fog forced me out his back door, where more perspiring buckets brimmed with empty shells all soaking in steaming white, eye-stinging bleach water. I saw Milton inside lower a foamy pot onto his dirt carpet. With two forks he lifted out a small steaming King's Crown. He stabbed one fork gently behind the lifeless black body's operculum, and tugged like a surgeon stitching a wound: "You gotta *ease* the meat out," he said. "Cause once they're boiled they're *really* soft, and sometimes..." He paused, concentrating on the delicate extraction.

His doorway gave me a different angle on Alana's house. I noticed a tall chicken cage outside Alana's bedroom window. I wouldn't have assumed she'd cage birds. Milton bade me look at the complete curlicue of black meat on his fork. "Sometimes the end a that tiny little curl'll break off inside," he explained. "Then I gotta soak it for *months* to rot it out. Fuckin hassle. That happens I usually just throw the bitch away."

"And you do this right by Alana's house?"

"Ooh, Alana. She back yet?"

"Tomorrow morning."

"Sweet." Never had this word disturbed me more.

I watched him clean a couple more shells and as the sun began to wake, it admitted to me that *this* is how Milton is killing himself. Like some inverted vampire he picks the flats during sunrise and sundown, then spends afternoons burning to a crisp, cleaning shells in his roofless maze. I left an hour later feeling sick, knowing I need to detach from him. I need to leave him to heal or die on his own.

But more than anything, I just want him nowhere near her.

* * *

I'd felt guilty leaving all my possessions back at Rosie's when Alana expects me to have been living here in her room. I stopped caring upon finding used condoms in Alana's trash can. Two, deflated, bright yellow. And who knows how many more, down under year-old napkins and tampons.

Alana has her very own bathroom, in a personal cabina almost as nice as mine. She's given the choice of two beds, both neatly layered in worn, comfy blankets. Unlike my all-white sanctuary, Alana's floor is a violet swatch of carpet atop clean, naked dirt. Her four walls are papered the same bright yellow as all the Compound's curtains: tripping flower yellow, wilted condom yellow.

On the positive side, these condoms mean Alana hadn't considered that a new boyfriend might enter her room unescorted. So I'll just blow my over-sensitive nose, cover the rubbers with the tissue, and relate this latest attack:

The Compound's razor wire supported my flip-flops like stirrups helping me over a loyal horse. I'd spent two discombobulated hours back at Rosie's, printing out all the letters I'd written to Alana and making them into a book. I first edited out my many promises to woo Alana's mother and replaced all mentions of Milton with more celebratory moments culled from my personal journal. I then decorated the outside in construction paper, markers and tempera paint I'd earlier bought at a village store for just 2000 colones.

Down in Alana's dark yard, Milton's stink abated, still the air tasted like wet trees and bird shit. I could see her distant chicken coop, and heard chickens moving behind me in the dark. When a light blasted on in the main house, I crouched. Something near me growled as I monitored the yellow curtains. When their glow died, I stepped cautiously toward the coop, and my fate.

Ten feet from Alana's door, the growling surged, suddenly ceased, then a hard flat object smacked my neck. *An ill-fated judo chop? Ilka brandishing a ping-pong paddle?* Alana had warned that big iguanas fall from her trees. Either way, I panicked toward her little cabina, and was met with another wooden *SMACK!* across my forehead. As the fireworks dissipated, I saw a fat, pale figure in the dark — big, but not Ilka's size. It shifted its weight, grumbled and quacked. *A giant duck?* I laughed at the big cartoon bird, before sensing a quick rustle, a rush, and then *WHACK!* another paddle to my skull. A sharp scream exploded all around my head. Hands over ears, I screamed back: my voice and the birds' wailed like ambulances through the sleeping jungle and I knew, *No way these are ducks...*

Assuming the next sudden silence meant imminent attack, I preemptively flapped my arms to scare the creatures back. My open hand connected with a bony, feathered skull. Webbed feet slapped away into the shadows. To my right and left they waited, breathing deep as obscene phone callers. I gained composure. When their stereo grunting paused again, I stomped toward the nearest tall white blur. The animal backed up flapping, tripping, squawking. In the same motion I grabbed the other bird's head. Her beak closed around my thumb, I felt the soft inside of her throat, but I never considered letting go. Not even when I realized these were actually two swans.

My flip-flop foot like a lion tamer's chair held one swan at bay. The swan's first strike split my shin. Still with a handful of beak, I hopped on my unpecked leg toward the house. Somewhere in the melee, I noticed slivers of bright yellow shifting at the edges of Ilka's window – she hadn't ever turned out the light; she merely eclipsed it while watching me struggle. Things can always get worse.

At Alana's door I tossed the one swan away, and brought forth my own loud "*SSSSSSSSsssssssss!*" A warning. The swans backed off and opened their vast wings in tandem, creating an unreal cave of white. I hissed as loud and as long as it took to get inside the cabina, slam Alana's door behind me, and collapse into her mattress and her smell.

Lying in the dark now, I hear soft, girlish laughter reverberating somewhere outside. Raphael's down in this hole somewhere too.

And none too soon, Alana herself.

BOOK 3:
swan song

(THE EXIT PROCESS)

3.1 REUNION

I didn't quite wake in Alana's room, on my stomach, trapped beneath tabby kittens as softly pretty as Rosie's daughter Mimo. One half-open eye counted three purring orange blurs across the bed, equidistant like landmines. Two kittens lay limp against my hips. The other fussed and rustled in my crotch. The sun was up, but her room was still cool. The sun was up but still no Alana.

The most intimately placed kitten yawned and stretched her extra-sharp, dime-sized claw up my shirt. My body rocked in warning, squeezing her. She broke free and squirmed farther up into my shirt and the shock of all her naked claws at once flopped me completely onto my back. She survived only by maneuvering around onto my chest where she emitted an eerie childlike whimper of surrender and I stretched my collar open to illuminate her exit and cried laughing as she clawed toward the light. More awake now, I was faced with a swarm of freckles. Orbiting brown human cheeks? *Raphael!* my fried mind celebrated. *But why's he on top of...*

Alana's sisters, I realized. *I'm in bed with...*

Fighting a strong first instinct, I did not jump up and scream out. My morning stiffness (painfully tight in anticipation of Alana) wilted between the girl's knees as she purred back to sleep. Hung over and afraid, I easily avoided action in favor of silently wondering, *Should I wake them? Am I guilty? Is this illegal, here?* Thinking, searching for answers in the hypnotizing tapestry hung above Alana's bed, I accidentally fell back asleep and dreamt I'd finally found that other octopus hiding between the pages of Alana's *Book of Letters,* still alive and longing for her mate.

She finally exploded into the room loud as a lawnmower. Her sisters scattered like from the path of a moving collectivo. Alana frowned down. I shined up at her, shivering, tearful, *finally! You!*

"I told you *this* bed," she insisted, ready to fight, and I remembered how I love her *readiness.* Her naturally perfect eyebrows pointed down at the rusted bed frame against her calves. "*This* one!"

"I didn't even know they were there. I just woke up." I did not want to talk yet. Definitely didn't want to fight. Yet. For now I wanted only dolphin squeaks and giggles and so rose up on my tailfin, crossed the wrong bed and shoved Alana back — forgetting that all mattresses aren't American. Cheap metal thundered. Alana winced and grabbed her skull but didn't cry out. "Baby!" I shouted but did not apologize, just followed her down onto the cot, kissing her lump. The pain would not let her kiss back. My face pressed into her black hair until there was nothing. Nothing but her, here, finally. Alana groaned, swatted me away, rubbing her lump.

"I thought this was just your room," I said. My grateful eyes reacquainted themselves with her small, perfect — if slightly angry — face. "Why were they in here?"

"My sisters have three of their own beds next door but sometime they sleep in here when I am gone, because they *miss* me." Her face scrunched like she found their love distasteful. Her English sounded so streamlined now. Confident. Slightly alienating – until she rolled her featherweight onto me, squeezed my whole body with her whole body, and again I was forgiven.

"Oh man! Alana. Your swans at*tacked* me!"

She quit squeezing, did not laugh along.

"Look!" I lifted my split shin. "Why didn't you warn me about them?"

"They never hurt no one else." Alana poked the green-purple bruise. I did not cry out, afraid she'd judge me a pussy. She continued pressing the bruise like dialing a phone until she conjured a, "Yee-ow!" Then she laughed.

"Laugh all you like," I shot back. "I smacked that fuckin bird *crack!* upside her fuck*eeYEEOW!*" Bright hot pain lit my testicles.

She released them. Minutes of throbbing silence later when my breath was caught I lectured, "Alana, I like that you're rough. It's fun. But *not* my balls. Understand?" I lifted her face manually, forced her eyes up, feeling awkward taking the liberty. "That *really* hurt. You understand?"

She nuzzled deeper into me. "*You* don't hit my *babies!* Papi saved Romeo and Juliet *lives* right before he died, and he gave them to me."

I backpedaled, "Well, it was an accident, anyway. I didn't *punch* her. I was just trying to keep them at bay and… She's fine."

"Wait!" Alana sat up. Her eyes leapt to my bruise: "When this happened?"

"Last night," I admitted. "I just got here last night."

"You just came in Tiburon *last night!*" she shouted, regaining her accent while losing her cool.

"No, no, no," I faked a matter-of-fact tone. "I've been here the whole time, staying at that lady Rosie's cabinas." Before she could reprimand, I lied, "I came by a bunch of times but there was no one here." Then a little more truthfully, "And I just don't speak enough Spanish, Alana, to explain my side to your mom — our side."

She laid her ear back down over my heart. I couldn't see if she was seething. "Mami tell that you are good, without talking," she said. Her small hand slid under my shirt, kitten-like. The other rested on the drawstring of the same trunks I've warn for almost a month. "I understand," she cooed, "you are not used to our family way, the *simple* way without so much words. But if you just *be around* Mami, she will know you are good."

"Ticos have sonar?" I nervously joked. "I'm not confident I'd pass a *character x-ray…*"

"Ticos," he laughed, biting my lips for the first time in weeks-like-years. "Cute!" She patted my crotch before springing up.

"Wait. Where are you going?"

"You stay here," she commanded, stepping out the door. "I have not talked to Mami yet. I am going to say hello and try to make things good for you."

I had laid in her bed too long already, however. I needed to get up, move, smoke and swim and roll in the sand — now, finally, with her. "Let's get Raphael and take a walk to the pier or something!

I haven't even been out on your pier yet," I let slip. "I wanna see your pier! I wanna see *you!*"

"Joss wait," she insisted. "When I come to get you, things will be better." She leaned in and kissed the pocket between my eyes. Watching her leave, I felt a silly but nonetheless deep, deep dread upon noticing the Pizza Dive logo across her back. I've still never seen her in *any*fuckingthing else.

Outside of Alana's window, the symphony's nightshift had taken back over. Under its *tick-tick-tick*s some nocturnal animal loudly sobbed. I hoped to god I didn't injure her swan; though ordered to wait, I needed to go check. Sitting up was hard after so much laying, but I forced one long stride across the room and carefully peeked out the door, expecting a beak in the eye. The sobbing was pronounced, almost human. But no swans, so I stepped out.

Across the yard I spotted one bird, much smaller-seeming now, balled-up sleeping beneath that Ladder to Nowhere, silent. Pitiful moaning came from beyond her. Maybe from inside Ilka's house. Maybe Alana's negotiations weren't going well. Maybe we cannot be forgiven. Might just be about money since really you'd have to work at Pizza Dive your entire life to pay for a ruined wedding. I would chip in, if I didn't fear we might need to fly the fuck out of here.

Sure Alana was crying, I could no longer hesitate wrapping on Ilka's door. No one answered. I opened it onto an office chair, its back cloaked in Alana's black hair. Before Alana, on a small kitchen table, two cups of ice sat with two small boxes of cornstarch, each stuck with a straw. Ilka comprised the scene's entire background, a fleshy mountain range, her sausage fingers lifting a cornstarch to her severe, unblemished face and smiling faintly, sucking its straw. She then emptied ice into her dump-truck mouth and, crunching it like bones, mumbled Spanish to her sobbing daughter, who reached for the other powder-blue box.

"Oh hey, Alana, what are doing? Don't do—"

She spun in her chair, face and hair soaked with tears. She bawled.

"Oh no!" I dropped to my knees beside her. "Baby, what?" Instinct compelled me to hold her. She pushed me off, making room for her pussy-willow fist to swing hard against my temple.

"*Shit!* Alana! What's the matter!" I begged. She sprang up, her confusing Spanish pushing me against a wall the texture of wheat thins. I acquiesced to her drama, flinched at all the right times. But when she swung on me again I grabbed her wrists. In them I felt all her real, frail youth as she screamed and spit and wriggled in my big-seeming hands. *Why is she doing this? What am I doing to her?* Afraid she might break off in my hands, I dared release her wrists. She immediately put all 98 pounds behind one more punch that clipped my ear.

"Don't *hit* me Alana!" I shouted louder than I'd expected.

She crumpled to the floor, shrouded in wet hair. "Don't tell me what to do!"

I remembered the hot chocolate I'd spilled on her, how she'd silently let it scorch her and if *that* didn't hurt her then again, *What am I doing to her?* My hands crept into her black mess, searching for an ear, an eye... "Alana, what's the matter? What happened? I love you. Tell me."

"You kill Romeo," she barely said.

"Who's Romeo?"

She exploded again. This time, her fist found my ear.

"QUIT FUCKING HITTING ME ALANA!" I screamed even louder. "I AM FUCKING *SERIOUS!*" My high voice lacked control and reminded me Ilka was watching. My eyes scaled her mass, up to a much-too-wide smile that made me realize: Romeo was Alana's swan. My own tears surged. "No," I promised Alana. "No way."

"You break his neck!" she cried.

"No way." On sandy knees, I let my mouth fall where I thought the ear might be: "They were both fine last night. I swear on my mother's *life.*"

"You *say* you hit him! You told me this! And Mami saw you too!"

From behind my own private waterfall, I watched Ilka drink cornstarch into a smile that admitted outright *she* killed Alana's swan. "Alana look at her!" I wailed and pointed. "Look at her *smile!*"

By the time Alana cleared away her hair mat, Ilka's frown chewed ice.

My knees hurt like I'd suffered too much church. Or like I'm too old for this. "Come outside with me, Alana. Now," I ordered, standing. "We need to speak in private."

"No-o-o-o-o" she sang staccato with renewed tears. Her

grieving body fell back and crashed against a loud metal wall. Deprived of options, I turned and walked out, alone.

The Compound was silent, no chirping crickets, birds or geckos. Feeling through the darkness down in their yard, I couldn't even hear the Gulf. I thought to look for the swan's new grave, but assumed Ilka probably ate Romeo's huge body like feasting on the father himself. Juliet slept still beneath the Ladder to Nowhere, her neck folded in a heap upon her breast. Eyes closed, she growled when I stepped close.

I climbed up out of the yard, and left her be.

* * *

HOLY SHIT MANDY!

YES it's me! I can't BELIEVE you found my little story on the Web! How embarrassing. I should have changed your name. I mean, obviously I changed some details, such as, it was NOT "easy enough to let [you] go." Either way, I'm glad you loved my fictionalized account of our friendship. It's the only creative piece I've ever had published — my other clips are obituaries. I didn't even get paid for that piece, but now I got YOU out of the deal! MANDY! THANK YOU FOR FINDING ME!

I'm glad to hear you've thought of me all these years, but it sounds like you've also learned that NO ONE is worth idealizing. I'm as rotten as any other adult. I'm not as ugly anymore, maybe. My red hair has faded and my acne cleared up. I guess I'm more confident now, too. I found love! Or thought I had… I am currently at terrible odds with MY significant other, as well. She hates me right now. Not as bad as your situation, but I feel your pain, all the way from COSTA RICA — yes, seriously. My lady's a native. I pen this email from a tiny crazy village in a rainforest. So at least there's that…

As far as you and your daughter moving out of Pennsylvania (DAUGHTER? Holy SHIT!): move anywhere but Ft. Heathen. If your ex-husband does allow you to take your daughter out of state, DON'T choose FLA! I know we had fun there as kids, but today it's completely sterile, soul-dead, WRETCHED. I JUST finally escaped. I do understand wanting oceans, swimming pools, warm winters and new clean schools for your child, and I'll help you any way I can but… If it must be FLA, maybe try Sanibel Island if you can afford it. Sanibel's very near Ft. Heathen but peaceful, protected, no strip-mall sprawl. There's a book about Sanibel you should check out called *Almost*, by this sort of famous FLA author, Milton Chapman, whom I've actually become friends with here in Costa Rica. I will tell you more about that when we see each other, which I am sure we will!

Wow Mandy! I could keep writing forever if the internet weren't the only expensive thing in C.R. I haven't checked email at all since I got here and only visited this internet cafe because the owner has my fishing pole. I have it now, still I'll check my email A LOT more often if you promise to PLEASE keep me updated!

Tujo compadrisimo!
Patrick

3.2 BIRDS' NESTS

Optimism followed the rain and me back down the slope into Alana's yard. Moonlit Juliet, still balled-up defeated and now soaked beneath that ladder, did not growl at my approach. Her eyes have remained closed almost as long as mine today. Tiptoeing through the sopping grass to not disturb her, I almost stepped on Alana's fingers. She sobbed against the nowhere ladder, head down, black seaweed hair draped over knees. I squatted and risked, "I'm so sorry Alana…" She fell into me. Her limp arms caught my neck, her fingers locked like prayer. The memory of her earlier violence toward me still glowed hot, but her tears extinguished my pride. "We should go inside," I suggested, longing to remove her goddamned work shirt. She replied with louder tears. Between the rain and holding her, I was soon just as wet. I dug into her hair and brought her naked face to mine and kissed it and tasted saltwater and wondered if *Maybe I could follow the water down to its source, down into her well of heartache and…* Then what?

Unable to accuse Ilka outright, I lied again to Alana, "I looked out your window before I went to sleep and they were both fine. Alana I *know* I didn't hit him hard enough to…do *that*…"

"She."

"She?"

"Her."

"Romeo is a boy?"

"I don't know," she said. Her eyes closed. Regarding her like a concussion victim that shouldn't fall asleep for fear she wouldn't wake, I shook her sharp shoulders: "Alana. Look at me." *How could her own mother destroy an innocent, beautiful creature? And that swan.* "I would *never* hurt an animal, Alana. You know that."

"You promise?" She placed my own hand above her breast and pressed my fingers into her heart, which I did not feel beating.

"Yes," I answered, praying to whichever god exists, that I did not kill her pet. "Let's go in," I tried again. "It's not good to be out in this rain."

"Juliet need me."

I've so often fantasized about sleeping outside with her, here. But not like this. I slid out from under Alana, collected dead palm fronds from around her strange yard, and arranged them up and down the Ladder to Nowhere, creating a protective lean-to over Juliet.

When I'd finished, Alana managed a smile: "Thank you."

"She'll be fine tonight." I extended my hand. "Please come inside."

Her head fell forward, which I took as a *yes,* and pulled her body up. She rose light as a ghost. Over the *tap-tap-tap* of rain on so many plants, I heard Juliet growl as I dragged limp Alana away.

The sleeping triplets bolted upright on their sister's bed, their three small, sleepy pink mouths open and their bleary-yet-fearful eyes locked on their big sister. Freckles swarmed their small faces, long arms and little-girl underwear. Alana pointed to the door. They shot up and out synchronous as fighter planes trailing flame-like hair out into the rain.

When they'd gone Alana whimpered, "Let me fall. Onto my bed."

"Wait." I couldn't help smiling, working her wet shirt up over her slumped torso and unhooking her bra. Contrasted against her loud depression, her breasts and brown nipples were as long and swollen as I'd obsessively remembered. Her cool nakedness made her smile too, almost. We stood holding each other until I gave her permission: "You can fall now."

She collapsed on her bed, fetal. Kinked black hairs peeking from her underwear surprised me as, curled up, she seemed her sisters' age. Looking up at me, her eyes questioned mine, even as she reached above her head, grasped her headboard, yawned and *ssttrreettcchheedd* out, looking again like a long, full woman. She relaxed and I let her close her eyes. The sound of my shorts hitting the floor re-opened them. She smiled, then turned back away, onto her side.

I slid in behind her, parted her hair and massaged the little wing nubs on her smooth back. She moaned gratefully. Her fragile shoulder squirmed into my kisses. She reached back, pulled my hand over her cheek's wet horizon and pressed it to her mouth. "Your hair on your arm is *very* red," she whispered and pulled my hand between her long breasts. I stiffened painfully. I closed in slowly, insinuating myself into the triangle formed by her skinny thighs and that smooth plane of cotton...

"Patrick, no," she whimpered, and resumed crying.

I slipped the sword out from the stone. "No, no, I know. I didn't *want* anything," I claimed. "I know you're too depressed. I just... can't help getting turned on, being here with you like this."

Her soft tits hugged my hand like she believed me.

Throughout the long night I lay there trying: trying not to be depressed about trying not to fuck her. Trying not to even brush against her. Trying not to move. Trying to just fade out after 20 hours of sleep. She needed only to be held, and I feared it would upset her if I went and slept on the other bed where I could cough and twist and masturbate. Eventually I compromised: "I'm taking a walk, Alana." I slipped my shorts on. "I'll go check on Juliet for you." I hoped this might elicit something positive. I received only her heavy bad-dream breathing, and the rattle of her doorknob on my way out.

Outside the rain had stopped, but there was the smell of more coming. Trudging up out of the yard, my eyes met just the brief top of the sun peeking over the mountains — as if the sun and I were climbing opposite sides of the same Earth and had paused for a staring contest. Whenever the sun rose an inch, I took a corresponding step up, then waited...stepped up, waited...determined to keep this slow pattern until the sun and I faced each other at full height. *By that time*, I figured, *my erection will have subsided.*

But not far into our game, I remembered Juliet. I'd walked right past her. Across the yard I saw that most of her lean-to had blown away. She looked more pathetic and sad than her keeper. I collected more palms and fixed her shelter, wondering how much longer she could live like this.

Then, remembering our game, I turned back around — only to find the sun looking down on me already.

Either The Gulf filled up with recent rain, or Alana brought this water back with her — water and so much confusion I forgot to wear shoes or sunscreen. I tromped along the beach, accepting the burns and inevitable cancers and worrying where I will go if forced to leave here, leave her. I haven't even given her the *Book-of-Letters* yet, and already it's *this*.

I choked my Dad's rod with both hands. The reel was dusted with salt. The guy'd obviously absorbed it into his collection, maybe even rented it out, put it away wet. You can't trust white people. Earlier as his truck's graffiti blurred away from me I grabbed a fistful of his cast-net and held on until he'd towed his dust cloud over the bridge and around the bend, out of sight. Now I had a pole and a cast-net to catch bait *and I'm in Costa fucking Rica woohoo! And Mandy of-all-people! And Alana will eventually calm down... Our love is real...* I felt almost good skipping out onto the tiny pier.

Standing before a rippled sea of silver baitfish, I remembered I'd never thrown a cast-net. I'd seen it done plenty: first snuff out your joint, loop the rope leader around your wrist, grab two handfuls of the big net's small lead weights at both 10:00 and 2:00 — most fishermen also *bite* the net at 6:00. Not I. Which is surely why my first throw like a clenched fist punched the million-minnow school. Ideally, a giant, perfect spiderweb cleanly crashes the water, sinks for a second then you jerk the leader, contracting the web, trapping whatever creatures it landed atop. My net returned tangled and knotted, holding captive just one finger-mullet. With a hook through her tail, I cast her out.

She landed far out in the channel, the death zone — where a human head now bobbed, buried in water to the chin, the face aimed at the sun. I assumed it was Milton. As my bait drew fanged fish to the vicinity, his face lowered and yelled, "Pat? Zat you?"

His hair was muted by water and distance. I did not shout back for many reasons; it felt wrong to antagonize the silent morning. I reeled in to go search out another fishing hole as his singed shoulders – the same violet color you'd find *beneath* the epidermis – paddled toward the pier. Emerging from the water, up the stone steps, his pink eyes widened. "Holy shit! A *cast-net!* Damn! Where'd you git this? Damn!"

"It isn't mine," I said, my dangling finger-mullet gasping for water.

"Then you definitely don't mind if I…" He scooped the net off the dock and frowned, "Ah, shit. Some dumbass fucked it up, didn't even try t'fix it." Milton plopped down and began picking at the nets' knots, the world's most important task. The sizzling dock drank water from his dripping shorts. "We gotta watch out who sees us usin this thing though," his catfish lips whispered. "Cast-nets are illegal here. Backward-ass country; you kin rent a teenage hooker outside the goddamned police station, but you can't throw a cast-net. S'true what they say bout Ticos, 'It ain't the heat, it's the stupidity.'"

"Stupid like Alana you mean."

"Naw, naw," he chuckled, untangling knots three-at-a-time like a magic trick. "Yr girl's definitely the exception."

I didn't like how he said that. I don't like how he says most things (except for the little I've read). I noticed my bait no longer breathing and dipped her in the water: dead as a popsicle stick.

"Don't worry man, I'll catch a *shitload* once I fix this bitch," Milton promised.

I cast out anyway. My electric-green line buzzed in a high arc that should have lasted days, but the reel shuddered and unraveled into a green bird's nest that prematurely jerked the bait down from the sky. "*Fuck!*" I disregarded the quiet morning and slammed Dad's rod down onto the dock.

He laughed. "Frustrated, ol Pat?" I sat but didn't answer. "Y'know Pat, I been thinking, how brave it was a you to follow yr girl all the way to this fucked-up place. Senseless, but brave. I ackshly *admire* you Pat. Enough that I'll even ask — and I never ask *nobody* — what's botherin you, dude? Why you bein such a little bitch?"

I couldn't help laughing. I now realize he was simply aroused by my obvious depression: an emotional jackal desiring to feast on the black emotions he'd sniffed out. In that moment though his compliments and rare concern softened me, and I regurgitated everything. I told him of my battle with the swans, about Ilka killing Romeo, even my sad sexual clash with poor, broken Alana. By the time I'd vomited it all up, the sun was brutally awake, the tide had fled back out, the jungle orchestra was wailing and Milton's wet hair had fluffed back to dry life. He finished untangling the net and sat in a zombie state, off somewhere deep inside his red head. He'd been this way since the very first line of my story, "Alana finally got back the other night..." I'd assumed he squinted down into the water so intently monitoring baitfish.

When I'd finished he asked, "She's at her house? Now?" Then noticing something in the water he grabbed handfuls of the cast-net at 10:00, 2:00 and yes, a mouthful at 6:00. His perfect spiderweb sailed out and out and — too far out, trailed by its entire whipping yellow leader, which he'd forgotten to tie around his wrist.

"Ah *shit!*"

We watched the net sink, pinning hundreds of baitfish to the Gulf's floor. The trapped school exploded in a synchronized silver panic, repeatedly, like a giant mirror being shattered over and over. Milton shrugged it off. Another casual holocaust. "Now see man, *that's* what you should write about," Milton declared.

"You losing the cast-net?"

"Naw dude, that story you just toll me bout you and yr girl. That was *awesome.*" He nodded. "I almost wish that'd happened to me."

"That is *fucked* up!" I erupted. "You're heartless, Milton. You think I should write the 'story' of Alana crying too hard to have sex with me?" *I can see where even your mother would hate you,* I didn't dare say.

"Ah shit, never mind, bro." Milton squeezed his pink temples white. "Just givin you the writing advice yr always askin for."

"Asking for?" I stood up, brushed fish scales from my shorts. "When did I ask you what I should write about? Never! And I *definitely* wouldn't ask your advice on what I *shouldn't* write about. I've never asked you for shit. I didn't even ask your real name when I knew you were lying. I didn't even ask why Alana would be friends with such a *fucked-up person!* I never asked that one because I know the answer: same reason *I've* been hanging out with you, or why anyone is interested in you at all: because you wrote a book and we assume you are smart and sensitive when in reality you are just a *stupid fucking redneck!*" Snatching up my Dad's electric-green bird's nest by its now cracked handle, I recognized its resemblance to all my other botched shit, and remembered my earlier decisions to avoid Milton *and* the sun. Without a care for his sizzling skin, I turned and...

Couldn't go back to Alana's, where I left my sunscreen. And no way could I sleep more at Rosie's — sleep being all there is on a Tiburon Sunday, besides church. Only the Gringo Restaurant is open today. Which sounds pretty bleak, but at least I'm not trapped in fucking Pennsylvania, like Mandy. *I should get Mandy's phone number.*

Either way, I turned and finally left him.

* * *

Oh Alana,

Sorry drunk and maudlin here at Nos Barra, waiting to follow Tiburon's social universe out to another jungle dance without you. I hope you'll be there, but then I hope you won't. Fuck. Of course it could be worse. Like Orlando's current scenario: his Alpha Jennifer has held Tiburon's belle-of-the-ball title my entire stay — until she tripped away to some far-off beach this weekend, and returned to find herself replaced by a tall fifteen-year-old gringa with long hair curlier than yours, and a protruding mouth like Orlando's. Across this bar now, their similar mouths grapple. Amazonia's not my fetish but immediately upon her arrival, your village celebrated her, and Orlando claimed her. Orlando's made the rounds twice already this evening, letting every Tiburon resident but you slap his bare back and congratulate him on his newest (and from their fuss I must assume FINEST) conquest.

Rolando gave me all this new drama's details. Do you remember kissing Rolando once? How about me? It was more than once, I think, me, though not much more... Sorry: my fifth Heineken. It and I both sweat at the bar beside Rolando, whose sunglasses continuously aim at his cousin's new prize. "Jennifer gonna be at this dance tonight too! We gonna see some SHEET, mae!" he laughs, breaking my fucking heart.

And now, not ten minutes later, Alpha Jennifer stands on my other side, flanked by her two Jennifers (maybe you're friends with them; how would I know?). Upon their entrance, Orlando abandoned his new one's long slender side under the guise of making the rounds yet again, this time alone. The three lovers now stand spread around the bar in a literal triangle, peeking at each other then looking away fast, as everyone but you watches on, smiling, shameless. I don't want to be like these people, Alana.

The most infuriating thing though, to me: though Alpha Jen doesn't CONGRATULATE Orlando, she seems as easily adapted to this new situation as everyone else! I sniff for HATE in the air around her: nothing. Insane. In this same scenario you, Alana, would rip me apart. Or, I hope you still would.

I still hope for no mercy.

I couldn't attend the dance. I'm staying the night at Cabinas Del Mar behind the Main Road. But first I stopped by your house, to give you this.

I've been so caught up dodging the backdraft of my mistakes I haven't found the right moment. NOW isn't ideal either, but I'm scared you'll never get this if I don't give up waiting for the right time and just: here. It's a book of letters I wrote for you, while waiting for you. This book is yours. As am I.

Of course I'm sorry, baby. I know you don't feel asexual ON PURPOSE. I know the pain you're in; I too have buried beloved pets. And I understand that in the gnarled face of your sadness I've been selfish. I've been extra afraid feeling like this relationship and my last one are running the same course. I know it's not the same. But in my panic, it felt the same.

I know you hate "I'M SORRY." But it's the truest thing I can say.

I hope you love this book. And me.

Love, still,
Patrick

3.3 Y'ALL'S PROBLEM (DOMINICAL PT. 1)

The book still sits outside her door. She's gone. Milton's nowhere either. The tide is too low for him to simply be off shelling. They've gone to *Dominical* together. Whatever Dominical is.

Stepping back through the Compound just now, I heard Ilka's thick staccato breathing and "She go! *You* go!" She was inside, on the phone I assumed (with a gringo?). The conversation sounded heated. I knelt outside her curtains, hoping I might overhear her admit she killed Romeo. I'd brought my tape recorder out this time, as I will henceforth, so no valuable evidence escapes. For now I gleaned only "She go! You *go!*" before realizing these commands were aimed at me.

Caught, I asked the sunny confessional drapes, "Where is Alana?"

"Go!"

Louder, I attempted, "*Donde - esta – Alana?*"

Somewhere on the Compound, little girls laughed at Mami's growing anger. "She go a Dominical!" she roared.

"Dominical? *Que es Dominical?*"

"Dominical. She go. You *go!*"

"Who'd she go... Er. *Con quien?*"

"*You go!*" she shrieked, meaning *get the fuck away*. She cranked on her thunderous garbage disposal, ending the first conversation we'd had since I called their house in Tampa.

Dominical? I stumbled onward, in the direction of their bright white washer-dryer I hadn't previously noticed rattling outside, near Alana's neglected *Book-of-Letters. Washer and...? Dominical? Garbage disposal?* Blinded, I did not register Raphael, standing at the washing-dryer there folding several versions of his same school-blue uniform.

"Pa-treek!" he spun, knocking his clean pile to the dirt.

He seemed a bigger, taller, *riper* version of his old self. Also less freckled; Raphael's yellowish pallor and thicker upper-body — which cracked my ribs with a bear-hug — made me wonder if Ilka hadn't been keeping him locked away in a hole with no sun, and nothing to do but push-ups. She hadn't beaten down Raphael's sweet, unassuming spirit though. He patted my back and called me "brother."

"Where have you been?" I asked.

He bent and, collecting his uniforms, claimed, "I don't know..." Then, "Where have *you* been? She say you would be sleeping *here!*"

"Your sister is upset at me."

"I know. She shouldn't be." His unstoned eyes sympathized. "You did not kill Juliet, I know."

"Well, either way your sister is gone now. To Dominical. And I think she ran off with Milton."

"I hate that fokeen guy."

"Me too."

We both flinched when a large animal roared, somewhere near. Fear engorged Raphael's eyes. "That is Mami. I have to go." He hugged me again almost violently then hurried away with his clean uniforms, directly into that continuing roar.

* * *

Dear Mandy,

Thanks for your compliments on my pretentious episto-
lary prose. I do most definitely empathize with your struggle; I too
am sick with grief. My girlfriend — a young but amazing, beautiful, fiery, hilarious, all-around well-written character — has been
gone from my life for two miserable days now, to DOMINICAL, a
city the travel website I just clicked described as a "party town"
north of where I stay (I just stopped myself from typing 'where
I live.' I'm not sure I'm alive anymore). Worst of all, she may have
gone with this scary alcoholic sociopath. I'm not worried she'll
cheat; he is disgusting, a sketchy pervert more than twice her age.
He's an interesting specimen but. I'm not worried she'll cheat.
     Still she just left with him without goodbye and it's scary.
Now I can't decide whether to take a $3 bus four-hours up to
DOMINICAL or just wait her out here, in her village. Or maybe just
go the fuck home — or rather, FIND a home, and then go there.
Could I come be your live-in maid and babysitter while you're out
jobhunting under the stark FLA sun? Kidding. Though I do hope
your ex lets you and your daughter move wherever you decide.
Even FLA.
     Until then, DON'T burn your wedding album! Don't even
joke that way again. I understand how easy it is to hate photo-
graphs of past mistakes, but hide the album away somewhere
until your daughter is old enough to ask for it directly. Which she
will. So don't.
     Eerie though, that we had simultaneous book-burning
urges; I handmade Alana a beautiful book of letters I wrote to her,
but we've fought so much recently I left it outside her door and it's
just lay there since. The wet jungle air already has it looking like
an artifact from a sunken pirate ship. I was SO ready to chuck the
damn book into the Gulf, or burn it — until I realized that if she
does betray me HEY at least I got some good writing out of it! If
the book is still rotting outside her door tomorrow, maybe I'll take
it back, flesh it out, and submit it around. Publication might com-
pensate for the heartbreak, right? Really, I hope to never find out...
     More (and hopefully better) later...

* * *

Buck moped into the internet cafe, mumbling about Jonathan's plans to drive them somewhere they hadn't yet decided. "Anywhere," he said. "Matters not. Got any suggestions?" Bummed Buck admitted that he and his wife aren't getting along. I strategically confessed that the girlfriend I'd traveled here for had run off to Dominical, "a little beach town, not far from here, supposedly a *really* fun place..."

"Aw damn, baby," Buck predictably nodded. "You need to go to Dominical? We'll drive ya. Jonathan'll be cool with dat. We'll leave the mornin after next."

Then back at Alana's using their machine to wash clothes for tomorrow's trip/hunt, I noticed another condom in her garbage can. Flesh-colored. I plucked it from atop the trash and studied it closely but couldn't tell how recently... It looked chalky, but... I turned it inside out, lifted, sniffed and finally, with shaking fingers, touched the reservoir tip — just as their truckload of laughter roared up.

Milton's industrial headlights screamed through her bathroom window. I ran up the slope out of the deep yard and faced the beams like a gator being poached. Milton stepped down from the cab in a wetsuit and disappeared around the tailgate. Alana leapt from the truck and onto me, pawing, kissing — *in a new clean Pizza Dive polo?* And just small bikini bottoms. Her beak pecked the corners of my mouth until I pried her off, barely able to breathe. "Man what the hell?"

"'*Man*'" she giggled, "All gringos call even girls '*man*'."

"What the *fuck*?"

"We go *sir*-feen!" Alana bubbled.

"In Dominical. I know. What the fuck? What the *fuck*, Alana?"

Beyond her, Milton's eyes avoided mine. He watched Alana's bare legs while dragging a long red kayak from his truck, then away into the maze of cement walls he calls home.

"Why you ask '*what the fuck*' if you know already?" she joshed, hugged me, jumping up-and-down, then rolled down her hill into her yard, leaving me with Milton.

Wetsuit peeled down around his bacony torso, Milton unloaded surfboards and beer coolers and *She and I have never even had a fucking beer together*, I realized. "So you guys just went surfing, huh?" I challenged. Milton clanged and banged tackle in lieu of answer. "Huh? Just surfing?"

When he'd unloaded everything he finally scoffed, "What else would we be doin?" He grabbed a hose the same red as his skin, twisted it on and rinsed his red truck.

"Well you certainly weren't wiping out whole colonies of defenseless animals together, I'll bet."

Trickling water.

"No, you weren't. And why not?" I asked.

"In Dominical? Ain't no shells in Dominical."

"Bullshit. You didn't go shelling because Alana would never talk to you again if she knew what the fuck you are doing here in her village!"

"I dunno bout that."

"I do."

He hosed as I throbbed and trembled. "You know Milton," I said limply, "she didn't tell me you two were going to Dominical. She *didn't even mention* that she was *leaving for two days. With another guy.*"

Nothing.

"How would that make *you* feel, Milton?" I exercised diplomacy. "How should *I* feel about it? Huh?"

"'At's y'all's problem," he replied, squeezing the last drips from his hose.

3.4 FOR SPECIAL OCCASIONS

I remember drinking three guaros at Nos Barra, then flopping back to the Compound where Alana slept in the thicker of her two beds. I vaguely remember drunken anger when she did not wake for me and beg for me inside her. Still in the morning I woke to her, whispering kisses: "When you sleep you go, '*mmm... mmm*'. It's cute."

"Thank you," I ached.

Raphael's teacher (and Milton's) had asked Alana to decorate a room for the younger kids' birthday parties. "Come help me and Raphael paint the birthday room," Alana ordered, her new clearer diction chaffing my hungover ears.

"Let me wake up first."

"Oh you *never* wake up," her voice grimaced on her way out the door. "I meet you at the school."

I could hear Alana's sisters, somewhere, berating each other in Spanish. Then giggling? In a fast angry jumble, one sister cursed another as "Alana!" which confused me, until another sister accused "Pa-treek!" Then they all died laughing. Dozens of them, it sounded like. Finally I heard the real Alana shout — effectively silencing her sisters and the rest of the jungle.

Finally outside the swan coop, I was immediately hit with green clouds of death stink boiling in from Milton's yard. I couldn't see Juliet. Breath held, I rushed up the slope toward fresh air, the Gulf, the school, and Alana's waiting arms.

I found her outside Rosie's, catching up. She joyously dragged me onto the Main Road and at first it felt like *me* showing *her* around; she skipped and hopped, so *enthralled* by this place, as I told her all the gossip I'd learned in a month. Along our way, her beak pecked every long-lost Tico friend. Her animal eyes flickered at every fleeing parrot and lizard. Each sad stray dog received personal minutes. Tiburon is definitely *not* her Tampa.

In yet another first, Alana escorted me inside the school's fence to a tiny, windowless room. There, the Teacher's missing tooth balanced out her conservative blue skirt-suit. Her creaky drinker's voice volleyed headache-inducing Spanish with Alana. She didn't seem to remember me – until the end, when she winked, "Make it pre-tee for me, Pa-treek." Her behind swayed out the door, leaving us to our imaginations in a tiny, windowless room.

We had no paint though. Alana stayed and waited for Raphael to arrive while I smoked pot on my walk to Tiburon's biggest General Store, which stocked only primary colored paints but whole cans for less than a dollar! Plus glitter and glue and 10-cent brushes that shed plastic hairs. Though unfortunately, no tinfoil. Smoking had imposed upon me a great stoned vision of the school's Birthday Room as *outer-space scene*: red-ringed planets, flaming meteors and yellow stars floating upon a vast navy-blue *nothingness* among satellites and rockets cut from tinfoil. But for foil, it seemed, I needed to seek Jordano.

I found him pleasantly hustling at the Gringo Restaurant. Waiting for him to close his current deal, I peeked into the Book Exchange: still no *Almost*. But among the romance novels, Steele, Grisham, Kerouac and *Siddhartha*, I found *Astronauts Like You: An Illustrated Book of the Cosmos*! I had worried that space travel fantasies may have eluded Alana and Raphael, out here in the jungle. So this book of examples was serendipitous.

Jordano was less so. "What can I do for you my frient?" he finally asked. "How is Alana? She back? What you got there, paint? What you gonna paint, mae?" — a thousand questions meant to prohibit all answers. Finally he repeated, "What can I do for you, amigo?" and paused.

"I need uh, tinfoil."

"I cannot get."

"You can get me a *laptop* but not tinfoil?" I scoffed. "C'mon Jordano, it's for the school. We're decorating a room for the kids. A Birthday Room."

"There is no teen-foil."

"But you know what I'm talking about though, right? Tinfoil? How do you know about tinfoil if there's none in the whole village?"

He led me to the back of the restaurant, far enough from gringos for him to safely admit, "Okay, I get the foil for you." Jordano removed his sweaty ball-cap and wiped his doubtful brow. "How much you need?"

"A lot, actually," I answered, imagining the room's whole ceiling foiled silver. "Ten rolls?"

"*Ten fokeen rolls*?" he hissed. "*No way*, mae! I cannot."

I led our voices back down: "Well, how many can you get?"

"OK, I get 10," he conceded. "I get 10 foils for...Fy-tousand colones."

"Jesus!" I exclaimed. "Fifteen bucks? For tinfoil? That's insane. That's as much as *mota*. As much as a *puta*!"

"Shhh!" he insisted. "I get the foil for you or no?"

"Shit. OK. Go ahead." I gave him all but my dinner money.

"Stay here," Jordano commanded, pushing my shoulder down as if planting me to the spot. He scurried off.

Waiting there though, I happened to glance inside the service window at two rolls of tinfoil beside a cutting board... Suspicious, I crossed the patio and leaned out over the Main Road to witness Jordano entering a grocery store just *two doors down! He walked 10 feet for 15 bucks?* My sense of justice flared. *Goddamned weasel!* I stomped down the steps and tapped my foot outside of the store until Jordano sauntered out carrying heavy-seeming brown bags (*booze!*).

"Weasel!" I shouted. Passing tourists paused. Rosie's relatives cut their *collectivos'* engines.

"Whot?" Jordano flinched, startled but unafraid. He lowered the bags to show me the foil. "I get the shit for you. Whot?"

"You went *right next door* for 15 bucks? That's robbery."

"Thass how mush it fokeen cost, mae," Jordano defended, stuck holding the bags. "You don't fokeen tross me? I don't even make no money doing dis for you. I do for you as Alana frient!" He wasn't pleading though, just admitting to himself the mistake he'd made in dealing with me — me, whom he finally judged "Gringo fokeen asshole." He dropped both bags in the white dirt, stepped over the foil and away down the Main Road.

Raphael! He bounded into the Birthday Room, a pubescent superhero, again crushing my ribs. His hand clamped my shoulder as I detailed my artist's statement for the Birthday Room. Sister and brother did not, in fact, jazz on my outer-space theme. Not at first. They'd watched space-shuttle takeoffs on the Costa Rican news, but this Birthday Room called for aliens, ray guns, unrealistically flaming comets, big fat Mother Ships — and they'd never even seen Star Wars. I couldn't tell whether I felt grand, or patronizing, exposing them to all these pop-culture concepts. Either way we were, for a moment, distracted from our real problems — like her goddamned Pizza Dive shirt. Maybe she'll throw it away, now that it's ruined with paint...

Raphael also wore a uniform: school pants the same navy as our spacey *nothingness*, and a light-blue dress-shirt he peeled down to a tight white T, before participating in our hedonistic, paint-splattering laughter. Everything was perfect again, finally. When our first ecstatic wave settled, we got down to the details of both the mural, and our lives. Raphael asked if I'd written anything new. "I wrote a little *book*!" I announced. "For your sister..." Alana flared her jealous little beak, mad that I hadn't told her. I had taken it back to my room at Rosie's. Now she was excited and wanted it. Everything was perfect again, finally.

"I try to write too," pale Raphael disclosed. "I try to write my story of going from Tiburon to Tampa. But it's too hard," he sighed. "I need help..." My instincts considered referring him to a Semi-Famous Author, but hell no.

His sister's brow furrowed. "Learn gee-tar, not writing," she nodded gravely. "Or pain-teen."

So we painted. My cosmic picturebook American memories plus Alana's recent angsty mourning made for good art; she wet her brush with a tear to paint space-swans piloting the deep, deep blue.

Raphael *nailed* the shadowy imposition of HUGE, monolithic star-fighters. But his details were cramped and sketchy. I knew exactly why: "That's great Raphael," I assured him. "But try holding your hand further back on the brush…"

"It is *'farther,'*" Alana corrected. "And don't tell my brother he is wrong with *art.*"

"Baby, I didn't say he was wrong." I looked to Raphael. His face subtly shrugged. "I'm just saying he'll be more relaxed," I explained. "And he'll have more control if he…"

"It is his art! Let him do how he want!"

"O.K. Fine. Jesus."

Sunset meant the start of Raphael's classes (the young kids attend day classes, the older kids go at night). He stepped back and studied our unfinished masterpiece, buttoning long sleeves over his paint-stained T. We hadn't yet foiled the ceiling, and already it looked like the work of asylum inmates. Little kids dig that aesthetic though. Raphael himself had never seen anything like it, and stood, clothed and smiling, long after his school bell had rung. Finally he kissed our cheeks and closed the door gently on his way out.

I surveyed our work, thinking, *The teachers are gonna* hate *this…* Turning to consult Alana, I found her standing on a chair tacking up foil. I was faced again with that big, round PIZZA DIVE logo halfway up her back. "*Christ* Alana," I said. "Take off that god-damned *shirt* and burn it with the roadside trash."

Unexpectedly, she lifted the logo and all that ropey hair out through the neck-hole, leaving me eye-level with her long nipples, which I clamped onto gratefully. She held my dull-red hair in small hands, moaning. Emotional walls crumbled, finally, returning us to what we had in FLA, almost. She smashed my face into her so deeply I could not hear but *felt* her whimper, "I love you Pat-reek."

Atop each other on the thin blue carpet, we smoked our first joint together (exhaling into her balled shirt so the schoolkids wouldn't smell), which intensified the pleasure of nursing sweat from her long breasts. I never touched her *munaki* — not with my hands, just my knee and, at one brief point, my furry orange wrist. This restraint because I do understand her current despair. I also don't think it will take much more of just my wrist, to break her without begging…

Retracting from our romantic tussle, I noticed fingertip-sized bruises on her thin arms. "Your fiancé do this?" I asked, changing the mood like a colored spotlight. She faced away. "Guess I don't have to ask how your birthday was," I joked, strangely unaffected by her bruises. She appreciated this and smiled teary eyes, her breasts sloshing gently to her sad laughter. Then, in changing the subject, I really lit the wick: "So I assume you know Milton's name now."

"I always know Meal-tone's name," she frowned.

"Before I left, you said you forgot his name," I softly reminded. "I have that letter where you said he had red hair, but..."

"That's not true. I always know his name. Meal-tone is famous!"

"I don't know about that."

"His book ease *so* good!"

"You read it?"

"Two time! *San-ee-bel* sound like Tiburon!"

Jealousy compelled me to add, "Then you probably know he pays to fuck Raphael's teacher."

"Oh, Patrick, shut up!" Alana snapped. "She was my teacher too *and* she babysit us when we were little. She is my good family friend. And Milton is my good friend too, so just shut up talking about my friends, O.K.?"

As she snatched her shirt from the paint-splattered floor, I leapt again to her nipple, glad she hadn't yet read her book of letters. Still time for another re-write...

Alana had cranked me up terribly. After hours of painting and sweating and suckling, on the walk home she squeezed and tugged my swim-shorts gently, pulled at my elastic, peeked down in and "Oh Pa-treek," she gasped, kissing my ear, squeezing it again, before suddenly skipping ahead, sliding away between her familial razorwire, and down into the Compound.

Now that things were good again, I knew I shouldn't press her. Still I shouted down, "You sure you don't want to take off these clothes and jump in the Gulf and um, I dunno..."

"No Patrick. Please," she whimpered up from the grave. "I am too upset. Please baby. I look for Juliet."

"I'm not pressuring you," I claimed, and continued on my

own down to the water.

In the Gulf just beyond Ilka's pier I floated alone in water to my jaw, every appendage stretched out stiff, except the one arm stroking rhythm beneath the tide. I scanned the beach again for witnesses as the arm churned faster and faster and tension built until finally the biggest wave came, and I did too: a wondrous *seagasm*, akin to a pleasurable version of a plugged-in TV thrown into the pool while you're swimming. Sun exploded inside my underwater eyelids as I heaved it out, toes extended, breathless, near to drowning — free enough to cry without shame as the ocean drank both discharges away, before they could exist, almost.

3.5 Post-Juliet

DEAR MANDY,

    Thanks for caring... And CONGRATULATIONS. Did your ex DECIDE to ALLOW you to take your daughter to Ft. Heathen or did the judge FORCE him to let you? I'm sure that, for all of their faults, my parents (though they might not remember you) will help you find an apartment, maybe a job in Ft. Heathen. Maybe they'll even babysit. I myself was only kidding about being your live-in nanny/maid. I honestly wasn't fishing for your magnanimity, though I do appreciate your offer to take me up on that. It does sound fun, and if things continue so badly with this woman, who knows where I'll end up...

    For now though, I feel I should stay and fight for this. That sounds emotionally fatal, maudlin at best. In Shakespeare's plays it seems romantic, brave — not that I need to be a hero, either. It's just that sometimes happiness must be fought for, they say. So I'm not leaving Costa Rica any time soon. Hopefully.

    Please do send along your phone number though.

Love,
Patrick

* * *

Juliet's dead now too.

I knew this as I chased Alana's scream down into the Compound and kneeled again outside yellow curtains, listening to her sob. Understanding only conjugations of *morir*, I flopped back to her bed to await punishment. An hour-and-a-nap later Alana's wet eyes smeared across my cheek: "Juliet... Juliet is..."

"I know, baby, I'm, it's, it..." Took everything I had to not agitate her with apologies. Knowing the answer, I asked out of simple self-hate, "How did she..?"

"Because she was *lone-a-lee!*" Alana wept and growled and pounded her small, frustrated fist against my diaphragm. Again. Then again, hard. Then harder.

"Baby stop. I know it hurts but... That *really* hurts."

"*I* don't *really* hurt?"

"Alana, that's not what I meant." She went cold on my chest. I even thought I smelled hate. We lay still for a bad half-hour, in which time I noticed, on the tree-stump nightstand in the dirt beside her bed, a small pink copy of *Almost*. The tattered paperback lay far enough away that grabbing it would mean stirring Alana, who would not appreciate my losing myself in literature during her misery. But I couldn't resist at least *skimming* the thing. "I'll bury her for you," I offered, sure this topic would raise her head from my arm, to meet my eyes. "Maybe they'll let me bury her by the airstrip," I mused, holding her gaze, *readjusting* my shoulder and snatching the novel.

"Mami already threw away the..." She choked on the thought. "She threw her away!"

I pushed her head back down onto my heart: "Shhh. Baby. Shhh." But no 'sorry' no matter what. I opened *Almost* one-handed and read the inscription — For Mama — as Alana studied the green fog rolling through her yard. She wiped her eyes, "What in hell is *that?*"

"Death," I enjoyed answering. "It leads right to your *friend* Milton. He's boiling animals alive. Rare animals. What do you think about that?"

"I don't know…"

"'I don't know?' How long do we have to know each other before you stop pulling that with me?"

"Four months, at least?" she barely laughed and wiped her eyes again, to see the fog more clearly.

"You know Alana," I couldn't help myself, "I've spent a lot more time with Milton than I think you have, and it really scares me to think of you alone with him. Let's just say, if he came into Pizza Dive, I might've spit in his food…"

She scoffed, "You joss don't like him because he don't like you."

"He doesn't like me?"

No answer.

"He said that? You defended me, right? Or you let him change your mind about me?"

"Well, he *is* very very smart man," she laughed. "And famous!"

"He is *not* famous! And *fuck* that guy!" the village idiot shouted for all the village to hear. "You admire him? He's a monster! Go to his house right now and see. Go! You'll see what I'm talking about." I sat up, rolled her off me and shooed her from her own room: "Go! Go *fuck* Milton since you won't touch *me* anymore."

"Aagh!" she bellowed and aimed a small finger at the book in my hands: "You *read* while I *cry* to you, Pa-treek! *You* kill my Romeo and I watch Juliet for *six days* get more lonely and lonely until she *die!* And *you* don't even say you are sorry!"

"It was only *three* days, Alana, and you told me not to…"

She punched me harder than she ever has. Her small, balled paw fit deep in my eye socket so perfectly that both my eyes screamed. "Alana! Stop! I'm sorry! You *know* I'm sorry! You *know* I love you!" She ripped the book from my hands and with it slapped her name from my mouth: "Alana, I'm *sorry!*"

From behind my wet blur, I saw her door slam. I wiped my eyes and watched her Pizza Dive logo flee up into his green fog — *Almost* under her arm.

Her bedroom remained empty through the night. In the morning I went to *Cabina's Del Mar* to brush my teeth, and found Jonathan and Buck eating breakfast at Rosie's window. "We were just comin up to get you to go to Dominical," Buck announced.

"I'm sorry, man," I sighed, "but I can't go anywhere today."

"S'cool, bruh," Buck grumbled. "I don't necessarily feel like goin nowhere neither." He turned to Jonathan: "I'll just wait, and go to San Jose with you this weekend, buy a ticket back to New Orlins. MY wife's not comin back here…"

Rosie told us of a much closer beach. Jonathan's wimpy blue mini-van panted us out past the airstrip cemetery to a patio bar hung with long, empty hammocks pinned to the underbelly of a small, seaside hotel. A retired ex-pat couple from Michigan had only recently bought this "property" — without knowledge of the Costa Rican law allowing anyone to camp 50-feet above any high-tide line. "Legally, folks were allowed to sleep under our house," the husband chuckled, satisfied with his new situation. "We figured we might as well make money off em, so we opened the place up."

Jonathan griped about the gringo-priced beers. After two apiece plus ceviche, we all rushed the ocean, sans sunscreen. The North Pacific was just one vast churning silver *muscle,* pulling and pushing us under and around. Only one of us remained consistently buoyant: that same white dog who'd stolen Milton's flip-flop. His name was Chester, we were informed by the bar owner, who did not own Chester. Saltwater never seemed to sting his big vacant eyes. As we flailing humans coughed out our nostrils, clumsily battling the sea, Chester remained calm, not seeming to notice the swells lifting him up into the sky then setting him down slowly, safe.

We eventually fought our way back onto the beach. Chester remained in the surf. Feeling suddenly like I might cry, I stepped away from Jonathan and Buck, down to the shoreline to stare out across the muscular ocean at Chester — in such deep maudlin contemplation, I didn't feel my arm toss a plump stone at his bobbing head. Then another. Each time, dumb Chester would swim out to where the rock broke water, as if to fetch. So I'd toss another, farther out, then another, even farther. Chester was just a speck on the horizon, vainly searching the dangerous whitecaps, which carried him *stories* into the sky.

"Hey Patrick, man!" Jonathan finally shouted, "What the fuck? Cut that shit out! Leave that poor dog alone."

I woke, and jogged back to them. "Man. I'm losing my fucking mind. I *love* animals."

"Especially octo*pi,*" Jonathan scowled.

The rest of the whole hot morning and afternoon, Chester gave us true, unconditional friendship on a level that genuinely threatened my sadness — and also gave me an idea, "We should start a business here in Costa Rica!" I shouted, as our four white heads bobbed in the rough surf. "Rent out big loyal dogs, by the hour, to tourists who are here by themselves and need companionship!"

"Beach buddies!" Buck seconded. A wave swallowed all but Chester. Buck's smiling beard emerged: "Our slogan could be, 'Lonely? Well we've got a *bitch* for *you!*'"

"A dog whorehouse!" I gurgled.

Jonathan rolled his eyes and ducked under, allowing Buck to casually add, "Bruh, I need me a regular whorehouse right about now..." And for a weird moment, Chester was forgotten. "You been to one yet, Pat?"

"A whorehouse?" Actually, I've never interacted with a known prostitute, aside from Milton's Ticas on that beach — and I *passed* that test, for whatever that was worth. Though Tampa's streetwalkers were all male crossdressers, after many lonely drinks at the end of long restaurant shifts, I had driven down Nebraska Avenue with a knot of tips in my wallet and a wild drunk pulse in my temples and crotch and if I'd seen a real, even semi-pretty girl for rent... Still now, I simply copped to, "I have a girlfriend."

"Y'all's problem cleared up?" Buck asked.

"Not really."

"Well, my wife's gone, bruh. Took the baby."

"I'm sorry."

"You know," he smirked, "it sketches me out when people apologize for things they didn't do." He tried laughing as he turned and swam for the shore, followed by Jonathan and me.

"What sucks though, honestly bruh!" Buck shouted, back on land, "is all the *pussy* I've turned down in Costa Rica! You know what I mean, Pat?" Under the patio he continued, and let me record it: "I know Jonathan doesn't approve of prostitution, but I for one am fascinated; it's such a shell-game here. When I first got to Costa, I took this trip to Puerto Viejo on the Caribbean coast, to cook at some tourist hellhole for the week. On my day off I'm hangin by the water, alone, drinkin beer, smokin dope. Even by myself it was just, one of the greatest days of my life. Then the *finest* black chick I ever seen, about 24 years old — don't tell *nobody* this, Pat. She wasn't built like black chicks back in New Orleans — I love New Orleans' girls, but this black Tica wasn't *thick* like them. Tall and *svelte* bruh, but also nice and round up top, and around back. Guys always claim that girls they fucked looked like models, but she did. She definitely had a little more meat but. She had these long-ass braids. I don't know where the hell she got em done out here in the jungle, or how she paid for em. At the time I almost kinda suspected she was an American, pretendin to be Costa Rican? But that makes even less sense than the truth: homegirl accosted me on the beach and just flat-out says, 'Let's go fuck.' Course I'm like, 'Look, I'm not givin you any money. I ain't got any money.' She says, 'I don't want money,' in English, with this beautiful kinda Jamaican accent. Damn, bruh. Course I figured even if she *did* let me fuck her for free, she'd prolly rob me afterwards. But the bottom line being: I shouldn't be thinking about screwin *no bitches at all.* So I keep sayin, 'I ain't got no money' and she keeps sayin 'I don't want money, I just want to fuck. Let's go.' 'I got a wife,' I tell her. 'Is she here?' she asks, then she *laughs* at me: 'Well then, you don't have a wife *today!*' Man, aside from being hot, she was like this really funny and warm person with a *beautiful* fuckin voice and beautiful laugh. Definitely woulda been the prettiest girl I *ever* had.

"So anyway, after telling her for the twentieth time, 'I'm not giving you money for sex,' until she's almost *mad* at me, I finally say, 'Listen, how about you just show me a place where I can go swimmin' — cause there aren't any real beaches in Puerto Viejo, just this dry volcanic rock that slices your feet up bad. It's hard to get *out into* the water there. I tell her, 'You show me a good swimming hole, and I'll give you some money.' By now she's *shoutin* at me: 'I don't *want* any fucking *money!*' Still she takes me to this amazing little swimming enclave. Soon as I jump in the water, she stands on the edge of this volcanic rock — which don't hurt *her* beautiful little feet at all, right! — and right there in front of God and everyone, she stretches that lean black body up to heaven and peels off her tiny little tank-top. God*damn,* bruh. Just the most nice, full, tight, smooth tits. She jumps in with me, all grabbin my dick and... Just *torture.* I tried to bail. Told her I couldn't bring her back to my cabina cause the owner lady was Catholic. She says 'I buy us another room.' I'm like *huh?* How is this *possible*? Don't tell nobody Pat, but I ended up in a tent with the girl, with a condom, *just* *about* to do it. *Almost.* She was *right there* buck-ass-beautiful naked. But I honest to god couldn't go through with it. What shoulda been the defining sexual fantasy of my goddamned life was just *torture,* bruh — specially now that I'm prolly gettin a divorce... I think about it so much, how *damn* I shoulda done it. What difference would it a made? I keep thinking about goin back to Viejo and lookin for that chick. Biggest regret of my life, hands down."

Then once more, "Don't tell *no*body..." before the tape runs out.

Under the hotel, the air was cool and our sandy sunburns began to prickle. We ordered a strange doughy pizza with more gringo-priced beers and watched the bar owner organize glass jars across his shiny wood bar top for our viewing pleasure: jelly jars filled with formaldehyde and animals too dangerous, or just too exotic, for him to resist killing and keeping. "We found all these critters in just our couple months cleanin off the property!" the Owner laughed. His jars held bats, scorpions, snakes' heads and rattles, peach-sized beetles, shin-length millipedes, "And this," he announced, bringing the last jar up: "We found this one just a few days ago."

It was some sort of mollusk, or octopus or squid, limp inside a delicate white spiral seashell.

"We didn't know *what* the hell it was," he continued, "till this redhead guy came in, said he wrote a famous book about seashells."

"Milton Chapman!" Jonathan bleated, and gave me a look that spoke of kayaking. "That guy's a dick."

"Seemed O.K. to me," the Owner laughed. "A little nuts. I never heard of his book — but I'm not the best-read fella. I knew he had to be *some* kind of famous though, ugly sunburned mug like his with the *cutest* little Tica squirmin in his lap. She had the most beautiful long flowing hair. I knew she wasn't a prostitute neither; smart little chick, spoke English real good. The kinda Tica that regular guys — ugly guys like us — can't get. Unless we *pay!* Right?"

Everyone snickered but me. I stared into the weird jar to keep from crying.

"Anyway," the Owner resumed, "fella called this a *Paper Nautilus*. Said they're rare, specially on this coast. Said he woulda gimmee 20 bucks for it if he wasn't leavin Costa Rica soon – gotta envy that jetsettin *author's life!*"

"Was she going with him?" I asked.

"The Tica?" he laughed. "Now, why in the hell would I know *that*?"

Everyone laughed again.

In the jar the Nautilus floated, its pink skin flaking.

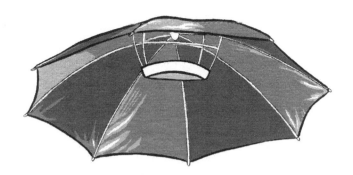

3.6 COMATOSE

Poor, poor Milton,

I laughed horribly loud when the village doctor asked if I was your brother. He didn't even flinch, because he hates you like the rest of the village. He allowed me more laughs when he informed me, "Mr. Chapman will not wake up for some days, he's a berry bad sunstroke, berry dehydrate, berry weak. He almost die. So its hard for him waking up. His skin is so bad, he need a hospital en San Jose, or Los Estados Unidos." And the whole time I couldn't stop thinking about what you've said so many times about Ticos, "It's not the heat, it's the stupidity." Sitting over your swollen purple body right now, it looks to me like a pretty good mix of both.

You look dead. Or at least gone enough you couldn't have witnessed my lowest moment just now after the doctor left. But if you did just see me smack Alana, then you also know she hit me first. Three times. And SO many times before that, by the way. If you are faking this coma, then you heard me warn her, and yet you saw her swing again. And again. You also saw only half my hand graze just the BACK of her head, before you saw me crumple onto her bed.

No. You could not have repressed laughter hearing us argue over YOU. I do believe you're out cold –- or out HOT, given the circumstance. I also believe you planned this, positioned your nearly dead carcass on the beach by the Ephraims' pier RIGHT where you knew they would find you and "give care to his burns, until he is well," because Alana doesn't realize yet that you're UNwell on the inside. A scorched soul.

Don't let her pity mislead you. It IS pity, and ONLY pity. "Milton is sad," she laughed to me. Your cancerous resemblance to her father is the only reason she cares about you. That and your book. And though you might've tricked Alana into caring, if her mother wants MY red head on a platter, wait till she sees YOURS! Ilka will go a long, hard way toward exorcising the GHOST of her husband…

Just to be sure, I plan to tell Alana EVERYTHING you haven't admitted, about all the animals you've killed, and the women you've bought. She'll consider your crimes against nature more unforgivable than my little three-fingered slap to the back of her head.

One way or another, you will wake from this coma alone.

Your protégé,
Patrick

* * *

Alana wasn't back home as the sun began setting. On the Main Road I hoped to stumble into and collude with Raphael, or Jonathan, or shit even Orlando, anyone who could help me rid her bed of Milton's carcass. I stopped by the internet café – Mandy hadn't written back yet. *I don't want Mandy I want Alana,* I knew, walking out near the school, where I was dumbfounded by a terrible smell, a waft of sulpher. And there was Milton Chapman.

Conscious, unfortunately, but alone, thankfully, with many bags of groceries stockpiled as if for disaster beneath the colorful shade of a wide umbrella hat, striped like a beachball. A wacky weatherman's hat, the ultimate cancer protection. Milton's face drooped, his lips melted like those of the schnauzer I owned as a child, who bit into a live lamp cord, recovered, but never again looked or acted right. Milton's arms glowed red and purple beneath a thick crust of white medicinal lotion like pink cake frosting. The doctor had estimated a weeklong nap, but in not 24 hours Milton's eyes shone whiter and clearer than I'd ever seen them.

"Learned *your* lesson now I guess, huh?" I mocked.

I stopped laughing however, upon noticing, emblazoned in black script across his white T-shirt:

MILTON CHAPMAN
Regresala Ephraim.
Puerto Tiburon
El Muelle Grande.

Return it to Ephraim... "What the fuck?" I asked myself, knowing Milton would not answer, especially not after that hateful letter I pinned to his chest — his chest, which now advertised Alana's name and address. This though, was a shadow of a smaller version written on the hat's single white stripe. Late-afternoon sun shone through Alana's feminine script, projecting it large across Milton.

"Why's Alana's name on that hat?"

"S'*my* name." His smile cracked his cheeks' dried lotion.

"Oh right, I didn't recognize your *real* name. I thought you didn't want people knowing it."

"Naw." Milton adjusted his groceries. "Just you." He turned and flip-flopped away.

"*Why is her fucking* address written *on your* hat, Milton?"

"Her mama gamy it!" he shouted haughtily. "Wuzzer daddy's. Guess he ain't usin it...I gotta go!"

He picked up his step, running almost. The whole village might've heard me yell, "She'll never love you Milton! *Never!*" Children gawked from behind the school's fence. My eyes watered and blood pumped as if I actually *had* run up behind and elbowed that *stupid fucking hat* off his skull. In reality, he continued fading into the distance and I stomped up the steps of the Gringo Restaurant to start drinking — unwittingly giving her time to pack up all of the clothes I will never see her wear...

I paid my tab and skipped up the soccer field with a buzz and a more hopeful heart. The Gulf was full of water and I was sure I had a shot at fixing this – nothing fixes itself. And yet things get fixed. *So there must be hope*, I thought until, up on the lip of the Ephraim Compound, I spotted that loud umbrella hat, and her Pizza Dive logo, zigzagging together up the opposite slope, up into the jungle. Towards Milton's house.

I sprinted silently around the bowl's rim. Ahead of me they scampered between Milton's walls. I followed, pressing against the rough cement outside, hoping to beat them to his truck and... *Then what?* Through glassless windows and watery eyes I could barely see them in there. I could sense, though, a new cleanliness: no cookware around, no books or seashells. I scurried behind them through the dark, followed them out and around the corner. I saw Alana look behind her like her name was being called but neither of them saw me. I noticed their hands locked together: a team, dashing away... My heart heaved. I collapsed on wet dirt.

I sprung up at the growl of his truck. "No! Alana!" Sweating, trembling, I scrambled toward his headlights. "Not with him! No! ALANA!"

The truck screeched backwards, spitting sharp gravel at me, and giving me one last view of their cold profiles.

I found no solace in diving back down into the Compound to scour and trash her room and count *six* condoms in her garbage, altogether. The jungle cawed mocking laughter.

3.7: THE UGLY ONE

Alana,

You know what hurts? Not this. This is almost painless. Telegraphed TOO far in advance for tears. I've always known that I don't know you. Not enough to trust you. So how could this hurt now? You don't even know ME as well as some childhood sweetheart I haven't seen in 15 years — her name is Mandy, and I'm leaving C.R. to go be with her. A nice consolation prize for me. While YOU, Alana, choose poison. Dumb little girl. You don't even know.

For one thing, Milton killed Romeo. As he surely has every night you've ever been home, Milton was watching your cabina out his window when Romeo attacked me. He killed your pet, to turn you against me. It worked. Or really, you let it work.

Because I suspect your point all along has been to eventually make me suffer, I will have you know that in my 27 years I've suffered MUCH worse. My ex, Natalie — that name you "hated" hearing. Why? Just to FUCK with SOMETHING? Well Natalie, Natalie, Natalie, Natalie, Natalie, Natalie, Natalie was crazier than you, even. So was I. I got over it. I don't necessarily think you will. During our four years together, Natalie and I broke up more than 100 times. To this day I've NEVER witnessed two people clash so hard, so often, like fucking rams, loud enough to sometimes attract police — anger I can't conjure anymore even when I need it. The up side is, nothing HURTS like that anymore either. Thanks to people like you. And Milton. And Natalie. Natalie gifted me with scars far more pronounced than this new one on my chin. Whereas, during my three-week wait in Tiburon, I many times totally forgot about you. For many long moments you did not exist. So it should not be hard from here, to forget entirely.

So just for the record: there will be tears from neither us. Nor will Milton cry when you inevitably pull this same shit on him. No. We're all masochists and nothing is worth our tears. It's not even worth this letter — which I won't give you two the satisfaction of reading together.

This story is all mine.
Thank you for it.
Goodbye,
Patrick

* * *

"No *way*, bruh! She's a fucking *school*teacher?" Buck slapped his eyes, laughing. "*No*-ho-ho *way*. That's *sick*, bruh!"

Across Nos Barra, the Teacher's forced smile unveiled a second missing tooth as she bounced in the hairy lap of a large gringo, who dug simian fingers into her chocolate flesh. Entranced by his steamy pink face, I recalled how my parents always vehemently differentiated *owners* from the mere *renters* in their condo development; *renters* have no rights, no say. Whereas this renter acted like an owner, calling the Teacher "*my* piece of ass" to his buddies, laughing in her oblivious face.

Buck and I considered who else in Nos Barra might be for rent, and Jonathan never once laughed. Buck announced to more people than intended, "*No thanks* on that raggedy teacher over there, but I have decided I *am* gettin a hooker before I leave Costa Rica. No way around it. I mean, why not? I ain't spent a dime on nothin else the whole time I been here. My baby girl's nowhere around. I need a grudge fuck. So there you have it."

Buck's hopeless laughter attracted Orlando, still beautiful when drunk, and Rolando, whose sunglasses masked his intoxication level. Their silent slaps stung my burnt back — I'd choose a thousand lashes over one mention of Alana. "Yah yah, *putas* all around!" Orlando joined our conversation. His beer bottle circled the air. "*All* of these girls are *putas*."

Jonathan squinted. "These girls do not look like hookers."

Orlando and Rolando laughed.

"Don't be fooled cause they ain't wearin makeup, bruh," said Buck. "They ain't like American streetwalkers. The game is more vague here. They can be just regulars girls you're hittin on at the bar who aren't attracted to you, but maybe right then she needs some extra money so she exercises the legal option." His every 'she' lashed Alana across my memory. Buck continued, "They got places in San Jose you can go and just straight-up pay. But in little villages like Tiburon, it's vague."

"Sounds like you've been researching this," Jonathan frowned and studied my response to Buck's conspiratorial grin.

I switched subjects: "So what happened to your new girlfriend, Orlando?"

"Jennifer?"

"The one I *kick away* Jennifer for? Oh the tall one was *so fokeen* sexy! But she stay for only one weekend." Orlando shrugged.

Alana and I didn't have even one Costa Rican weekend together. I gestured to a murder of young Ticas across the bar: "What's the deal with your sister's friend?"

"Your *sister?*" Buck and Jonathan shouted in tandem.

"Yes," Orlando said. "My sister like a sex very mosh."

"Then why's she always with those geriatric gringos?" I wondered.

"Dey have much money," shrugged Rolando, cousin of the girl in question. "She do anything they want, mae. I seen these one video they make of her, with all fat gringos stickeen a feesheeng pole in her ass, stuffing money up there..."

"Ugh fuck y'all, no." Jonathan couldn't take it and walked off. And he was right, it was sad; though she did radiate sex across the bar, her clean, bright smile belonged to a simple, nice person, someone's relative who babysits, trapped here on the head of a pin occupied not by angels but by burnt, leering sport-fishermen.

"Hit was fokeen *hot* video, mae!" Rolando laughed.

I rewound: "But what about her friend?"

"The ugly one?" Rolando asked.

The Ugly One's sensual brown skeleton, topped with short greasy hair and big maroon pout, belong on a Paris runway. Her plump mouth compelled me to ask, "So how are you related to *her*, Orlando?"

"No," he claimed, palms up. "I don't tink." Then mischievously, "You like? I go tell her that you are famous book writer making *thirty-thousand dollar* for your book!" Before I could ask where he'd cribbed that figure, Orlando's bare feet slapped away, around the bar. He spoke in her ear while pointing across at me – all so fast and shocking I never had the chance to look away. She stared me down unsmiling as Orlando returned to us. "She have sex for fy-tousand," he announced.

"Orlando! No, geez, I wasn't... I didn't..." I couldn't tell if I was faking. "I didn't even know she... I just..."

Buck laughed. Orlando slapped my sunburn again then focused all his attention on two California hippy girls that Jonathan had quickly teamed up with. Attempting to (tonight at least) try and get laid naturally, Jonathan and Buck planned to take the girls to build a fire on some beach, any beach they wanted. Buck was afraid to leave me alone at Nos Barra in my condition. Still he did.

Deserted, I focused on the captive Teacher. Above her smile her eyes projected 'save me.' But this all seemed her choice. I could maybe offer her more money and get her away from him as Milton had done, but... Morbid thoughts swarmed like *no-see-ums* until her ape drug her off like he owned her. When in truth he was a mere *renter*.

Nos Barra was empty by 1 a.m. when I checked Tweety's Daffy Duck watch and saw that it was actually 9 p.m. The village had evacuated to another jungle dance to kick-off of a three-day rodeo fair. I returned to my cabina for money to hire a wildly expensive private collectivo. My last jungle dance, ever.

The fairgrounds were much like FLA's department-store-parking-lot carnivals: high-flying, decrepit steel rides and food-on-a-stick. Except here we also got bullfights and hard liquor. The collectivo dumped me out directly beneath Jonathan and Buck and their girls, all screaming in plastic chairs attached by thin chains to a monstrous robot squealing louder than all those at its mercy. Stepping back in case any parts flew off, I reflexively swatted at a gray moth fluttering toward my face. She skirted death, to land on my heart, where I let her be.

Jonathan and Buck wobbled off the ride. Their bra-less dreadlocked California girls (one a redhead, though I couldn't have cared) are much groovier than the Jennifers. Also grimier, having spent months caked in Costa Rican salt and sand and drinking so many nights in a row and sleeping it off in a hot tent — a lot of us look to have crawled on our bellies up the face of the Earth.

The couples kept company and I followed them around, exchanging glances with the moth on my shirt. I stayed always on flat land, drinking twice as much whiskey as any of them and so not needing further disorientation. During a rare moment alone ordering drinks together, Buck described to me, "This thing I seen on T.V. today, one of those *When Animals Attack* shows. I fuckin love those, bruh, when the animals finally fight back — though they *are* usually killed in the end... But there was this one guy who'd fight animals, different kinds. Hand-to-hand! On his cable access show. He had his wife tape him doin it. Anyway, homeboy was fighting some kinda moose, or deer, and the deer pins him to the ground just *wailin* on him with its hooves and antlers, just kickin the shit out of the guy. The guy's wife's screaming her head off but her husband's shoutin back, '*Don't stop taping! Don't stop taping!*'"

When I asked where he'd been watching TV, Buck's laughter tapered off. "Oh, I rented a cabina. In Tiburon. Next to the Post Office."

"I live there too!"

"I'm only stayin one more night," Buck mumbled. "John's takin me to San Jose tomorrow, to get a flight back to New Orlins." I made him promise to take me. "To New Orlins?" Buck sipped an icy spill off the side of his cocktail. "You'd like it there. It's cheap and wild. But San Jose, sure bruh, we don't mind you taggin along. You leaving Costa too?"

Yes, I am. To where, I don't know.

Their scraggly girls wanted to dance, so even I paid 2,000 to follow everyone onto another dancefloor in a humungous chicken coop. Orlando's sister was nowhere. The beautiful Ugly One stood pouting alone. I doubted whether or not I could fake a seduction in miserable air so thick with cow dung. Then *she* asked *me...*

Not the Ugly One, but a pretty, white Tica (Mom's tourist guidebook claimed that Ticos proudly consider themselves Caucasian). Her dark hair was cut in a type of modern bob I haven't seen out here at all, and her white skirt-suit looked dry-cleaned. The only evidence of her authenticity were her cocoa-colored, withered parents on a bench behind her, gawking at the flashing lights and erotic dancing. I accepted the girl's silent invitation to dance and nodded to the mother and father before leading her away. With only tentative glances up from our feet, we danced three songs. The girl didn't mind my clumsy dancing, and I remembered Hochi's warning: "Costa Rican women will *impale themselves* on you to get to America." I was soon sweaty as the rest of the crowd. This girl remained powder dry, composed. I tried shouting Spanish questions, then hoped I'd understand her answers. She explained that she's in town from University of San Jose, on a break from studying architecture. I think.

When I paused to pant and offer to bring her a whiskey or beer, she shook her frowning head, "No. Coke." I bought one whiskey and one Coke, which she appreciated so much she brought it over to show her parents. I shook their hands — drunkenly willing to meet the folks and flex my Spanish, despite looking like I crawled on my belly up the face of the Earth.

Dragging their daughter back into the crowd, I asked her the last question I was able to in Spanish: *"Que es sus nombre?!"*

"Alana!" she yelled, dancing, dry.

This was enough to end everything. *But don't be so sensitive...* We danced on. This new Alana made a disparaging remark about my dripping whiskey. *Already trying to change me...* I defiantly gulped, glanced down at my wet shirt and remembered: *My lucky moth!* At least *she* was still with me. I thrust out my chest, showing her off to the new Alana. She stopped dancing, bent close, and smashed her against my heart.

Buck and I made tomorrow's San Jose plans with Jonathan before he dropped us at Rosie's. Lounging, smoking a joint on the bamboo balcony, Buck gave me every detail about his wife leaving with the baby and, "This *When Animals Attack* thing I saw on TV today!" I let him go ahead and re-describe: "*Don't stop taping! Don't stop taping!*" He laughed and before he could cry, Buck shuffled back to his cabina to "pass-the-fuck out." I remained out on the balcony, watching late-night passersby, seemingly up to no good — including Jordano, his unbuttoned shirt tucked up under his wet pits.

"Fssst! Jordano!"

"Hello, my frient!" he smiled up, drunk and seeming to have misplaced my mental file, so no need for apology. "You need anything tonight, my frient?"

"A girlfriend," I answered sincerely, but knowing how it sounded. The alcohol plus pot plus Buck's thoughts on the subject, now made renting a prostitute sound as reasonable as a deep-sea fishing charter. "What's Orlando's sister up to tonight?"

"Oh, she really busy girl right now. She almost a professional. I can get her for you in two days, you tell me now."

I didn't admit I'm leaving tomorrow: "I might be dead in a few days."

Jordano's wet finger tapped his moustache. "Oh! I have a good one for you! You like *ski-knee*?"

"Yeah sure. Skinny's better than fat I guess... "

"Oh she *ski-knee* man," Jordano promised. I followed him back down to the soccerfield, fantasizing that he would lead me to the Ugly One, who would be a much better last memory of Tiburon than *either* of the Alanas. "She very, very sweet too," Jordano campaigned. "Dis one I go with myself. I rent her for one whole week sometime."

A bolt of sobriety shocked my brain, bounced down into my crotch and ricocheted out my mouth, "Wait! Is she missing a couple teeth?"

"*Si, si.* But she *sweet*, mae! And it's a good with a missing teeth."

"No! No way." I grabbed Jordano's shirt, which ripped when I tugged him the opposite direction. "Not the Teacher."

"She a actually Counselor or someting, I tink."

Our comedy of errors was interrupted by a thin form trickling toward us, a skeleton from the shadows: the Ugly One. I jogged to her. "Venga a mi cuarto conmigo," I commanded. She smiled passionless agreement and we left Jordano without goodbye or a tip.

Under the orange streetlamps I could tell she was young. She revealed only her name, Pamela, and her monetary value: 6,000 colones. A thousand too much. Still I stuck beside Pamela, trying to make her laugh the way I do free girls. Through drunken gringo eyes Pamela was perfect: thin shoulders wrapped in tight brown skin and backless shirt. One of the most beautiful women I've ever made laugh. 6,000 was still a bargain.

Upstairs we sat on my bed, splitting her beer. I stripped off my stinking socks and offered her *mota*. She said she only smoked cigarettes, never pot, but that she would smoke with me now. Her first puff choked her out of bed. Eyes watering, she coughed into the bathroom. Hacking and snapping her fingers, she spit thick into the toilet then breathed, sipped her beer, laughed it off, and returned to my bed to try again.

I asked her how she likes to be touched. She extinguished the joint without permission, pantomimed some bodily pointers, and inquired about condoms. "Oh si, si." I plucked my lone condom from its hiding place between the mattress and box spring, and dropped it on the floor beside the dead roach, her empty beer bottle, and my rotten socks.

I first *needed* to brush the night, the week, this whole disaster off my teeth. Over the scrubbing sound echoing inside my skull, I heard Pamela announce that I would have to pay her first. "Diez mil."

"Ten thousand? You said six thousand."

"Diez mil."

"I'm sorry. I misunderstood you then," my mouth foamed. "I can't pay you 10,000. You can just go." I pointed my toothbrush to the front door.

She clucked and squawked then finally conceded to stay. "Pero no sexo," she stipulated.

"That is a lot of money for no sex." I used English since it's my money. "No. You can just go." I think I wanted something to go wrong so it wouldn't happen. She stomped her foot as I rinsed and spat, but silenced when I returned to bed, flashing a new clean smile and 6,000 colones. She copped to our initial deal, and tucked the money into her tight white jeans.

Now she seemed happier. She swung her spider legs over the bed and told me to remove her suede pumps. On my knees I obeyed, revealing long perfect toes. She peeled her white jeans down past tiny underwear just darker than her skin. I unsnagged her cuffs from her pretty, pointy ankles, and accepted that this was really going to happen.

Against the headboard, I asked her to lay back on my chest. She'd said she liked it soft, and so do I, so I tried to barely touch her while exploring all her soft dips and bones. She did not seem to notice. So I repeated, "Que quieres?"

The huge mouth she'd forbade me kiss, frowned. She laid back on the mattress, knees up, eyes closed, arms above her head. "Do it," she muttered. By the wisp of light from the cracked bathroom door, she looked asleep or dead. I hovered over her big closed eyes. I pecked her throat. Her beautiful corpse didn't quiver. "Oh c'mon." I warned, "If you are not present, I can't pay you." Though I already had.

She sat up and lurched toward me. Like starting over, she grabbed my crotch through my shorts and told me I was big, I think. I understood "grande." Then just as suddenly, she released me, and flopped again onto her back: "Do it." She did not want to participate. She wanted me to shut up, do my business in her, stop, then disappear. When I didn't comply, she opened her eyes and argued herself back into a sitting position. Then a standing one. She took her clothes and all the cabina's light back into the bathroom, and locked the door.

Listening to her dress, I knew I wouldn't get my money back. *Unless I surprise her when she comes out, reach fast into her pocket and...* No, she would scream and Rosie would hear. Or I would scream. I tried accepting all this as a lesson learned but *I've learned* enough *lessons lately...* When she re-entered the room clothed, suede heels dangling from her long hand, I pointed out, "We didn't *do* anything. Please give me my six-thousand colones back."

"No," she defied, and tried to snake past me. My two fingers on her bony shoulder kept her from the door. She ducked down but I blocked her like playing basketball. "Soy pobre!" I shouted. "Dame mi dinero!" I even tried coaxing her back into bed: "Fine! I'll fuck your corpse, *fine!*"

"No," she repeated, finally gaining enough ground to grab the doorknob.

This now all felt like an honest-to-god travesty of justice. Hot, red and helpless but temporarily unafraid of waking Rosie or anyone else, I shouted "*Why! Why* are you trying to *fuck me over*? I am a *good person!*" I knew if I kept going I would cry. Before my tears could wake the village, I had the presence of mind to reach down and rip her shoes away from her, hard and dramatic. She gasped. Her face wilted. She pressed her empty palms together like they burned. Her intensified sadness failed in its objective. A sense of power shocked me: *I won!* Her shoes, now *my* shoes, surely cost more than 6,000 and I'd wrenched them from the jaws of defeat! *For once! I won!* "OK! Go now," I laughed. "Take off. Go ahead! Keep the damn money. I'll keep *these!* Fair trade. Go! GO!"

Finally she wedged her hand into her white pocket and retrieved my 6,000. When I reached for the bills, she pulled them back: "Mis zapatos." I handed her one — though I was supposed to have given her both so she could dash down the stairs with the shoes, and money for a new pair. But I've been tricked enough in Costa Rica. I made sure to snatch the money before dropping the other shoe.

Transaction complete, we stood inches from each other, looking like real failed lovers. Opening the door for her, I apologized. She smiled her gorgeous swollen mouth, cocked her head back, and spit. As her clearly telegraphed, dime-sized clump of white came to rest on my shoulder like a jellyfish on flat water, my hands reflexively jumped to block it. My pinky poked her eye. She let herself fall against my door, touching her face like I'd punched her.

I am done for, I believed, and made the mistake of profuse apology.

"Soy Tica, mae! Soy *Tica!*" she shouted, hand over her eye: *I'm a* Tica, *motherfucker! You don't mess with a* Tica! *You* are *fucked!*

"I'm sorry! It was an accident! I'm *sorry!*"

She revealed her age – 16 — and threatened to go to the police. She barked a thousand more words I understood only as threats. I contemplated giving her the money after all, to pay for her silence. But I'd done nothing wrong. *She'd* tried to screw *me* over. I tossed the 6,000 on the floor beside my bed, placed my hand on her back and escorted Pamela out.

Descending the stairs, she suddenly seemed to fear *my* telling someone: "Tranquilo, mae," she whispered, "tranquilo." She placed a finger across those lips, "Shhhhh." I locked the gate behind her.

Back in my room, I could see Pamela still sitting down on

the roadside, perhaps waiting for *La Fuerza Publica*, or an older brother who would exact revenge. But before worry could overtake me, I noticed the tableaux that had organically assembled beside my bed during our episode: two dirty socks, condom, beer bottle, half a joint, and 6,000 colones. I found my mom's camera and snapped several pictures of this Costa Rican still-life while chanting, *"Don't stop taping! Don't stop taping!"*

Hoping to photograph her sitting down there, I opened my pink drapes. But Pamela was gone. I laid down alone, excited to tell Buck and Jonathan this new story tomorrow, on our long drive to San Jose.

3.8 RAPHAEL'S GOODBYE

Dear Mandy!

Miraculously, I bear hardly any scars from the teenage acne you thankfully never saw. I attempted and abused every possible remedy from tetracycline pills to NAIL-POLISH REMOVER (that first week, I SWEAR it seemed to be working). Instead of "Oh honey, it doesn't matter, they'll go away some day," my Mom shared my same end-of-the-world horror. She gave me humiliating brown base make-up to cover my pink cheeks, nose, forehead, chin, and neck. From a client who visited Mexico she once procured a kind of black-market acne ointment, which we lathered on me together. I woke the next morning with my chin eaten away, wet scabs up the sides of my mouth, like the victim of a grease fire. I stayed home from middle school for three days, then spent the next week hiding my made-up face in my arms on my desk. When the burns finally healed, my Mom and I agreed to try the ointment again. Same results. I never tried again, though at times I did contemplate, 'Maybe just a little LESS this time...'

That's maybe another way I've changed since we were kids; not that I'm a quitter, but I've learned when to quit. To that end, I am leaving Costa Rica and was hoping I could, in fact, take up your earlier offer to come stay with you in FLA, help you get set up, babysit while you jobhunt, etc. Ft. Heathen will also be the perfect distractionless place for me to drag out and fix up all I've written here, edit the mountain down into a proper book. You could help me? You SAID you "loved" my writing! We'll help EACH OTHER!

If you've changed your mind, or were only joking or offering out of pity, don't worry; I have enough savings to begin a small new life almost anywhere. I was also thinking about trying New Orleans, on the suggestion of a friend I made here in C.R. I think right now I need the OPPOSITE of third-world though. So my childhood home it is. If you'll have me.

Please send along your phone number.

Love,
Patrick

* * *

Keeping an eye out for those who want me dead, I said my last goodbyes to Tiburon's stinking, sunrise-tinted mudflats, smoking one last joint on the flats outside Nos Barra. There I fell asleep beneath the seawall. I was awoken by the cries of five motherless ducklings, sucked along in the current. The Gulf had filled up and now circled, slowly and powerfully. If not for the loud baby birds, the fast rising water might have taken me. Before I could thank the birds, a large shadow fell over the chicks, followed by what at first seemed like a comet: a large rock, or small boulder, crashed atop the ducklings. In the next frozen moment, not one bird resurfaced.

I whipped around to face not a meteor shower but Raphael, standing up on the seawall. Rivers poured between his freckles. The rock had been meant for me. "*You*, suppose to pro*tect* her!" he shouted down at me. "*You!*"

"I tried Raphael! I'm sorry. I've never felt so helpless."

"But you fokeen *heet* her! You fokeen *heet* my *seester!*"

"I…"

This would have been a pathetic last word. Raphael took a long, trembling moment, deciding whether to jump down and beat me back to sleep. Instead he shouted some last Spanish curses then bound off down the crescent seawall, past the small pier, along the sand, toward the big pier…

I rose to leave as well.

3.9 A Last Sunset (Dominical pt. 2)

Jonathan's two-wheel-drive AstroVan bound for San Jose first detoured to *Dominical.* I doubt she and Milton would return here. I really can't imagine why she would visit this tourist trap to begin with. Only gringos gather on this beach to watch the sun set behind dramatic waves exploding against cliffs like spray from a boxer's mouth — while closer up the beach a smaller sun sets between her legs... Lying on her back, this lone, skinny Tica's hip-bones lift her bikini up and open, affording a beautiful view over her stomach and down into the shadow. The way she peeps over her sun-glasses, the only local on this corny beach, even I realize she's for rent. Wish I'd owned these powers of discernment before meeting Alana...

A pale young surfer's now introduced himself to her, half cocky, half scared... He already has her up on her elbows, closing off my view of that sunset. She's reaching out now, taking his hand to stand up. Already, the handsome new couple leaves together. And I wonder why I would have ever expected any more than what that boy expects, right now.

If one can call this living, I temporarily do so inside the

booming bowels of *Hammerheadz*. Jonathan and Buck share the quiet minivan on the breezy beach for free and I pay $6 for this wood-walled sauna cell attached to a bass-thumping meat-market. *Hammerheadz* danceteria is in every way a replica of FLA's fratboy beach bars, right down to the *z*.

So no way was Jonathan even eating dinner there. A trail of hand-lettered signs led us far down Dominical's technically gorgeous beach to an empty patio restaurant that sent crackling vinyl record-ings of crusty punk-rock out over the ocean. Unpopular music, of which Jonathan approved. The bartender/cook/owner, Angel origi-nally from *"Bar-tha-lo-na"* Spain, spoke baritone, radio-announcer Spanish. Angel's wrinkled face was that of a distinguished doctor, but framed in long, gray brillo-pad hair. His sun-bleached black t-shirt bore the logo of a Death-Metal band *from Tampa! Tampa's the Death-Metal capital of the world!* I had no way of bragging to him. *My old band practiced in a warehouse right between Morbid Angel and Deicide!* I couldn't muster the energy or heart to bang my head and air-guitar, to get my point across. I just want the hell out of para-dise.

After filling us with seafood and beer, Angel turned off his "heart-core ponk," and we all shared jungle-quiet peace. For nearly an hour, brushed by breezes in wooden patio thrones, we watched the moody nighttime ocean peel back and back and back. At low-tide's peak, herds of young Ticos began passing across the tight wet sand in their best clothes. "Disco *loco* a noche," Angel explained, writing us a bill for 1,500 apiece. As gratuity, I scribbled down a list of great American heavy metal albums for Angel. He smiled, appreciative, then hugged Jonathan and Buck.

By the end of our goodbye, the crowd had migrated far ahead, reduced in the distance to music, laughter, and fire glowing high atop a cliff. This afternoon's two-story waves had evaporated down to lunar ocean floors. We passed a joint while hopping be-tween shifting moonlit shadows, across giant slippery orange boul-ders specked with green-glowing phosphate globs. The shoreline finally ended in a deep dark pit of what looked like sharp rocks. A long anemic tree branch reached across the pit like a bridge: the only way up to the party. Judging from the festive noise up there, many others had dared and succeeded (in their best clothes, too). As did Jonathan and Buck, who both scoffed disappointed when I balked, said goodbye and walked back here, to live inside the booming bowels of Hammerheadz.

Or if not live, then at least write.

3.10 WHORE CORRESPONDENT (SAN JOSE REDUX)

Our drive north through endless wet, rocky cliffside jungle shook the van's brain loose. The engine lived on, though all of Jonathan's dashboard gadgetry died. I had time and a receptive audience for my story. Mostly Buck. I began back at Pizza Dive and recounted everything for the first time. From first meeting Alana, to Milton's shelling, to the Semi-Famous Author killing Alana's swan to steal her away from me, my story flowed, and more than once forced laugher even from Jonathan. I know I have a good one here. I'm just still not sure about its bleak ending…

Darkness seemed to encourage the capital city's famous criminality as we wandered searching for cheap lodging. On the street outside Hotel China, a drug-addled, smiling Tico offered us a duo of too-young girls with similar druggy smiles and dark-circled eyes. I recognized the name Hotel China: where Milton killed his mother via heart attack. We took two rooms. I didn't have the courage or the Spanish to ask the young deskman in which wood-paneled room it had occurred. In my bunk above Jonathan, I imagined it was ours.

Buck decided to shave for the first time in six months, and I knew he was planning to rent someone. He also petitioned to occupy the separate room, with the stipulation that, if he and I both partook, Jonathan would then inherit the single. But now lying against the dank cardboard ceiling, I was sure, "I'm over this hooker nonsense."

"Pat!" Buck pointed his razor at the bottom bunk: "I'll let you lie to John here. And I'll even let you lie to me. But I can't stand by and let you lie to yourself."

Despite Buck's shave, in holey t-shirts and surf shorts we did not look like ideal marks on San Jose's streets. Still, I stepped alertly. When I told Buck that Mom's travel book described San Jose as "worse than pre-Giuliani Times Square," Buck shouted at the night, "You kiddin? Shit's a *joke* compared to New *Orlins*, bruh. I mean, I love Ticos to death, but they got *no* game, no hustle. I see um tryna scam these gringos and it's like they're kiddin! They need to come to New *Orlins* and learn the real hustle."

Finally, as must be the fate of all male tourists without women, we passed under a million tiny colored lightbulbs, in through the doors of a madhouse. Its slot machines were loud, its beers five dollars (possibly the most expensive in the country). Its women, abundant and perfect, nuzzled old gringos' dewlaps, or sparkled and posed alone at the bar. Jonathan used the attended restroom and Buck and I hadn't even wished for our drinks before a braided black girl in a tube-top and black silk shorts draped herself over me. Her white Tica friend sat her tight, ocean-blue dress down in Buck's lap, smiled in his ear and whispered funny dirty Spanish. The black girl's breasts massaged my back when she laughed and tousled my hair in seemingly sincere wonder: "I never been with no *pele rojo.*" Beneath my dirty shirt and dirtier skin, my heart swelled, the poor blind thing expecting love. The women did seem genuinely happy just to talk with the youngest guys in the place. Still their flirtation tasted like force-fed chocolate. Buck remained calm, and in blunt, capable Spanish, interviewed the girls, first asking their income.

"$100 for one hour," the black one answered in clear English. "$300 for a whole night."

"Jesus!" Buck laughed. "Y'all buy *us* drinks then!"

The girls playfully obeyed. Our $7 whiskey-and-coke's landed before us just as Jonathan returned from the bathroom, perplexed, amazed and disgusted, watching the black girl reach up my shorts to happily find her magic working. But like a doll that announces its hunger, when she gave a squeeze to my hard, bare penis I blurted, "*Soy pobre!*"

Beautiful women laughed all around us. My cheeks flushed deeper when the black girl's free hand slapped my face. "Shut up, pele rojo," she smiled and continued taking my pulse under the bar. For free. Whether or not I could enjoy it.

"*Es verdad* though," Buck assured her. "Only these old-ass gringos got money."

"No, no," the white Tica argued. "I am with many young gringos with money! Many."

"Well, we have very little," Buck laughed. "*Money,* that is."

"Then we go to the bar," the white Tica laughed back, "talk to *old-ass* gringo."

In reaching down for her friend's hand, the white girl gripped me too. The two women gave a simultaneous smiling squeeze, then floated away.

* * *

DEAR MANDY,

Great talking with you today! I can't wait to see you! I found out afterwards that Hotel China's payphone charged LITERALLY $14-a-minute to my credit card! Worth it though, definitely. I was shaking for the first minute! Your voice and laugh haven't changed at all! I can't wait to see you!

I hope you won't rescind your offer when I admit I'm currently emailing you from a real-life whorehouse. Don't worry, I'm too heartbroken (among other better traits) to PARTAKE. This place is pretty nice, actually: a casino/bar in a gold-trimmed hotel lobby full of truly pretty Latin women all wearing a little too much makeup. From certain angles it looks like a Calvin Klein modeling audition in Miami. Old American men rent the girls for $100/hr apiece, or $300/night – thus, the hotel can afford to offer this free internet by the slot machines. I sit at the second of three computers, between two SWEET-smelling women both struggling to type with long fake nails as my friends Buck and John lounge across this room with two young working girls. Jonathan seems to have become genuine friends with one of them. She's attached herself to Jonathan and I know HE isn't shelling out hundreds of dollars like these older dudes. She must really like him. Does that ever happen, you think?

By now you probably don't want me NEAR your daughter! To reiterate, I am NOT messing with hookers myself. Just seeing the crazy sights. Please believe me. Assuming you do, I'll see you in Miami tomorrow! This is so great! I can't wait!

Thank you SO much, Mandy, for saving my life!

Love,
Pat

* * *

The cabby asked our destination. Buck deferred to me: "To another club? With women?"

"Putas," the driver assumed, and entered lawless San Jose traffic.

"Not $300 ones though," I said.

"We *like* the $300 ones," Buck qualified. "We just can't afford em."

The driver dumped us outside Las Margaritas with the warning, "Go right in. No walk around outside." On the sidewalk, a light-skinned Tica with short sweaty hair flicked her tongue at us. The doorman's tuxedo had us worried we'd been taken to the wrong place — until the $3 door price included one free beer. Inside, Las Margaritas was a dank stripclub lit by purple bug-zapper lights and gynecological porn glowing from small TVs reflected in many mirrors. Stoic Ticos in too-small chairs watched a featured Tica lazily hump the dreary pole, accompanied by stale rock music. Beyond the pole, other women in cotton underwear led patrons to a service window — to make transactions involving towels? — and then down a dark hallway.

The featured dancer finally pulled her tight tank-top and tighter white underwear back on, and beelined to the absolute whitest guy in the bar: "You will buy me a drink?" she asked me. She

ordered a guaro shot, which she still hadn't touched by the time she
invited me into a back room.

"Cuanto cuesto?"

"Fy-tousand."

A roaming old Tico offered up a basket of nylon roses. She
wanted one, but luckily I had the presence of mind to stop nod-
ding, and refuse at least that. Shotglass in one hand, my fingers in
her other, she not-so-happily led me past a new girl on stage. At
the service window I gave 5,000 to a man who handed my Tica a
towel plus a new role of toilet paper, a condom and a tube of lubricant. My heart beat harshly down a dim hallway of many ill-fitting
doors. She opened one door onto a much more beautiful, younger
girl riding a handsome Tico youth on a cot. They shouted and their
slammed door's breeze brushed my face like ghost's fingers. Behind
the next door in a wood-paneled closet, she found an empty, single
bed. She flicked the clinical light on, locked us inside and threw her
bundled supplies on the bed — the toilet paper reminding me that,
despite her very real flesh, I was still, theoretically, a hair's breadth
from masturbation.

"Not yet, please," I gulped when she began removing her
tank-top. "*Despacio.*"

She complained that she was hot (*near my frying nerves?
my hellfire soul?*), then made me remove my shirt. For a moment, I
stared masochistically at my florescent-lit fishbelly folds, my frowning bellybutton encircled in red hair like some sad bearded pirate.
She hung my shirt on a hook in the shelf where her untouched guaro
balanced. "*Pantalones,*" she urged, nowhere near as sweet as that casino's $100-an-hour girls. Nerves, embarrassment, borderline terror
made me do exactly as I was told.

Sucking my stomach in and concentrating my eyes on her
full shot, I asked, "What do you want to do?"

"Sexo?" she frowned. "Si? No?" She commanded me to
stretch across the dirty bed in just my white socks and orangest hair.
My attacking heart stood my dick up like a baton, impressive or just
different enough from the rest of my body to hold her gaze as she
ripped open the condom.

"*Despacio,*" I repeated. "Not yet." I sat up and asked her to lie
back on my chest as the Ugly One had. She obeyed, finally removing
her shirt. The stark lights announced flaws in her skin as well: black

nicks and scrapes on her shoulders, stretch marks on her breasts and stomach. My white hands looked even deader crawling across her. Back at the service window I had noticed her rubbing her shoulders, so I now rolled her onto her stomach and dug my thumbs into her back. She smiled at first, but quickly grew impatient; she was at work. She rose and again rushed the condom.

"No! Not yet. *Primo*, uh...*con sus manos?*" I requested, preferring warm hands to a condom.

She scoffed, grabbed me and began pumping, a hard, fast, mechanical blur. "*Despacio!*" I coached. "*Despacio.*" She squirted lubricant onto her palm then began again, rolling slow slippery fingers down, then up, slowly, the complete ocean-smooth motion of her petite fist back down, then up, so perfectly I beseeched, "Oh, hang on. Wait, wait. Wait a second..." Instead she took the advantage, gripped tighter and sped *updownupdownupdownup* until, thinking nothing of my $15, I emptied what felt like my soul down her pretty brown knuckles.

Everything immediately turned ridiculous. I sprang up breathless, snatched my boxers from the hook, almost tipping the shot. She cleaned and wiped her hands, threw the towel on the bed, dressed quickly, and left me her full guaro.

Because Buck understands, and Jonathan mildly dislikes me, they left me alone be on the taxi ride back to Hotel China. I wanted only to return to my bunk, lie against the dank ceiling and think too much and too hard in too much silence about tomorrow's escape. After a joint.

Even Jonathan smoked, readying for bed. On the roach's third full orbit, Buck requested, "Let's hear your new story, Pat." Meaning, describe my handjob.

"No, no," I laughed, uncomfortable at the thought — until my sixth hit. Depressing as tonight was, my sad sex anecdote made Buck and Jonathan hoot loudly enough for someone outside our window to hear and, "*Fssst!*" The same sexy mating hiss heard on La Avenida: "*Fssst!!*" I kneeled on my bunk to peer out a window over a brick alley, into a similar room. The same two black and white $300-a-night girls from the madhouse casino beckoned us from their beds: "*Boys! Fssst! Hey!*" Buck and Jonathan joined me up top to witness the white Tica's tiny blue T-shirt and microscopic black underwear.

The black one wore a matching white bra and g-string.

"What should we do?" Buck worried quietly.

"You two invite them over," I suggested. "I'll take the other room. I've had enough."

Stoned Jonathan's hasty agreement impressed me; he shouted the women over.

"No," they laughed, "Venga *aqui!*" The girls announced their room number and Jonathan and Buck were gone.

I turned off the lights and from my bed secretly watched the girls adjust their hair and lipstick and underwear. Jonathan and Buck knocked on their door and the girls giggled and hugged them. Buck laid right down on a bed with the black one, Jonathan with the white. They all adopted a quiet, indiscernible tone. The guys must've told the girls I'd stayed behind; intermittently the girls called out, "Pa-treek? *Venga*, Pa-treek!"

But I'd been disarmed, and I was now better off as voyeur, watching the four of them over there talking, laughing, caressing. Eventually I grew bored and laid down. Then sat back up to check their giggling progress. They'd catch me peeping and, "Pa-treek! Venga!" My stoned suspicion inflated into solid paranoia: *Why do they want all* three *of us over there?* I even thought I heard scratching at our room door. *Someone picking the lock?* I leapt down from the bunk and whipped our door open, startling the hotel's sweaty front deskman, on his knees at our doorknob. He jumped up and stuttered Spanish I couldn't follow but which reeked of defense. Across the alley the girls laughed and called my name. He pointed at my window, squawked about "putas!" shook his finger meaning we're all in trouble, then hurried off down the hall, rat-like.

My heart leapt back up onto the bed. *It's a set-up!* Buck lay outside my sightline. Jonathan and his white Tica stopped kissing when I hissed, "*Fssst!*"

"Pa-*treek*! Venga!" the girls continued. When their door slammed open I noticed they didn't squeal. I watched the same front deskman barge in and declare that there would be none of *this* in *his* hotel! Jonathan and Buck chased their bouncing erections out of the scene. The front deskman sat on the white girl's bed for a casual talk.

"Man!" I announced when they slunk back into our room. "We were being *set up!*" I told them the newest tale, which Jonathan refuted:

"No way, man." He shook his earnest head. "I *know* when a woman really likes me."

I woke on my knees with a view over the sunlit alley to "our little black friend," as Buck dubbed her. She applied make-up, naked. "Buck!" I pounded my bunk. "Buck, look!"

Buck scrambled up, red-eyed. "Why am I leaving Costa Rica?" he asked himself. Our mutual plane to Miami leaves this afternoon. But only Buck is asking *why*.

Painting and powdering her face and bare brown body, our little black friend caught us peeping and smiled. "Hola!"

We ducked out of sight. Then back up, slowly...

"Hola! Hombres!" she'd giggle, and we'd hide again, playing the game like those ducks in the story I wrote for Alana – I should incorporate that piece into my book somehow...

Jonathan knocked on our door suggesting *"desayuna con putas?"* He shouted over to our little black friend, inviting her for breakfast. Buck and I dressed and smoked the last of my weed, then slouched downstairs to wait in the lobby for the girls. I considered complaining to the old woman now snoozing behind the front desk, about last night's attempted break-in. But the culprit was probably her son. And we're leaving today. *Just expel me safely, and I'll go without a sound...*

Waiting, waiting and waiting for the girls, Buck asked to be reminded why Jonathan had won the single room last night. "We spent the night together," Jonathan disclosed with post-coital calm. "It was incredible. She is indeed a professional."

"You paid!"

"Hell no," Jonathan scoffed, "I told you, she really likes me."

The girls finally emerged wearing matching electric-blue stretch pants and swoop-front, backless shirts. Last night, even at the casino they'd seemed less done-up, cleaner than now. This morning they looked like transvestites. Huge drawn eyebrows arched across their foreheads. The white Tica hid beneath coats of the same beige base foundation Mom daubed on my high school blemishes. Their beauty was almost buried. Still we followed the giggling girls up *La Avenida Central*. They walked far ahead of us, in case a better option opened. I appreciated the honesty of our situation. Hundreds more fast-food restaurants seem to have bloomed in San Jose just since I last stayed here. The girls led us into McDonald's, but Jonathan led us directly out, next door, to a greasy red table inside a Tico diner.

Jonathan's girl stamped beige face-prints on his arm. Buck continued quizzing the girls regarding their profession. Our little black friend explained that they work 1 to 11 p.m. on *La Avenida* "all the time, since I was young." They are both 22. After sunset, she said, the girls keep fixed rates and expect tips, but on boring afternoons like today, San Jose's heat melts their expectations.

"But it is *so* much money we make just for *sexo!*" our little black friend laughed. To illustrate, when a small boy approached us peddling pens bearing bootleg Warner Brothers cartoon characters, our wealthy lady friends thought nothing of buying the table a round of pens. Waiting for our breakfast, we sketched each other on napkins. Drawing me the black girl realized: "Wait! *You* are *Pa-treek?* No? Why you did not come to our room when we call? You were scared?" Buck and Jonathan laughed. Before I could decide whether she was either very brave bringing this up, or else simply not in cahoots with Hotel China, her plastic fingernails invaded her cleavage, pushed her bra clasp down and revealed...

Buck leaned over, looked in and winced.

I craned across the table. A tattoo on her dark skin read: PATRICK

"Oh." Buck sat back. "It looked at first like a hideous scar."

Covering herself, the black girl stared and smiled like she owned me. But I also sensed sadness, as if the real PATRICK had left her when she hadn't wanted him to. I suffered a false triumphant twinge, and for the next two minutes she was, in fact, mine. Her watery eyes poured over me as Buck, Jonathan and his white Tica too-busily scarfed fried pork, eggs, beans, rice and coffee. Under the table, her high-heel tap-tap-tapped against my crotch, inflating me with blood. *Tap-tap-tap-tap-tap* as Buck and Jonathan rose to pay our bill. When the girls and I were alone, the black one motioned for her colleague to look beneath the table at my erection straining against her heel. Their sudden laughter sent all blood to my face. And she was no longer mine. Easy as that.

Back on the ferociously sunny street, PATRICK's little black friend rustled and primped and then pecked my face goodbye — nothing more for free. Jonathan and his Tica joined mouths so solidly we all turned away. When they'd finished, the white Tica reapplied her lipstick, then plucked a hot-pink datebook from her hot-pink purse. She flipped its small pages, read a line to herself in Spanish, then closed her eyes and mouthed English words.

"She is not yet very good with English," the black one explained. "I teach her now, so she makes more dolares."

I smelled their powdery make-up odor when we all leaned in to read the list of phrases the girls would need for today:

- Me nombre es Angela: My name is Angela.
- Quieres comprarme un bebe: Would you love to buy me a drink?
- Quieres tener sexo conmigo: Would you love to make love with me?
- Soy un estudiante a la Universidad, no una puta: I am a student at the University, not a whore.
- Uno ciento dollars: One hundred dollars.
- Me amas: Do you love me?
- Tienes un cuarto por nuestros: Do you have a room
  for us?
- Te amo: I love you
- Neccesito a ir: I need to leave
- No se: I don't know

PHOTO BY AUBREY EDWARDS

A lifelong resident of New Orleans, **JEFF PASTOREK** received his BFA from Loyola University New Orleans and his law degree from Tulane University. Since 2003, he has worked with gouache and ink on chipboard, BFK paper, and butterboard. His work focuses on the banal, confusing, and delightful experiences of human existence. His work has been featured in *I Heart Magazine, The Oxford American, Constance,* as well as numerous gallery showings. Nearly all of his work can be found through www.jeffpastorek.com

The author enjoying the luxuries his talents afford him. PHOTO BY ZACK SMITH

MICHAEL PATRICK WELCH is the author of the diary *Commonplace* (Screw Music Forever Press), the novel *The Donkey Show* (Equator Books) and the music and art book *New Orleans: the Underground Guide* (University of New Orleans Press). He served three years at the *St. Petersburg Times* daily newspaper, and his freelance writing has appeared in *Newsweek*, *Spin*, *Filter* and many Village Voice publications -- not to mention hundreds of articles in New Orleans' *Gambit Weekly*, *OffBeat* and *AntiGravity* magazines. When not teaching his rap class for public school students (youngaudiences.bandcamp.com), Welch leads the psychedelic-rock-n-r&b band, The White Bitch, and hosts NoizeFest and other concerts in his yard. He currently lives in New Orleans with his wife Morgana King, his daughter Cleopatra and their pygmy goat Chauncey Gardner. Write to him at michaelpatrickwelch@gmail.com